A TAPESTRY OF DREAMS

ROBERTA GELLIS

sourcebooks
casablanca

Published by Sourcebooks Casablanca, an imprint of Sourcebooks, Inc.
P.O. Box 4410, Naperville, Illinois 60567–4410
(630) 961–3900
FAX: (630) 961–2168
www.sourcebooks.com

Originally published in 1985 by The Berkley Publishing Group,
New York

Library of Congress Cataloging-in-Publication Data

Gellis, Roberta.
  A tapestry of dreams / by Roberta Gellis.
      p. cm.
  1. Nobility—England—Fiction. 2. Knights and knighthood—Fiction.
I. Title.
  PS3557.E42T37 2011
  813'.54—dc22

                         2010043656

              Printed and bound in Canada
        WC 10 9 8 7 6 5 4 3 2 1

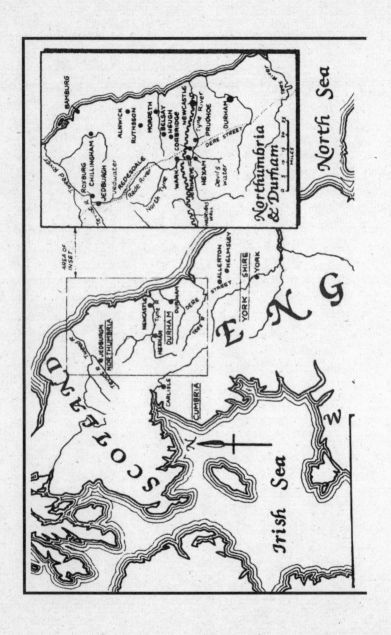

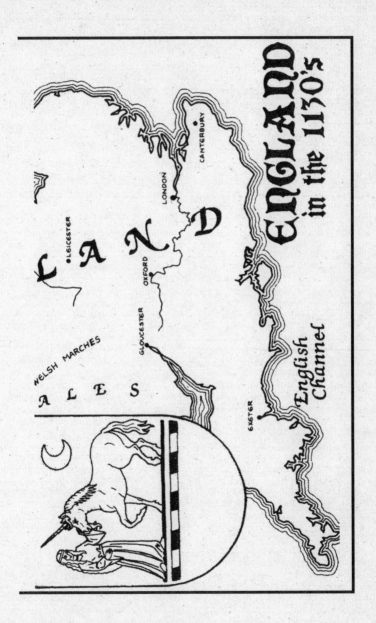

ENGLAND in the 1130's

CANTERBURY

LONDON

LEICESTER

OXFORD

GLOUCESTER

EXETER

WELSH MARCHES

ALES

LAND

English Channel

Prologue

THERE HAD ALWAYS BEEN AN IRON HAND ON THE HILL CALLED Iron Fist. A strong man could see immediately that the hill was a most desirable place for defense, a rocky outthrust around which the river had worn a deep valley. Where the river crossed the foot of the promontory, there was a shallower area that could be forded; however, it was a deep and dangerous ford. Erosion had carved gullies into the harder stone of the hill so that the protruding mass showed four huge bulges and, lower on the hill, a smaller fifth, which ran crosswise. The river ate away at the base, over the aeons wearing even the hard stone into a shallow curve under the crosswise bulge. From across the river, when the light glanced along the hill just right, a huge fist of stone appeared to threaten any who approached.

It was an ideal place to make a stand to protect the cultivated fields in the river valley below and behind the promontory. It was easy to club one's enemies as they climbed or push them off with sharpened sticks. Even the primitive tribe that settled there found signs that a still earlier people had defended the great fist. But they did not hold it long.

Another group with a far more ferocious leader took the place. The assault cost half his fighting men, even against the poor defense the less aggressive leader contrived, but it did not matter, for he closed his iron hand over the defeated and enslaved them, eventually melding them into his own tribe to bolster their numbers.

When the Romans who built Hadrian's Wall found the place, it was clear that it had been used as a fort for a long time. The native slave who acted as translator told the centurion the name of the site, translating the Pictish words into *Pugnus Ferreus,* Iron Fist. It was stone, of course, but iron was the wonder metal that could defeat bronze and black magic, too.

The Roman wall itself could not cross old Iron Fist, for the slopes were too steep and the valley surrounding the promontory was too low; the wall was built on a ridge some half mile to the north. However, Iron Fist was an obvious site for one of the great forts that would house supplies and serve as a base for the soldiers who manned the mile castles. One spring already welled sluggishly from a fault in the rock. The Romans, being fine engineers, widened that fault so that fresh, sweet water flowed freely; probes found others.

Some of the rock that made up Hadrian's Wall, eighteen feet high and eight feet wide when completed, was hewn cleverly from the slopes of old Iron Fist, hewn so that the promontory became even more isolated and only a tortuous, curving road approached the summit. There was no need for the construction of so elaborate a defense. The Pictish tribes were more a nuisance than a threat, but the centurion was an engineer at heart, and in this isolated post he needed amusement.

A lesser wall, not so much for defense as to mark out the limits of a settlement, was built from the great wall to the foot of the hill where it met the river. But Romans built walls to last; even the lesser wall was built of stone, as were certain storehouses and, of course, a prison. There were plenty of slaves, and the soldiers were often idle; why not keep them busy? The centurion's name was Artorius—but by the sweating soldiers and exhausted slaves he was most often called Iron Hand, *Manus Ferrea.*

The Romans were recalled to defend their native land and abandoned the wall and the *castellum,* but Iron Fist remained a prize to the fiercest, so that the men who held it were called, by custom, Iron Hand.

For those who raided from the sea, the river was a tempting road. A few centuries after the Romans abandoned Iron Fist, the first boats ventured so far upriver, scraped their keels on the ford, and stopped. They raided the rich river valley that time. Their second foray, some years later, was not a success. Fire rained down from old Iron Fist. The ships burned; the warriors died. A few who escaped told the tale, which lost nothing in the telling as time passed, and it came in the end to the ears of a needy younger son. He was clever and strong and hard, but he had brothers of equal merit; his father had no land for him.

So the language in which the name Iron Fist was spoken changed again. The local people learned the words if not the grammar and called the place Jernaeve. Before the Normans came, they had made the conqueror's language their own— but the original place name stuck. And the hard-eyed mercenary who was given Jernaeve by William the Bastard had an odd romantic streak. He liked "Jernaeve" better than "Poing de Fer." Moreover, because he had no name himself—other than Oliver le Bâtard (like his lord)—and because he did not wish to give that suspicious master any uneasy thoughts by taking the name Main de Fer, which went with the castle, so to speak—he used the ungrammatical inversion himself and became Fermain: Iron Hand.

William the Bastard, hard and clever, ruled, then died in his bed. His son, William Rufus, harder but not nearly as clever, was shot by an arrow while out hunting after only a few years as king. William's youngest son, Henry, followed. As clever as his father, Henry, too, died in bed—but he had no living sons, for his heir had drowned in a crossing of the narrow sea.

Before he died, Henry forced his reluctant barons to swear they would make his only surviving child, his daughter Matilda, queen. But death loosened Henry's powerful grip on the barons, and some repudiated the oath forced on them and invited Henry's nephew, Stephen of Blois, to take the throne.

Thus, the seeds of civil and foreign war were sown, for in England there were barons who decided to stand by their oaths to Matilda, and in Scotland to the north King David felt he must support his niece. The whole land seethed with rumor and counterrumor, and atop old Iron Fist, a new Oliver

Fermain prepared to defend Jernaeve, knowing King David would not dare leave so strong a keep, astride a main road between his realm and England, in the hands of one who would not swear fealty to him and might oppose his purpose.

Chapter 1

A HORSE FLOUNDERED THROUGH THE TREACHEROUS FORD, almost toppling its wavering rider. The man, numb with cold and exhaustion, clung desperately, casting only a single glance at the threatening fist of rock that towered over him, the tips of its great knuckles just gilded with the rising sun. Although he could see the walls that projected above the stone knuckles like awkward, ugly rings, he knew the angle would prevent him from seeing the men who walked guard duty on those walls.

The horse slipped and slithered among the ice and rocks of the bank and at last heaved itself onto solid ground. As the horse came around the curve made by the largest knuckle, the man raised his head at last. The narrow riverbank was clean and empty. No blood stained the rocks; no corpses fouled the river.

The rider was too tired to smile, but his breath seemed to come more easily after he had seen with his own eyes that what the men on the north wall said was true, that indeed he was not too late with his warning, and he spurred his tired horse so that it quickened its plodding walk to a heavy trot. The touch of the spur was a mark only of the man's eagerness, not of the distance still to go. Only a few of the horse's lengthened strides brought them to the point where the stone of the cliff met the stone of a Roman-built wall, mended and reinforced over the centuries. The river turned with the curve of the hill, too, so that the bank on which the narrow road ran was no more than fifty feet wide for a quarter mile or so. But he did not have to go so far. The gate he sought was close by.

Already the rider could hear the challenge of the guards. He gathered his strength and bellowed, "It is Bruno, Berta's son."

What his name meant to anyone now, after so many years of absence, he did not know, but one man alone was no threat to Jernaeve keep, and some of the men-at-arms might remember him. In any case, the gate was open when he reached it, and he went through without further challenge, turned sharply left to pass through the narrow space between the wall and the side of the hill on which Jernaeve—old Iron Fist—perched.

The passage, a hundred feet or more long, widened suddenly, stretching out into a series of fields some half-mile square that sloped gently upward to the north until they met the great Roman wall. It was a fertile piece of land. The close furrows of the winter planting could be seen under the mantling of snow, but Bruno did not ride the path toward the cottages that backed against the Roman wall and housed the demesne serfs.

He kept his horse on the frozen mud of the snowy track that turned to the right, past the wooden buildings that served both as living quarters for the men who guarded the lower walls and as guest quarters for visitors' men-at-arms. Those buildings lay in the shadow of Jernaeve's cliff, where fire and missiles could be rained down on them—in case a guest developed ambitions of permanent residence. Almost halfway around the base of the hill, the track Bruno followed met the road that wound left and right in sweeping curves to climb up Iron Fist, each curve exposed to the narrower one that hung above it.

At the end of the last curve, the road made a short, sharp turn, nearly a right angle, and went under a portcullis between two towers, called east and west. The wall that stretched beyond the towers, enclosing nearly the whole of the flattened top of the hill, was far more massive than the one below, a wall built of ancient stones culled from the Roman ruins and newly set by skilled Norman masons. The portcullis was lifted, permitting entry to the dark passage through the wall, fifteen feet thick at that point, with another portcullis at the far end.

There were slits in the roof of that passage, Bruno knew, slits for shooting arrows and for pouring boiling oil, but he did not raise his head to look.

Had he been an enemy, he would have been dead long since—shot as he rode along the bank, or as he strove to burst through the gate or traverse the passage between the wall and the cliff, or as he climbed each curve in the road. There would be many, many dead enemies before any reached the passage between the portcullises and were trapped there. It was a warming and comfortable thought. Tired as he was, Bruno turned to look back over the formidable defenses, which were only the least and outermost. Those of Jernaeve itself, which crowned Iron Fist, were far stronger. They might be strong enough.

Beyond the second portcullis, the bailey opened out into a rough rectangle dominated by the massive keep. The noise, reflected back from the thick stone walls, struck Bruno like a blow. From pens and kennels against the east wall, cattle lowed, sheep and goats bleated, pigs grunted, and dogs barked. Within the yard, men and women moving about at their morning tasks laughed and shouted at each other, and from the area between the men-at-arms' quarters and the north wall of the chapel came the thud of wooden weapons, an occasional shout of pain or surprise, and the regular clang of hammer on anvil from the small smithy.

Just beyond the east tower against the north side of the wall were the stables, and a groom ran out to take Bruno's horse. His knees buckled as he dismounted, and the groom dropped the rein to support him, calling out for help. Bruno started to shake his head, and then glanced toward the wooden forebuilding, which sheltered the steep, unrailed stair that led to the entrance of the great hall. He uttered a weary chuckle. It would be just his luck to have escaped so many dangers only to fall off the stair and be killed.

By then he had been recognized, and a lounging man-at-arms ran ahead to tell his master of Bruno's arrival. Sir Oliver, as dark and strong as the keep he held, was at the door when Bruno had struggled up the stair, and Bruno said,

"The Scots are at war. Norham and Alnwick have yielded to King David—and Wark is besieged."

"Wark," Sir Oliver repeated, his voice expressionless. "How long since?"

"I meant to sleep there last night, thinking David's army would keep to the coast, but parts of the village were still burning. I have been all night coming those few leagues, dodging the Scots."

"Can you remember how far north you saw the last raiding party?" Oliver asked.

"I do not think they *were* raiding parties. They were hunting someone, I could swear. I was driven far to the east, keeping clear of them," Bruno replied. "The last I saw was a league north or a little more."

After frowning for a moment longer, Sir Oliver nodded and gestured with his head toward the fire, newly fueled. From the embers of the logs that had burned slowly through the night, new flames leapt along the dry branches, spitting and roaring. Without more words, Sir Oliver went out and down the steps. Bruno knew that he would send more men to protect the great wall to the north, and possibly to warn the serfs to make ready to come up into the castle in case the Scots should succeed in breaching the lower defenses. For the time being, Bruno had no further duties—and he was good for no more anyway.

The groom had melted away from his side when Sir Oliver appeared, and Bruno took a careful step toward the fire, watching where and how he put his foot down. He had been numb with cold from riding through the day and the bitter night, unable to make a fire to warm himself even when he stopped for brief rests, lest the light and smoke draw his enemies. Immersion in the freezing water of the North Tyne when he forded the river had added the final touch; Bruno had no feeling in his legs from knees to toes.

Eventually he reached a bench set to the side and well away from the hearth and let himself down on it. To come too close to the fire for the sake of warming himself quickly would only increase his misery later by inflaming his chilblains. The area was quiet because it was the high end of the hall, the place of the noble family. Bruno was glad of it. He did not wish to be asked for news.

There had been a normal bustle of activity—but at a decent distance—while he had spoken to Sir Oliver; the serfs had known better than to crowd their lord when a messenger came. But he had spoken softly and apparently no one had recognized him—or, if they had, did not know what to do. Now the servants were busily clearing away a few scattered sleeping pallets and snatching at the remnants of the bread, cheese, and ale with which Sir Oliver and those entitled to break their fast with him had started the morning. Bruno just sat, trying to cudgel his tired brain into deciding whether it would be less effort to call one of the servants to help him or to remove his wet shoes himself. Suddenly the activity stilled and a silence fell.

By the time Bruno's dulled reactions had brought his head up, light footsteps were rustling the rushes in a hurried advance, and a soft voice cried, "Bruno! Brother! Is it you?"

Small, warm hands pulled at his helmet, lifted it off, cupped his face. Pale blue eyes, made deep as bottomless pools by the darker ring around the iris, glinted happily. Rosebud-pink lips parted in laughter, and a flush of happiness colored cheeks translucently fair and framed by long, thick braids of palest gold.

"It *is* you! And you have not changed at all," she exclaimed joyfully, carefully setting the helmet down and feasting her eyes on her half brother's crisp black curls and dark eyes. His face was strong and square, with the handsome aquiline nose and the thin, well-shaped lips of the Fermains, the line of the latter somewhat blurred by several days' growth of black beard stubble.

The silence that had startled Bruno into seeking its cause had ended by the time she spoke, and the warm pleasure in her voice drew a smile, in spite of Bruno's exhaustion. "And you have not changed either," he said, "although you should have. Will you never grow up, Demoiselle Audris?"

"Alas," she said, lowering her eyes for a moment in mock sorrow, "I fear I am as grown as ever I shall be. Have you lost count of time, brother? I have put two and twenty summers behind me. And you are unkind to call me Demoiselle, as if—"

"No, Demoiselle," he interrupted her gravely. "You are unwise to call me brother. My mother—"

"Oh, Bruno, I do not care a rotten apple about your silly mother. Do you not know that you could shave yourself by looking into Uncle Oliver's face?" She laughed merrily. "Except, of course, that he is bald and gray."

"My looks make no difference," Bruno said severely. "In fact, they are a good reason for you to mind your tongue. I was not speaking only of your inches when I asked if you would never grow up."

Audris released Bruno's face and started to seat herself beside him on the bench. In doing so she touched him and became aware of his condition. Her eyes widened, joy being replaced by apprehension. "Oh, heaven! You are cold as ice and soaking wet!"

When an old maidservant had come timidly to her door to tell her that Bruno, Berta's son, had come home, she had been delighted, thinking that her uncle had changed his mind and invited her bastard half brother back to Jernaeve. Now she realized that some dire emergency must have brought Bruno. She jumped up to call to a manservant, only to see her uncle standing and looking at them with a frown.

Audris met Oliver's eyes steadily, lifting her chin and straightening her back. "Uncle," she said, "I see that Bruno has come to us at no small risk bearing heavy tidings." Her voice, although not raised, could be heard throughout the hall because a new silence had fallen as soon as she faced Sir Oliver.

Oliver nodded and came closer. "Yes," he said, watching her keenly and somewhat nervously. "The Scots are attacking. Wark is taken."

Audris stared back, startled by the news at first, but then she shook her head, refusing to be distracted. If the Scots came to attack Jernaeve, they came, but it would not be in the next few hours, and she could see no reason why poor Bruno should sit wet and cold while they waited.

"Even so," she said, "I cannot see why you could not spare

one moment to bid Eadmer to see to Bruno's needs. Now I will take him to my own chamber—"

"No," Bruno said.

But the rigidity of Sir Oliver's lips relaxed just a little, his frown lightened, and he nodded. "Yes, Bruno. Go with her. You will be no good to me until you have rested anyway."

Bruno might have protested again, but Oliver had already walked away, and it was useless to argue with Audris. Besides, she had slipped away too, beckoning to the nearest menservants and telling them to help Bruno as she ran ahead to her quarters in the south tower. He watched her go, thinking with the old stab of anxiety that her feet barely stirred the rushes as she went, so light and frail she seemed. He remembered his terror when he had first seen her, only a few hours old, at his mother's breast. He had been sure Audris would die, like the other legitimate children Sir William had sired. Then Sir William would find a hundred excuses to beat him and, even when he could not, would stare at him with burning, angry, hate-filled eyes because of all the young he bred, only the one the castle whore *said* was his survived. But the lady, Audris's mother, had died instead.

Suddenly Bruno smiled, remembering how his mother had laughed at him when he began to weep because he was afraid and also because so tiny and tender and beautiful a creature as Audris should die.

"*She* will not die," Berta had said, "not this one. Do you not see how hard she sucks, for all she is so small? And it is *my* milk she takes," she added proudly, lowering her voice so that none but her son could hear, "not that sour whey that leaked from her mother's tit."

The men helped Bruno back across the hall and up the narrow stairway to the third floor of the south tower. The door, thick and ironbound—a last, strong defense should enemies fight their way into the great keep—was open. Bruno blinked, for the light was strong compared with the dimness of the hall below. The true windows of the hall opened only inward, on the bailey, where the high walls that surrounded the whole hilltop blocked the sun of early morning and evening. Here the windows opened southeast and southwest over the cliff above the river, and even though they were set deep in the thick wall and closed against the worst of the winter cold by thin-scraped hides, the room was bright. The men paused uncertainly in the doorway, and Bruno noted with dull surprise that they had both turned their heads away from the loom that stood near the hearth.

"Come! Come!" Audris cried, waving them toward the chair on the other side of the fire.

They brought him to the chair and fled, as if there were something to fear in the bright, quiet room. Bruno hesitated, knowing it was not fitting for him to sit in Audris's chair, but she laughed and pushed him with one finger, and his numb knees buckled so that he would have sat hard enough to jar him had not a bright, embroidered cushion softened his collapse. Then she clapped her hands, and from behind him came a maid, who laid the robe she was carrying across the back of the chair and knelt to remove his shoes.

Audris came to his side and began to struggle with the buckle that held the ventail of his mail hood. It was plain she had never undone one before.

"Let me," Bruno said, but his fingers were swollen and awkward, and in the end, seeing what he was trying to do, Audris unhooked it.

He would not allow her to continue undressing him, however, and when she saw that he was truly being made uncomfortable by her presence, she went away to fetch salve for his chilblained hands and feet and left him to the maid. When she returned, he was wrapped in the warm robe, dozing in the chair. Audris was as gentle as possible in applying the salve, but when she looked up from her task, he was watching her.

"I am sorry if I hurt you," she said softly.

Bruno lifted a hand as if to touch her cheek but did not, just shook his head, smiled, and said, "Your fingers are as light as feathers. It was your gentleness that woke me."

"You are ill cared for in your service." Audris sighed as she shifted her position from kneeling to sitting on the cushion she had used while she was salving Bruno's hands. "Bruno, will you not come home?"

"No," he said firmly. "I will help fight off the Scots if they come, but then I will go."

Audris's bright eyes examined his face for a moment and then dropped. Under Bruno's calm, she sensed a deep uneasiness and uncertainty. She lifted her eyes again. "If I asked Uncle Oliver—"

"No!" he exclaimed, cutting her off, and then, seeing how shocked she was, he went on hastily, "Audris, you must not think Sir Oliver put me out. He is not a cruel or unjust man. Had he wished to be rid of me, he could have driven me away when I was a child—or had me killed. Instead, he trained me carefully, found honorable service for me, and even gave me as much as many men give their younger sons—good arms and armor and a good horse."

"Of course Uncle Oliver is not cruel or unjust," Audris agreed. "Who knows better than I? A babe a few months old left heiress to a rich property—how many men and women, who were the next heirs, could have resisted allowing that babe to take a chill or be carried away by some other sad illness or accident? I owe Uncle Oliver and Aunt Eadyth my life. I understand that it was right for you to be in service with some other household, but now, when Uncle Oliver is growing older—"

"Audris, you are foolish. Your well-being and your right to Jernaeve have always been first in Sir Oliver's mind. That is why I had to leave and must not return."

She stared at him for a moment, then slowly shook her head. "You cannot mean that my uncle feared you would harm me or take Jernaeve from me."

He shrugged. "I hope not, although I fear he has not the same trust in me that you have," Bruno said. "Audris, you said yourself that I resemble Sir Oliver—and if he and his brother were much alike, then I resemble your father—"

"I am sure you do, brother."

"Do not call me brother! Cannot you see there is a danger for you there? I would not take Jernaeve from you, but others might prefer me to a woman."

"Well, and so what if you ruled Jernaeve?" Audris asked

with a shrug. "Would you drive me out? Would you not allow me to live quietly as I do now with my loom and my garden and my hawks? I am not unhappy, and if I had you for my companion, I would be happier still."

"It is not right!" Bruno exclaimed. "You should be married. Your husband is the one who must take Jernaeve into his hands when Sir Oliver is too old. Why have you no husband?"

"I have not seen any man I favor," Audris replied lightly, "and my uncle is too kind to force a man on me."

Bruno frowned. "Kind" was not the most appropriate word for Sir Oliver. He was a hard man, although honest and honorable. He did what he felt was right, whether or not he liked the doing, and made others do the same. Bruno doubted that Audris's preference would count for much if Sir Oliver wanted her to marry.

"You are in the direct line," he said, avoiding any remark that might seem critical or suspicious of Sir Oliver, "and it is right that your son should be Fermain of Jernaeve. If you choose a strong man who will be kind to you, what more favor need you feel?"

Audris lowered her eyes. "I do not know, but... Do you remember, Bruno, when Father Anselm told us the story of Jacob, and how he labored seven years for Rachel and was given Leah, and though Leah was all that any wife could be, he so desired Rachel that he bound himself for another seven years?"

"Merciful Mary," Bruno groaned wryly, "Father Anselm was a very holy man, but not overly wise. He filled your head with the *most* unsuitable things."

"And not yours, Bruno?" Audris asked mischievously. "Besides," she went on, smiling up at him and not waiting for an answer, "if your hands and feet feel more easy, it is owing to Father Anselm's unsuitable teachings."

"I never said herb lore was unsuitable," Bruno replied, then sighed. "And do not think you can lead me so easily away from what is needful to be said. It is time for you to marry."

"Perhaps soon," Audris temporized, climbing to her feet and beckoning to Bruno to get up too. "But it is time for me to get back to my weaving, and long past time when you should have been abed and asleep. I am a fool to have kept you talking."

Without waiting for an answer, Audris called her maid, who hurried from some work she was about behind the loom to open the bed curtains and lift the covers invitingly, while Audris turned to her weaving. Bruno glanced at her, knowing he had been put off, but he was too tired to argue and was asleep as he tumbled into the bed.

Audris heard the curtain rings rattle back across the rod with relief. She did not want to discuss the subject of marriage further because she knew Bruno would be horrified to learn she had decided never to marry—at least not while her uncle was alive—unless Oliver himself pressed her to do so. How blind Bruno was not to see that her husband would be a greater danger to her uncle than Bruno's own presence could ever be to her. Perhaps had she married very young, a boy equally young, her husband would have come to accept her uncle's role as master. It was too late now. If she married a man strong enough to be the Iron Hand in the Iron Fist, he would not wish to be second in authority.

It would be her husband's right to be first, yet her uncle, she knew, was not the kind of man who could bear to take orders from one younger and less experienced than he. There could be only one solution to such a situation: Oliver would leave Jernaeve. But Audris felt that would be unbearable. Her uncle had spent most of his life protecting her and her lands. How could she allow him to be driven out in his old age? And where could he go? His own small keep was held by his elder son, and Oliver and Alain were birds of a feather. Alain would not take kindly to his father's seizing command of the property he had ruled alone for many years.

Nor, Audris thought, was she as simple as Bruno thought her. Right or wrong, it would have suited her very well if her half brother had been willing to rule Jernaeve after her uncle was dead, for she loved Bruno dearly and knew he loved her and would always be kind to her. She could be content to continue to live as she now did, free to watch the birds and beasts, to examine what grew and how it grew, and to weave the stories the animals and plants told her into her tapestries. Audris sighed. Bruno would never consent. He was, she realized, as obsessed with her right to Jernaeve as was her uncle. No, Bruno was worse because he was more selfless. In his desire to do what was best for her, if given the chance he would probably force her to marry.

At least Uncle Oliver had never urged her to marry; he knew as well as she that his role as Fermain of Jernaeve would end when she chose a man. Possibly he hoped she never would find one to suit her and that his son would rule Jernaeve in her name after him. Yet she had not lied to Bruno when he asked why she had not married. It was true that she had not yet seen any man to whom she was willing to entrust her life and lands. Her uncle dutifully brought to her each proposal made to him for her hand. But those who had asked for her had mostly done so before they ever saw her. And when she had been introduced, the suitors barely glanced at her in their eagerness to learn the extent of her property.

While these thoughts ran through her mind, Audris had reached blindly for a spindle of yarn. A rainbow assortment, strictly ordered by color and intensity, lay in racks ready to her right hand. As necessary, these were refilled and replaced, but the location in which each spindle lay was never changed, and by the habit of many years' use, Audris did not need to look to choose the proper shade or depth of color. Her fingers ran over her work, found the spot where the color belonged, and fastened the thread of woof in its proper place. Then her left hand lifted the warp threads while her right pushed the spindle through.

As she pulled the spindle out, her fingers were already seeking the next portion of the pattern in that color and lifting alternate warp threads again. The spindle followed unerringly, her wrist twisting to release the necessary amount of thread from it each time it came free. At the end of the warp, she changed hands, taking the spindle in her left. Still without glancing at the work, her right hand changed the order of raised and depressed warp threads and her left shot the spindle back. She did two more rows, then broke the thread and reached for the ivory comb that fit between the threads of the warp to pack down the woof.

Her mind still busy, Audris continued to stare at the closed bed-curtains as she replaced that spindle and chose another. Often she enjoyed "watching" the growth of the pattern she wove, although she could not really see it, because she faced the wrong side of the weaving. Just as often, however, her mind roamed free, and her hands, seemingly with a life of their own, wove a picture at which Audris herself would express surprise.

❧

The next day a knight bearing the banner of David, king of Scotland, appeared before the great north wall with a small troop. The men were armed but clearly had neither the capacity to attack nor the intention of doing so. Jernaeve was too strong a place, and the knight was not even riding his destrier but was astride a strong palfrey. Sir Oliver had come from the keep to the outer wall as soon as the troop had been sighted in the distance, and he called down to ask the business and identity of the arrivals.

"Do you have a guest who arrived last night riding a fine chestnut destrier with a saddle bound and bossed in silver and a richly embroidered saddlecloth? Or has such a man been seen, if he did not stay or is already gone?"

"No," Oliver replied, in a voice replete with surprise, although what he was thinking was that Bruno had been right. This troop was hunting someone. Oliver wondered who could merit so intense a search as he went on, "Certainly I have no such guest, and if such a man has been seen, it was not reported to me. If that is your purpose here and your only purpose, you are welcome to enter and question my men yourself."

There was a noticeable hesitation, as if some inner struggle were taking place in the knight, but at last he shook his head. "That is a small matter," he said, although his voice was choked with anger. "The loss of a mare's son to a son of a bitch must be put aside. I am William de Summerville, liege man to King

David. In his name and that of the Empress Matilda, rightful queen of England, I bid you join us in rejecting the usurper, Stephen of Blois, who has seized the royal rights and by lies had himself crowned king."

Briefly Sir Oliver clenched his teeth. When he had been asked about what seemed to be a thief, he had had a spurt of hope that Jernaeve would not be challenged to declare loyalty for either Matilda or Stephen. That hope was now dead. Oliver had known when King Henry forced his barons to swear to accept his daughter Matilda as queen that the device would not work. While the king was alive, the hold he had on his men could bend them to obedience. As soon as Henry was dead, however, few regarded their forced swearing as binding—particularly since no one could abide Matilda, who was as arrogant as she was foolish. Scotland's King David was Matilda's uncle and might be expected to support her—of course, David was also the uncle of Stephen's wife, Maud—but whichever way David eventually leaned, Oliver felt no doubt that the Northumbrian castles now taken in Matilda's name would remain in King David's possession as the price of that support.

As for himself and Jernaeve, Oliver thought, they were caught between the kettle and the coals. No matter what he did, either one side or both would call him traitor and claim Jernaeve forfeit. Furthermore, if the Scots remained involved in the struggle between Matilda and Stephen for England's crown, the war would roll back and forth over Jernaeve's lands. All Oliver could do was try to maintain a careful balancing act, hoping that neither side would attack him as long as they believed they could induce him to join them, and pray the war of succession would be settled quickly.

Thus, Oliver kept his voice as bland as it could be when he had to shout to make himself heard, and his answer was mild. "It is not for me to decide such high matters as who shall rule in England. When Stephen of Blois and Henry's daughter Matilda and the great lords among them have decided who shall hold the royal dignity, I will be glad to accept their verdict."

"King David told me you would say some such thing,"

Summerville called back. "He bade me tell you that this time it would not be sufficient. If you will not stand with us, he will account you an enemy."

"I am sorry for that," Oliver replied politely, although he tried to make clear that the threat left him unmoved. "I admire and respect the king of the Scots and would wish always to be on good terms with him. With all courtesy, Sir William, tell him from me that in spite of these harsh words, I will think of him as a friend until he does me harm."

"Have you not heard that all the north has come over to King David and the empress?" Summerville shouted, a note of anger coming into his voice. "Only a few fools in Wark denied my summons, and they soon yielded."

Sir Oliver raised and dropped his hands in a gesture equivalent to a shrug, for Summerville could hardly have seen the movement of his shoulders. "I think Sir Walter Espec will not be pleased, for Wark is his. But Espec is well able to see to his own affairs. As for me, if you did not know, I hold Jernaeve for my niece, Demoiselle Audris. Thus, I am not free to do my own pleasure but must think first of what is best for her."

There was a brief hesitation, and Summerville's horse suddenly backed a step and sidled, indicating that his master's hand had moved incautiously on the reins. Sir Oliver knew the hint of uneasiness had nothing to do with the fact that he did not hold Jernaeve in his own right. Summerville would discount Audris's nominal possession as of no importance. Walter Espec's displeasure was another matter.

Espec was one of the great men of the area, regarded as *dux et pater* by the other barons of the northeast, although he had no great title. Apparently Wark castle had capitulated easily, and from that Summerville had assumed that Espec either favored Matilda's cause or would prefer David as an overlord to either Stephen or Matilda. Oliver could see that his remark had raised doubts in Summerville's mind. Sir William knew that if Espec supported Stephen, Espec could rouse Yorkshire, Durham, and Northumbria to fight for the new English king, and it would be far more difficult, perhaps impossible, for King David to hold Northumbria.

It was easy for Oliver to follow Sir William's thoughts that far. He could not determine the result the doubts would produce. Summerville might decide against expending time, blood, and money in attacking so impregnable a place as Jernaeve if David could not hold the shire. It was equally possible for Summerville to feel that possession of Jernaeve would be sufficiently valuable in controlling Northumbria to merit an instant, overwhelming attack. It might depend on whether Summerville knew how strong Jernaeve was; Oliver could not remember him, but he hoped Summerville might have accompanied King David, who had guested at the keep more than once.

Summerville's reply, however, did nothing to encourage the hope that he feared Jernaeve's impregnability. "It will not be best for Demoiselle Audris to have a war going on about her," he snapped, harkening back to Oliver's remark that his behavior was constrained by Audris's best interests.

"Let us hope it does not come to that," Oliver said, but Summerville made no answer aside from turning his horse and signaling his troop to ride away.

Chapter 2

SIR WALTER'S CHIEF SQUIRE, HUGH LICORNE, HAPPENED TO be in Wark when Sir William de Summerville and his army arrived, and he had no intention of yielding tamely, although he had no power to prevent the castellan of Wark castle from doing so.

Hugh Licorne was no boy in training. Measured by age, skill, and experience, he should long since have been knighted, but Hugh had neither family nor patrimony—nor even a real name of his own, for there was no one he had ever heard of called Licorne—or "Unicorn," in the common tongue—and he could see no reason to assume honors he could not support. In fact, Hugh could have had his spurs and a fief as Sir Walter's vassal if he wished. Sir Walter had generously offered those to Hugh when he turned twenty years of age, but Hugh had said, quite truthfully, that he preferred to stay and serve as his lord's squire.

Thus, when Summerville's demand came that Wark yield and declare for Matilda, the castellan had little choice but to include Hugh, who had come as surrogate for Sir Walter, when he convened a council of the officers of the keep to discuss the Scottish threat. He had summoned the men into the keep itself instead of meeting with them in the hall in the lower bailey. If that was a device to create a sense of urgency in those gathered around him, it did not work with Hugh. The dimness of the building, lit only through the open door and the arrow slits in the walls, gave Hugh a sense of security rather than oppressing him by implying they were reduced to a last hope, and Hugh spoke out boldly against yielding.

"I have no choice," the castellan had answered angrily, glaring at Hugh. "We are not manned to fight an army."

"But you are victualed to withstand a siege," Hugh urged. "If you think them too strong, at least make one foray so that some men-at-arms can ride to warn Sir Walter. He will—"

"Ride all the way to London?" the castellan interrupted, sneering. "And who knows if Sir Walter is there? He might be anywhere. A man could be weeks, even months finding him. And then, having found him, it will doubtless be only to discover that Hugh Licorne is less clever than he thinks in his understanding of Sir Walter's intentions. Sir Walter is not a man who breaks his oath. *I* think it more likely that he has decided to hold by his homage to Matilda. And even if Sir Walter has done homage to Stephen, as you seem to believe, Wark could be destroyed before he could return north and gather an army."

Hugh's bright blue eyes blazed, and his lips parted as if to speak again, but he did not. He dropped his eyes and closed his mouth in a hard line. Hugh knew his protest against yielding was not misplaced, for he had not been alone in his opinion of Wark's ability to resist; the castle marshal had said he felt Wark was strong enough to hold out for several weeks, at least, and the steward reported that they were well supplied. But the castellan had brushed off the advice of his own officers, just as he had more angrily rejected Hugh's more direct suggestions. He was now pointing out that if a keep were yielded in good condition, it could always be returned intact, whereas if it were destroyed by attacks or even razed for spite, great expense would be involved to restore it.

Hugh's wide, mobile lips thinned even more as he held back a hot rejoinder. Seldom was a yielded castle returned without a stiff payment of ransom. It was a moot point whether it would be more expensive to rebuild or buy Wark's freedom, but the question was irrelevant. Sir Walter was the kind of man who would gladly pay double the cost to rebuild rather than pay ransom for what had been meekly delivered into enemy hands.

And Wark keep was no fragile house of cards. The huge logs of the palisade and the strong wooden keep, two feet thick at their bases, were well sunk into the motte on which the keep was built and the rampart above the ditch that surrounded the lower bailey. The logs were soaked with winter rain and snow and could not easily be set afire. As far as Hugh had seen, the Scots had brought no mighty siege engines to batter down the log wall, and even if they had, the stones shot from mangonel or trebuchet lost so much power coming across the deep ditch and up the rise on which the wall was set that it would take a long time to damage the fabric. And that was only the outer wall. The keep was set even higher and surrounded by an even more formidable palisade.

Hugh also knew it was useless to argue when he had no power to enforce his opinion, and he saw that the castellan's mind was made up. In fact, it seemed to have been made up from the first sighting of the Scots... or had it been made up even before Summerville's army appeared? The idea should not have occurred to Hugh; for a castellan to yield a castle entrusted to him because he believed it would best benefit his overlord might be excusable, but to arrange in advance of any threat to hand over his trust to an enemy was deeply dishonorable. Nonetheless, Hugh wondered. There had been oddities in the castellan's behavior from the time he had arrived.

Hugh had come to Wark to collect the lord's share of the produce of the demesne and the rents of the tenants. Usually Sir Walter came himself, using the opportunity to examine the property, listen to any complaints, and look over the men-at-arms and the defenses of the keep, as well as go over the accounts. This time, because of the urgent political situation, Sir Walter had sent Hugh to take back to Helmsley what was owing to him. Instead of producing the tally sticks and giving orders to make ready transport for the cheeses, salt meat, and other items due Sir Walter, the castellan had claimed to be too busy to attend the matter that day or the next. He had told Hugh jovially that a few days' delay could not matter. Hugh was to amuse himself, and on the Monday he would make up the accounts.

At the time, Hugh had accepted the excuse, feeling only mildly irritated by the castellan's assumption that he would be glad to take advantage of his master's absence to idle away a few days. Now, in conjunction with the castellan's fixed intention to accept Summerville's terms, the reluctance to fulfill his commitment to Sir Walter took on suspicious overtones. And one suspicion bred others. Doubtless, Hugh thought furiously, the terms of yielding would contain an agreement that the castellan would continue to hold Wark—or would be adequately compensated, perhaps with an estate of his own in Scotland. Whether the terms would be equally generous to those who had urged resistance was questionable. Possibly, also, the castellan would not be eager for Sir Walter Espec to learn too soon that Wark had been yielded to King David. In that case, Hugh thought, Sir Walter's most trusted squire was unlikely to be allowed to leave soon—or, perhaps, at all.

Hugh dropped his head as if abashed by being made a fool by the castellan's reasoning. Then, pretending his embarrassment made him wish to be less conspicuous, he eased his way back in the group surrounding the castellan's chair until he was in a patch of shadow. Just now, Hugh knew, the man was intent on justifying his own actions, and perhaps almost had himself convinced; however, Hugh did not think the castellan was really a fool. When the man reconsidered what had happened, he might well become suspicious of Hugh's quick capitulation and realize that Hugh had not been convinced and still intended to warn his lord that Wark was lost.

Quietly, while the castellan talked about the terms he would demand for yielding, Hugh moved farther back and then down the hall until he was able to slip out the door. To his relief, the drawbridge was still down between the wooden keep atop the motte and the bailey below. He had not heard the castellan give orders to have it raised, but he might have done so secretly. Since he had not, it was probable that he had not given any other special orders. Hugh came down the steps and crossed the bridge without signs of haste, although he was moving as quickly as he could, and made his way to the large hall in the bailey where he had been quartered among the men-at-arms.

In the hall, he swung off his cloak and undid his belt as he walked toward the chest where his arms and armor were stored. Opening it, he lifted out his hauberk. It was the finest mail, and his hand stroked it lovingly as he thought of the giver. For a man born as he had been, Hugh thought, he had been singularly blessed. As if to make up to him for having no father in blood, he had been granted two fathers of the heart.

His hauberk, a costly work that he would have been hard pressed to pay for, had been a gift from Thurstan, archbishop of York, into whose care he had been given when only a few hours old by his dying mother. An odd gift, some would have said, from one like Thurstan, who was not one of the fighting warrior bishops but a truly holy man, but to Hugh it was a mark of his foster father's true goodness. Thurstan would not twist his ward's nature to satisfy his own desires. Having seen that despite gentle persuasion Hugh had no inclination for a religious life, he had not forced the child in his care into the Church. Instead, Thurstan had placed the boy in Walter Espec's household, where Hugh could become what he wished to be—a fighting man.

His lord's name reminded Hugh that this was no time for memories, no matter how dear, and he straightened the hauberk and laid it front down on the chest so he could lift the back and slide his head and shoulders into it. Having drawn in his arms and worked each upward, Hugh stood, feeling for the armholes. The weight of the mail pushed the garment down as soon as his arms were through the sleeves. No one paid any attention to him. With an army forming outside the keep, there was nothing surprising in a man's arming.

He reached into the chest again, brought out his spurs, and pushed them into the belt pouch, which he slid onto his sword belt, then belted on his sword. That, too, was a finer weapon than a man of his status would ordinarily have. Sir Walter had given it to Hugh when he had said he would like to remain in his lord's household and serve him. Hugh's fingers moved to the silverbound hilt and caressed it fondly, but a faint frown formed between his wide-spaced eyes. Aside from his love for his master, his reason for remaining a squire had been to quiet the envy Sir Walter's open affection for him bred in other members of the household, and even in Sir Walter's nephews. The gift of the sword, which had been made for Sir Walter's dead son, had rendered virtually useless Hugh's rejection of knighthood and an estate. In some ways, the situation had become even worse. There had been nasty insinuations that Hugh's action was the first step in a campaign to become Sir Walter's heir.

Each time this thought occurred to Hugh, he felt sick with fear that Sir Walter would hear and—even if he did not believe—be hurt. The solution to the problem was extremely simple: leave Sir Walter. But to leave without a reason after saying he wanted to stay would also hurt his dear lord. So, as he had done each time before, Hugh thrust both problem and solution out of his mind. Immediately, other problems—practical difficulties concerning his escape from Wark—flooded in to take the place of the nagging worry he had dismissed.

An armed man afoot is at a great disadvantage, but Hugh knew that even if the castellan were willing to let him go, which he doubted, to ride across the drawbridge of the lower bailey would simply deliver him into Summerville's hands. Hugh's mobile lips twisted briefly into a grimace. The alternative was managing to hide in the keep until dark, going over the wall at night, and stealing a saddled horse or a horse and saddle separately from some knight in the Scottish army. The chance that he would succeed in escaping and getting to Sir Walter was growing slimmer and slimmer as he thought about what he must do, but Hugh's stubborn chin just set harder. There *was* a chance, and that was better than sitting in Wark for months… or dying here.

Hugh took up the cloak he had laid aside while he donned his armor, and another problem, minor but irritating, made him draw up the hood. Hugh had the misfortune of having a remarkably distinctive face. No one failed to remember him, even after just glimpsing him briefly once. The flaming red hair, so red that occasionally some simple soul touched it to see if it were hot, was bad enough since it drew attention, but it was his eyes that really marked him. They were large, bright blue, and set so wide apart under a broad brow that they appeared unfocused. A strong Roman nose and a mouth a bit too wide for the long, stubborn chin below completed an appearance that seemed to make many uncomfortable and was totally unforgettable.

Thus, if he did not use his hood to conceal his face, every person he passed would mark his doings. And, of course, if he did shadow his face enough to hide his eyes, there was a chance someone would remember that. Still, of the alternatives, the concealing hood seemed better to Hugh because the serfs in this keep did not seem overly curious or likely to run to their master to report an oddity. He had one piece of luck, too. Although Summerville's herald had brought his demands soon after sunup, the castellan had not called the council to discuss the problem until after they had eaten dinner. Thus, there was no particular place that Hugh would be expected to appear, and his absence might go unnoticed altogether until the evening meal was laid out.

When Hugh came out the front door of the hall, he was relieved to find that there was more defensive activity in the bailey than he had noticed when he entered the back. Serfs and men-at-arms were soaking hides in troughs of water and dragging the hides up to the walkway built about four feet below the top of the palisade in the areas considered most vulnerable to fire arrows. Other soaked hides were being laid over the roofs of essential storage sheds. Arrows for the short bow and quarrels for crossbows were being piled at intervals around the wall, as were strong poles with forks or hooks at one end for toppling scaling ladders. Last-minute repairs were being made to arms and armor by the harried smith in the small smithy. Men hurried from place to place, carrying items demanded by the smith and by the master-at-arms.

In the shadow of his hood, Hugh smiled; no one would notice one more hurrying figure. He made his way quickly to the storage sheds, glancing in and passing by one and then another. The third held what he wanted, and he entered and took a coil of rope, which he looped over his shoulder where it was hidden by his cloak. He then walked purposefully to the palisade and climbed to the walkway.

Once on the wall, Hugh did not hurry. He paused often and carefully examined the disposition of the Scottish troops. Some were settling down and making camp, but small parties were riding out to forage for supplies at outlying farms, and others were in the village that had grown up below the keep. Even as he watched, the thatch of one hut burst into flame. Hugh cursed softly under his breath. The villagers should have been taken into the keep for protection, but there had not been time enough. Either the invasion had truly taken the castellan by surprise, or he had known too much and dared not expose his knowledge by warning the villagers. Hugh shook his head as another roof was set afire. Summerville was growing impatient and had decided to hasten the decision of Wark's castellan by demonstrating his power to burn out the village.

Hugh watched thoughtfully while several more fires were set, but he saw that mostly smaller, isolated places were burning. The most distinctive building in the village, the two-storied house of the alewife, was well away from any threat of fire. They would not burn that—at least, not until all the drink was gone. Hugh glanced anxiously at the sky. The morning had been bright, but it was clouding up now and would be dark enough for him to go quite soon. A flicker of movement to his left drew a sidelong glance, and Hugh saw that several men-at-arms were converging on that section of the wall, drawn by the signs of fire in the village. Hugh moved west quickly. Fortunately, the men's interest in the action to the southeast was intense enough to make insignificant the oddity of Hugh's hooded form, but when one of the men called the news down into the bailey and the master-at-arms ran off toward the keep to report to the castellan, Hugh felt his period of grace might be over.

He moved more quickly, dividing his attention between the area outside the walls and the stairway to the motte, and it was not long before men began to emerge from the keep.

Someone in that group was shouting; it was too far for Hugh to recognize the face or voice, but he thought he heard his name. He ducked down so that his head and shoulders would not be outlined against the sky above the wall and made his way, crouching, to one of the ladders that connected the walkway with the ground. Just as he turned to descend, he caught sight of a man running from the base of the motte drawbridge toward the stables. It could be that a horse was to be readied to bring the castellan's submission to Summerville and prevent further attacks on the village, but Hugh had the feeling that the castellan wanted to know whether his horse was still in the stables. Another man running toward the guards at the bailey drawbridge convinced Hugh that the castellan had become aware of his absence and was seeking him.

Hugh came down from the walkway at once and slipped behind the supports close to the wall. Here he paused to turn his cloak inside out to expose the dark fur that lined it rather than the emerald-green cloth. The footing was terrible, since no one ordinarily walked in that area, and refuse was often dropped from the wall or tossed under the walkway by anyone passing. Hugh stumbled and grimaced with disgust when his foot came down on something that squished and gave off a sickening odor of putrefaction, but eventually he reached his goal, a place about midway on the westerly side of the palisade where one of the storage sheds was built right against the walkway braces.

Here Hugh moved away from the palisade, setting his back against the rear wall of the shed just alongside an upright brace. Now, unless the search for him grew so frantic that every inch of ground was to be examined with torches, Hugh felt he would be safe. He leaned on the wall, crossed himself, and offered up a prayer for help to the Mother of God and to Saint Jude, the champion of lost causes. Although Hugh had not found in himself any vocation for the religious life, Archbishop Thurstan's influence had had a powerful effect on him. His faith was strong, and it had been encouraged by Walter Espec, who was himself deeply religious. Comforted, Hugh relaxed. He continued to listen intently both for sounds of anyone approaching and for any hint of whether the search for him was intensifying or diminishing, but Hugh's mind was now busy with what he had seen from the wall.

By the time it was dark enough for Hugh to move from his shelter, it was also very quiet there. Hugh had begun to think his original assumption was wrong and the castellan had never been searching for him. If so, the rushing to the stables and the gate guards was preliminary to negotiating the submission of Wark. The thought made Hugh angry, but the situation was advantageous to him because both the guards of Wark and those of Summerville's army would be relaxed rather than alert for an attack.

Hugh moved quietly to one end of the shed and peered out. Nothing. Slipping back, he worked his way to the other end and still saw no one moving in the area. Not once since dusk had he heard footsteps on the walkway above him. There was a mounting ladder not far away, and Hugh came out of concealment and climbed it. He paused with his head just above the walkway to look right and left. As far as he could see in the dark, the walkway was empty. If there were guards, presumably they watched where the army was camped. Hugh climbed the rest of the way up, bending to keep below the line of the palisade. Still crouched, he pulled the coil of rope from his shoulder and fastened one end around the sharpened top of one log of the wall—and froze as a shout of warning rang out and a torch, plunged into a firepot, burst into flame.

The paralysis of surprise was very brief. Tightening his grip on the rope, Hugh flung himself over the wall and let himself slide down a good deal faster than he had intended. He bit his lips against the pain as friction burned his hands and pieces of hemp found soft spots in his callused palms and were driven into the flesh, but he was not tempted to slow his pace. The rope jerked as a sword was brought against it, but swords are not efficient chopping weapons, and the rope held for two more blows. When the last strand parted and dumped Hugh, his legs were bent to absorb the shock and he was near enough to the ground to land without injury. The slope of the ditch below the rampart was steep, however, and he rolled helplessly down, bumping and scrabbling for a hold on the rocky, fire-scored earth.

Hugh did not mind the bruises, although each time he rolled over, his sword, dagger, and pouch dug painfully into various parts of his anatomy. What he objected to was the noise he was making. One of his gyrations gave him a flashing sight of the wall, but it was enough to show several more torches. Then fire blossomed just below him, and he twisted wildly to avoid rolling onto the torch that had been thrown down to light the area. His body would not extinguish the flame; most likely the soft, burning pitch would stick to him and set his cloak afire. Other torches followed, but none so close, as Hugh finally hit the bottom of the ditch in a shower of earth and stones.

In the quiet that followed his impact with the far side of the ditch, Hugh heard the whirr and thunk of arrows behind him. The men on the wall had expected him to be stunned and lie quiet or to waste time trying to climb to his feet, and that first concentrated flight had missed because Hugh had crawled forward immediately, straight ahead for a few feet, and then irregularly from side to side. Still, the only thing that saved him was that the excited men began to shoot separately instead of blanketing the area with a series of flights.

A moment later, Hugh was out of the lighted area, and he stopped abruptly, swept up a handful of earth and pebbles, and threw them a short distance ahead. As he levered himself painfully to his knees, he grabbed for more with both hands, letting fly first with his left hand and then, harder, with his right.

To Hugh, the spattering did not sound much like a man running or crawling, but the noises must have been very faint by the time they reached the palisade, and for a few minutes arrows whirred off into the dark, well ahead of Hugh's position. The brief respite gave him a chance to stretch himself face down, not along the bottom of the ditch but vertically against the rise of the slope toward the palisade, and he lay immobile, trying to quiet his gasping breaths.

More torches began to rain down at last as the archers realized they had lost their target, but the dirt-encrusted fur of

Hugh's cloak was an adequate disguise in the flickering, uncertain light they gave. Lying flat and still, he seemed no more than another irregularity of the rain-carved side of the mound. Finally the chase moved on around the palisade. By then the torches that had been thrown first were guttering out, the soft pitch having picked up enough dirt to leave little surface to burn as they, too, rolled down the slope. Quietly, Hugh turned over, eased himself upright, and returned, as near as he could estimate, to where the rope still hung from the wall. Of all the places they would look for him, the last, he hoped, would be where the symbol of his escape marked his route.

Slowly and carefully Hugh began to climb the other side of the ditch, feeling for handholds and footholds that would not set loose stones rolling. Fortunately, this side was not so carefully burned over to eliminate brush to make it difficult to climb. The purposes of the ditch and rampart were first to discourage attackers and second to make it hard for them to get into the keep. As a result, the mound rising to the palisade was denuded of anything that might assist climbers or shelter them.

No one cared how fast invaders ran away, though, so only brush large enough to divert the aim of archers was cleared from the far side of the ditch. Hugh found well-rooted plants to set his feet against and to steady his hands. True, most of them were brambles, and a variety of thorns were added to the splinters of hemp in Hugh's abused hands, but speed and security were more essential than comfort, and he did not complain at the pricks.

Over the edge of the rise, Hugh went forward about twenty strides and then stood still, listening. A winter quiet lay over the land; no birds sang or chattered, no insects hummed, no frogs or toads peeped and croaked. Yet, at the edge of hearing there was faint sound, a low grumble comprised of the noise of many fires, many snores, many animals moving and breathing, a few voices. What was significant to Hugh was that there was no sharper level to the grumble to indicate a group of guards watching without a fire in the dark. Had there been any near, they would have been moving and talking, for they would have been witnesses to the excitement caused by his escape.

Satisfied, Hugh began to walk rapidly toward the Scottish encampment. As he went, he removed his cloak and shook the dirt out of it as carefully as he could. Then he raised the mail hood of his hauberk and fastened it so that it hid his hair. Pushing up his mail sleeve, he used the cloth beneath to clean what little of his face showed and to rub what dirt he could off his hands. Actually he was more concerned about his own comfort than afraid that dirt would betray him; men in an army on the march were not known for their cleanliness.

When he saw the first campfires, Hugh slowed his pace and tried to estimate their distance from the edge of the ditch. After a moment, he smiled grimly and walked on. He was almost certain he could pass the outermost groups without being noticed. If that were true, when he did have to pass through the encampment it would seem as if he had walked down to look at the rampart rather than that he was coming from outside the camp.

This expectation was fulfilled; at least, no one challenged him. Hugh guessed that those who did see him clearly enough to know he was not a fellow man-at-arms going to the latrine or seeking a friend assumed from the richness of his fur-lined cloak that he was one of Summerville's Norman companions. To further this deception, Hugh strode along boldly, looking neither left nor right, as if he knew exactly where he was going.

That much was true, although Hugh would gladly have diverted his goal had he seen a saddled horse he could seize. There had been no horses on the outskirts of the camp, for most of those men were peasant levies who were foot soldiers; as he penetrated more deeply into the encampment, he did see some tethered animals, but there was no hope of obtaining one of those and escaping.

When Hugh saw that the campfires ahead seemed to form a line, he began to wonder whether he had angled his path too sharply and was approaching the southern edge of the camp. Nonetheless, he dared not ask any questions or seem to hesitate. If challenged, he had a haughty reply ready that might save his skin, but there were no looks of surprise or questions as he passed the last line of fires, and soon a large, solid block of shadow loomed ahead: a house.

Breathing a soft prayer of thanksgiving and another fervent one for continued help, Hugh turned sharply right to walk well behind the cultivated patch usual at the back of each house, and then left when a second solid shadow appeared to pass between the two dwellings. There was an ugly stench of burning as he drew closer; Hugh's generous mouth tightened with anger and pity, but he was already doing what he could to help. If he got to Sir Walter, he would mention the villagers who had been sacrificed—and sacrifice it was, not the ordinary chances of war. Since the castellan had already decided to yield, he should have told Summerville at once instead of idling away the morning and waiting until he had eaten; then, likely no burning would have been ordered or permitted.

Those angry thoughts did not divert Hugh from necessary caution. He slowed his pace, watching for fallen beams or rubbish. Even so, he tripped on something soft and almost cried out when the hand he extended to break his fall struck a cold and rigid face. At least it was a man, Hugh thought, recognizing gender and age from the short hair and bristled chin. A dead woman or child would have made him sick and so angry that he might have lost his sense of priorities. Even so, he dropped to his knees beside the body for a moment, closed the eyes, and murmured the prayer of absolution and then another to Mary, begging her infinite mercy for this poor soul who had died with his sins upon him and no chance to confess them.

Hugh knew he had no right to give absolution and knew it was probably too late anyway, but he thought it could not hurt. And Hugh's trust in the mercy of Christ's mother was infinite. He had adored the Virgin since he was a little boy. Hugh had come to believe that his early interest was probably owing to the fact that he himself had no mother. As an adult, however, he felt just as strongly about the Virgin because, unlike many other saints, Mary was not at all rigid and unbending. Not only was she tender and merciful, but she had a quixotic sense of humor, and many legends concerning her described her defense of downright sinful behavior when it was self-defeating and naughty rather than cruel and hurtful to others.

Having done everything he could for the dead man, Hugh edged around the body and continued on even more cautiously. He found no other corpses, and soon recognized his goal, the house of the alewife. There Hugh hoped to find the horse of some leader of the Scottish army who was making free with the alewife's brew, but no animals were tethered in front of the building. Hugh hesitated, then came ahead anyway. He thought he remembered a shed at the back of the house. There was a chance the family owned a horse, and it might still be there.

A structure did protrude from the back of the building, as he remembered. Hugh advanced cautiously, sniffing to determine whether the place smelled of animals or cooking, for such an extension could as easily be a kitchen as a shelter for the family's animals—or both. The attempt was defeated by an overwhelming smell of woodsmoke and an underlying mixture of stenches from manure, animal and human, vomit, stale beer, and other assorted refuse.

A crash and a scream from inside the house behind him froze Hugh for a moment. He realized then that there were Scots in the house, and he hurried around the corner, where he would not be in sight if a window or door opened. He was feeling for the opening into the shed when he was brought up short by treading on a chain. Hugh froze again, expecting the dog to leap at him barking wildly, but knew, even as he stiffened, that the animal would have given the alarm already if it had been able. To make sure that the beast was not inside the shed, trained to give voice and attack only if someone entered, Hugh crouched and felt for the end of the chain. His hand touched another stiff body, this one covered in fur. Hugh stroked the still form automatically, apologetically. He was very fond of animals, and it saddened him when a beast was killed in a quarrel among men.

The brief pause saved him. As he drew his hand back from the dog's body, Hugh heard the crunch of a pebble grinding underfoot and a faint clink of metal against metal. He had his knife out as the man came around the side of the building, and he rose and thrust the knife against the throat in one swift motion, grasping for the back of the man's head with his other hand so that his victim could not jerk away. But the blade did not come to rest against leather or mail as Hugh had expected. To his surprise, it slid in right to the hilt. The body convulsed against his, but Hugh had been prepared for resistance and automatically clutched it against him. In the next instant it sagged bonelessly, and Hugh eased down with the weight.

Only when the man lay alongside the dog did Hugh quickly draw his knife free of the wound it had made, for he did not want to be covered in blood—blood made horses nervous. As he wiped his knife blade and the edge of his hand, where a trickle from the wound had run, on his victim's tunic, Hugh again muttered absolution and a prayer for the sped soul. He was sorry about having killed when he did not intend to, but the man was an enemy, after all, and it was his own fault for being careless about his armor. Hugh had killed men before, and another death did not trouble him.

Paramount in his mind was the question of whether the man had been a guard sent to watch the shed, and, if so, whether another guard waited inside to be relieved. He did not think so, because no glow of light showed and there was no reason for the guard to wait in the dark. Still, he carried his knife bare in his hand, hidden by the edge of his cloak. Now, however, he walked boldly toward the open side of the shed, as if he were expected. At the entry he stopped, but the only sounds were the breathing and low snorting of resting animals and the stamp of a horse's shod hoof.

Hugh's eyes were adjusted to the dark, so he was able to make out the forms of several horses crowded together in the small shed by the very faint light coming through a crack here and there. But none of the horses wore a saddle. Hugh bit back an exclamation of disappointment. Even as he did so, his hopes rose strongly again. He knew that even the alewife could not afford so many horses and would have no use for them. It was cold, and there was a nasty wind. Likely some of the captains had chosen to lodge in the alewife's house rather than in tents. As the thoughts passed through his mind, Hugh's eyes roved around the shed and at once caught a faint gleam of metal from a dark heap near the rear wall. There were the saddles!

Relief made him incautious, and his foot again struck a soft body as he hurried toward his goal. The form jerked, proving it was alive, but made no sound other than a faint grunt. Hugh was down beside the man in a moment, his knife pricking the throat. This time he was more careful, and there was no accident. There was no need, either. An intense odor of beer and vomit assaulted Hugh's nose as he leaned over to command silence, so he saved his warning. It took no more than a moment to cut the man's crossgarters and tie his hands and feet. Another minute sufficed to use a strip of his tunic to gag him.

Stepping over him, Hugh reached for a saddle. His hand grazed a lantern over on its side, its candle out. He hesitated a moment, then got flint and steel from his belt pouch and lit the candle. If the man on the floor had been the guard and the one he had killed had been his relief, no one else was likely to visit the shed. There was only a small chance, then, that the light would betray him, and it would permit him to saddle so much faster that Hugh was willing to take the chance.

As soon as Hugh held up the lantern, he began to laugh heartily if silently. The saddle he had reached for was bound and bossed in silver, the saddle cloth near it was embroidered in silver and gold. Hugh turned to look at the horses, and the sight of a tall, powerful destrier among the lesser animals made his grin grow wider. It seemed Sir William de Summerville himself was lodged here. Now Hugh was thankful for the castellan's delay in yielding Wark, for Summerville would surely have lodged in the keep if it had been turned over to him.

A moment later Hugh's hands were busy gentling the high-bred warhorse. Most men would have thought twice about trying to saddle a strange destrier without help, for the warhorses were taught to be fierce and to attack strangers. But Hugh had a way with animals, and he murmured dulcetly to the horse as he offered a handful of grain from an open sack near the saddles. This form of bribery, combined with Hugh's lack of fear, worked quickly. Bit and bridle were slipped in place while the horse nuzzled for the last kernels in his hand. Then Hugh led him to the sack, which occupied him happily while cloth and saddle were swung into place and cinched. This done, it was easy enough to take the stallion outside, where sound was less likely to disturb those in the house, and jab him violently in the ribs so the cinch could be properly tightened.

Grinning from ear to ear, Hugh swung up into the saddle and trotted out of the yard and onto the road. He had often been told that virtue and devotion to duty, being good works that smoothed the path to heaven, were their own reward, but this time the reward was tangible. Hugh was now richer by a very fine horse and all its valuable accoutrements—and all taken from a rich enemy, too, so that he would not need to feel guilty about depriving some other poor man of his means of livelihood.

Fate had another twist for Hugh, however. He did not succeed in escaping unnoticed. By chance, one of the men drinking with Sir William de Summerville in the alewife's house stepped out to piss just as Hugh was disappearing down the road. The man was somewhat fuddled with drink, but not so fuddled that the sight of a mounted man riding south out of the village did not raise doubts in his mind. He shouted a question and then an order to stop, which, needless to say, Hugh did not obey.

In fact, Hugh kicked his horse into a gallop and kept the pace until he was through the armed camp, staying carefully on the road that ran due south. But when he judged that the sound of pounding hooves could no longer carry back to the camp, Hugh checked the horse and turned west. He knew he would be pursued as soon as Summerville discovered whose horse had been taken, but he would be far away by then and, he hoped, the pursuers would believe he had continued south or would turn east to find protection in Prudhoe or Newcastle.

The thought generated a doubt in his mind. Since King David himself had not come to Wark, doubtless he had other, more important castles to subdue. It was impossible for Hugh to guess which places had been attacked, and he decided that safety lay in avoiding all towns and all fortified places until he was well south in England. That made him think of the great wall that crossed England. He would be much safer once he was south of that. It was a ruin except where it had been repaired, but it was a formidable ruin, as much as ten or twelve feet high wherever it had not been deliberately breached. Hugh frowned. He had no idea where the breaches were, and off the road, with the stars hidden by clouds, he was not even certain of his direction.

Chapter 3

WHEN HUGH THOUGHT BACK ON HIS ESCAPE, HE WAS SURE Saint Jude or the Blessed Virgin herself had had a hand on his horse's bridle all the way. With neither moon nor stars to guide him, all he could do was keep the wind, which he remembered as being from the northeast, at his back. Nonetheless, he did not travel in circles; he came to the great wall before dawn—and without seeing or hearing a sign of pursuit.

By daybreak he had found a breach, where the small river that ran along the wall sent a branch southward. He and the destrier drank, then followed the river valley for only a little way before they came on a road. This ran somewhat westward of south, but Hugh took it gladly, for this part of the country was strange to him, and a road meant people. He had reason to doubt the wisdom of his decision all morning, because the country was desolate, but by afternoon he had come to a crossroad that went east and looked better traveled, and late in the day he came to Brough keep, where there was news of King Stephen.

The king was in Westminster, they told him, and directed him south by way of Richmond and Pontefract, grateful for the warning he brought about the danger from the Scots. Fortunately, Hugh did not need to ride all the way to Westminster. Somewhere on the road—he never remembered where, for after that night at Brough he stopped only when either he or his horse was failing—he heard that the king had come north as far as Oxford. When Hugh came there, in the afternoon of the fifth day, he and his horse were hollow with exhaustion. Still, the quality of his mount could not be mistaken, and the richness of his saddle and armor contributed to the alacrity with which Sir Walter was sought and Hugh brought to him. Hardly able to keep on his feet, Hugh blurted out his news about Wark without noticing anything except his master.

A tall, fair man, who had stepped back a few paces as Hugh approached as if to give Sir Walter privacy to speak to his visitor, came closer again and repeated, "The Scots have taken Wark, you say? Where is Wark? Why should my uncle wish to seize it?"

In turning toward the voice, Hugh staggered and would have fallen if Sir Walter had not put an arm around him to support him. And it was Sir Walter who replied. "Wark is in Northumbria, Sire, north of Jernaeve. As to why King David should desire it, I have no idea. There is no route south from Wark, for Jernaeve guards the valley to the south… unless King David intends to use Wark as a base from which to attack Jernaeve. But before I make more wild guesses, let me ask, Hugh, do you have any other news?"

Hugh had steadied himself and removed his weight from Sir Walter's arm. His lord was still strong, but he was not young, and Hugh stood equally tall. "The king was not at Wark," he said slowly, trying to be sure his answer was coherent, "and the army, from what I could judge, was small. One of his men, Sir William de Summerville, called on us to yield in the name of the Empress Matilda to oppose—"

"This," Espec interrupted hastily, gesturing toward the tall man who had asked the questions about Wark, "is King Stephen, Hugh."

Hugh blinked blurrily at a broad, good-natured face with kindly gray eyes. There seemed no threat in it, but Sir Walter could only have interrupted him with such information as a warning. To give himself time for his tired brain to work, Hugh undid the laces holding the throat piece of his hood and pushed the mail off his head.

But the king had understood Sir Walter's warning, and he shook his head. "I will not blame the messenger for ill tidings," Stephen said. "Did Summerville call me a usurper?" And then he added inconsequentially, "With that flaming hair, you look like a Scot yourself, young man."

"I do not know," Hugh said, feeling more confused than ever by Stephen's personal remark. "My mother died soon after I was born, and I was a ward of Archbishop Thurstan, who gave me for fostering to Sir Walter." But then his mind reverted to what he had been thinking about all during his long ride. "King David did not come to Wark," he repeated, "and although I have never been inside Jernaeve, I have passed by that keep. The army with Summerville could never take that place. I think the main army must be with the king, perhaps attacking Newcastle or Prudhoe."

"But Hugh," Sir Walter protested, "for the Scots to be as far south as Newcastle would mean—"

"That the whole north of England has fallen," Stephen interrupted harshly. "Why should you think the king of Scotland so far south?"

Hugh blinked his burning eyes again, but he answered readily because he had thought out the whole subject on the long way south. "First because Wark is no great bastion of the north that must be taken to make holding the land possible. Thus, any leader but a fool would leave that for last, to be swept into the net after the big fish were taken—and my reason must be good because no large force was sent. The manner of the demands made on Wark was another piece of evidence, and the way the army settled in, a third. They were too easy on all counts and too sure. It was as if they knew they had nothing to fear."

"Nothing to fear, eh?" Stephen growled furiously. "We will see if they have nothing to fear."

Sir Walter's hand tightened on his squire's arm, and Hugh was appalled, realizing suddenly that a meaning he had never intended could be found in his words. "My lord," he exclaimed, "I did not mean—"

Stephen patted his shoulder. "No, no, I know you meant no insult."

"Indeed I did not, Sire," Hugh assured him. "I meant that it was as if they were sure Wark must yield and knew no help would come to Wark from Alnwick or Morpeth or any other keep nearby."

"I thought you said the north would be safe," Stephen said, turning on Sir Walter.

Hugh stiffened, but Sir Walter tightened his grip on his squire's arm to keep him silent and shook his head at the king. "Not safe from the Scots, Sire. I said there was no sympathy for the empress's cause there, and I think that still to be true. King David is another matter... not that the northern lords wish to do homage to the Scottish king, but that they are uncertain of you."

"My uncle *did* lean toward me at the end," Stephen said uneasily, and then more surely, "and I have been crowned and anointed with chrism. I am king."

"Yes, my lord," Walter agreed. "I did not mean they doubted your right. What they doubt is your will or your ability to protect them from King David. They are willing to fight the Scots, but not alone. Compared with the south of England, the north is poor. Perhaps they fear you might believe it too costly to bring them help."

"Rich or poor, all parts of my kingdom are in my care!" Stephen exclaimed.

Sir Walter bowed slightly. "So I believed you would feel when I did homage to you, Sire."

Listening to this exchange, Hugh felt there was something odd in Sir Walter's manner and phrasing, but he was too tired to pick out what disturbed him. The brief spurt of energy supplied by his nervousness at being the focus of the new king's attention was ebbing rapidly. He wavered on his feet, then caught himself steady and upright, but not for long. A sharp order in Sir Walter's voice made Hugh brace his body again, but the order was not for him, and he began to sag once more. A minute later a firm arm around his waist steadied him. It was not Sir Walter, who had turned back to the king, and Hugh looked down to see that John de Bussey, Sir Walter's nephew, was supporting him.

"Come along, my sleeping beauty," John said. "My uncle has given orders that you be bedded down."

Hugh started off willingly, then hesitated. "My horse—"

"I will see to him also," John assured him. "Where did you leave him?"

Hugh remembered describing his new mount and accoutrements as well as the area of the bailey in which he had given the reins to a groom, but he did not remember anything after that, until he was wakened by a toe in the ribs to see Sir Walter standing over him, fully dressed. He sat up immediately, apologizing for oversleeping and failing to help his master dress, but Sir Walter laughed at him.

"Wake up"—he chuckled—"you are dreaming of the past. Robert and Philip dressed me as they have these two years agone." He laughed again as Hugh shook his head as if to free it of dreams and went on, "You have nearly slept the sun around, and I thought you might be more hungry by now than sleepy. But I do not need you, so you may choose for yourself whether you wish to come to dinner or finish your sleep."

"I will eat, my lord, thank you," Hugh replied.

He rose to his knees, trying to smooth the worst of the creases out of his tunic. Apparently John had let him tumble down on a straw pallet and had thrown his fur cloak over him for warmth without urging him to undress. His tunic was loose, and he looked around the room in which he had slept for his baggage before he remembered that he had come away without anything. The glance showed a nearly bare chamber of fair size with a steeply sloping roof and a stone fireplace and chimney not far from his pallet at the rear of the room. Closest to the hearth was a cot, farther away another, and by the side wall, a clothes chest. Hugh turned around, absently pulling at his chausses with one hand and gathering his tunic together with the other. At the other end of the room, taking up most of the front gable, was a large window with its shutters folded back and scraped hides keeping out some of the cold.

Clearly they were not in Oxford keep but in the solar of a house in the town. Hugh frowned, wondering if that meant that King Stephen did not value his master highly enough to lodge him, or, more pleasantly, whether Stephen had taken Sir Walter's measure and felt he did not need to watch him constantly.

His thought was interrupted by Sir Walter saying, "You need not stand there picking at your stockings and holding your tunic together like a modest maiden. I will lend you my clothes, those on the chest there. You would split John's at the shoulders, and his chausses would probably only reach midthigh on you. But you had better take one of John's belts. Mine will go around you twice."

"Thank you, my lord," Hugh mumbled in a muffled voice as he pulled off his stinking, sweat-soaked garments and donned one of his master's fine linen shirts. He did not protest, for he and his master stood a head taller than most men and were broader in proportion. It was fortunate that Hugh was redheaded and fair as well as so distinctive in feature, rather than black of eye, hair, and beard as Sir Walter was, or worse would have been said than that he was the lord's favorite. A pair of woolen stockings with attached feet and underpants was drawn on under the shirt and, over all, one of Sir Walter's plainest tunics. But Hugh did not go to John's baggage for a belt.

"I will just unhook the sword from my belt," Hugh said. "You are not wearing yours in the presence of the king, I see, and my sword will be safe with yours."

Sir Walter looked at him and raised his brows, but he did not, as Hugh had feared, insist that Hugh make use of John's belt or ask why Hugh preferred the nuisance of removing his sword from his own belt. Instead he said, "I gather from the fact that you came away from Wark without shield or helmet or saddlebags, not to mention on a horse I have never seen, that you left without my castellan's blessing."

"Yes, my lord," Hugh said. Then he grinned. "The horse and accoutrements were Sir William de Summerville's. I told you, did I not, that he led the Scottish force. Forgive me, but I do not remember very well what I said yesterday."

"You came in bawling halfway across the chamber that Wark had fallen to the Scots without a battle," Sir Walter said dryly, "but you did tell us about Summerville and that you thought all north England was in David's hands after the king began to ask questions."

Hugh looked up from tying long cloth strips around his legs to keep his borrowed chausses from sagging. He had lost his grin and paled. "If I have spoken amiss and brought trouble to you, my lord, I beg your pardon. Perhaps—"

"No, no." Sir Walter shook his head. "In this case you could not have done better than you did, and now that you know the king by sight, I am sure you will speak with more caution in his presence."

"I hope not to need to speak at all in his presence!" Hugh exclaimed. "Who am I to speak to kings?"

Sir Walter laughed at Hugh's vehemence, but shook his head. "I am afraid your company has been requested. You have taken King Stephen's fancy. He was much impressed by the devotion that drove you beyond exhaustion to bring me the news. And since he no longer regards it as bad news…"

Hugh had been about to protest the notion that his ride south had been anything extraordinary, but he was so startled that he echoed "Not bad news?" in amazement. "If I am right and the northern keeps are all taken or yielded, he has lost almost a third of his kingdom to the Scots. How can that be good?"

"Not good, perhaps," Sir Walter replied, "but an opportunity to convince the northern barons of his intention and his power both to support them against David and to control them. Nor is he wrong in so thinking. He has in hand the treasure amassed by the late king, and an army of Flemish mercenaries to pay with that treasure. Combined with the men I can raise from Yorkshire and Durham, we will easily overmatch King David's forces, especially if he has left men in the royal castles in Northumbria. But come, we will be late to dinner. And while we go, you had better tell me why you needed to flee Wark without your arms and baggage and how you came by Summerville's horse—his prize destrier, if I am not mistaken."

"The answer to the second question is tied into that for

the first," Hugh began, and explained what had happened from the time he arrived in Wark until he stopped at Brough keep.

While he talked, they went down the stair and out into the town. Hugh had been too exhausted to see anything except his goal when he had arrived, but now he looked about curiously. Because he had so often thought over the events that led to his escape from Wark, Hugh was able to describe them without much need for thought, leaving most of his attention free. To his surprise, he found they were heading downhill to the castle, which, in violation of usual practice, was built on the lowest land, near the river. Then Hugh realized that the town had not grown up around the castle; in this case the keep had been built to control the town. Oxford must have been one of those walled burghs that were what the English thought of as defended places before the coming of the first William.

The town looked prosperous, too. Hugh and Sir Walter had come out of the house onto a busy street. Most of the people were hurrying in the direction opposite to theirs, toward the lively market not far up the road from Sir Walter's house. Hugh cast a longing glance toward the noisy confusion of beasts and men and women.

Banners flapped invitingly before open storefronts; peddlers threaded their way through the crowd crying aloud of hot pies, roasted chestnuts, and other tasty tidbits; merchants held their wares aloft to draw notice to them, bellowing praises of their beauty and fine craftsmanship; buyers poked inquiring fingers through the feathers of squawking chickens and the fleece of placid sheep and examined hogs, cows, and asses. Trade was brisk if judged by the people's voices, shrill with the excitement of chaffering.

If only, Hugh thought resentfully, he had had the sense to say he was still sleepy, he could have bought himself some hot pies to eat in the market and spent a delightful day. Now, instead of enjoying himself, he would have to mind·his manners and his tongue every minute.

They had come by then through the town and past the hundred or so yards of wasteland on the far side of the moat.

Hugh noticed fleetingly certain regular lines breaking the even ground cover of dry grass and dead weeds, which showed that houses had been pulled down to clear the area and remove anything that might shelter attacking troops. Most passersby in the street were now well behind at the market or had turned off onto side lanes, but Hugh and Sir Walter were not alone. Well-dressed men, singly and in pairs and small groups, were converging with them toward the bridge that spanned the moat. Hugh and Sir Walter crossed in silence, although Sir Walter nodded to some men and raised his hand to others as their long legs carried them past smaller mortals who walked more slowly.

Sir Walter's brow was furrowed in thought, and he rasped his beard up and down ferociously, occasionally giving it a good tug. Hugh watched him in sidelong glances, wondering what was troubling him. Sir Walter often fingered his beard when thoughtful or puzzled, but he only did violence to it when deeply distressed. Even odder, several times Sir Walter turned his head and seemed about to speak, only to grunt, growl, or hawk and spit—but never a word followed. Hugh would have said that his lord was showing typical signs of embarrassment, if it had not been impossible that Sir Walter should feel that emotion with regard to him.

Inside the castle, the great hall was a scene of chaos. Some servants were scurrying about setting up trestle tables, others were bringing in sacks of day-old bread to serve as trenchers, still others dragging wooden cups, bowls, and spoons from where they were stored. At the head of the room, one table on the dais was draped with bleached linen and laid with several silver plates and one gold one.

A blond squire with curled hair and a lavishly embroidered tunic was placing precious glass goblets near each plate. The butler, even more richly dressed than the squire—which was not surprising since he was an earl and one of the great men of the kingdom—kept one eye on the elegant squire and the other on the flagons of wine being readied to fill the cups. His shouted orders sometimes overrode, sometimes conflicted with, those of the chief steward, the sewer, and the pantler, creating a cacophony of sound and a swirl of bodies dropping one task to rush off in a new direction.

Getting ready for dinner was always a busy time in any household, but this was like nothing Hugh had ever seen, and he paused on the threshold of the hall, startled by the chaos. Sir Walter thrust him forward with a hand between his shoulder blades and then passed him to weave a purposeful path toward a doorway at the rear. This led to a much smaller chamber with its own hearth, near which stood a canopied chair of state. The king was not seated there but was standing near the middle of the room within a loose half circle of men, flanked on one side by his brother, Henry of Blois, bishop of Winchester, and on the other by William Pont de l'Arche. Hugh knew neither of the men, but Sir Walter rumbled their names and the fact that they had been instrumental in getting Stephen crowned. Curiously, Hugh studied the expressions of the men as well as their faces with his bright, wide-set eyes, noting that neither man looked very cheerful.

His intense scrutiny, although brief, did not go unnoticed. First the bishop's head turned in his direction and then that of Pont de l'Arche. Both heads promptly turned back to Stephen, and both spoke eagerly, almost as if they did not want the king to notice who had caught their attention. It was too late to divert Stephen; he had already looked the same way, but his face broke into a pleased smile of recognition, and he beckoned Hugh and Sir Walter toward him.

"You are well come, on the very moment I need you," the king said genially. "Here, gentlemen, is the young man I mentioned, Hugh Licorne. And Sir Walter, you know."

Hugh bowed; Sir Walter nodded, receiving nods of recognition in return.

"We are concerned—" Winchester began.

Before he could say more, he was cut off by a peevish voice from one of the men who had been forced to move by their entry into the circle near the king. "Licorne?" the man cried. "Licorne? What sort of name is that? I do not believe it is real. The man is a Scot himself. Just look at him."

"Pembroke, do not talk nonsense," Sir Walter growled.

"Whatever his looks, Hugh has been in my household since he was eight, and his name is a name like any other. I have never known anyone but Sir William here to be called 'bridge of arches,' either, but I do not claim his name is false."

Gilbert de Clare, earl of Pembroke, a head shorter than Sir Walter and round as a barrel, glared up at him with red-veined, malevolent eyes. "So, he is *your* servant. And he rode all alone from the north to cry of King David's trespasses and makes claim that all Northumbria has fallen—although the only place he has been is *your* keep at Wark, where he admits the attackers were only a small force. They could have been a band of outlaws, hoping by a clever ruse to find easy pickings. You are asking us to believe that in the entire north of England there is not one other who would come to warn the king of a Scottish invasion. Is not one young man's word a frail thread on which to hang the rush northward of a whole army?"

"It is not so frail a thread," Hugh answered calmly before Sir Walter, who had stiffened with anger, could speak. "The force was made up of Scots and was no band of outlaws. I walked among them and heard them talking. The force was led by Sir William de Summerville, who is known to be a liege man of King David. I took his horse during my escape, and you may look at the destrier and accoutrements and tell me how an outlaw would come by such."

"Usually the outlaws in those hills are reduced to eating horses by this time of year," Sir Walter put in dryly. "And Hugh came first because he rode harder and faster."

Stephen nodded and smiled. "He was certainly all but asleep on his feet when he arrived."

Hugh bowed acknowledgment of the king's support, but his eyes were still on Pembroke. "As to my guesses about the invasion, my lord, if you can find causes other than those I offered for the attack on Wark, those causes must certainly be judged against mine. But if"—Hugh's voice suddenly lost its tone of calm reason and hardened with naked threat—"you are suggesting that this is some plot of my own or my lord's to deceive the king, I will meet"—he hesitated, ran his eyes with open contempt over Pembroke's rather flabby rotundity, then went on—"I will meet your champion and prove on his body that I have spoken the truth."

Stephen laughed. "So, Licorne's temper does grow out atop his head. I wondered at so calm a reply from one of that color hair. I like a man who will pledge his body to support his word. But it will not do. Those who love me must not fight among themselves."

"Certainly not," Winchester agreed. "Nor do I wish to cast doubt on this young man's veracity, for I believe he spoke what he believed to be the truth. Still, it does trouble me that no other message has come from the north. Does not Summerville have lands in Roxburgh? Is it not possible that the attack on Wark is some private act? And if that is so, will not it seem an offense or a threat to King David to bring a large army north?"

"I must agree," Pont de l'Arche said, shrugging. "A guess, no matter how good the will behind it, is still a guess. Sir Walter may be right that Licorne is only the first to bring this news, but it seems to me also that we should wait until we have some confirmation."

"Which might not come for another week," Sir Walter protested. "Then more time will be lost in readying the army to march. By then, King David will have his own men in all the royal keeps, and it will be said throughout the north that King Stephen would not defend the land against the Scots. Delay, and you could lose a third of your kingdom, Sire."

"Run north on a false scent," Pembroke, whose lands were in Wales, snarled, "and you will lose Wales."

"The Welsh," Sir Walter pointed out, "are not one nation. There may be a rising here and there, but no king like David can draw all the Welsh together. A king must oppose a king. You, Lord Pembroke, and the other Marcher lords can hold down the petty princes of Wales."

Hugh's face was expressionless as he listened, but he had to clasp his hands behind his back to keep them from trembling, and he was cold with fear inside. What if his reasoning were wrong? What if the taking of Wark were an act of collusion between Summerville and Wark's castellan and had nothing to do with King David? He had jumped to a conclusion because Sir Walter had discussed with him his concern that David might try to use the disputed succession as an opportunity to annex Northumbria and Cumbria. Hugh wished passionately that Sir Walter had not espoused his harebrained idea with such enthusiasm, but he dared not now say he was mistaken. Others in the circle, who had been listening, now joined the argument, and all seemed to oppose an expedition to the north. The only advantages were that in their eagerness to speak they pressed in front of Hugh and their vociferous remarks occupied the king's attention until all were summoned to dinner.

Since he sat at one of the lowest tables, Hugh contrived to escape without further notice. He spent an uneasy afternoon, unable to divert himself at the market, which he had previously wished to visit, and a restless night. Although he did not want Stephen's attention, he was worried all the next day because he had not been summoned to the king again; worse yet, Sir Walter seemed to be avoiding him.

Not that Hugh lacked companionship. John de Bussey insisted on Hugh's company to celebrate his appointment as castellan of Wark. Hugh was truly glad for John's sake; Sir Walter had offered the place to Hugh himself first, and he had refused it and recommended it be given to John. To spare John's feelings at being second best, Hugh knew, Sir Walter would not have mentioned his refusal, although he would certainly have told John that Hugh had suggested his name. Thus Hugh could not refuse to join the merrymaking lest he be thought sullen at losing to a rival a prize he desired, but he was worried sick about the position in which he had placed his master.

Relief of one kind came the next morning. John was on the watch for Hugh when he came out of Saint Frideswide after hearing a second Mass—at the moment, Hugh felt he needed all the help he could get, and Frideswide was a notoriously gentle and sympathetic saint. The summons from Stephen had come. But Hugh's heart sank right down into his shoes, making him feel hollow and empty inside because John brought no advice to him from Sir Walter on how to act or what to say. John had been sent to fetch Hugh to the king's page because the boy did not know him—and that was all.

He was halfway through the great hall before he realized what a fool he was. Sir Walter had never failed to support any loyal man who made an honest mistake; had he guessed wrong, Hugh was certain, Sir Walter would have been walking beside him into the king's presence. On the other hand, if praise were due his man, Sir Walter would absent himself so that the honor need not be shared with him. Stephen's smile as Hugh crossed the smaller chamber in which the king did business was the final proof that confirmation of the invasion of the Scots had come.

"Sir Walter was not mistaken in his trust of you," Stephen said. "You judged aright. My uncle has taken all the royal castles north of the Tyne." He gestured to a broad-shouldered, dark-haired man in mud-splashed clothes who stood to the left of his chair. "This is Bruno, who came late last night with a message from Sir Oliver Fermain of Jernaeve to say that Summerville had ordered him in King David's name to yield his keep, and when he refused, threatened to bring an army to assault that place."

Hugh nodded at Bruno and bowed to the king. "I am sorry to be right," he said. "I would I had been wrong and that there would be peace between England and Scotland."

"We may still have peace," Stephen said. "I am not lacking in the ability to judge a man any more than Sir Walter. I was so sure you had not mistaken the case, I ordered my army to gather near Leicester soon after you brought the news. Tomorrow I will join them, and we will march for the north. David may have taken the royal keeps, but Sir Walter has assured me that his vassals and the men of Durham and Northumbria will rise to support me."

"That is true, my lord," Hugh agreed eagerly. "They do not love the Scots and will be quick to join you if they are able. So, if your army comes before the lesser keeps are taken, David will have little hold on the land."

"And if King David starts with Jernaeve," Bruno put in, smiling grimly, "he will need his whole army, and it will be long before he is free to turn elsewhere."

Stephen looked at Bruno with surprise and doubt, and the man flushed slightly. Hugh had a sudden feeling of recognition—not that he knew Bruno personally, but the signs he had noted subconsciously had suddenly fallen into place. Although he was well beyond the age for knighting, no "Sir" had preceded Bruno's name, and not even a place name, like "Bruno of Jernaeve," had followed it. Yet Bruno's speech was the language of the nobility, fluent French, pure of accent, and his clothing, like Hugh's own, was far better than that of any ordinary man-at-arms. What Hugh recognized was a condition similar to his own: a man who was a part of the ruling class and yet had no recognized place in it. A wave of fellow feeling made Hugh want to offer support.

"That is no idle boast," Hugh said. "I have never been in Jernaeve, but I have seen it. It is very strong, and my lord will testify to Sir Oliver's tenacity in holding his lands."

"They are not his," Bruno pointed out. "Jernaeve belongs to Sir Oliver's niece, Demoiselle Audris."

"His niece?" Stephen repeated, interested. "Is the lady free to wed? Has she an heir—other than her uncle?"

"She is a maiden," Bruno answered.

Hugh cared nothing about the lordship of Jernaeve, and he saw that Stephen's interest had made Bruno uneasy. "If Jernaeve holds until you arrive, Sire," he put in, trying to bring Stephen back to the Scottish invasion, "King David will be in evil case. His army must be smaller than yours. He will have to retreat from Jernaeve and any other keeps that are under attack to protect what he has already taken. Yet, if he puts his men into the keeps yielded to him, he will have no army with which to oppose yours and will himself be in danger of being taken prisoner. If he musters his men into an army, the keeps will fall back into your hands easily, either through being undermanned or by a change of heart of the garrison when they see your power. And all will be more fixed in their loyalty to you, seeing that you came so swiftly in strength to their support."

Stephen nodded. "So I think also. And I have not forgotten

your part—or Bruno's—in adding to my chances of success. I can use men of proven loyalty and hardiness of body. Will you both come into my household?"

"No!"

"Yes, my lord."

The voices mingled, but there was no doubt about who had agreed and who had denied the invitation. Bruno's dark eyes shone with relief and pleasure; Hugh's had widened in shocked dismay. Before Stephen could add anything, Bruno had dropped to one knee before the king's chair.

"Thank you, my lord!" he exclaimed. "I will serve you faithfully, I swear. When Alnwick yielded, those of us who were unwilling to accept the terms were given leave to go, and I lost my place. Thus, I am free to give my service where I will."

"You owe no fealty to Sir Oliver?" Stephen asked.

Bruno shook his head. "I was born in Jernaeve and trained there by Sir Oliver's kindness, for which I am grateful, so I rode to warn him of the coming of the Scots. But I have no place in Jernaeve."

Bruno's quality, age, and lack of position had not escaped Stephen's notice any more than it had escaped Hugh's. "Are you Sir Oliver's son?" the king asked.

"No, I am not," Bruno replied flatly and without hesitation, but then he flushed and an expression of anxiety crossed his face. "I swear I am not Sir Oliver's get," he added, "although we are said to look much alike."

Stephen nodded kindly. "I will not press you, and honor you for making no claim to what you cannot prove. Nor will your parents' sin be held against you in my service." Stephen turned in his chair and gestured to a clerk seated at a table by the back wall. "Enroll Bruno of *Jernaeve* among my squires of the body," he said, emphasizing the place name to give Bruno the status he had not claimed, and smiled when he heard Bruno gasp. Then he turned to look at Hugh and raised his brows.

Hugh was prepared, since Bruno's intervention in accepting Stephen's offer had given him time to think, and he also dropped to one knee, answering without hesitation, "I am not free, Sire. I know my lord would free me to serve you, but I beg you will not ask him. His squires are both young, he has no son, and he has just offered his nephew, who also was in his service, the castellanship of Wark when it is retaken. Without me, there will be no squire strong enough to stand by him in battle or to do those errands that a man rather than a boy must do."

Stephen stared at him, and Hugh held his breath. It was no light thing to refuse service to a king. He had gambled on the good nature and generosity that Stephen had displayed at their previous meetings, but it *was* a gamble, for kings seemed always to be suspicious. Old King Henry would have taken such a refusal as a sure sign of intended treachery, but Stephen finally smiled and shook his head.

"You are very loyal, Hugh Licorne, for I am sure you know there is much to be gained by serving a king. But you should have understood that I have already spoken to Sir Walter. I would not cozen away his man without permission. Does this knowledge change you answer?"

Hugh swallowed, knowing he was treading dangerous ground, but he muttered, "No, my lord."

The king shrugged. "Ah, well, it is true that Sir Walter deserves your loyalty, for he said nothing of his own need. He spoke only of your good qualities and how I would never regret advancing you, so I thought I had found a reward that would benefit us both. Now you must name your own reward, for good service must be rewarded."

Since Hugh had never given a thought to Stephen's good or ill when he had decided to escape from Wark, he did not feel especially deserving of any reward; however, he was well aware how unwise it would be to utter another refusal or to admit how indifferent he had been to the effect of the Scottish invasion on the holder of the English throne.

"If I may have my choice," Hugh said, "I would beg of you only a token that I could bring you at some future time to ask for service with you then. I cannot leave Sir Walter's service while war threatens, Sire, but when there is peace and his squires are older so that my master no longer needs me, I would like to come to you."

"*Fiat!*" Stephen exclaimed, his reserved expression melting into a beaming smile. He was a kind and generous man and honored Hugh for his self-sacrificing loyalty; nonetheless, he had felt some pique at being rejected. Now that pique was soothed. His offer was not refused; it was not that Hugh preferred Sir Walter, but that duty and honor delayed acceptance.

"But what token shall I give?" Stephen mused. His fingers toyed with a ring, and he began to draw it off, but then pushed it back on, threw back his head, and began to laugh. "No," he said. "One ring is much like another. Such purity must be marked by a special token. Before we ride tomorrow, your token will be brought to you."

Chapter 4

MORE THAN A WEEK BEFORE BRUNO HAD ARRIVED AT OXFORD and been taken into Stephen's service, Sir Oliver had tried to determine how serious Jernaeve's situation was by questioning him. When Sir Oliver returned from speaking with Summerville, Bruno was rested and able to give many details that had previously escaped his tired mind, but everything he remembered only confirmed that the parties he had avoided with such trouble had not been raiding but hunting a thief. Unfortunately Bruno had been driven too far north and east of Wark to be able to judge the number of campfires or even how far these had extended around the keep. Thus, there was now no way to determine the size of Summerville's army or whether he would be able to come down on Jernaeve with a host large enough to attack the outer walls all along their extensive east-west fronts.

Such an attack could not be long withstood and would mean retreat into Jernaeve keep. The keep itself was nearly impregnable and was stocked for a siege of weeks or months, depending on how many of the serfs were taken in. But Oliver knew that if he were penned up inside Jernaeve, the Scots would be free to raid southward. Although sheep grazed on the lower hills to the east and west and pigs rooted in the forests that crowned those hills, the wealth of Jernaeve came from the farms of the fertile river valleys to the south—and from his niece's loom in the south tower.

Since he could learn no more from Bruno, Oliver sent messages with what information he had to his sons: Sir Oliver, the younger, held the wooden motte and bailey keep above Devil's Water, and Sir Alain, the elder, was building a strong castle in stone about three leagues southwest of Jernaeve. They were not to come, Sir Oliver said, unless he sent further word, but they were to be alert to drive off any parties of Scots that might wish to raid for supplies. A third man was dispatched to Prudhoe keep but warned to be sure it was not in Scottish hands before he entered. Prudhoe would warn Newcastle if it were not yet taken.

Then Sir Oliver sat staring at his bastard nephew. After a moment he sighed and said, "A pox on these kings with their lands on both sides of the narrow sea."

The remark was such a non sequitur and so unexpected that Bruno simply gaped.

"If Henry's son had not drowned," Oliver went on bitterly, "we would not be in this coil."

Relieved that his uncle had not gone mad, Bruno laughed. "It was doubtless God's will that the prince perish. If it had not been drowning, there are plenty of other ways to die."

Oliver shrugged dyspeptically and looked away into the fire. Bruno was a sore spot in his mind and heart. He had never doubted that the young man was his brother's son, and he felt he had treated him fairly in the past. Now matters were not so simple. He knew Bruno had lost his place by coming to warn them of the Scottish invasion, yet he could not allow him to stay in Jernaeve, particularly if there were to be an attack on the keep. Oliver knew Bruno's strength and skill as a fighter—he had trained his nephew and nearly been overmastered before Bruno had gained his full power—and Bruno loved Jernaeve. He would surely distinguish himself in its defense... and that would be dangerous. A strong impression of Bruno's prowess plus Audris's obvious preference for her half brother would make him a strong contender to rule Jernaeve instead of his own son. But Alain would never accept that, and the situation could erupt into war.

"The news must go south," Oliver said heavily. "I did

not wish to take sides between the new king and Henry's daughter, but I will not yield Jernaeve to the Scots. It will be best for you to go."

Bruno's expression froze, and he dropped his eyes to his hands, which had clenched suddenly into fists.

"I do not know where the king is just now," Oliver continued, still staring into the fire rather than at his nephew. "He was crowned at Westminster more than two weeks ago and will have left there, I believe, but there should be word either there or in London of where he went."

There was another short silence before Bruno could completely control his voice. When he could, he said, "I will go."

There was no other reply he could have made, and though it wrenched his heart to leave the only place he loved and Audris, the only person who loved him, Bruno knew Oliver was right. Had he not himself said to Audris only the day before that he was a danger to her? He had known from the beginning that he could not stay long, but he had hoped to be warmed by his sister's affection for a few weeks and to be there to protect her if the Scots chose to fight. It hurt to be driven away so soon. What could he tell her? He was aware, too, that those who brought ill tidings to kings were often the innocent victims of the royal wrath.

As if he heard the last thought in Bruno's mind, Oliver said quickly, "The king may not be pleased to hear the truth, but he is said to be a kind, good-humored man. In any case, Sir Walter Espec is with him. If you are in need of any kind, go to Sir Walter and tell him any help he can give you will be a favor to me." His lips twisted wryly. "You need no letter or token to warrant your word. You carry that in your face."

❧

The next day and the next, all was quiet. Each day Sir Oliver was out by dawn seeing to the defenses of the lower wall and to the moving of all supplies from sheds and storehouses to the keep itself. There was no sign of the Scots, neither army nor raiding parties, but before supper of the second day Sir Oliver's messenger returned from Prudhoe to say that Newcastle was in King David's hands. Sir Oliver waved the messenger away with a nod of acknowledgment. Prudhoe was not a royal castle where a new king might change the castellan, so Prudhoe was likely to resist the Scots. But after supper he sat by the fire considering the situation, and one uncomfortable thought recurred to his mind until he sat chewing his lower lip in unaccustomed indecision. At last he turned his head to his wife, who was sewing on a low bench near the fire.

"Eadyth, when did you last see Audris?"

His wife raised her head, and the firelight touched her gray braids under their dark veil, giving them a gleam of their original bronze. That thick bronze hair had been Eadyth's one claim to beauty, for her features were undistinguished— rather dull gray eyes, a round snub nose, and a small pursed mouth, fallen in somewhat now with loss of teeth. The generalized anxiety on her face changed to a sharper fear as Oliver spoke.

"Not since Bruno left," she replied. "Audris insisted on going to the gate with him, but I warned her strictly not to go out and reminded her of the danger from raiding parties. And her maid has been taking food…" Her voice faded, and her shoulders hunched just a little. "Do you think she is weaving… something special… again?"

There was a hesitation. Sir Oliver would not have admitted under torture that his niece was a witch; he would not admit it to himself. And Father Anselm, a very holy man, had said there was no harm in her or in the pictures she wove. And, mostly, there was not; in fact, there was much good in the glowing scenes of hunting, of work in field and forest, of men and women at play, and of birds and beasts. The tapestries were eagerly sought by traveling merchants, and some noblemen who discovered their source came themselves to buy or pledge for anything new Audris wove. The weavings brought good coins of silver and gold into the coffers of Jernaeve, and fresh news also came with the visitors, so Oliver was more aware of events than most masters of northern keeps.

But sometimes the pictures were not bright and lovely. The

spring two years past, Audris had woven a terrible pair: one showed dry fields and dead cattle near the well of a house; in the doorway was Death kissing one child with his fleshless lips and tucking another into his black robe. The other panel had been of the countryside buried in snow and ice, even the river frozen, with skeletal animals scattered dead in the icy fields and skeletal people trying to climb the walls of Jernaeve while Death stood atop, reaping them with his scythe.

Sir Oliver restrained a shudder thinking of those panels and then shook his head when he remembered the price they had brought. He had been sure no one would want them, but the pair had been exchanged for a heavy purse of gold from a visiting Cistercian abbot with a taste for memento mori. Nor had the scenes come to pass exactly as depicted—but only, Oliver knew, because he had learned to take warning when Death showed himself in Audris's weaving.

The drought had come, but Oliver had culled the herds so there was water and forage for all the beasts that remained. And heat and sickness had killed many children—about that Sir Oliver could do nothing—but no one starved during the famine of the bitter winter that followed, for Oliver had been prepared and had fed those who had need, thereby profiting greatly by gaining new tenants and new lands with blessings and gratitude rather than with hate and fear.

That was what Father Anselm had said—that only good would come of Audris's weaving. Still, foretelling made Oliver uneasy, and he felt a fool now to look to a girl who could know nothing of war or politics for answers in a time of crisis. Nonetheless, he nodded his head to his wife's question, and because he was aware of Eadyth's increasing nervousness, spoke sharply.

"You did not question her maid?" he asked suddenly and harshly.

"My lord," Eadyth protested, "you know Fritha is mute. Audris insisted—"

"Then you go up and try to see what she has on that loom," he interrupted, annoyed with himself.

Oliver remembered now that Eadyth had objected to

Audris's choice of the mute serf girl when her old nurse had died, and he had called his wife a fool, thinking it an excellent idea that Audris's maid should not be able to blab anything she saw in her mistress's chamber. It had slipped his mind because he so seldom saw the maid.

Without complaint, although she felt faintly sick, Eadyth laid aside her work and picked up the oil lamp that stood on the bench beside her. The hall was dim, with only a few torches blazing in the holders on the walls. The candles in the iron candelabra had been extinguished soon after the evening meal was eaten, for Oliver did not believe in waste and most of the household went to bed soon after dark. She should have known, she told herself, when her husband continued to sit by the fire and think, that there was immediate danger, but she had assumed Oliver was only disturbed about Bruno or about Audris's distress at her brother's leaving so soon.

On the stair leading to Audris's tower, Eadyth lifted the lamp high, for the curving narrow stair was blacker than she expected. Usually it was faintly lit by the illumination spilling through the open door of Audris's room. Was Audris asleep already, or was the door closed? Eadyth shivered when she reached the landing, telling herself it was only the cold of the icy stone passage that made her shake, but knowing it was fear. She did not want to see what Audris was weaving, but she did not blame Oliver for sending her. It was not any lack of courage on his part. He had never set foot in Audris's tower lest it be said by those who had asked for her in marriage and been refused that there was evil between himself and his niece.

A soft, repeated thudding came to Eadyth's ears, and she shivered again and bit her lip. Audris was not asleep, and the door was open. That was the sound of the comb beating down the new-woven threads. Audris was weaving in the dark! Eadyth stood a moment longer, fighting the desire to turn and run back down the stair. But Eadyth knew that running away could not help, and most often the evil that Audris pictured could be averted by care. Her panic passed, and she forced herself to step into the room.

"Why are you in the dark?" Eadyth asked.

There was the sound of something falling, and then Audris's merry laugh. As Eadyth came closer, the feeble lamplight showed Audris blinking like an owl and smiling.

"Oh, aunt, how you startled me!" she cried. "I had no idea it had got so dark. Fritha must have fallen asleep waiting for me to make ready for bed." She turned her head and called, "Fritha! Fritha, light the candles."

Above the sound of the maidservant's sharply drawn breath and the rustle of her stirring, Eadyth asked, "But how can you weave in the dark?"

"I was only doing the border," Audris replied, "and anyway, with the tall loom one cannot see the pattern. A good weaver does not need to see, aunt. Surely you know that the women often talk to each other or even close their eyes when they weave. It is not like embroidering."

"They weave plain cloth," Eadyth protested, though her mind was not on her words.

The fear that Audris's laugh had diminished had returned in full. She had forgotten for the moment that Audris herself might not know what was depicted in her work. When the first of the scenes with Death had been woven—Audris had only been a child then, and the work was crude, barely recognizable—she had screamed with terror when she saw it and had run weeping with it to Father Anselm. The priest had talked with her a very long time, and she had come from his cell soothed and showed the panel to her uncle.

Oliver had called the tapestry a child's nonsense, although Father Anselm had talked with him about the work also—but the river *had* flooded in the spring and drowned the winter wheat, and the sodden fields could not be replanted until too late in the season for a good second crop. Sickness had followed the flooding, too. Eadyth felt tears rise to her eyes; two of her own children had died in that sickness, and Oliver himself had nearly died, babbling in his fever of paying no mind to the serfs who had warned him of damage to the lower reaches of the river.

In the seconds it took for the memories to flit through Eadyth's mind, the maid had lighted the candles. Audris had stooped to retrieve the spindle she had dropped, but when she rose and saw her aunt's face, she cried, "What is wrong, aunt? Why do you weep?"

"Your uncle desired me to look at your weaving, Audris," she replied.

Audris looked puzzled. "But why do you weep?"

"I am not weeping. It was only the brighter light that brought tears to my eyes."

Since it was not only the tears in her aunt's eyes but the expression on her face that had startled Audris, she did not believe the excuse. It was strange, too, that her uncle should ask about her work. Although her tapestries brought wealth, he never urged her to weave, as a greedy man would have done. But sometimes he did tell her that a particular scene had been requested, and usually she would weave a picture to fit the request the next time the desire to work took hold of her. That could be the answer. If her uncle had bade her aunt tell her of a demand for a special design and Eadyth had forgotten, Eadyth might be beaten.

"Did you tell me that a special piece was desired?" Audris asked. "If so, I will tell uncle that I am sorry it would not come to me, and… No, that is not the answer you desire."

"Audris, stop!" Eadyth cried, backing up a step before she could stop herself. "How do you know what is in my mind?"

"Fritha, turn the loom so we can see the work, and bring some candles," Audris ordered, ignoring her aunt's question.

She knew what Eadyth thought because Father Anselm had showed her how to read people's hearts from their gestures and expressions, from the way they moved their bodies and the way their breath came, but when she tried to explain what she saw to others, they would not believe her. Even Bruno had not believed her. It had been a game between her and Father Anselm, but after he had died, no one else seemed to understand. They were afraid when the pictures on the tapestries… And then Audris understood. Her uncle feared this new work would show Death. But there was no reason. Audris did not wait for Fritha, who was pulling the heavy loom farther from the wall, to fetch candles. She brought light herself and peered around the maid's shoulder.

"Sweet heaven," Audris exclaimed, "it is all changed from what I began." Then she laughed. "That is what comes of listening to men talk. Come see, aunt."

Relief had washed over Eadyth when Audris ignored her question. She never intended to ask Audris how she read thoughts and did not want any answer. For although Eadyth would not say the word aloud, knowing her husband would kill her for doing so, she did sometimes think that her niece was a witch, but a *white* witch, a good person. Father Anselm had said that Audris was good; he denied she was a witch of any kind. Perhaps that was true. Eadyth knew Audris cast no spells and practiced no evil sorceries; she went often to Mass—perhaps not so often as she should, but often enough—and to confession, and the raising of the host did not drive her from the church or chapel or turn her into a monster.

For months, sometimes years, it was easy to dismiss her fears of what Audris was, to laugh at the castlefolk and villagers, who were in great awe of her and would fall silent when she appeared, until it was clear her business was one of ordinary life. It was easy to put her fears out of mind because Audris kept much to herself since Father Anselm's death. She was usually in the garden and drying shed or out in the hills or in her chamber weaving. Often she did not even appear at meals, and when she did, she was so small, so frail-appearing, and withal so merry and easy of disposition that one did not, could not, think of witchcraft. Still, when she looked into a person's heart…

The thought was broken off by Audris's words, and Eadyth's breath caught at the surprise in her voice, but the light fell on her face and there was no fear in it, only wonder. Eadyth came forward and looked at the work displayed in the candlelight. It was not a large piece, perhaps a yard square, and at first glance it seemed a merry scene, the colors bright even in the uncertain light. A second look brought Eadyth's heart into her throat when she realized the bright colors were penons, tents, and the shields of knights, and the scene was of a keep besieged.

"And look," Audris continued, "it is not finished. I thought it was the border that I worked because it was the same pattern over and over, but it is the beginning of a new piece. Those are the crenels of a wall. The border is there"—she pointed to a dark strip with sharp edges like dagger points reaching down into the finished piece and up into what would become a new panel.

"I see," Eadyth said. She saw also that Audris was staring at her work with a bemused expression, and she added hastily, "I must go down. Your uncle will wonder what has become of me."

Audris nodded, but the concept of the second panel had leapt whole into her mind, and she did not answer her aunt. "Let us push the loom back into place, Fritha," she said. "It is not very late. I will work a little longer, for the sun is a laggard in January, and I can lie abed until it is well up if I wish."

She put down the candles she had been holding, only vaguely aware that her aunt had left the chamber, and helped her maid replace the loom. It moved more readily when Audris assisted because despite her diminutive size she was strong, her muscles hardened with much climbing of trees and cliffs. When it was precisely in place so that the spindles of yarn were exactly where they should be, she picked up the one with which she had been working before her aunt interrupted her, and began to weave. Her fair brows drew together in a worried frown, and she turned her head toward her servant, her pale eyes glittering like ice in the flickering light.

"Fritha, do you think it would have made my aunt easier in her mind if I explained that Bruno and I had talked about what the Scots might do and it must have been that talk that was in my mind when I wove this picture?"

The maid turned fully toward her mistress and the candlelight caught the ugly split in her upper lip, which was one outward sign of her muteness. The other was the too-broad nose with its flaring nostrils, which drew all attention, making most people miss the large and beautiful blue eyes above them. Audris looked only at her maid's eyes and hands; she was accustomed to the deformity of her face and also to the fact that though others with harelips could grunt or gobble, sometimes even speak in a distorted way, Fritha could make no sounds at all. There were times when Audris noticed that Fritha looked much older than she, although they were only a few years apart—but tonight the lines of ill-usage on her maid's face did not wake the spark of anger they usually roused.

Fritha put down the spindle from which she had been unwinding a small amount of yarn, shook her head, and held up her fingers, clenched them into a fist, and then repeated the gesture several times.

"You mean I have already tried to explain many times?"

Fritha nodded, and Audris sighed.

"Yes, I know," Audris continued, "but this is different. I do not *know* that we will be besieged. I wove it because of what Bruno told me and what I heard him and my uncle say during the evening meal when he was here. I even know what the next picture will be. It will show the besiegers fleeing away at the top, beyond the great wall, and in the center the king and his knights entered into the lower bailey, having come to our rescue. But this is not a real thing that will come to pass, Fritha. I do not really suppose the king will come to Jernaeve. It is only a picture."

Fritha just shook her head again as she reached up to a particular peg set into the stone wall and took down a hank of yarn. She did not look at the color because it would have been impossible to match color in the dim yellow light of the candles. Nor was it necessary. Each spindle on the rack matched a peg on the wall—except for the special yarns of silk with gold and silver thread, which were kept in a chest—so there could be no mistake. And no matter what Audris said, Fritha would not have believed the weaving was only a picture. She was convinced that her mistress had supernatural powers, but she did not use the word "witch" either. To Fritha that word implied evil, and she knew Lady Audris was good. But Lady Audris could read the words in her mind even when she kept her hands still, and Fritha was sure that whatever appeared in the tapestry would come to pass.

It was just as well that Audris had resisted the impulse to explain to her uncle and aunt how she had come to weave the two-picture panel. Actually, the events of the next month did not match the scenes, except in a very general way, but to those already convinced that Audris could foretell the future in her weaving, her denials would have smacked of dishonesty.

❧

A week after Eadyth had rushed down the stairs and related breathlessly that Audris had depicted a siege, Sir William de Summerville brought his army through a breach in the great wall some miles to the east. One halfhearted attempt at assault was thrown back without difficulty, for the defenders were able to rush from all parts of the inner walled area to the place under attack, and Summerville did not have enough men to mount several assaults simultaneously. After being beaten back, Summerville settled his men into camp beyond arrowshot from the eastern wall with a small force to guard the ford. It was not a siege in any real sense because the western wall was not blocked by enemies, so the people in Jernaeve could come and go.

Although Sir Oliver made sure that adequate watch was kept, he was certain the assault had only been a test to determine whether he trusted his tenants to fight, which he did. Unlike the south, where most of the English had been reduced to oppressed serfdom and bitterly hated their Norman overlords, most men in the north were freemen who could bear arms. After the harrying of the northern shires by William the Bastard, so few remained alive on the land that most of it was left waste. The present inhabitants were largely immigrants over the past fifty years, men seeking land of their own. And overlords like Sir Oliver's father, who needed tenants to till the soil and herd their sheep and cattle, did not ask too many questions. If those who came were runaway serfs, they did not want to know and gladly accepted their oaths that they were free.

So Sir Oliver, who had no more than fifty men-at-arms, still had defenders enough to hold his walls against twice the force

Summerville brought. But the fact that Summerville had made camp after having discovered that there were enough defenders to hold him off easily meant that he expected a substantial addition to his forces. It was a matter of time, Sir Oliver thought, considering his alternatives. If Prudhoe held out, King David would not have men to spare to add to Summerville's force; and if King Stephen were not engaged in putting down some other rebellion against his assumption of the crown and came north, Summerville would be called away.

In either case, the "siege" was also a test of Sir Oliver's temperament and judgment, or rather a temptation to him. Summerville was trying to reduce their numbers by drawing Oliver out into a battle to drive away the troop at the ford, who blocked their escape route and the route by which succor could be expected to come. To the proud or the hotheaded, that small group might have proved an irresistible target, since it would seem that it could be overwhelmed before help could come from the men in the main camp. Sir Oliver had pride, but not that kind; he was a wily old fox and doubted Summerville was such a fool as to leave the small troop unprotected. Besides, he had not the smallest desire to escape. If necessity demanded, he would die defending Jernaeve; he would never leave it.

Assault might not even be attempted. Even if David took Prudhoe soon, the Scottish king knew Jernaeve and might be reluctant to assault old Iron Fist. David would prefer to starve them out—and Audris's picture showed only a siege; that thought crept unbidden into Oliver's mind. But if news came that Stephen was on his way or gathering men to come north, then David might assault Jernaeve, for it guarded the road to the central northern shires. Newcastle and Carlisle were far more important. Doubtless Stephen would make for one or the other first, but if David held Jernaeve, he would have an easy road east or west to attack Stephen's army and a mighty fort from which it would be difficult to evict him. He might then think the price Jernaeve would cost in blood worthwhile… and Audris's work was not finished, Oliver's unruly mind reminded him.

It must be finished now, he thought. Audris had been on the wall this afternoon and had joined them for the evening meal. But she had said nothing about her work and had not brought it down to show him so he could send out word to the buyers that a work was done. Well, that was not surprising. Audris was not an idiot and must know that sale of the tapestry must wait until they were free of the Scots. Or could there be a darker reason? Could the work show Death embracing the whole keep? Oliver felt cold, and then, remembering how full of laughter and teasing Audris had been, he put the fear aside. Still, a remnant of doubt clung to him, and though he told himself a dozen times that he was a fool, he still sent Eadyth up to look when Audris was in the mews with the falcons the next day.

Thus, Oliver felt no great surprise when, ten days later, the fruitless siege was lifted and Summerville's army marched away. He was not entirely pleased; he had learned to accept Audris's infrequent predictions of impending natural disasters and her occasional verbal warnings that certain men were not to be trusted—she had always been right about the men, too—but he felt this depiction of the outcome of military action was more unnatural. Father Anselm had babbled some explanation for Audris's abilities, but no watching of birds or beasts or the amount of snow that fell in the hills nor judging little twitches of face, limbs, and body could give signs as to when an army would march or retreat.

Oddly, the same thoughts had occurred to Audris and were worrying her. She had never feared her tapestries—after the first one, which had given her a terrible shock—because she had accepted Father Anselm's explanation that what she saw in the hills and fields worked slowly in her mind until a picture of it grew from her fingers. And it had seemed reasonable enough to her that the new tapestries she created should reflect all the talk she had heard about the Scots and Summerville's threats and whether the new English king would come to support them. Still, the fact that she had predicted not only the siege but the coming of the king began to trouble her. She kept recalling how the picture of Stephen riding up the steep path to the keep while his knights waited in the lower bailey had formed in her mind. If Stephen did come, would that be true foretelling or only a chance coincidence?

Being pent inside the keep increased Audris's uneasiness by denying her her normal outlets of wandering in the hills. She restrung her loom and produced a handsome border of blue and silver, but found she did not want to weave and could not imagine a picture that would suit so rich and elaborate a surrounding. A further irritation was Fritha, who spent every free minute undoing a corner of the hide that sealed the southeast tower window and peeping out. The behavior was so unusual that Audris came to the uncomfortable realization that Fritha was watching for the king's arrival.

She scolded the girl for wasting time, but not even the slow passage of several weeks and the news that King Stephen had come north but was staying in Durham could discourage her. Audris's tapestry had shown the king in Jernaeve; Fritha believed, and it was Fritha who saw the royal cortege first, running to draw Audris to the window just as the lookout on the tower top called down that a large party was coming along the south side of the river.

Chapter 5

WITH A QUIVER OF MINGLED ANXIETY AND EXCITEMENT, AUDRIS began to undo the entire hide that covered the window. It seemed undignified for her to peep through a corner like a maidservant, but the process was tedious. By the time she had unfastened the top, bottom, and one side and was able to swing the hide out of the way, the leading riders had reached the ford. She heard a bass roar, muted by distance, and then her uncle's voice from the wall to the left of her tower shouting a welcome. The sounds came in the open window. Even on the third floor, the stone walls of the tower were eight feet thick, and only the sound of a battering ram or a mangonel-cast stone could penetrate them.

Audris assumed that her uncle had offered to show the party the best path through the ford, because instead of crossing, they waited on the bank. Ten men, closest to the bank, formed a divided group, two to the fore and eight unevenly spaced behind. From the depth of his voice, his size, and the huge destrier he rode, Audris was certain one of the leaders was Walter Espec. The other must be the king, but Audris did not look at him. Her eyes had been attracted to a shock of brilliant red hair on the man just behind and to the left of Espec. The distance was too great to make out his features, but at that moment Espec said something to him, and he turned his horse to ride back to the bulk of the party, which was forming a second group a short distance behind.

As the red-haired rider turned, Audris caught sight of the shield hung on his shoulder. She drew in her breath in surprise and delight, having suddenly perceived a subject that would suit the sumptuous border she had woven. For once her tapestry would be pure fantasy, incapable of any interpretation outside myth. Audris continued to look for a few moments more at the red-haired rider, who was now returning to Sir Walter, and she felt grateful to him for wearing a shield of blue with a silver unicorn, rampant. She noted how lithely his body moved to the destrier's stride, and then admired the superb destrier. If not quite so massive an animal as Sir Walter's, it was still remarkably strong and more beautiful, really, because more graceful. If it had a horn and were white, instead of a chestnut almost as bright as the rider's hair, Audris thought, it would make a perfect unicorn.

Smiling at the idea, Audris realized she was cold and stepped away from the window, telling Fritha to refasten the hide. It was only after she had picked up a spindle of grass-green yarn that she remembered she had not looked at the other man, who might be the king. But that hardly seemed to matter now. She was eager to begin work on her picture of a unicorn, rearing up on the bank of a river as if to display his beauty to a maiden who watched him from the window of a tower.

Audris did not realize that she had been observed as well as observing. Although Walter Espec had mentioned the strength of Jernaeve to Stephen, the king was still startled at the sense of threat generated by the overhanging fist of stone. Stephen was a brave man; nonetheless, as they approached the ford, he felt uneasily vulnerable and found himself scanning the walls and towers. The movement in the window brought a low, startled exclamation from him and the beginning of a gesture of defense.

Bruno, just behind the king, leaned forward and said, "There is no danger, Sire, I swear. That is Demoiselle Audris's window, and she is probably curious."

A moment later, to vindicate Bruno's assertion, Audris stood staring out at the men. Stephen's raised head attracted Hugh's attention, and he, too, glanced upward briefly before his master bade him warn the remainder of Stephen's cortege that the ford was treacherous and they should follow the path Sir Oliver took as closely as they could. Hugh glanced up again as he returned to his position, just in time to see the small figure in the pale gown fade backward and the blank sheet of hide close the window. There was a haunting quality to that image, a fairy-tale feeling of untouchability about the girl as the blank hide replaced her.

The odd impression dissipated as Sir Oliver came around the curve of the lower wall with four men and a substantial length of sturdy rope. This was stretched across the ford as a guide, while Oliver spoke a more formal welcome than could be shouted from the wall. The words were more smoothly said than Hugh had expected from what his master had told him of Sir Oliver's general reluctance to commit himself to any purpose other than holding Jernaeve. Bruno, too, had mentioned Sir Oliver's indifference to political matters that did not directly affect his own, or rather his niece's, property. The thought caused Hugh to glance again at the closed window in the tower—the girl must have been Demoiselle Audris.

But neither Walter Espec nor Bruno knew of Audris's tapestry, and it was the weaving that provided King Stephen with the warm welcome Sir Oliver had extended. Although it made him uncomfortable, Oliver had no more doubted the validity of the picture Eadyth described than Fritha did. He had therefore been considering his response to the king's arrival ever since Eadyth had told him what Audris's second panel portrayed. Had he truly been surprised by Stephen's visit, as Stephen had intended, his distaste for becoming involved in the struggle for the crown would certainly have showed—and that, Oliver had decided after considerable thought, was what the tapestry was warning against.

Oliver would have preferred greatly that Stephen leave him strictly alone; however, he recognized that none but a fool would pass Jernaeve by. It was too great a prize, a strong point blocking one of the main roads between Scotland and the wealth of England. Since Oliver believed he had already burnt his bridge to Matilda's side by rejecting Summerville's offer, all that was left was to make Stephen so sure of his support that he would leave him to his own devices. The decision had brought Oliver to the southeast wall to call a welcome rather than suspicious questions, and now made him seem eagerly solicitous to protect Stephen and his entourage from the dangers of the treacherous ford.

Oliver's care resulted in so smooth a passage of the ford that his guests were hardly splashed by the low waters of the North Tyne River. Nor was the narrow pass through the west gate and the easy defense of the long, steep road up to the keep lost on the men who entered there. Eadyth was waiting to greet them at the doorway to the great hall, curtsying to the ground before the king.

"This is my wife, Eadyth," Oliver said. "You need only tell her what you desire for your comfort, Sire, and it will be provided."

Stephen's acknowledgment was genial, and after he and his companions had been unarmed and attired in warm, dry garments, he returned to the hall to apologize for his unannounced arrival. "I hope it will be no great trouble to you, Lady Eadyth, to provide us with an evening meal?"

"No, my lord, it is a great pleasure and no trouble at all," Eadyth replied calmly, for she was secure in the efficiency of her domestic management. As soon as Oliver had come down from the wall, orders had been sent to the cooks for extra dishes and whatever delicacies they could add to the evening meal, and Eadmer had tapped the tun that held the special wine. Eadyth was accustomed to exalted guests and Stephen was not the first king who had guested in Jernaeve. "We are well provided," she explained with a smile, "for we were under siege until your coming to the north. I assure you that it is with a grateful and glad heart that I will use those provisions for an occasion so much happier and that does us such great honor."

"My wife speaks the truth, Sire," Oliver added as he led the way to his own chair of state.

The high-backed, elaborately carved chair had been moved to the side of the eating dais closest to the hearth, where a huge fire leapt and roared, a position affording warmth without being in the direct path of the gusts of smoke and cinders that occasionally billowed out. The fireplace was hollowed out of the thick wall of the keep that faced into the bailey, set off-center near the high end of the hall. Below the dais, to the left of Stephen's chair, was a short bench; to the right was a smaller chair with a low back, which Oliver used when he wanted to be closer to the heat of the fire or wished to dispense with ceremony. Beyond the second chair, facing the hearth, were several benches, and two others beyond them, at right angles to the fire, faced the king's seat.

With a lesser but still respectful curtsy, Eadyth led Sir Walter Espec to the smaller chair and gestured with a smile to the benches for the other knights. "We have not had you as a guest for years, Sir Walter," she said. "I am very sorry about Wark, but for me the loss has been lightened by the pleasure of your company."

Since Eadyth and Sir Walter were following close behind Oliver and the king, Stephen heard. "Ah, but there has been no loss," he said with a pleased smile as he seated himself. "Wark has been returned to Sir Walter, and he has benefited by being rid of a treacherous castellan."

"That is good news, my lord," Oliver said. "We knew you had come north when Sir William de Summerville broke off his siege, and I had heard you were to meet with King David in Durham, but we had no news of the results. I am very glad indeed to hear that a man of Sir Walter's will still be my neighbor. To speak the truth, I had no lust for a Scottish keep less than three leagues from Jernaeve. I would not have had a sheep left on the hills by the end of the year."

Espec and the three northern gentlemen who had come with Stephen from Durham burst into laughter, but the king and the knights of his personal entourage, all from Blois, looked surprised. "The Scots," Sir Walter boomed, "start their instruction for roasting mutton with, 'Go out and steal a sheep,' and those for beef or chicken with the same phrase suitably altered."

More laughter greeted Sir Walter's explanation, this time including hoots from Stephen's men, but the king himself looked uneasy. Eadyth, who was behind Sir Walter's chair, stepped closer to Stephen and, with well-trained alacrity to smooth over the slight awkwardness caused by the joke, asked, "Will you have wine, my lord?"

"Yes, that would be most welcome," Stephen replied quickly.

Eadmer poured wine from the flagon he held into a chased silver goblet, which Eadyth presented to the king. From behind the seated knights, several squires moved to help the steward, the younger boys pouring from other flagons set ready beside cups of wood and horn, many carved beautifully. Jernaeve keep held other silver vessels and some of gold and gold-framed glass, equally precious, but Oliver had warned Eadyth not to display them. It might do the king honor, he snapped impatiently in reply to his wife's faint protest, but it would also give Stephen the idea that Jernaeve was too rich. When the wine had been served to the knights, the squires took their own, but while the others were dispersing to where they could hear, Bruno plucked Hugh familiarly by the sleeve.

In Oxford, one of Bruno's first duties as Stephen's squire had been to bring Hugh his promised token—a shield, azure, painted with a rampant unicorn, argent, above which was a scroll bearing the word *incorruptus*. Hugh had been appalled, and Sir Walter had been convulsed with laughter. Bruno, who was still in the first throes of gratitude to the king, had showed that he felt indignant on his master's behalf. His reaction had sobered Sir Walter, who hastily explained that neither he nor Hugh felt the gift to be humorous or inadequate, nor were they laughing at King Stephen.

"No." Hugh sighed and then laughed himself. "The jest falls on me, and the king could not know that I was much tormented in my youth for being 'pure' like the unicorn. But that is long past. The shield is beautiful, and I will carry it gladly and proudly."

This time it was Bruno who recognized the wealth of past misery in the lightly spoken words, and again like called to like. So when Sir Walter suggested that Hugh go back to the castle with Bruno and ask whether Stephen had time to receive his thanks, Bruno had spoken of what being taken into the king's service meant to him. Hugh had responded eagerly, and during the following weeks, as the army moved north, the two young men had met often, spent a good part of their free time together, and became good friends.

As they talked, both Hugh and Bruno gave a small part of their attention to their lords, a habit ingrained by long experience of service. Suddenly, there was a check in the easy conversation and occasional laughter among the men surrounding the king. Hugh and Bruno were instantly alert, aware of the uneasy silence, in which the sound of the fire seemed very loud.

"But you must know, Sire, that I do not have the right to do homage for Jernaeve." In the tense quiet, Sir Oliver's voice was just a shade too loud. "I only rule the property in the name of my niece, Demoiselle Audris. Did not Sir Walter tell you that my brother had a child?"

"Ah, yes, I remember now," Stephen replied, not very truthfully, for he had given considerable thought to the heiress of Jernaeve. "But it was Bruno who told me. I suppose Sir Walter did not think it needful to mention it because I have taken your… er… Bruno of Jernaeve into my service."

"Into your service?" Sir Oliver echoed. "You are a generous man, Sire. It is not often that the bearer of bad news is so kindly rewarded."

Stephen laughed. "Bruno was only the confirmer of the news. My unicorn—" Stephen stopped and looked around, and Hugh and Bruno came forward and bowed. "Ah, there you are. This is Hugh Licorne, Sir Walter's man. He carried the first word of the Scots' invasion."

Sir Oliver glanced at Hugh and nodded. He had seen him once or twice over the years when he met Sir Walter at gatherings of the northern nobles ordered by King Henry for tax collection or some legal deliberation, but no one ever forgot Hugh's appearance. Then he smiled at Bruno with real relief and pleasure and turned back to the king.

"I thank you, Sire, from the heart," Oliver said to Stephen, "for you have lifted a great weight from me. Bruno is a good man, the best. You will never regret your kindness to him."

"I am sure of it," Stephen replied. "He has been infinitely useful already. You have some odd customs here in the north, and he saved me from giving offense where I intended none. But your niece, how is it she did not come to greet me?"

Sir Oliver shrugged. "Audris is not just in the common way of women," he said. "She has little taste for company, except those well known and comfortable to her. She seldom does come down from her tower to greet guests."

As Oliver spoke, Hugh's memory brought forth an image of the girl stepping back from the window of the tower, and a wave of fierce interest and sympathy coursed through him. Here was a poor soul, he thought, in a worse state than he. Was she a prisoner in that tower, afraid even to look out for long? Or, if not truly a prisoner, had she been so cowed that she feared everyone? From the glimpse he had of her, it seemed she was very small and frail. He felt angry and protective—and foolish, too, because whatever Demoiselle Audris had suffered, he was powerless to help her. Then a more effective ally took up cudgels in her defense.

"Come, come," Stephen said, smiling but with a note of suspicion in his voice. "I hope I do not appear like a monster who eats young maidens." He shook his head playfully. "No, no, my good wife would never permit it. If the Demoiselle is my vassal, she must do homage to me, so if she is shy, she had better be fetched down to grow accustomed."

"I never said she was shy," Oliver muttered, but he nodded at Eadyth, who was now seated beside him on the small bench to the left of Stephen's chair. She beckoned a maidservant to her and ordered that Demoiselle Audris be asked to come down to greet the king.

Although he seemed a trifle sullen, Oliver was not at all displeased with the way events were moving. He was, in fact, attempting to hide his satisfaction, again blessing both the tapestry that had given him days to think and plan and Audris herself for clinging to her habit of indifference to company, even when that company was the king. Any other maiden would be agape with curiosity, but Audris's seeming isolation had so fixed the king's mind on her that Oliver had high hopes Stephen would take Audris's fealty and forget to ask for his own. That would leave a postern gate for escape if Stephen's bid for the crown ended in failure. Oliver could truly say he had *not* given any oath of homage and swear support to Matilda. He hated the twisting of true honor of engaging in such a practice, but he would do it if necessary to save Jernaeve. As for Audris's oath... well, a woman's oath was not worth anything.

Knowing that any woman summoned to a king would spend some time putting on a new gown and recombing her hair, Stephen had expected a delay. He was relieved that Oliver had not persisted in keeping the heiress mewed up and held out his goblet for more wine. He intended now to ask how old Audris was so that he would have an opening to say directly to her that it was time she married. Four of the gentlemen who had accompanied him had been asked specifically because he felt they would make suitable partners—suitable from his standpoint because they were penniless and out of gratitude would be devoted to his cause; suitable from Audris's, he assumed, because the gentlemen were young, strong, and not of repulsive appearance. But before Eadmer could refill the king's goblet and return it, the maidservant came running back to Eadyth.

"Oh, I feared to go in," she gasped. "The Demoiselle is weaving."

"Holy Mary," Eadyth breathed, "again? So soon?"

"Eadyth," Oliver's voice overrode the last three words his wife said, "go yourself and bring Audris down."

"Take her from the loom?" Eadyth whispered.

"The king has asked to see her," Oliver snarled. "Just tell her that her presence here is required."

A new surprised silence had fallen, and although Oliver also felt a wave of uneasiness, he told himself that Eadyth was only a superstitious fool. No doubt Audris had not realized she would be summoned down, had assumed the guests would be with them for several days, and had merely started an ordinary picture to occupy her time. In any case, he wanted no rumors that Audris was... He checked the thought without finishing it and shrugged casually as he turned toward the king.

"Women are damned fools," he growled. "My niece is a weaver of surpassing skill. I sell her pictures for a good price, but she only weaves when she chooses, so I have given orders that she is never to be disturbed when she is at the loom. But women... Even my wife does not seem to understand that a rule may be broken for an exceptional circumstance."

"Woven pictures," Stephen remarked, distracted from his intended question about Audris's age. "They are not so common. I have seen my grandmother's great work, which shows the destruction of the usurper Harold and William's conquest of this country, but that is embroidered. I would like to see Demoiselle Audris's work."

"I have not any to show you," Oliver replied, trying to subdue his uneasiness. He was worried about what Stephen would think if he saw his own coming pictured. No one could believe Audris had woven the piece in the short time the king had been in Jernaeve. He did not want to be caught in an outright lie either, and went on, "I believe my niece finished weaving a piece a few days ago, but something more must be done to it, I understand, before it is truly complete. I must confess, Sire, that I have never inquired about it. When Audris is finished, she brings the work to me, and I send word to those who are interested in buying."

"The Demoiselle Audris seems to have many talents," Stephen commented.

Sir Oliver laughed, his hard expression softening for a moment. "Not many, for I suspect she does not know boiling from baking, nor sewing from spinning. Eadyth used to complain that we would all starve and be in tatters if the running of Jernaeve were left in the girl's hands. She would not learn any other woman's skill from Eadyth, only weaving, and she will not do plain cloth, only pictures. No, I am wrong, she is also skilled in herb lore, Eadyth says."

This answer, which was perfectly truthful, quite unplanned, and actually bred of Oliver's sometimes exasperated fondness for his niece, only made Stephen more suspicious because it seemed to denigrate Audris as a wife. But the king was saved from needing to make a reply by the unexpectedly swift arrival of Audris and Eadyth. Because she had been the subject of the conversation—and because four of Stephen's companions had a special interest and the others knew or guessed his plans for her—all the seated men turned to stare at her as she walked toward them.

Chapter 6

HUGH HAD BEEN WATCHING THE DOOR EVER SINCE THE MAID had first gone up, and thus was the first to see Audris. Clearly she had not been given time to prepare herself. Her braids, pale as moonlight, showed no glint of pearls or golden threads, not even a bright ribbon to support her spirit and give her some assurance of being fine. Her dark blue tunic and pale blue bliaut were of fine wool but unadorned by embroidery or jewelry, and they were speckled with short threads of different-colored yarn from her work. She seemed very small when compared with Eadyth, and it looked as if she were being pushed along by her aunt's more massive figure behind her. It took all Hugh's self-control not to go to her and whisper a kind word.

Catching a glimpse of the king's face, Hugh felt that Stephen probably regretted demanding that the Demoiselle come down. The king could, Hugh thought resentfully, have gone up to see the shy child and spared her this torment. But then he reminded himself of the king's purpose in bringing Demoiselle Audris down. Sir Walter had told Hugh he was sure Stephen intended to marry the girl to one of his own men to guarantee that the holder of Jernaeve would remain loyal to him. Hugh felt a twinge of odd and inexplicable anger, but fought it, telling himself he had nothing about which to be angry.

Demoiselle Audris's fate had nothing to do with him. The heiress of Jernaeve was far, far beyond his reach. Besides, there was nothing real to arouse the ridiculous protective urge he felt toward her. The king was probably doing the girl a favor. Hugh knew Sir Walter suspected that Oliver had refused all offers for Demoiselle Audris—of which there had been many—and prevented the Demoiselle from marrying because he wanted to keep Jernaeve in his own hands and possibly wanted his son to inherit it from his cousin. In addition, Hugh told himself impatiently, Stephen was being kind in presenting several suitors to the Demoiselle Audris, all of whom were young and pleasant-faced. And not one of them, Hugh thought with a fresh spurt of anger, had any more than he—except the knowledge of who had fathered them.

Hastily he buried that foolish notion by recalling Sir Walter's comments on the unusual idea of offering Demoiselle Audris a choice. Ordinarily a husband would be chosen by a male guardian to suit himself. The very last and least consideration, if the subject were considered at all, would be whether or not the woman would like the man to whom she was given. But in this case, Sir Walter had said, the king must induce the lady to oppose her uncle.

"If the girl wants a husband and Oliver has been refusing decent offers," Sir Walter had said, frowning unhappily, "she has a right to be married, and I will not stand in her way, but I wish Stephen did not so openly intend her for one of those landless hangers-on he brought with him." Then he sighed. "Well, I suppose he thinks a man who owes him everything can be better trusted. But I am not so easy in my mind about replacing Oliver with a young man bred in Blois or France who does not know our ways and who might be greedy as well as poor. No, I do not like it, and I am going with the king to Jernaeve and taking a few friends, too, to make sure Demoiselle Audris is not forced into marriage with Stephen's man."

So, Hugh thought, his eyes fixed on Audris, who had threaded her way through the benches and was nearing Stephen's chair, the king dared not give the impression that he was usurping without cause Sir Oliver's position as Demoiselle Audris's warden. Hugh's lips twisted. Of course, that was why

the Demoiselle had to come down. The king needed witnesses
that she wished to marry and that Sir Oliver's refusals of all
offers for her were a violation of her rights.

Hugh's mind had been so busy that it took a little while to
register what his eyes were seeing. But now he noticed that
Demoiselle Audris's quick, light gait was eager. Actually, the
swift approach changed his feeling that she was being pushed
forward; now it appeared as if the small, quick figure was
towing the larger, reluctant form of Lady Eadyth behind it.
Nor, Hugh saw, did the Demoiselle Audris seem to cower
away from the stares of the attentive men or to be at all
disturbed by their silence. And when he could see her face
clearly, he perceived that her eyes were bright with interest
and her lips curved into a half smile as she sank to the floor in
a deep curtsy. Could she have guessed the king's purpose? If
so, it seemed Demoiselle Audris would jump at the chance of
being free of her uncle's domination and would gladly choose
one of the four young men with Stephen. A disappointment as
unreasonable as his earlier resentment made Hugh draw back
farther behind the king's chair.

"I do beg your pardon, Sire." Audris's head was bent in
seeming submission, but her voice, low and sweet, held, to
Hugh's surprise, a note of merriment, and her next words
shocked him. "I was taken of a sudden notion for a new picture,
and I quite forgot we had so exalted a guest."

"Audris!" Eadyth exclaimed, horrified.

"No, do not scold her," Stephen said kindly.

Although Hugh could not see the king's face from his
new position, he was certain Stephen was delighted that
Eadyth's remark had given him the chance to show himself as
a protector against her oppressors. Now Stephen had reached
out and cupped Audris's chin in his hand to lift her face. Her
head came up without resistance, and her smile had broadened
so that her rosy lips displayed her teeth, a trifle too large to be
delicate, but strong and white.

"You are merciful, Sire, to forgive me so easily," Audris
said, spoiling the deferential words by a confident chuckle.
"But to show my true contrition, I have brought you a gift."

She rose and peered behind the benches, then nodded and gestured. Fritha hurried to her side, holding a rolled tapestry in her arms. Oliver stiffened, inwardly cursing his wife for being such an idiot as to allow Audris to show this work, but he did not rise or speak. It would be worse to protest against displaying the picture than to pretend indifference to it. The best way to protect Audris now was to act as if there were nothing out of the ordinary about the panel. Audris herself, Oliver realized, did not seem to attach any significance to the piece. She had asked for someone tall to hold up the work and was waiting with a pleased smile for Stephen's opinion.

The king's first word was "Beautiful!" but as he took in the subject, he glanced at Oliver and frowned. Oliver merely nodded his agreement with Stephen's judgment, seeming not to see the expression that had followed the word. Stephen's lips twisted. "So," he said softly, "my coming was *not* a surprise. This cannot have been woven in a few hours or even a day. Who—"

Audris's smile had frozen on her lips. She had noticed the way her uncle had stiffened and realized that bringing down the tapestry had been a mistake. What a fool I am, she thought, not to have seen that my aunt was troubled by more than a fear of foretelling. I should have tried to learn what was going on beforehand. I could have sent for it later. And she blamed herself all the more bitterly because she had not stopped to think through the results of offering the gift to the king. She had only wanted to be rid of the piece, which made her uneasy.

"Oh, but it was a surprise!" Audris cried, interrupting Stephen. "I swear I did not know you intended to come here. The picture was only what I hoped for—wished for. Bruno had told me that he was going to you to find help after Summerville threatened to take Jernaeve by force when my uncle would not yield. And I was... afraid." That was not true; Audris could not remember fear, only a concentration on the work she was doing, and because she was unaccustomed to lying, her voice shook, immediately convincing everyone that she had, in truth, been terrified. "So I wove a picture to comfort myself," she finished.

Stephen was smiling again, for Audris's explanation was both reasonable and flattering. He nodded at Oliver, but it was to Audris he spoke. "I did not mean to frighten you, child."

That drew a return smile. "I am no child, my lord. I know I am small, but I fear I will grow no larger. I am near three and twenty."

"And still unwed!" Stephen exclaimed. "How does that come about?"

Audris had seen the trap, but only after she had fallen into it. Stephen's too great satisfaction with her answer was betrayed by the slight preening of his body, by the way his fingers moved and his head tilted, even though he had kept all but an expression of sympathy from his face. That satisfaction told her of his intention before his words defined it. The king, like Bruno a few weeks ago, was going to blame her uncle for keeping her unmarried. But the king, who had power, could call her uncle neglectful and give her a husband of his own choosing.

For an instant panic held Audris frozen; then her quick mind found a solution. So the king wanted to trick a poor, ignorant girl and force a husband on her, did he? Audris was sure her uncle had the *right* to choose what man she should marry, and if it was not his fault she was still a maiden, Oliver's right could not be taken away.

"Alas, Sire"—Audris sighed, dropping her head guiltily—"it is through my own overgreat particularity, I fear. My poor uncle must be near to wringing my neck, for it is he who must bear the wrath of those I refuse. He has brought a bushel of offers to me, but I could not, among them all, find a man to please me, and Uncle Oliver is too kind and too fond to force me."

This time it was Stephen's smile that froze on his face. Hugh, who had been drawn forward again in his desire to see the tapestry clearly, had seen the stiffness around the king's lips. He was not surprised that Stephen was somewhat stunned. Hugh could hardly believe his own ears. He had been certain, when Demoiselle Audris's head bent, that her next words would be the traditional, "I do not know why, Sire, but I will have a husband according to your wishes."

Now Hugh held his breath, torn between a delight whose cause he refused to recognize and anxiety that the king would react with rage.

But Stephen had no chance to reply. Walter Espec laughed loud and heartily. "Demoiselle, I think you have been made naughty by overindulgence. Still, if your uncle is willing to put up with you, it is none of our business."

The words were addressed to Audris, but the last phrase was clearly a warning to the king. Had Sir Oliver given some sign of reluctance to accept Stephen, Espec and the other northerners might have accepted his ambivalence as an excuse for the king to press the issue of the heiress's marriage. The warmth of the welcome Sir Oliver had extended, however, closed that loophole.

But Stephen had recovered from his surprise, and if he was aware of the hidden warning, he gave no sign. "I do not think the Demoiselle naughty," he said. "One who can produce work of such beauty"—he gestured toward the tapestry—"may indeed have a particular taste. Perhaps among my gentlemen she will find one to suit her."

Another trap. Panic rose again in Audris. All she wanted was to escape. If she could save herself now, she swore that she would disappear into the hills. It would be safe enough now that the danger of Scottish raiding parties was gone. The weather was still too cold to make roaming all day and sleeping out-of-doors pleasant, but there were shelters aplenty, and she hoped the king could not spare more than a day or two. Jernaeve was strong, and the lands, under her uncle's care, had grown wide and rich. Still, Jernaeve must be a small matter when compared with the affairs of the whole kingdom. Audris clasped her hands nervously and then opened them as if in supplication.

"But I do not wish to marry," she cried. "I am happy as I am. And if my wish alone does not merit your indulgence, Sire, still you cannot believe after what I have said of my uncle's kindness that I would marry any man who did not have his goodwill. Sir Oliver alone can judge whether the lands of your gentleman would be well fitted to mine."

"All women wish to marry," Stephen said, his voice growing sharper. "And lands are not all in all. These gentlemen have my *favor,* and a king's favor is worth much."

The sharpness of Stephen's tone brought both Bruno and Hugh forward. Hugh stopped after a single step, again crushing down a surge of protective rage, but Bruno took the chance of coming right to the back of the king's chair and shaking his head in warning. When Audris had first approached, Bruno had deliberately placed himself out of sight, for he feared Audris was so heedless that she might run to him before she greeted Stephen. Now, however, he felt it more important to stop her from saying any more. She might anger the king by further argument when she could safely leave her case in the hands of the northern barons, who, Hugh had told him, did not want to see her married to Stephen's penniless henchmen any more than Sir Oliver did.

Fortunately, Bruno's motion caught Audris's eye, and instead of saying rebelliously, "Such favor is not of much worth to me!" she cried aloud, "Bruno! Dearling!" and then clapped her hands to her mouth, but almost at once she removed her muting fingers to say in tumbling haste, "Oh, I am sorry, my lord. I will think on what you have said most dutifully, but I beg you to give me leave to speak to my brother, Bruno. I thought I had lost him again, and you have brought him back to me."

"Brother?" Stephen repeated, glancing at Oliver. The displeasure smoothed from his face, and he turned back to Audris and smiled. "Yes, I will let you go in a moment. I must just ask if you know what it means to do homage."

"Yes, my lord," Audris replied, infinitely relieved that the subject of marriage seemed to have been put away. "I did homage once—no, twice it was—to King Henry."

"And are you willing to do homage to me?" Stephen asked.

A flicker of her eyes had caught her uncle's urgent nod. "Yes, with all my heart," Audris replied. "Shall I kneel now?" She started to bend and then looked anxious. "Oh, but our token is not ready."

"It will be readied by the time supper is eaten," Sir Oliver said, rising to his feet and bowing to Stephen. "Eadyth, see to the folding of Audris's picture in oiled cloth and then in leather so it will be safe for the king to carry with him when he chooses to leave us. And you, Audris, curb your time with Bruno. You must be fittingly dressed if you are to do homage. It is no wonder if King Stephen thought you neglected. You come down like a beggar maid, all besmottered with stray threads. For shame. I am grateful I have not been accused of starving you."

Audris had turned her bend into a curtsy to Stephen and now whirled to throw her arms around her uncle's neck and kiss his cheek. "I am sorry, uncle," she cried, laughing. "Aunt Eadyth bade me change my gown, but I thought it better to mend my first rudeness by coming quickly than to delay to be fine." And on the words she was away, to throw herself into Bruno's arms.

"I have told you over and over—" he began, but Audris, clinging tight around his neck, whispered into his ear, "Come away. Come away."

Bruno was so startled by Audris's urgent whisper that his eyes flew to Hugh, and he made a beckoning gesture. The moment he had done so, he felt ridiculous. He trusted Hugh, but this was not an alehouse brawl or a rough-and-tumble in an army camp. There was nothing Hugh could do to help—or was there? Hugh had Walter Espec's ear, and Audris could not have a stronger champion. Bruno was grateful to Stephen and was coming to love his generous master, but when he had urged his sister to take a husband, he had not meant a penniless adventurer. Moreover, although he understood why Stephen wished to place his own man in Jernaeve, he knew the king would do his cause more harm than good by accomplishing his purpose. Thus, as he followed Audris across the hall to a spot out of the sight and hearing of the king, he looked over his shoulder and beckoned Hugh again.

"You are still saving me from scrapes," Audris sighed, kissing Bruno's cheek and letting her arms drop from his neck. "I was about to say something highly improper to the king. How dare he think he could force on me a pauper henchman and push out Uncle Oliver? Thank Saint Bede I saw you and found a way to escape. Now, if I can only stay out of his way—" She stopped speaking and her eyes widened as she saw Hugh. "The unicorn!" she cried, recognizing him by the shock of red hair.

"Do you know Hugh?" Bruno asked, surprised.

"No," Audris replied, smiling. "But I saw his shield from the window—and his hair. There cannot be many with heads as red as that."

"Then let me make known to you Hugh Licorne, who is Sir Walter Espec's squire."

Audris smiled again, and Hugh bowed gracefully. "I must thank you," she said, "for putting into my head the subject for a new picture. And I must find a way to thank Sir Walter for supporting my uncle."

"Sir Walter spoke for us all—I mean for all the northern barons," Hugh replied, his fair skin reddening under its weathered tan at his slip. "As to finding a way to thank him, there can be no problem. I will take you to him whenever you wish to go. But you must not be afraid of his loud voice. He cannot help it, and I swear the words will be kind."

Audris touched his hand gratefully, knowing he wished to be consoling, but she could not help laughing as she denied any fears of Sir Walter. Hugh was barely conscious of the rippling sound of mirth. The gentle touch on his hand had made him breathless, and his heartbeat had quickened. Hugh was annoyed with himself. Demoiselle Audris could never be anything to him. She was not even beautiful, he told himself; he had seen many women more beautiful, and had felt no great interest. The Demoiselle was too pallid for beauty—pale hair, pale brows and lashes, pale eyes—but those were different and perhaps the source of her power, for her eyes had a depth and luminosity rarely seen.

"Hugh, do you not agree?"

"Forgive me," Hugh said, tearing his eyes away from Audris's face and looking determinedly at Bruno. "I did not hear. Agree to what?"

"That the king is a good man, and Audris must not leave immediately after the ceremony of doing homage," Bruno repeated, looking with some surprise at his friend.

"Leave?" Hugh echoed. "Leave for where?"

"My own tower," Audris said, smiling questioningly. "I can say I must get on with my weaving."

"No," Hugh protested, not quite looking at her and missing the unspoken question. "That will sound as if you are kept at your work night and day. And Bruno is right, I do not think you should hide yourself away. If you do so, it is possible Stephen will claim it is by your uncle's order that you are sequestered and the words you spoke were not from your own heart but learned out of fear of him. Better that you mingle freely with the guests."

Now that Hugh had pulled his eyes away from her face, Audris examined his, though somewhat more covertly. She had been oddly disturbed by his intense scrutiny, which was so different from the awed staring of the superstitious common folk and the measuring yet indifferent glances of the men who offered marriage and wished to be sure she was not too deformed to bear children. Hugh Licorne's face might be called ugly by some, with those wide-set eyes over a strong nose and long chin, but it was a fascinating ugliness, and his mouth was beautiful, tender-looking and expressive. But what Audris read in the eyes and from the movements of his body was even more fascinating. For the first time a man was looking with avidity at *her* rather than at her uncle as he described the prized estate.

"But most of the guests are those—those suitors with hungry, gaping maws that he brought with him," Audris pointed out. "I am afraid if I say one word or nod my head to one of them, the king will have a priest saying the rites of marriage over me before I can turn away."

"No, Audris. He would not," Bruno assured her. "King Stephen truly thought you were being kept a maiden against your will. He even intended to offer you a choice, an uncommon kindness."

"A fine choice," Audris snapped contemptuously. "Each one so poor he would have holes in the behind of his chausses if the king had not provided patches." Then her eyes and voice softened, and she slipped her arm around Bruno's waist and kissed him again. "He has been good to you, brother—"

"Do not call me brother, Audris—"

"It is too late to worry about that," Hugh said, "since Demoiselle Audris named you brother to the king's face. Moreover, you must not deny it because—"

"No!" Bruno exclaimed, not loudly but with great force. "My mother—"

"Hush, Bruno," Audris interrupted. "I do not need to hear that stupid excuse again, and I think what Hugh wants to say is to my benefit, not to yours."

"Yes, it is, and to the benefit of Jernaeve and the northern shires as a whole. Bruno, you do agree that it would be better for Jernaeve to remain in your uncle's care than for the Demoiselle to be given against her will to Warner de Lusors or Henry of Essex or—"

"Yes, I agree," Bruno growled. "I have tried to tell the king that the companions he brought are not best suited to holding a keep like Jernaeve. He has seen that the north is not like the south, but as for Jernaeve, he thinks I say the holder must be a northern baron out of loyalty to Sir Oliver. But still I do not think he would try to trick Audris into marriage—"

"No, nor does he need to try it as long as he thinks he has a suitable master for Jernaeve in you, Bruno. No, do not interrupt me." Hugh held up a hand. "I am not implying any dishonorable threat to Sir Oliver, but surely you must realize, Bruno, that your uncle"—he shook his head at the instinctive, mumbled protest and continued—"is not a young man. If some ill should befall him and the next holder be less trustworthy, then you can be brought in to contest the honor of Jernaeve."

"Oh, Bruno, stop shaking your head," Audris urged. "I have told you before that I would rather have you hold Jernaeve for me than have some greedy boar of a husband take it away from me. But Hugh, are you sure the king has given up the notion of marrying me to one of his friends tonight or tomorrow? Bruno has so soft a heart that he trusts everyone."

"Audris—"

"I do not deny the king would like to see one of his hungry gentlemen settled in Jernaeve." Hugh answered

Audris's question as if Bruno had not spoken. "But he did stop pressing the subject of your marriage as soon as you called Bruno 'brother.' There is an easy way to be certain no false claims can be made, though. Bruno and I need only make sure you are never alone, Demoiselle Audris. Bruno's evidence might be suspect, but I do not think I could be considered to be serving Sir Oliver's purpose."

"And speaking of Sir Oliver, Audris," Bruno remarked wryly, "he is glaring at me right now. I think you had better go up and change your clothes."

"We will walk to the tower entrance with you," Hugh offered, "and wait below for you to come down. You need not then fear to find an unwelcome escort."

Audris reached out and took Hugh's hand. "I thank you," she said softly. "Your care for me, a stranger, is gracious and generous."

"You are no stranger to me, Demoiselle Audris," Hugh replied gravely. "Bruno is my friend, and you claim him as brother. I owe you my care." He hesitated, then laughed. "And is it not the duty of the unicorn to protect the fair maiden?"

"The unicorn," Audris repeated. "My unicorn."

She remembered then the tapestry she had begun, the unicorn saluting the maiden in the tower, and a faint chill passed over her as she recalled herself saying that the subject was a fantasy into which no meaning could be read. Another foretelling? But she did not release Hugh's hand until they reached the stairs to her tower, and when she looked over her shoulder from the seventh stair, he was still standing there watching her go up. She smiled down at him, marveling at the bright beauty of his blue eyes and wondering why she had first thought him ugly.

Chapter 7

IN THE QUIET OF HER CHAMBER, AUDRIS STARED FOR A TIME AT her loom, then shivered slightly. The unicorn in the picture in her mind had eyes of the same lambent blue as Hugh's. She turned away abruptly and saw that Fritha had already opened the chest and was lifting out tunics and bliauts for her to choose among. She had not seen the maid leave the great hall, but was not surprised. Fritha had surely heard her uncle tell her to dress more fittingly. A chill of fear flicked through Audris. No doubt Fritha thought it a fine thing to be a great lady, but Audris wished heartily that she could *give* Jernaeve to her uncle and free herself of the recurring threat of being used as impersonally as a seal for the transfer of the property.

She began to reach for the nearest garment, and then bit her lip. No more heedlessness, Audris warned herself. She must show that she was denied nothing; but she must not appear too rich either, lest she whet the appetites of those who thought of her as a prize to fill their pockets. And there was a new need, too, the need to enhance her looks for the sake of the blue eyes that saw her instead of a strong castle.

Audris had no doubt that Hugh's interest in her was purely personal because she knew he was totally unacceptable as a prospect for a husband to an heiress. Had he the smallest property or access to power, he would have been knighted at his age—and without wealth or influence, there could be no question of asking for her in marriage. He knew it and she knew it, so his admiration—or whatever it was he felt—was for her own sake.

Audris smiled and looked with more interest at the tunics, pointing at last to a fine wool gown dyed a soft rose. Strong, bright colors were more commonly favored, but she had learned that such colors faded her light eyes and hair into nothing. Unlike her work clothes, which Fritha had pulled off over her head, this gown was embroidered lavishly with a repetitive pattern of thick columns in thread of gold around the low V neck and hem and around the enormously wide bottoms of the long, fitted sleeves. Since the neck of the gown was cut low, Audris removed her plain shift, too, and replaced it with a finer one. This also had embroidery around the neck, and six narrow bands of gold circled the base of the sleeves, which were deliberately too long. When pushed up over the hands, they folded so that the embroidered bands looked like glittering bracelets and showed under the wide edge of the sleeve of the gown.

Having pulled down the shift and settled the tie and sleeves, Fritha eased the tight gown over Audris's head. For daily wear, Audris favored the warmth of a long undertunic and short overtunic, both garments full and loose for free movement and fastened with a simple girdle to prevent them from getting in the way. Fashionable wear was quite different, impossible to don without help since it was molded to the figure with laces at the back.

Had Audris been wearing such a gown when she first came before the king, he would never have called her "child," for as Fritha tightened the laces, it became apparent that Audris was a well-developed, if small, woman. Her breasts, high and firm, were full, her waist narrow, and her hips well rounded. These were further emphasized by the heavy golden girdle, which went around the waist, crossed in the back, and tied in a decorative knot just above the pubis. With the eye directed by the V of gold at the neck and girdle, there could be no doubt about the ripeness of Audris's womanhood.

Last, Fritha undid Audris's plaits, combed her hair, and rebraided it, twining the strands around gold ribbons. The ends of the plaits were tucked into gilded leather cylinders decorated with small pearls. Audris had no need to use false hair or any other device to fill out her braids; her hair was thick and would have curled had it been loose, and it hung nearly to her knees. The maid smiled broadly and clapped her hands together softly to show her pleasure in her mistress's appearance, then fetched a piece of metal polished to a mirror sheen for Audris to see her handiwork. Audris sighed and then smiled. Not only was she reluctant to spoil Fritha's pleasure, but she found that her spirits had been lifted by the image she saw.

Normally, Audris would have waited for her aunt to summon her down, but she did not want to begin weaving when an interruption would come so soon, and doing nothing left too much time for uneasy thoughts. She asked Fritha to give her the blue cloak, also embroidered around the border in the pilaster pattern, clasped it around her neck with a gold broach, told Fritha she was free until bedtime, and went out. Male voices floated up the stairwell, but Audris recognized them and did not hesitate until she came to the last step but one. There she paused, her full lips thinning as she heard what she thought was more bad news.

"I am afraid David will invade again, and not long in the future," Hugh was saying. "The temptation to break off another piece of Northumbria as he did with Carlisle will be too great."

"Do you mean we are not free of the Scots?" Audris asked anxiously, coming down the last stair.

Both men turned to her. "There is no danger now, Demoiselle," Hugh said, and Bruno spoke simultaneously, "You will be safe, Audris." And then, as Hugh appeared to have lost his voice, Bruno went on, "Hugh fears that the peace King Stephen has made will not hold, but I am sure King Stephen is aware of the temptation to David. Is that not why he arranged for Prince Henry to accompany him back to England? And I do not believe David will break the peace while his son is in Stephen's power."

"But Henry was not named hostage, was he?" Hugh asked. "That means he can find some excuse to leave the court any time."

"There is that danger," Bruno admitted, "but I know the king has given orders that everything be done to please Henry. And how could Stephen call him a hostage when Henry had just done homage for the shire of Huntington and been named earl?"

Audris had listened to this exchange with a frown. "No, this is not what I meant," she said. "What I want to know is whether the Scots are back in our hills."

"The soldiers are gone," Bruno answered, "but there may be stragglers about." Then a look of horror appeared on his face. "Audris, you do not still run about the hills all alone? How can my uncle permit it? Anything could happen to you."

"What could possibly happen to me?" Audris asked, laughing merrily. "There is not a man or a woman for miles around who does not know me, and none of them would do me harm. Nor is this the crossroads of the earth where a hundred strangers pass every hour." She put her hand persuasively on Bruno's. "Come, brother, do not frown. Most times I take Fritha—"

"A mute!" Bruno exclaimed. "She could not even scream if you were set upon."

Audris's laughter rippled out again. "But *I* could scream, and Fritha is very strong. No, do not scold me, dearling. In all the years, I have never met one person I did not know, and the shepherds all call to each other to mind where I am when I am on the cliffs. If I am long out of sight, one of them looks to be sure I have not fallen."

Hugh had been listening to this in stunned silence. First he had been much taken aback by the change made in Audris's appearance by her clothing. When he had seen her first, she had seemed pale and pathetic. Now he was put in mind of a thin alabaster cup holding red wine; Audris, like the cup, glowed from within, but her beauty was so fragile and delicate that, had he had the right, he would still have been afraid to touch her, lest she shatter. And while those thoughts were going through his head, she and Bruno were arguing about her wandering loose in the hills.

"Audris, you are not still climbing..." Bruno did not seem able to finish the sentence and exploded, "God curse my thoughtlessness in teaching you to climb!"

"Oh, hush," Audris whispered, "you will attract just the attention we wished to avoid."

But the warning came too late. Warner de Lusors, the handsomest—and hungriest—of Stephen's young men, had glanced around at Bruno's anguished exclamation. Lusors could not hear what was said after Bruno's voice attracted his attention, but he caught Audris's swift glance across the room and the frown that followed, and interpreted those in his own way. The Demoiselle, he was sure, was annoyed at being trapped by her brother and Espec's squire, both local boors, and was longing to escape into more worldly and amusing company.

Lusors had heard Audris say she did not wish to marry, but like Stephen, he assumed that to be the result of female modesty—or deviousness. As to the many refusals she had mentioned, either she had lied—all women lied—or she wanted something better in exchange for her handsome estate than the barbarians bred in the area. He had had considerable success in the past and did not believe any woman could resist him, especially a shy, ignorant girl who had spent her life buried in a northern wilderness. In the past, fathers and guardians of heiresses had cut short his progress to a marriage that would give him a livelihood, but now he had the king's support. Lusors was certain he need only present himself to win this girl.

It took Lusors a few minutes to extricate himself from his conversation without drawing attention to where he wished to go. Nor could he take a direct route to his goal because the servants were setting up the tables for the meal, but quick glances allowed him to keep track of his prey and to note the glitter of gold about Audris's gown. It would be a good match, Lusors thought as he made his way toward Audris and her companions. There would be no need to molder in this wilderness longer than it took to get the girl pregnant. He would allow Sir Oliver to stay and manage the place if the old man did not interfere. He himself could continue to follow the court to pick up additional gleanings—only he would now have a full purse to buy his own pleasures and would not need to pay for them with flattery to fools.

Had Lusors heard Audris's contemptuous remark about cuckoos—a bird that lays each egg in the nest of another species, where its young, once hatched, casts out the true nestlings so it can eat all the foster parents glean—he might have been more cautious in his greeting. As it was, he bowed slightly, smiled, and extended his hand, saying, "Let me escort you away from this cold corner, Demoiselle. Such loveliness should be where all can see it."

"Thank you, but I prefer the quiet of this corner," Audris replied stiffly, ignoring his hand. "And I am not cold."

She was not immune to flattery, and Lusors's words might have had an effect had not his eyes seemed to move so swiftly from her face to her rich dress, the pearl-sewn braid enclosures, and the elaborate girdle. She was also distracted by sensing that Hugh had tensed. Glancing at him, she saw that his mouth, soft when he had spoken to her, was now in a hard line, and his long chin thrust forward aggressively. Clearly he did not like another man to flatter her. Audris was thrilled by the signs of jealousy, but she did not realize that it was not Lusors's words alone that had provoked Hugh. He had seen that Sir Warner's eyes were as attracted by Audris's breasts and hips as by the gold on her gown.

"Ah, but I will protect you from any annoyance," Lusors murmured. "You need not be shy with me, although I find it charming and delightful." He used the rejected hand to gesture at Bruno and Hugh, and when they simply stared at him, said, "You may go. I will see to Demoiselle... er... to the Demoiselle's comfort."

"No, stay," Audris said angrily, gripping both Hugh's and Bruno's wrists. "And you, sir, I give *you* leave to go and discover my name before you give orders to my companions and dare to assume that you are better able to see to my comfort than my dear brother and my friend."

Actually, neither Hugh nor Bruno had given any sign of obeying Lusors's order, and Audris knew there was no need to hold them to stop them from leaving. In fact, her grip was designed more to prevent her outraged companions from assaulting Lusors than it was to keep them with her, as her arrogant speech to Lusors was designed to deflect his rage from her companions to herself. There was, after all, nothing he could do to her, whereas if he complained to the king, Bruno or Hugh might suffer. Color suffused Lusors's face, and the lifted hand clenched, but before he could release the angry bellow that was building in him, there was a burst of laughter to his right.

Another of the king's young gentlemen bowed deeply and raised a smiling face to say, "Demoiselle Audris, I am Henry of Essex. May I apologize for Sir Warner—"

"I do not need your apology!" Lusors roared. Then, recalling his purpose and the presence of the king not too far away, he swallowed and forced a smile. "Demoiselle," he said in a slightly choked but much lower voice, "I assure you I knew your name. It seemed to me too precious to be freely mouthed. I wished to ask your permission to use it. Sir Henry is too bold. And as to ordering away your companions, I only wish them good. You do them wrong to hold them. They have been loitering long enough. They are only squires, and their duty is to their masters."

"Who will forgive them, I am sure," Audris said, wondering what kind of idiot Lusors thought her, to mouth such obvious lies, "when I report that Hugh and Bruno awaited me by my asking."

"To shield you from the attack of so many too-eager suitors?" Henry of Essex asked, grinning. "There was no need. See, here come William Chesney and Richard de Camville. In such a crowd, Demoiselle Audris, you can come to no harm."

"You mistake me, sir," Audris said, more gently than she had spoken to Lusors because she was amused by Sir Henry's cheerful frankness. "I fear no harm, because I know my own mind and I am in my uncle's care. Perhaps you did not hear what I said to the king. Bruno has been away from Jernaeve for years. I have missed him sorely, and I wish to spend every moment possible in his company."

"That is most unkind to us, however," Richard de Camville said as he and William Chesney joined the group.

"Yes, indeed," Chesney put in. "You give riches to him who has plenty—for Bruno knows you well—and you deprive the starving—for we hunger to make your acquaintance so that we may learn to please you."

"You had better learn to please my uncle," Audris riposted. "I have said already that I will consider only such men as he presents as suitable."

"And he has said," Henry of Essex reminded her, "that you have refused every man he has presented. This comes near to the merry question of whether the chicken came before the egg or the egg before the chicken."

"Sweet Saint Bede, listen to them," Audris remarked, looking from Hugh to Bruno. "One speaks of starvation, and the other compares me to a chicken or an egg." Then she swept the half circle of men with a purposeful glance. "I think all of you gentlemen are troubled by empty bellies, but I assure you, you will suffer a violent disturbance of the bowels if you try to satisfy your appetite with me."

Hugh burst out laughing. "Indeed, I think so too, Demoiselle, for you are all pepper, vinegar, and sharp spices. But see, gentlemen, the king is sitting down. The evening meal is being served, and I am sure your bellies will be filled there with milder, more digestible dishes."

He lifted the hand Audris still held, and she had the presence of mind to relax her grip on his wrist so that only her fingers lay on it. Stephen's gentlemen had glanced around when Hugh announced the king was ready to eat, and Hugh used their momentary distraction to lead Audris between Henry of Essex and William Chesney. Bruno followed close behind, effectively sealing Audris off from the others.

Richard de Camville shrugged. "I think trying to win that girl a waste of time unless the king destroys the uncle or removes him by force. Espec's squire and her bastard brother were not waiting for her by accident. They were surely watchdogs. So, either Demoiselle Audris truly does not wish to marry and asked them to stand by, or her uncle *did* know of the king's coming and arranged a pretty scene to which Espec agreed."

"Either way, I agree that Demoiselle Audris is probably out of reach," William Chesney said. "The king will not force the issue. Did you not see how Espec and the others watched him? Sir Oliver is highly respected, known to be a man of honor and narrow interests. Sir Oliver will not mix in affairs of state, and he will have nothing to do with Empress Matilda as long as her cause is allied with the Scots. Thus, Stephen has no excuse to act against Sir Oliver, and if he does, Espec and his friends will assume they, too, will be unjustly treated." He smiled wryly. "The king may love us, but finding one of us a rich wife is not worth the loss of the whole north."

"On the other hand," Henry of Essex remarked, "if the Demoiselle could be brought to say she wishes to have one of us for a husband, the king would support her—and I think Espec would, too, for he watched her closely also."

"Too much trouble," Richard de Camville repeated. "I am not sure I wish to be isolated here in the north, and, in any case, I do not believe anyone will be allowed to discover what Demoiselle Audris truly feels. We will not be here more than another day at the most, and in that short time she will keep to her chamber or be well guarded."

Warner de Lusors had said nothing in the beginning, for he was still choked with fury at Audris's rejection. As he listened, however, he had a revelation that restored his good humor. Naturally, if she wished to deceive her watchdogs, the girl would attack most viciously the man she favored most. He also realized that neither William Chesney nor Richard de Camville was much interested in the prize, because both seemed to have overlooked the uncle, who would surely be grateful to be allowed to stay in Jernaeve and would gladly pay for his place with the profits of the land and the girl's weaving. So much the better. They would not even seek to catch her alone. Essex's interest was more doubtful, and he would have to be watched, but Lusors did not think Henry of Essex prepared to watch the girl's every move and seize her even on her way to the garderobe if she were alone. No doubt she would be startled, but it would be easy to soothe her and hide her until she could be brought before the king while her uncle was absent.

The remainder of the evening showed Richard de Camville to have judged correctly. Audris was never alone except for the brief time when she swore fealty to the king. During the meal, she sat on one side of the king with Walter Espec beside her, while her aunt and uncle sat on the king's left. They did not linger long over eating, for the delay caused by preparation of enough to feed the "unexpected" guests had ensured unusually sharp appetites. Then, too, although plentiful, the meal was simple, consisting of a single course: meat and fish pasties, cold sliced brawn, a hot, spicy fish soup, and the cheese for which Eadyth was famous in the area. No special ceremony was observed, except at the king's table, and even there it was curtailed, for Stephen bade the knights and squires who served him to leave the dishes and go to their own places.

Having been dismissed, Bruno joined Hugh at the last table, covered by a cloth and set with trenchers of white bread. Below them and the squires who had come with the northern barons were the servants' tables, where the food was of a coarser kind and somewhat less plentiful.

"I told you all would be well," Bruno remarked between gulps of his cooling soup. "She is telling the king of her early attempts at weaving and her ineptness as a housewife."

Hugh glanced at the high table, which he had made an effort to avoid, just as the king, who had been laughing, broke off a particularly succulent piece of pasty and popped it into Audris's mouth. "She is making a merry tale of it," he commented dryly.

"She always does," Bruno replied, chuckling. "Audris is the most lighthearted little wretch, and by the time you are done laughing, she has flitted away, and you discover that you never said to her what you intended—particularly if you wished to scold her, forbid her to do something, or order her to do anything she did not wish to do."

Whether it was Audris's clever conversation or the king's own decision not to raise any controversial subjects until

Jernaeve had been sworn to him, both Hugh and Bruno could see that those at the high table were at ease and enjoying themselves. And when the meal was over, Audris rose, took a basket from the steward, Eadmer, and began to collect for the poor, who came each day to beg at the gate, those scraps that had not been tossed on the floor. It was a task often left to servants, but equally often a noble lady would perform it as a humble, charitable good work. Stephen did not even think of forbidding Audris to do it, turning his attention to Sir Oliver to discuss setting the scene for taking Audris's homage and oath of fealty.

The ceremony was simple, but no less impressive for that simplicity. The chair of ceremony was placed in the center of the dais. Just below it to the right and left, Walter Espec and the northern barons stood as witnesses, the king's men next, with squires and servants behind them. The thick candles impaled on the spikes of the wrought-iron candelabra that hung from the blackened beams cast an uneven golden light on the dais and down the center of the hall. Torches blazed from holders in the walls, flaring and waning as drafts swept in from the ill-fitting window enclosures and the open doors. Now and again a red or gold gleam flashed from a rivulet of moisture trickling down the stone walls or a glittering spark leapt from a mote of mica or quartz in the stones themselves.

Similar bright points flickered from the embroidery of Audris's dress and the gold threads woven into her hair as she came from the side of the room and walked down the aisle formed by the witnesses. Simultaneously, Sir Oliver came across the dais and stood respectfully behind and to the left of the king's chair, and a priest, hurriedly summoned from Hexam abbey with holy relics to swear upon, moved to Stephen's right. When Audris reached the dais, she stepped up on it and knelt, and the king stood. Some of the men shifted uneasily; Audris was so small compared with the king who towered over her that an impression of threat and domination was created even though none was intended.

"You are Demoiselle Audris, rightful heir of Sir William Fermain, holder of Jernaeve keep—" Stephen hesitated, and Sir

Oliver prompted him softly, naming the other estates Audris nominally controlled, for Stephen to repeat in a louder voice.

"I am Demoiselle Audris, heir and holder," she confirmed. Her voice was strong and clear. Those men who had seemed uncomfortable nodded approvingly.

"And do you of your free will and without fear or reservation wish to become my man?"

There was a soft murmur of amused sound, and nearly all of the watchers smiled.

"I do so wish," Audris replied steadily. Now she clasped her hands together and raised them, and Stephen enfolded them in his own. "My lord king," she continued, "I enter into your homage and faith and become your man, by mouth and hands, and I swear and promise to keep faith to you against all others, and I swear to guard your rights with all my strength."

That brought another wave of amusement, one or two chuckles breaking the silence; even the king smiled, but he replied clearly: "We do promise you, vassal Audris, that we and our heirs will guarantee to you the lands held of us, to you and your heirs against every creature with all our power to hold these lands in peace and quiet."

He then bent and lifted Audris to her feet and kissed her firmly on the mouth. The priest stepped forward, extending a golden box with jeweled crosses on all four sides and an elaborate representation of Saint Cuthbert on the lid. Audris placed one hand on the box.

"In the name of the Holy Trinity, and in reverence of these sacred relics, I, Audris, swear that I will truly keep the promise I have made and will always remain faithful to King Stephen, my lord."

Sir Oliver now handed a leather gauntlet sewn all over with steel plates to the king, and he passed the glove to Audris, saying, "By this token, you are my man."

Audris took the gauntlet and kissed it, curtsied to the king, and stepped down from the dais. She carried the token purposefully back down the aisle, seeming intent on getting somewhere, but as soon as the formal arrangement of men broke up behind her, she veered off toward the huddle of servants who had gathered to watch at the lower end of the room. There, Bruno and Hugh closed in on her. The king's men, who had been watching in case de Camville had been mistaken and Audris would become available after her fealty was sworn, nodded knowingly to each other and did not bother to pursue, which resulted in a delightful and profitable evening.

Instead of fleeing to her chamber as soon as possible, Audris was able to talk at length with Walter Espec and each of the other local barons. She left no doubt in any mind that she loved her uncle and was well treated and content with her present condition. Moreover, she made clear to each man that if she should choose to marry, it would be to one of her own kind, a man bred in the northern shires who understood their lands and their ways and, last, that she had no prejudice against those who had already asked and been denied. This stroke was her cleverest, for it gave renewed hope to anyone with a marriageable man among his family or friends and stimulated his desire to prevent her from being given away to one of the king's needy supporters.

A few tentative openings in conversation soon showed Stephen the way the wind was blowing, and he abandoned his initial intention—actually without much regret. He liked Audris and did not wish to force a husband on her. She had made him merry enough to forget the worries that seemed to grow more intense and complicated with each day of kingship, even as success followed success. He longed for his wife, who could always soothe and divert him and often take his worries into her own capable hands. Had Maud been with him, Stephen thought, likely enough the little minx would already have been married to whomever he thought most suitable, but the thought was a tender praise of his wife, not an angry blaming of Audris. He was not dissatisfied with the hold he would have on Jernaeve. Stephen believed Sir Oliver would keep his word—and if he did not, it would be easy enough to replace him with Bruno, who owed him as much as the others and who would be welcomed warmly by Audris.

Stephen's easy acceptance of Audris's refusal to take one of his men as a husband pleased Walter Espec and the others. Sir Oliver was enormously relieved at having escaped from swearing his own private fealty to the king. In fact, everyone except Warner de Lusors went to bed in high good humor that night. Sir Warner was in a foul temper because he had decided to wait until everyone else had bedded down and then move his own mattress off the bench that had been provided for his bed and use it as a pallet on the floor, away from the warmth of the banked fire in the hearth, in the icy area near the doorway to the south tower.

It was only there that he would have a chance to catch Audris before her watchdogs did. Lusors was still determined to obtain Audris as a wife. He knew the other men were counting on new opportunities turning up, but he had suffered enough slips between his expectations and reality that he preferred a bird in the hand. He settled himself, pulling only his furred cloak over him. The cold would make him restless, and he knew he would wake at any sound or movement.

There was another restless sleeper that night. Hugh was warm enough, although he was farther from the hearth than the knights. He was happy, too, for he had a new friend, one who did not care about his birth or his position. Audris's loyalty to Bruno and her manner to him showed her warmth of heart and lack of pride. But Hugh was also uneasy, and each time he slept, he dreamed his true desires, so that he woke more than once, cursing his virility.

It was a sin to have such desires, Hugh thought, and for the first time in his life he was not thinking of sin in religious terms. Even if he accepted Sir Walter's offer to knight him, he had no right to think of Audris in that way. Sir Hugh Licorne would be as landless and as fatherless as squire Hugh Licorne and as unsuitable as a husband for Demoiselle Audris.

Hugh wished Audris had not spent most of the evening hinting that she still might agree to marry some northern-bred landholder. Unfortunately, the castellanship that Sir Walter had promised him would not qualify him as a landholder. Sir Walter was not a young man, and when he died his lands would be divided among his sisters, whose husbands or sons might not wish to retain Hugh in his position. In any case, a castellan, except for those great men to whom the king gave many castles to be held by deputies, must live on the lands he governed. Perhaps Audris could leave Jernaeve in her uncle's care, but for what? To live with him in a little log fortress?

It was easy enough for Hugh to convince his waking mind and suppress desires he knew to be unobtainable; once asleep, however, the chains he had fastened to his aspirations shattered, and in his dream he climbed the stairs to Audris's tower to find her waiting for him with open arms. She was warm and soft and naked, and he bent to suck the rosy nipples of her breasts, then sank to his knees to kiss the pale curls of her mound of Venus, to seek with his tongue the little one in her nether mouth. She held his head to her, tickled his ears, stroked his neck, trembled, and cried out… and Hugh woke again, gasping and appalled at his dream's lewdness. Only it did not feel like lewdness.

Hugh knew lewdness. While he was still a boy, he had been goaded by the taunts of his fellow squires and the other men with whom he served to lose his virginity to one of the castle whores. He was aware that the act was weak and sinful, and his pleasure had been mixed with horror and disgust. Confession, and a surprisingly light penance, had soothed away the horror, but the disgust remained and, though Hugh used women when his need grew strong, he had never enjoyed his couplings as a clean and unstained act. Nor had he ever caressed a bought woman as he had dreamt of caressing Audris; that knowledge had come from what others had told him, some intending honestly to instruct him and a few teasing, trying to incite him to further violate what they felt was a priggish purity. Yet Hugh felt no lewdness, no disgust, in the dream. His body had responded, yes, but with a pure joy that left no ugly stain.

Still, it was dangerous to allow himself to feel such desire for Audris. Awake, Hugh felt only a calm sadness and a strong determination that she should never know of or be disturbed by his passion. Not trusting himself to sleep again, he opened his eyes, grateful to discover that the dim grayness of dawn was seeping around the edges of the shutters. Hugh crossed his arms behind his head and wondered whether he would have the pleasure of playing bodyguard to Audris again or whether she would use the simpler defense of staying in her chamber. Involuntarily, his eyes strayed to the entry to the south tower and rested there. He hardly realized where he was looking, his mind dwelling with pleasure and amusement on various incidents of the previous evening. Slowly, as the light grew stronger, he became aware of the dark hump near the doorway—and then it moved, and Hugh realized someone was sleeping there.

Bruno, he thought. But Bruno had been beside him, and Hugh did not remember him leaving his place. He turned to look. Bruno was still there. Frowning, Hugh raised himself on his elbow, saw there was an empty bench among the group sleeping nearest the hearth, and uttered a muffled curse. Apparently one of Stephen's men had not given up and was waiting to catch Audris as she came down. Hugh started to push away the fleece under which he had been sleeping and then changed his mind. Probably Audris would not come down until it was time for Mass, and he did not want to provoke a quarrel with one of Stephen's men. He could watch from where he was until all woke.

Hugh had scarcely resettled himself, however, when a cloaked and hooded form came out of the tower doorway and moved silently across the hall to the outer door. This was latched shut but not barred—in fact, as they had been settling to sleep, Hugh had heard one of the squires joke to a neighbor that there was no sense in barring the door when the enemy was already within. The hooded form opened the door and slipped out. Since the person sleeping near the doorway had not moved, Hugh's eyes had naturally followed the figure in motion, and he had begun to think that either he was mistaken or, more likely, he had misjudged the size of the cloaked person and it was Audris's maid who had gone out on some errand.

By the time the door was pushed shut, however, the prone

form was up, slinging a cloak over his shoulders, and hurrying to follow. Hugh stood up too, annoyed because he had not thought, as soon as he saw the form near Audris's door, to pull on his outer tunic and his shoes, which were the only garments he and the other squires—who did not merit the luxury of a bench and flock mattress to protect them from the drafts while they slept—had removed. He was sorry if Audris was harassed, but no longer felt any anxiety about a marriage being forced on her by a false claim, so he did not hurry about adjusting his clothes, and even took the time to comb down his unruly red hair and rinse out his mouth.

Audris was vexed when Warner de Lusors burst into the mews on her heels and greeted her with a fulsome and ridiculous compliment, comparing her "blushing beauty" to the dawn, and she answered only with a brusque nod. She was aware of the anger he felt, but she was too eager to be rid of him to be cautious. With so determined a pursuer, cold courtesy might not be enough. Rudeness was more direct.

She turned her back on Lusors to face the falconer, who had been waiting in the mews for her since dawn in response to a message sent the previous evening. Both of them were standing by the perch of a magnificent gyrfalcon; the bird had turned her hooded head and opened her beak to hiss at the sound of Lusors's voice, mantling her wings slightly. Audris uttered a cooing sound and caressed her with a large goose feather, and the bird quieted.

"But is she well enough trained?" the falconer asked anxiously when he realized his mistress wished to ignore the intruder. "Only you have flown her, and as you see, she still does not like a man's voice, except mine."

"I know," Audris replied. "My uncle has had no opportunity to take her out. Yet she is the finest falcon we have had, and I wished to give the king a rich gift, since I have already denied him what he came for."

"What of Warlock?" the falconer asked, moving down the mews toward another perch.

Audris followed without a glance at Lusors, who gritted his teeth with rage. While she and the falconer discussed the merits of the second bird, he considered abandoning his project. He had actually turned to leave when Audris said, "I think this decision must be left to my uncle. Go and explain the problem to him." The falconer looked surprised, and Audris added, "I am going out, and I will not be back before the king leaves. Go now, Nils, and see if you can catch my uncle alone."

The falconer bowed and left. Audris chucked to Warlock and moved still farther down the mews, speaking to each bird and examining its reaction and appearance with care. She heard Lusors approaching and grimaced with distaste, turning her head ostentatiously away and hunching a shoulder angrily in his direction. She was therefore totally unprepared when he seized her, turned her forcefully about, and plastered his lips over her mouth. The attack stunned her. Within her memory, no one had ever seized her and held her against her will. Aside from instinctively pulling her head away from the repulsive, wet kiss that was smothering her, Audris was too surprised to struggle.

"You are as clever as you are beautiful," Lusors whispered. "I did not understand until you sent the falconer away and explained your absence and what you planned. We will be together—and then it will be too late. Your uncle will be forced to agree to our marriage."

"What are you talking about?" Audris asked. "Let me go!"

"Ah, how sweet, how innocent!" Lusors laughed. "But there is no need to play these little tricks on me. I understand that you felt you must seem to dislike me so that no one would suspect your favor—but we are alone now. There is no need to be coy. What I meant—well, we can find a private place, and I will teach you the pleasure to be had from that ripe, lovely body of yours. Then, when I have your maidenhead, I will take you to the king, and we will confess—and be married at once."

"You are mad!" Audris gasped, still not struggling because she could not believe her ears.

"Oh, no," Lusors assured her, misunderstanding. "I know you are afraid of your uncle, but there is no need. Once we are married, I will be with you and protect you."

"You idiot!" Audris exclaimed, but still in a low voice. "I am not afraid of my uncle. Let me go!"

And on the words, she kicked Lusors on the ankle and wrenched herself free. Her escape was possible because Lusors's grip had slackened while they talked. Now his surprise gave her a moment's time to step back, but rage at her "cheating" him soon flooded in, and he leapt forward to seize her again. He caught only her cloak. Audris whirled away, and the broach that closed the garment came loose. Lusors cast it from him with an oath and sprang again, this time catching her left arm. She swung back toward him, using the impetus of the turn to add to the full strength of her right arm as she struck him in the face with her clenched fist. Unprepared for any blow, Lusors did not dodge, and Audris's fist caught him in the eye and the side of the nose. Blood burst from his nose, and he howled, releasing his grip on her arm.

"Be still!" Audris hissed. "You cow turd! You will frighten the birds."

She was afraid as well as angry now, but she dared not run out of the mews lest Lusors, who she was sure was a madman, wreak vengeance on her hawks. Neither did she dare call for help; her screams would also disturb the birds and, even though they were hooded, might startle them enough to try to fly. If they rose to the length of the thongs that fastened them to their perches, they could be jerked out of the air and fall to hang upside down, doing incalculable damage both to their bodies and their spirits. She stepped backward, nervously fixing her eyes on Lusors, whose face was distorted horribly by rage and smeared blood. He had first raised his hand to cup his nose and eye, as if he needed the evidence of touch to assure him that Audris had struck him so hard, but then he had spread his arms so she could not dart by him and started to advance on her.

Chapter 8

"LUSORS!"

The deep male voice was not loud, but the authority in it froze Sir Warner in his tracks.

"Hugh!" Audris breathed, then cried out softly as Lusors, infuriated beyond reason, spun around and charged.

He was met by a single blow that caught him on the chin and snapped his head back. Audris ran forward, afraid that he would fall against a perch, but Hugh had already reached out and caught the unconscious man. In a smooth, experienced movement, he swung Lusors up on his shoulder and carried him out of the mews. Audris ran after them, snatching up her cloak as she went and catching Hugh by the arm to stop him. He turned his head toward her; his long jaw was set, his blue eyes blazing with a murderous rage, but Audris clung to him.

"Wait," she said softly. "It will be better if *you* do not carry him into the keep." Servants were now moving about in the bailey, and she hailed two men who ran over at once. "This poor gentleman tripped and hit his face in falling," she said, blushing slightly as she told the lie. "You must carry him into the great hall and ask my aunt to tend him."

Hugh relinquished his burden to the servingmen without argument. He was relieved to be rid of Lusors, for he suspected the man would have demanded satisfaction of him. Hugh would not have minded fighting Lusors; in fact, he would have been glad of an excuse to kill him, but he could not expose the true reason for the quarrel, and he knew Lusors would provide one that would cause trouble between either Sir Oliver and the king or Sir Walter and the king. Nonetheless, his rage at what he had seen and his frustration at not being able to vent that rage made him turn on Audris.

"What the devil were you doing in the mews all alone?" he snarled.

Audris looked surprised at his ferocity, but then she realized Bruno probably had not mentioned that she was mistress of the hawks of Jernaeve—as odd as that might be—so she smiled at him merrily, and said, "My unicorn. I do believe you have saved your virgin from ravishment—or attempted ravishment, at least." She laughed aloud as angry color flooded Hugh's face and added hurriedly, "I will explain, I promise, but do not bellow at me here. You will shock the servants, who have an unreasonable awe of me. Come, let us get horses and ride out."

The light promise to explain and teasing tone made Hugh want to laugh, but the urge only added fuel to the flames of his temper. He felt a flash of sympathy for Lusors. If Audris had invited the man into the mews as she had just invited him to ride out with her, it was no wonder Lusors had tried to seize her. At the moment Hugh himself would not have minded seizing Audris and giving her a good shake, but she had flitted away, her light, swift step carrying her halfway to the stables, where she stopped and turned around to wait for him. He was suddenly reminded of Bruno's loving and exasperated comment to him about Audris's proclivity for making people laugh and then disappearing before any reprimand could be administered. But Bruno was her brother and doted on her. She cannot play such games with me, Hugh thought furiously.

"Bruno warned me about you," he said as he came up to her and they walked on together. "How you make him laugh so that he forgets to scold you. But I am not so easy to manage. I am very stubborn and have a long memory. I will not forget that you promised to explain what you were doing in the mews."

"But it is my place," Audris said, gazing at him earnestly with eyes as limpid as pure water. "I bring in the hawks—most of them, anyway—and share their training with Nils, our falconer."

Hugh stopped dead again and glared at her, not sure whether she was teasing him, until he recalled Bruno's exclamation about her "still climbing," and her assurances that the shepherds looked for her to be sure she had not fallen. There was good evidence that what she said was true, but it was so shocking and unusual that Hugh merely stood and stared. Growing impatient, Audris took his wrist and pulled him into the stable. She ordered the grooms to saddle her mare and Hugh's stallion and turned back to him.

"It would not do for me to train them alone," she went on, as if he had accused her of dereliction of duty, "for then they would be accustomed only to a woman's voice. That would not serve the purpose, since it is mostly my uncle and those to whom he wishes to give the falcons as gifts who fly them."

Hugh blinked, again torn between the urge to laugh and a deep, painful anger. She had answered what he had asked—but without answering the real question. He looked at Audris sidelong. "It is not usual for a woman to catch hawks or to train them," he said, "but that still does not explain why you crept out of your chamber and into the mews at dawn. I told you I was not easy to divert from my purpose, and you promised to explain."

"*Crept* out?" Audris repeated not only the word but the emphasis Hugh had given it. Then her eyes widened and she burst out laughing anew. "You cannot think I went to meet that—that—brainless bag of vanity! Oh, Hugh, that is not proper at all. I am sure a unicorn is not supposed to have suspicions about the purity of his virgin! All wasted suspicion, too. I was not alone in the mews. Nils the falconer was there, at first. How could I dream that Lusors was mad and would attack me when I sent my man out?"

"What do you mean, 'mad'?" Hugh's voice was suddenly uncertain. The enormous relief he felt at Audris's contemptuous dismissal of Lusors as a "bag of vanity" had betrayed to him the true cause of his rage.

"I had refused to speak to him, turned my back on him— what man in his right mind would take that to mean I was afraid of my uncle and desired *him*?"

At that point the grooms brought the horses, and the conversation ended. Hugh lifted Audris to her saddle, and the feel of her body in his hands made him turn his head so that she could not see his face. Then he mounted, automatically checking the long hunting knife and short bow with arrows that were part of his saddle furniture. His thoughts were very far from the action of his hands, however; they seethed with discontent. He managed to keep silent while he followed Audris out of the walled upper bailey, down the steep road, and out through the east gate of the lower wall, trying to erase from his mind the one question that still nagged at him. When they were free and riding toward the hills that rose beyond the river valley, Audris laughed aloud, and her joy woke in Hugh a fresh wash of rage.

"But why creep out at dawn?" he asked suddenly, unable to control a last surge of ugly suspicion.

"Because I wished to escape before the king woke," Audris replied, grinning in triumph and looking back over her shoulder at the keep. "How could I be sure he would not begin anew to urge me to marry? To be at Mass with those greedy paupers and a priest so easily at hand… I could not bear to take such a chance. If I were out in the hills and none knew where to find me or how long I would stay, the king would have no cause to think of me or rethink his willingness to leave me—and Jernaeve—in my uncle's care."

Hugh had hardly heard more than the first sentence. With his jealousy finally gone, the knowledge that it had been fed by his own desire came alive, and he flushed with embarrassment. Unless Audris were as innocent as a baby, she must have realized why he had questioned her so sharply. No doubt kindness to her brother's friend had kept her from telling him flatly that her affairs were none of his.

"Forgive me," he muttered. "I had no right to ask any accounting of you."

Audris's grin changed to a gentler smile. "That is quite true," she said, "and, as you know, it is not my way to suffer arrogance in strangers, but I understood. You were frightened because you thought I might be hurt. You are like Bruno in that. He, too, used to shout at me when he feared for me."

Hugh shrugged angrily. "Perhaps."

"Perhaps?" Audris repeated, raising her brows. "Do you think I do not know why I do a thing?"

"I do not like crumbs of kindness," Hugh snapped. "I would prefer that you told me roundly to mind my own affairs rather than be treated gently because I am a poor squire who is your brother's friend—and in a similar case."

"Do not be so silly." Audris shook her head impatiently. "I answered you because you care, not for Jernaeve and its lands, but for me, for *me,* as Bruno cares for me, Audris, separate from Jernaeve."

"No!" Hugh exclaimed.

"No? You mean you do not care for me?" Audris asked.

"Yes, but—" Hugh stopped abruptly. "I think," he went on stiffly, "that we had better talk of something else. Where are we riding?"

Audris's laugh made a rippling music, but she did not explain it. Instead she asked, "Are you free to ride with me? I should have thought that you might have duties to perform."

"No—at least, none for the morning. The boys—Sir Walter's squires—will see to his dressing." Then Hugh frowned. "But we will miss hearing Mass."

"We will miss the breakfast meal, too," Audris said, her voice redolent with regret. "Like a fool I left my bag of supplies in the mews when I ran after you."

There was a brief pause. The casual mention of a bag of supplies had made Hugh's stomach growl, but the additional proof that her intention had been escape rather than flirtation made Hugh unreasonably happy.

"You seem to regret the meal more than the Mass," he remarked, trying to sound reproving but unable to keep his lightheartedness from his voice.

"I do," she answered, chuckling. "I can listen to two Masses—or even three, if needful—anytime, but no matter how much I eat tomorrow or how many times, it will not fill my belly now."

Hugh could not help laughing aloud, although he was faintly uneasy at her light view of what was owing to God. Still, he believed in Christ's love and His gentleness and understanding of human frailties. It would take a devil, not a God of loving-kindness, to punish the naughty twinkle in Audris's eyes or the way the corners of her lips curved upward. This was the mischief of an innocent, not evil.

But Audris had read the touch of uneasiness under Hugh's laughter. She recognized from that and from what he had said that he was deeply religious, and that he had not preached at her or told her another significant fact about him. He was, Audris thought, like Father Anselm, a person whose own deep faith did not lead to demanding all others follow exactly his own observance. The knowledge that Hugh would not scold her naturally made Audris contrite and made her want him to be as happy as she was. And there was a solution near at hand. She pressed left knee and left rein against her mare, turning her south, and beckoned to Hugh to follow.

"I have just realized," she said as he came level with her again, "that we need not lack food for either soul or body. If we ride south to Hexham abbey, we can hear Mass, and the good monks will feed us, too." Audris's glance sparkled with mischief again. "And since I know I never could convince you to let me ride about alone, you can send a boy to Sir Walter to tell him what has become of you."

"You could order me to leave you," Hugh pointed out, not sure himself whether he was teasing or testing—or, if he was testing, for what. "I have no authority over you."

"But I do not wish you to leave me, my blue-eyed unicorn," Audris replied. "I wish to know you better."

It was the truth, and although Audris had been warned that knowledge is often dangerous, she did not realize just how dangerous knowing Hugh better would be until the next day, after he had left Jernaeve. The day they spent together was all joy. Never had Audris felt such freedom in any equal's company—except for Bruno's—and there was something different in being with Hugh. She loved Bruno, but a sense of excitement thrilled her each time she met Hugh's luminous eyes.

At the abbey, after refreshment for soul and body had been provided, Audris offered to act as scribe for Hugh, so a fuller and more private explanation could be offered Sir Walter than could be carried verbally. This led to an exchange that made clear that both Hugh and Audris could read and write— unlikely skills for a woman or a simple squire—and to further elucidation of the youth and upbringing of each. Audris spoke because Hugh's deep interest was a new and wonderful experience for her; for Hugh, Audris's desire to know everything was painful as well as heartwarming, but when he had told her in plain words about his situation, Hugh felt better. He believed she had guessed from the first, but it was a sweet balm indeed to be sure she knew he had no father and little future, and did not care.

Actually, Hugh wrote his own note to Sir Walter, stating that Audris refused to return to Jernaeve and refused also to send for an escort from the keep or to remain longer in Hexham. He explained her decision in tactful terms and added that under the circumstances, he felt obliged to stay with her rather than let her wander alone. If Sir Walter left Jernaeve before he was able to return, he wrote, he would follow the king's party as soon as he could lay down his responsibility.

"You should have written 'burden,'" Audris teased, reading over his shoulder.

"I do not like to lie," Hugh responded lightly, as if he were jesting, but he was grateful that his head was bent over his writing. He had promised himself that he would keep knowledge of his desire from Audris, and he was sure at that moment it showed in his face.

"How inconvenient that is," Audris said, still teasing. "At least, I find it so. It is dreadful that I cannot tell the smallest untruth without blushing or my voice and knees trembling. It is Father Anselm's fault." But her tone changed on the last words, and there was affection and longing in it when she added, "It grieved him so when I did not speak the truth that the punishment for the fault I wished to hide was the lighter to bear."

Hugh twisted around and looked up at her. "Love is a harsher whip than a flail of nine tails studded with iron points."

"Is that true?" Audris breathed, shivering when their eyes met, as if Hugh's words were a dire warning.

But he had already turned back to his note, and his voice was flat as he replied, "So Thurstan said when I complained his love constrained me."

"Did you chafe at those bonds, too?" Audris asked, smiling again.

Hugh was so relieved at the renewed lilt in her voice, which he took to mean she had dismissed his mention of love, or at least applied it only to his foster father, that he finished writing in a hurry and told her the tale of his early divergence from Thurstan on the matter of his future.

"He loved me, truly like a son, and wanted the best for me, but to his mind, the best was a holy life. Alas, I was not fit for it. No matter how he pleaded or reasoned with me, I was forever running from my lessons to the men-at-arms. Not that I minded the lessons, but my longing for arms was so strong."

"Like my desire to climb for hawks." Audris nodded understanding.

"I made swords from sticks tied together," Hugh went on, his eyes staring off into the distance in remembrance. "And, worst of all, I tried to use the farthings Thurstan gave me to make offerings in the church to bribe the men-at-arms to teach me to fight. They would not take the coins, of course, being men of Thurstan's own retinue, and they even told me how wrong I was to wish for a hard, ugly, sinful life instead of one of peace and prayer." He shrugged and smiled. "I wept for my sin—but I did not change my desire. I think what convinced Thurstan at last was that when I confessed the sin and promised to sin no more and made the offerings, the prayers I uttered with them were for permission to learn to be a knight."

Audris nodded again, for she had similar, if less momentous, stories to tell. But more important than the memories evoked was the sense of kinship both felt, owing to the strongest influence in the youth of each coming from men of deep faith and deep wisdom. The difference in Thurstan's and Anselm's conditions—Thurstan's high office and worldly pomp and Anselm's rustic isolation and innocent simplicity—had burdened Thurstan with guilt and washed Anselm nearly free of all sense of sin. These attitudes had affected Hugh and Audris, particularly as their experience had mirrored to a great extent that of their mentors, but the devotion of each to the respective foster father and tutor was a strong bond between them.

Through the day, they found other bonds. Each loved animals and was fascinated by the habits of wild creatures. Audris knew most about birds, Hugh about the beasts of the chase and those that preyed on them. And both loved the harsh northern countryside. True, Audris had never seen the south, but she rightly assumed it was all much like the lush river valleys of the Tyne and its tributaries, which Hugh confirmed, and she found such tame countryside dull.

They had ridden west from Hexham, where all the lands that were not abbey lands owed allegiance to Jernaeve, and they could have stopped at several manors and been more than welcome. Instead they chose the rugged hills. For dinner, Hugh brought down two hares with his bow, and Audris dug wild carrots, horseradish, iris roots, and parsnip from the hard ground. They cooked these in an oven of hot stones covered with embers on the open ground in front of a cave—or niche—just large enough to keep the wind off them while the horses grazed on the brittle dead grass of the hillside. The hares were winter-lean, the roots tough and woody, but Audris and Hugh both felt they had never eaten so well.

Only once did they touch, when their hands came together by accident in sharing out the food. Hugh's reaction was so strong and so immediate that he could not restrain a gasp. That brought Audris's eyes to his face before he could mask his expression or turn away. The mingled pain and passion mirrored there were so vivid that the image remained as if branded on her mind, even though she looked away in the next instant. At the time, she only felt a shock at intruding on emotions so powerful and private, and she hastened to make some light remark behind which they could both hide.

It was only the next day, after Audris woke—rather late, for she and Hugh and her aunt and uncle had stayed in the hall long after the evening meal, first playing a foolish game and then talking of the doubts Hugh felt about the lenient treaty Stephen had made with King David—that she associated the passion and pain with herself.

She had been lying abed thinking of all that had happened since she had seen the unicorn shield below her tower. One by one she looked back at the events of the past two days. The memories as usual appeared as moving pictures in her mind, and somehow from her first sight of him to her last, when she glanced over her shoulder on her way to her chamber in the tower and saw him watching her go, every event revolved around Hugh Licorne.

The last image of him lingered. There had been no particular expression on his face then, but the line of his body and the turn of his head showed the restraint of his desire to follow her. And unbidden, the tormented image she had seen on the hillside replaced the controlled face in the hall. Audris leapt out of bed, dressed as quickly as she could, and ran down, but it was too late. Hugh Licorne had left at first light to follow his master.

She was filled with a sense of loss, but when thought replaced emotion, she realized that she had not the least idea what she would—or could—have said to him. It would have been very wrong to beg him to stay, for he owed fealty to Sir Walter and had duties. Nor, Audris realized, could she even invite him to return to Jernaeve. It would be more cruel than kind, for she could offer no hope his desire could be fulfilled. Even if she could somehow convince her uncle that Hugh would make a suitable husband—which she knew to be impossible—her marriage would mean the expulsion of her aunt and uncle from Jernaeve, and she had vowed she would never allow that to happen.

Throughout the days that followed, as the unicorn tapestry was completed, the image of Hugh's face rose up in Audris's mind to trouble her peace. She thought often of writing to him—a messenger need only find Sir Walter, and Hugh would be near—but she knew it would be foolish, for it would only remind him of a passion that could not be gratified. Another trouble beset her. She found she could not bring the picture of the unicorn to her uncle for sale or even pack it away out of sight. Against her will, for it, too, broke her peace, she had to hang it in her chamber. Nor was the inability to let go of the tapestry because she identified the unicorn with Hugh. She needed no reminder of Hugh, whose strange face and haunting passion bred a constant restlessness in her. She could not part with the tapestry because she knew the work was not complete—but no new images on any subject came to mind. Did that mean she would—or must—see Hugh before she could weave again?

At last spring came. Winter wheat thrust tender shoots through the dark earth, glazing the fields in a delicate haze of pale green; buds swelled on the tips of branches. Audris fled Jernaeve, saying she wished to keep watch on the nests of the falcons so that she could take a few of the young once they were fledged, but also because she hoped to leave her trouble behind her. Mostly she did, except when she saw the mating play of the beasts and birds—and she was never free of it, for each came into heat and rut in its own season.

The generation of young had never disturbed her before, but when in spring she saw a stallion cover a mare or in late summer a ram mount a ewe, Audris had to turn away, for the sight woke strange sensations—a dull, oddly exciting ache in her groin, intensified by a pulsing tickle that swelled and moistened her nether lips. Once while she sat as still as an image at the edge of a forest clearing watching a young sparrow hawk tear its first kill, a buck caught the doe he was pursuing there. Caught by surprise, Audris could not tear her eyes away, and when she saw him plunge and plunge again, both animals crying aloud in their mating, the sensation between her thighs grew so intense that she almost touched herself. But a fear came over her when her hand slipped under her skirt, and she could not even try. Had she done so as a child and been punished or threatened? Audris could not remember, but whatever had happened was effective; it blocked that path to relief.

From then on, she was more careful and watched the hawks where there was no chance she would intrude on the matings of other beasts. Even so she could never escape completely. The doings of the birds in the spring affected her differently. Their love play was more alien and did not arouse her physically, but it was also intermingled with building a place to rear their young. Especially when she knew the pair she was watching mated for life, a longing stirred in Audris for someone of her own, a person to whom she could belong as he would belong to her—but whether her body responded or only her heart, the face that haunted her desire was always Hugh's.

Still, such moments of acute distress were brief. There was always so much to do in spring, summer, and autumn: the herbs and flowers used for spices, treats, and medicaments were also Audris's responsibility, and it was under her direction that plants were moved or pruned, the seeds of the annuals planted, and the gathering done. The gardeners worshiped her, for when she put her finger in the earth and said, "Set seed this deep and no deeper, and cover them so," those plants grew. And when she felt the dry twigs of the perennials and said, "Cut here," the new growth on the bushes was lush. They did not call her witch because only good came from her touching—and because the eldest of them remembered that Father Anselm had done before as Audris did now.

Between one task and another there was little time for idle dreaming about unicorns. Moreover, through the spring, summer, and autumn that followed, there was more food for thought than usual. Bruno sent a regular stream of news, which Sir Oliver encouraged by paying the cost of the messengers. So far it seemed that Sir Oliver had chosen well when he decided to welcome King Stephen and have Audris do him homage. Most of the kingdom appeared to feel the same, for when Stephen turned south and held his Easter court in London, almost all the great nobles and bishops of England and Normandy were in attendance, even Robert of Gloucester, Matilda's half brother and most determined supporter.

Only one problem marred Bruno's satisfaction. As Hugh had feared, Ranulf, earl of Chester, was furious over Stephen's promise of lands Chester claimed to King David; the earl left the court in a rage. And when Stephen seated David's son, Henry of Huntington, at his right hand, the archbishop of Canterbury, who felt that place to be rightfully his, took offense and also departed. These events were all the excuse David needed. He insisted his son had been insulted by the English and called him home.

It was easier to deal with the few men who resisted outright, such as Baldwin de Redvers. Even Baldwin offered to do homage to Stephen after he saw that few others clung to Matilda's cause—but by then it was too late. The king decided that a lesson must be administered and refused to grant him the same favors he had granted those who came at his first summoning. Nor did Stephen mouth idle threats. Bruno sent a triumphant message describing how Redvers, who was castellan of the royal castle at Exeter, had intended to capture the city. But the people of the city favored Stephen and sent him a warning of what Redvers planned, so the king was able to bring his army into Exeter and besiege Redvers in the keep itself.

Not long after, however, the news grew a shade less satisfying. Bruno's next message bore a note of caution. Some who had sworn had not done so with clean hearts, he warned. During the siege of Exeter, the besieged garrison had been reinforced—and those responsible for preventing such a thing offered only lame excuses. Gloucester and others, Bruno feared, had connived in the plot. Now and then Bruno mentioned Hugh, who was also with the king, leading a troop of Walter Espec's men. Hugh had been knighted, and rightfully, Bruno reported, for he was a daring devil, strong as a bull, always in the forefront of any raid or beating back any sortie from the keep. Audris did not ask for any repetition of the facts about Hugh. She did not need repetition. Every mention of him seemed to sink into her soul and warm her body.

Then there was a long silence, and Audris began to fear that Bruno had been hurt. But she did not fear for Hugh; the unicorn could only be slain when trapped and held by the maiden. But Audris was thinking seriously of demanding that a new messenger be sent simply to determine whether her brother was well, when news of the fall of Exeter keep arrived.

Oddly, there was little triumph in this message. The wells had failed, and the besieged, seeing that their time had run out and only the choice of yielding the keep or dying in it remained, sent a deputation out to beg for permission to leave Exeter. This Stephen at first refused, even when Redvers's wife came out barefoot, with loose hair, weeping bitterly to beg mercy. But then Gloucester and his followers began to talk to the king, and suddenly Stephen changed his mind and not only gave permission for the garrison to depart without punishment or even swearing not to take up arms against him, but to take with them their possessions and to adhere to any lord they wished.

"What?" Sir Oliver said when he heard the final piece of information. "Tell me again."

The messenger repeated what he had said.

"The king is very kind," Audris said, but she sounded uncertain.

Sir Oliver glared at her. "Unless there is some matter Bruno does not know and thus has not passed on, I would say the king is a fool. Either he should have accepted the first offer they made, or he should have insisted on harsher terms, no matter what Gloucester promised or threatened. What he did almost cries aloud that the cause of the rebels is honorable. Rebellion *must* be punished. Only an honorable difference of opinion may be compounded by honorable terms of submission."

Audris remembered Hugh telling her that Sir Walter feared Stephen was the kind who would charge at once but, if halted and urged to think, would lose faith in himself and fail to chance a final confrontation. She had said, laughing, that to her that sounded like being reasonable, and Hugh had frowned and answered that if the king's actions were a result of reason, the nation would be most fortunate. But while he spoke he shook his head, making it clear that he feared it was not reasonableness that formed the basis of King Stephen's decisions.

Sir Oliver's concern, of course, was that King David, hearing of the events at Exeter, with even greater emphasis on how easy it was to escape retribution from King Stephen and remembering how much he had profited from his last incursion into England, might decide to take another bite out of the north. Fortunately, that did not happen, and the truce with the Scots seemed to be holding. There was some raiding, but that was common in any year, and the perpetrators were clearly small outlaw parties that had no sanction or support from King David.

The winter passed. Bruno's news was still largely taken up with Redvers, who had not mended his ways but only used to his own advantage the mercy bestowed on him. He had renewed his rebellious activities in the Isle of Wight, where Stephen had pursued him, but Redvers had escaped again.

The spring of 1137 was early and mild, but Bruno's news was less pleasing than the weather. Matilda's husband, Geoffrey of Anjou, had received Redvers with honor, supplied him with men and money, and set him to rousing Normandy against Stephen. The king, Bruno warned, intended to call his English vassals to his support and cross to Normandy by Lent to hold his province and settle with Redvers once and for all. Knowing his uncle, Bruno reported that he had already spoken to the king, who had graciously and generously—for Bruno's service was already pledged to him—said that he would take Bruno for "two men" and not require Sir Oliver to serve in person. All he would demand were the services of the men-at-arms Oliver was pledged to bring with him or scutage for their service.

Sir Oliver blessed Bruno, smiled grimly, and when Stephen's pursuivant arrived, he promptly dispatched with him five young troublemakers, roughly trained, wearing boiled leather armor, and carrying reworked swords, which strictly fulfilled the terms under which the Fermains held Jernaeve. The pursuivant was not pleased, but Sir Oliver explained that William the Bastard had left his father a ruined land nearly devoid of men to till the soil. William expected only that Fermain would suppress any new revolt in the north, not that his vassal could supply men for his king's other wars; thus, William had demanded only a token troop despite the wide extent of the estate.

The first William's heir, William Rufus, had not troubled his father, Sir Oliver said—in truth, he had looked at Jernaeve, shut tight against him, and decided to leave that problem until he had a full army to expend on taking it, but he died before that. The late King Henry, Oliver went on smoothly, expected only that Fermain would hold the border against the Scots, which, Sir Oliver pointed out, he had done most faithfully, and King Henry had never changed the terms of his vassalage.

The pursuivant nodded. There was nothing special in Sir Oliver's face or voice, but Stephen's pursuivant understood the purpose of his tale. What was more, he had looked up at old Iron Fist from the ford and traveled up the steep winding track into Jernaeve keep. He knew what it would cost to take such a place by force and decided that a mark or two or a few more men were not worth setting in Sir Oliver's mind the notion that his master might ask too much once his grip on Normandy was reestablished and all rebellion quenched. And Sir Oliver was content because his conscience was clear. He was not cheating the king. Those five devils, so discontent and rebellious on the land, would doubtless make good soldiers.

There was, however, little enough else to make Sir Oliver content. Within weeks after Stephen had sailed for France, reports began to come to his ears about a gathering of men and arms in Scotland. Sir Oliver cursed long and loud, but without much real spirit. Licorne had predicted a renewal of the war, and Sir Oliver had feared his reasons were good. Now Oliver was only expressing his frustration at the time of year. Spring was the worst time to withstand a siege. The stores of winter were used up, and nothing could be added to fill the storerooms until the first harvest. The sheep and cattle were breeding and could not be slaughtered without disaster. Nor could they be brought in and sheltered behind the walls, because there was nothing to feed them. Nonetheless, Sir Oliver sent warnings to the shepherds and the cowherds to keep the animals on the lower pastures so that they could be driven in. If the Scots came, they could feed the livestock on the new growing wheat within the walls—until the people inside the keep had to eat the sheep and cattle themselves.

Chapter 9

THE YEAR THAT HAD PASSED HAD BEEN HARDER FOR HUGH than for Audris. Oddly, this was because Sir Walter loved Hugh, who had filled his master's need for someone to instruct and care for at a time when his life seemed to have been emptied. Thus, Sir Walter noticed Hugh's strong attraction to Demoiselle Audris of Jernaeve. He never thought for a moment that any result could come of that attraction. Nothing he could give Hugh without infringing on the rights of his blood ties could make Hugh a suitable match for Audris, and Sir Walter never wavered in his conviction that his sisters' sons must be his heirs. But he did wish to ease his lovesick fosterling and sought distractions for him. The first was to take Hugh with him to the Easter court in London instead of leaving him behind to oversee his bailiffs and stewards on smaller estates, as he usually did. The great city, he was sure, could distract even a man on his deathbed. But in London, appearances counted far more than they did in Yorkshire, where everyone knew Hugh, so Sir Walter had Hugh outfitted in fine garments, a new furred cloak, and dyed leather boots and shoes.

In a sense Sir Walter was successful. Hugh had been to London before, but only when he was young enough so that every moment he was not serving his master was strictly supervised by some other responsible adult. Now all but a few hours a day were free, and he roved the busy streets. Most fascinating were the docks where ships came, seemingly, from the far reaches of the earth. The crews showed every color of hair and skin from the yellow and white of the men of the northern seas through browns of every shade to a startling black man who spoke a strange gibberish that no one could understand. The precious stuffs they brought in exchange for English wool and tin were unloaded on the wharves, but they were too well sheathed in boxes and bales to be examined. For that one had to walk the Strand, where stalls stood before rich warehouses, displaying a feast for the eyes of goods as common as woolen stockings and as rare as a unicorn's horn.

Hugh gaped at that. It was a fantastic and beautiful thing, pure ivory, long, slender, and straight, but with a spiral twist from base to sharp point. He thought for a minute of sending it to Audris, but when he heard the price, he knew the horn to be as far beyond his reach as the Demoiselle herself. Later, he was glad the horn had been so costly. It would have been wrong to remind her of him if she had forgotten. That thought hurt, and Hugh hurried on to his second rationalization, the hope that Audris would not wish to think of a dead unicorn.

Those thoughts only came to Hugh later, however. On the Strand even a sharp disappointment could not hold one's attention long. Not only one's eyes but every sense was assaulted. Odors came in waves as one passed along: the sweet, greasy scent of wool, the tang of fish, the welcoming, musty smell of beer. And at every moment a new cry dragged one's head from right to left, forward and back. Boatmen shouted from the river; eel wives offered baskets with their odd wailing but musical call. Hugh loved the Strand and never tired of it, because it was never the same no matter how often he came.

He only wore his fine clothing to the Strand once. The rich velvet tunic and high horseman's boots brought him bows and obsequious smiles, which he was fortunate in being able to measure because some of Sir Walter's minor servants treated him to the same false honors. The handsome clothing also brought doubly high prices, which he would not have known except that a passing cart splattered him with foul sewage before he could decide which item he wanted. It was far more important to hurry back to his quarters and try to save his boots and tunic than to buy a trinket, and when he returned a few days later in his old woolen clothes, he was offered the same items at half the cost.

Unfortunately, high prices were not the only problems Sir Walter's generosity brought him. More than once he had been mistaken for someone of wealth and influence. Then, when his state was discovered—for he refused to say he was Walter Espec's favorite—he would often be angrily rejected, and once he was crudely insulted. The rejections did not hurt Hugh—much—for he knew what value to place on the friendship of the lickspittles who hung on the rich, but they reminded him of his empty future.

Another complication was added when Sir Walter came upon him the time insult was offered. Hugh's lips were drawn back in a snarl, and his muscles, tense with rage, bunched under his elegant tunic. The insulter sneered at him, enjoying what he thought was impotent fury, for he did not know Hugh. But before Hugh could strike, Sir Walter's hand fell on his shoulder, and the man confronting him choked and backed away—he knew Sir Walter and the power he wielded. Hugh swung around, his eyes blazing.

"Enough," Sir Walter said firmly. Then, sensing Hugh's instinctive response to his tone of command, he added, "On Friday the king will give the accolade to five candidates for knighthood. I will ask him to add your name to the list, and he will be glad to do it."

"But—"

"But me no buts," Sir Walter snapped. "If you had struck that fool, you would have made trouble for me. That he deserved it is not the point. As long as you are my squire, I am responsible for you—and you are too old for that, Hugh."

The statement woke an immediate response in Hugh. He realized suddenly that he desired to be a knight. He was too old—and too strong in both body and will—to be a squire any longer. Four years earlier, when he had first made the decision not to change his status, there had still been something in him, despite his size and strength, that shrank from being called a man. But it was no longer true. When had that changed, Hugh wondered. And as if in answer to his question, a melange of memories of Audris filled his mind. He called himself a fool. Knighthood would bring him no closer to Audris; he knew that well. Nonetheless, his desire to be knighted remained. Nor did the way Sir Walter phrased his remarks arouse any sense of guilt in Hugh. In fact, he smiled wryly at his master.

"How does it come about that it is always to save you trouble that I receive favors?" he asked.

Sir Walter struck him a fond blow on the head that might have stunned another. Hugh merely rocked with it and blinked. He was accustomed.

"It will save us both trouble," Sir Walter growled. "Being knighted will not stop such filth from annoying you, but you will have the right to challenge, and silencing one will silence them all."

Hugh nodded grim satisfaction. "I will have to find one willing to take my challenge," he remarked dryly.

Sir Walter laughed. "They do not know you here. Some fool will think your size would make you slow."

Hugh never needed to issue a challenge; having been knighted so publicly by the king was evidence enough that Hugh had connections to match his garments and saved him that kind of trouble. It was only after Sir Walter had returned to his own keep, Helmsley, that the dark side of becoming Sir Hugh showed itself. Seemingly tales of the new, rich garments and the knighting by the king had worked their way to the ears of Sir Walter's sisters and renewed all their fears of Hugh's influence. Even his recommendation that John de Bussey be made castellan of Wark was turned against him. He had done it, he was told by Lady de Bussey not long after their return to Helmsley in the early summer, only to be rid of John so that he could bind his aging master still closer.

"That was not my reason," Hugh protested hopelessly. "But if you do not believe me, I beg you to tell Sir Walter to send me away."

"You are as subtle as a snake," the lady hissed. "But I am not such a fool as to try to pull the scales from my poor brother's eyes by force. Do you think I do not know how good and pure his heart is? I know well why you bid me vilify you. That will only make him cling more closely to you and think me cruel and spiteful."

"It is not true!" Hugh cried desperately. "I love him. I cannot leave him without any reason. That would hurt him. Find me a good reason, and I will go."

But that was not what the fearful sisters wanted. They wanted Hugh to expose his "true nature," for example by complaining of their insults and cruelty to Sir Walter. The sisters felt that if Hugh left while on good terms with Sir Walter, the young man's absence might be more dangerous than his presence, for their brother would then miss and long for Hugh.

Fortunately, Hugh did not know that. He believed that if he went away from Helmsley their animosity against him would be ended, and he sought desperately for an excuse to leave. But it was Sir Walter who sent him away, to the siege at Exeter—not to please his sisters but for reasons of his own.

While Audris fled to the hills and worked in Jernaeve's garden, Hugh fought at Exeter as the leader of his own troop. A senior vassal was in charge of the entire contingent, but Sir Walter wanted Hugh to have a chance to put into effect, all on his own, what he had been doing for several years with Sir Walter's authority behind him.

In a personal sense, Hugh enjoyed himself greatly. He was spectacularly successful in the few sorties and raids that enlivened the dull weeks of the siege, and it soon became clear that Hugh was a natural battle leader. Sir Walter relished his chief vassal's reports of Hugh's all-around success and laughed heartily at his fosterling's much more casual and often jocular recounting of his doings. Other passages in Hugh's long, detailed letters were not at all amusing. They related the same events that Bruno had described for Sir Oliver, but often in darker terms. Less blinded by loyalty and gratitude to Stephen, Hugh saw the disaffection of Robert of Gloucester and his adherents less as an affront to the king and more as a political danger. He was thus more shocked by Stephen's ill-judged mercy.

Sir Walter was more ambivalent than Hugh in his reaction

to these events. He had become aware during the time he had spent with the king that Stephen was persuadable, but this facet of his character had advantages as well as drawbacks. He was not overjoyed to learn that the homage of Robert of Gloucester was a clean patch over a festering sore—but he had suspected that all along—and if the king were busy watching the barons of the southwest, he would have less time to pry and poke in the north. Sir Walter's greatest concern was that any rebellion be contained in one place at a time and not be allowed to flood the entire kingdom. Thus, when Stephen followed Redvers to the Isle of Wight, Sir Walter allowed his levy of men to go with the king, but when they returned, having failed to take Redvers, he summoned his contingent home.

The entire family was gathered in Helmsley to celebrate the time of Christ's birth and the Epiphany. To most it was a period of great joy, but it was a time of penance to Hugh. Although Sir Walter was not so unaware of his family's jealousy as Hugh thought, he could not completely refrain from praising his protégé for his fine performance in Exeter; after all, it was he who had trained Hugh, and it was to his credit that Hugh had done so well. The result, naturally, was more nips and snaps and threats and lectures whenever any of the family caught Hugh alone. Thus, Hugh almost wept when Sir Walter decided to pay scutage rather than send men with the king to Normandy.

"But I would like to go," he said, trying to keep the desperation he felt out of his voice, "and I cannot see why you should have to pay—"

"I do not think I will be paying, and I believe I will need you here," Sir Walter replied. "My friends in the Scottish court tell me that although efforts are made to suppress them, rumors are about that King David is only waiting until the ships carry Stephen away before the Scots gather men for war. You will have fighting enough here, I fear."

Hugh was distracted from his own troubles. War was an enjoyable exercise… but only when fought on the lands of others. He had little taste for seeing his master's yeomen killed or injured and their farms burnt and stock stolen.

"Do we need to wait to be overrun?" Hugh asked.

"Are you suggesting that *I* break the truce with King David?" Sir Walter countered.

"No, my lord," Hugh replied, "but you could send warning to the other barons not to strip themselves of men and even to gather more—"

"That I have done already," Sir Walter said, and shook a finger at him. "Are you trying to teach your grandfather to suck eggs?"

Hugh laughed. "If I am canny, it is your teaching that has made me so. But you did not let me finish, my lord. What I wished to add was that King David must be told we are ready."

"If I have friends in his court, do you think he has no news gatherers in the north?"

"Of course he has," Hugh agreed, "but it is one thing to pick up rumors from a central place like the court and another to gather a word here and there. David will certainly have heard of King Stephen's request for men, and some will send men to save the scutage. He will also expect to hear that there is a readying for defense against his coming. What he may not understand is that it is not just this and that man preparing himself alone. If he is told that the north will unite to form an army—"

"By my soul, you have an idea!" Sir Walter exclaimed. "But will he believe it?"

"If he is told by a man whose word he would not question, he would believe," Hugh suggested. In the back of his mind he wondered whether Sir Walter himself would go to speak to King David and take him or, even better, send him as a messenger on his own.

Sir Walter stared at him so intently for a while that Hugh's hopes rose, but then he shook his head, "I cannot go myself," he said slowly. "I must call the lords together to explain. I do not really doubt their agreement, but the understanding must be firm before any envoy reaches David. Nor can I get agreement first and then go to Scotland. If David's army is summoned and on its way, it may be too late to stop them."

"A messenger from you—" Hugh began.

"No, to send a messenger is useless," Sir Walter said instantly.

"A messenger cannot discuss anything. And a messenger might make David suspicious. Would he not wonder if we were using the device to gain time? No, someone respected must go, a man who David will believe can give his word and bind other men with it. And it would not do to use a man who will lose his temper... *hmmm*."

"This is a matter of peace, not of war," Hugh said. "Could you not ask the archbishop for help? Perhaps he would send one of his bishops."

Sir Walter nodded. "You have it, Hugh. It was what I was thinking myself. You go to Thurstan and explain our fears to him. I will send out messages to the sheriffs and some others to gather opinions."

Hugh was doubly delighted. Not only would he be able to get away from Helmsley, where he felt spies watched him even after Sir Walter's family had left, but he would see Thurstan. He had not visited his father in God for some time—in fact, not since he had started for Wark the previous year, and there had been a three-year hiatus in his relatively frequent visits before that. As Sir Walter gave him more responsibility, Hugh had less free time although he had more freedom, and he found it more difficult to fit his visits into Thurstan's busy schedule. The time had simply slipped away, and there had never been any sense of absence, because if they saw each other less, they wrote to each other more.

When Sir Walter had gone south the preceding year in response to the news that Stephen had arrived in England to claim the crown, Hugh had found he had little to do. So on his way to collect Wark's dues, he had stopped at York to visit Archbishop Thurstan. In the back of his mind, he was considering asking Thurstan's advice about his increasing problems with Sir Walter's family, but all thoughts of himself flew out of his head when he first saw and embraced the old man in greeting. Suddenly, as he held Thurstan's frail body in his arms, he realized how aged, how worn the archbishop had become. It was inconceivable to Hugh that he should add to Thurstan's problems even so small a weight as his own discomfort.

Of course, it was one thing to make the decision, another

entirely to prevent Thurstan from sensing that something was amiss. In his preoccupation with the old man's physical fragility, Hugh had failed to notice that Thurstan's eyes were as bright as ever, and Hugh was assailed by searching questions as soon as he disclaimed any special reason for his visit. He had mostly managed to evade giving any answer he thought would worry Thurstan, but the archbishop heard enough to be sure Hugh's troubles were not of the soul. Believing implicitly that worldly problems could trouble but not truly harm the child he loved, Thurstan forbore to question further.

Nonetheless, Hugh had taken fright and knew that he could not hide his worries for long. Then his desire for Audris added to his dissatisfaction. It was easier to avoid burdening Thurstan by staying away from him and writing cheerful letters. The only trouble with staying away was that Hugh soon began to wonder whether his foster father was giving him a taste of his own medicine. Could Thurstan's assurances to Hugh's inquiries about his health be as false as Hugh's own cheerfulness?

Thus, Hugh was overjoyed at this new opportunity Sir Walter offered to make a visit with much serious news to discuss. Hugh was certain his real concern about the possibility of a Scottish invasion would mask any personal problems and permit him to spend some time with the father who had kissed and cuddled him when he was a baby and who, he greatly feared, must die before long. He wrote as soon as he was certain he understood clearly what Sir Walter wanted him to say—not always identical with what he might have said if left to himself—making clear in his letter that his request for time was one of business, although it would give him private joy. The answer arrived speedily, saying that Hugh must come at once, before preparations for the celebration of Easter absorbed all Thurstan's time and attention.

Remembering the fasting and penances that Thurstan invariably inflicted on himself before this saddest and most joyful of holy periods, Hugh was on the road that very afternoon. He was terrified that, frail as he already was, Thurstan might not survive, and when he was shown into the archbishop's quarters, he flung himself to his knees and kissed Thurstan's hands with a passion that made the old man free himself so that he could take hold of Hugh's face and lift it.

"My child, my dear child, what is wrong?" Thurstan asked anxiously. "There is no sin so great that God's love cannot forgive the truly repentant."

There were tears in Hugh's remarkable eyes, and his fear showed as he stared into the lined face and hollowed eyes that examined him so tenderly. He shook his head, as much as he could without disturbing the hands that cupped his face.

"Father, dearest and most beloved father, I have no sin on my soul so great that I fear God will abandon me," Hugh replied, knowing that he must explain or he would only create more anxiety. Then he covered Thurstan's hands with his own and bent his head so he could kiss the archbishop's palms. "I—I fear to lose you," he whispered.

Thurstan laughed, a hearty chuckle that was soothing to Hugh because there was nothing of an old man's cackle or wheeze in it. He extracted his hands from Hugh's hold again, and this time used one to ruffle his foster son's bright hair. "You cannot lose me," he said. "Do you think I will be less real to you after I am dead? I assure you it is not so. I will be more real. And do you think I will care for you and pray for you less?" A frown crossed his face. "There are those who say the soul loses all earthly care, but I agree only insofar as I believe all evil passion to be driven out. As Christ loved us on earth, so He loves us in heaven. He did not abandon us when He became one with His Father. Why then should I abandon you, as dear as you are to me?"

"I do not fear you will abandon me when you are in heaven, but I want you here where I can talk to you," Hugh said slightly sulkily.

Thurstan pulled Hugh closer and kissed his forehead. "So you can wheedle me into approving what you well know a pure soul would resist?" He chuckled again.

Despite his fear Hugh could not help but laugh too. "Father, whatever *you* think, you will never convince me that your soul will be purer in heaven than it is now."

Hugh was about to add a plea that Thurstan consider his age and abate his stern penances, although he knew such a plea to be hopeless, but suddenly a much better idea occurred to him. He knew that Thurstan believed in the separation of worldly and spiritual matters, according to Christ's dictum that what pertained to Caesar should be rendered unto him. Perhaps the presentation of the threat from the Scots would make him feel he had to save his strength for political action.

"But it was not only my personal fear for you that overset me," Hugh continued. "It was because I believe your entire see will need you in the flesh. Sir Walter fears King David will not abide by the truce once King Stephen leaves England, and then perhaps you alone may be a shield for all northern England. So I pray you, Father, to have a care to your strength and well-being."

Thurstan sat back in his chair, gestured Hugh to rise, and pointed at a stool. "So," he said, when Hugh had brought the stool close and seated himself, "what reason has Sir Walter for his suspicions?" And when he had heard Hugh out, he sighed. "David is a good man, but strong temptations beset him—his oath to Matilda, his wife's desire to hold what was once her father's earldom, the constant urging of his hungry nobles... I can see that the rumors might be based on truth. Well, the first thing is to be sure. I will send to the bishop of Saint Andrews, whom I consecrated, and ask him whether David will swear to him to keep the truce."

"And if he will not?" Hugh asked.

"I do not expect he will," Thurstan said wryly, "even if his present intention *is* to abide by the truce. Kings have become wary of making promises to bishops, some of whom do not take political realities into consideration. However, I will be able to discern much from Saint Andrews's answer, and I assure you I will do my uttermost to keep the peace. As to how, I have no answer for you this moment. I must think what would be best and pray for guidance."

Anytime Thurstan said he would pray for something, Hugh became nervous, but as the days passed and the archbishop continued to eat regularly and look no more tired or frail,

Hugh began to feel his ploy had been successful. In his prime, Thurstan had loved politics; he had been the late King Henry's favorite negotiator; even after he had fallen into disfavor with the king, Henry summoned him whenever he had a particularly difficult piece of bargaining to conduct. And within the Church the archbishop had been no less contentious, fighting for the preeminence of York over the Scottish bishoprics and for equality with Canterbury in England. As he grew older, his joy in the battle for worldly honors faded, and he began to sieve each situation more carefully with regard to its true value. Still, Hugh had hoped his foster father would consider holding off the carnage of war sufficiently important to merit his attention, and he had.

Hugh was not told what reply the bishop of Saint Andrews sent; apparently the answer had included a request that it be kept in confidence, but Hugh was assured that Thurstan's interest had not wavered, because Easter came and went without any sign that the archbishop was mortifying his flesh in any excessive manner.

When that crucial period had passed, Hugh rode back to Helmsley to learn from Sir Walter how his campaign was progressing. He had few doubts that Sir Walter would be successful, since the northern barons were accustomed to following his lead, but he felt it would be good to have definite information if Thurstan asked, and it was only twenty-four miles from York to Helmsley. Hugh always treasured the certainty that it was not only Sir Walter's good character and the loss of his son but Thurstan's own need to see Hugh often that made him decide to send the child he had raised to Sir Walter for fostering.

While Hugh was at Helmsley, the news came that Stephen had left for Normandy in the third week of March. A few days later, a letter from Thurstan arrived asking Hugh to come again and dine with him in private the following week. The statement that Thurstan wished to speak to Hugh alone caused some consternation because both Hugh and Sir Walter thought the archbishop would wish to coordinate his efforts with Sir Walter's if he intended to convince King David to abide by the truce. But Hugh discovered as soon as their affectionate greetings were over that the request for privacy had only a peripheral connection with Scottish affairs.

Thurstan signed for Hugh to serve himself from the Lenten fare: three tureens of fish stew and a dozen platters of variously prepared vegetables, fish, cheeses, and eggs the servants had been told to leave on the table. Thurstan took minuscule portions of two dishes onto his own gōlden plate, added four spoonsful of stew to a marvelous bowl, pure white and as thin as an eggshell, and said without preamble, "How necessary are you to Sir Walter, my son?"

"Not—" Hugh began, then stopped as he reconsidered his strong impulse to say that he was not necessary at all. The question Thurstan asked of course implied that he had some task in mind for Hugh that would take him away from Sir Walter, but Hugh dared not simply grab at an excuse for release. "It depends," he went on, "on the circumstances. On a battlefield, I am still necessary—and will be for a year or two more. Sir Walter's squires are not yet strong enough to guard him as well as I would like, and Sir Walter is not as young as he was. But for other things…" Hugh shrugged. "Now that Sir Walter is no longer attending King Stephen's court and has time to oversee his lands, anyone could do the tasks he gives to me."

Thurstan nodded and smiled. "You have become a man, Hugh, and such a man as is a joy and a blessing to those who love him."

He paused, watching Hugh's face. The young man had made a denying gesture with the hand that was reaching for a second helping of baked pike stuffed with chestnuts and shaken his head in amused denial, but he had smiled—a singularly sweet smile, Thurstan thought, for so strong a face. And over all and under all, the old man sensed sadness, a sadness that had grown stronger since he had first marked it a year before.

Thurstan believed that man was God's instrument to bring about good on earth. His fasting, scourging, and praying were purely personal, penance for his own evil thoughts and deeds. He did not scourge himself or pray in the expectation that God would intervene directly in the affairs of men by sending angels or miracles. And, although he had let his knowledge of Hugh's unhappiness lie fallow for a year, that was because he hoped it was some small problem that would work itself out. Thurstan did not believe that unnecessary misery was beneficial to the soul. Now he wanted to finish this business as quickly as possible and get on to what he hoped would give the dear child of his heart relief.

"Well, then," the archbishop said briskly, "from what you say, I would do Sir Walter no harm if I asked that you come into service with me for a time?"

"No harm at all!" Hugh exclaimed, his eyes lighting with eagerness and relief. Then, realizing such eagerness was not completely compatible with satisfaction in his present situation and that he did not want Thurstan to know he was not happy, he looked anxious, and to cover that, said, "So long as I will be free to fight at his back if the Scots make war."

"I hope to convince David to keep the truce," Thurstan replied, bending his head over his bowl and lifting a spoonful of stew to his mouth.

He was greatly surprised and disturbed. It had never occurred to him that Hugh's unhappiness was connected with his service to Sir Walter. He had assumed that it was Hugh's condition as a foundling that was haunting him. As a result, he had sought a parchment on which he had written out, a few days after Hugh had come into his keeping, every detail he could remember about that event and everything he had been able to discover in an admittedly brief investigation of it.

For years Thurstan had regretted not carrying his investigation further, but at the time he had felt he must keep his schedule of visitation, and he was sure he would be able to return to Durham very soon and pursue the facts at leisure. In that he had been mistaken. First he was so busy with his newly granted archbishopric that weeks and months flew by without his noticing them; then his troubles with Canterbury had begun, and he had been forced to write to the pope to plead his case. Success in the pleading had only brought King Henry's rage down on him and driven him into exile for years. By the time he was able to return to Durham to ask questions about Hugh's birth and mother, he was certain no one in the convent would remember her because the abbess had died and many of the sisters were no longer at that convent. He was so busy, too, bringing order to his archdiocese after his long absence that more years had passed—and then it was too late.

Oddly, Hugh had never asked any questions about his ancestry. He had accepted the fact that he was not Thurstan's son because, though sons were common enough to priests either through concubines or even wives, Hugh knew Thurstan would never lie. He had seemed satisfied, as a child, to be loved as a fosterling, and Thurstan had hesitated to damage the child's peace by intruding a subject he avoided either out of indifference or out of fear. Now it appeared that Hugh's parentage was not the problem at all.

"But if I am not successful with David," Thurstan continued, his mind still busy with whether or not to raise a subject that seemed not to be troubling Hugh, "you will be free to do your duty to Sir Walter."

"Then I am sure my service to you will do no harm." Hugh smiled broadly. "In fact, good will come of it. The boys will take over much of what I have been doing of late, and it is time for them to have more responsibility."

Thurstan, who had taken and swallowed another spoonful of stew, lifted his head. "Why are you so eager to flee Sir Walter's service that you do not even ask why an aged and peaceful man of the Church needs a knight?"

The question took Hugh completely by surprise, and he exclaimed, "I am *not* eager to leave Sir Walter!" Then, under the kind but piercing scrutiny of Thurstan's eyes, he flushed. "That is true, or nearly true, Father. I love Sir Walter and he me—and that is the source of trouble." And having said that much, Hugh realized he had better go on and describe the whole situation. He was able to do so with a clear conscience because Thurstan's request for his service would solve the problem, and there would be nothing more for his foster father to worry about.

But when he was finished with the tale of the fears and jealousies of Sir Walter's relatives and his own fear of hurting

Sir Walter by telling him or leaving him without a good reason, Thurstan shook his head. "Such foolishness, Hugh. Why did you not tell me this sooner?"

Hugh laughed. "Because I did not know that an aged and peaceful prelate of the Church would have need for a man of war. What is that need, Father?"

"I will come to it in time, my son, but first I wish to clear away this private matter. I am old, but not yet grown foolish with it—I hope—and it is plain enough that you did not speak to save me any worry over you. Do you still believe you succeeded in that?"

Mildly chagrined, Hugh answered, "No, Father."

"Self-deception in worldly matters, especially when meant as a kindness, is no sin, but it can cause unnecessary pain. Your trouble with Sir Walter's family is not all that hurts you, my son."

"No, Father," Hugh admitted with a sigh, "but it seems useless to me to speak of the other matter." Then he smiled. "Oh, no. I will give your answer to that before you say it. I have heard it often enough. 'The more minds that consider a problem, the better the chance that it will be solved. And if they all pray, too, guidance may be granted.' But it would take a miracle, not guidance, to solve my problem, and I am no saint to look for divine intervention, especially in this, since I am in the wrong. I have looked too high, Father, and seen a woman I desire who is far, far beyond me."

All the time he had listened to Hugh describe the jealousy of Sir Walter's relatives, Thurstan had been also mentally debating whether to introduce the subject of Hugh's ancestry. Now he asked, "Because you may be a bastard?"

"May be?" Hugh repeated. "But I thought my mother sought shelter with the sisters at Durham because she had been cast out by her own people. And I assumed from that she had ado with a—a man not fit for her station."

"Hugh! Who told you this tale?" Thurstan looked shocked.

"Indeed, I do not know, Father," Hugh replied. "I… it seems I knew it always. Could my mother—"

"You were not a day old when your mother laid you in

Saint George's arms in Durham church." Thurstan cut him off sharply. "And she died not half an hour later. She told you nothing—and me not much—your name, only that, really. 'Hugh,' she said, over and over, then 'Take care of him,' which I promised gladly, and then 'Yourself, yourself.' I tried to explain, but she could not understand and only wept and said 'Yourself,' so I promised again."

"And you have surely kept that promise," Hugh said, impulsively rising and embracing his foster father.

Thurstan raised his head and kissed Hugh, but then sighed. "I have loved you always, so it is no merit in me to have cared for you. Indeed, I have wondered sometimes if what I felt when I lifted you from the carving and carried you in my arms out of the church—I let you suck my finger while I sought a wet nurse for you... Hugh! That silly woman!"

"My nurse? I can scarcely remember her."

"But it must have been she who made up that tale. Perhaps I told her your mother was a lady to ensure close and good care for you, and—yes, I remember now, she asked if you would be taken from her or if she would go with you when your father came. I must have said I did not know who your father was—"

"And she added the most likely story to those few words of yours." But Hugh was smiling when he spoke, and he kissed Thurstan again and added, "Do not look so distressed, Father, I beg you. No harm was done. It is best to believe the worst, and it saved me from dreaming false dreams and putting on airs."

Thurstan shook his head slowly. "You do not understand, Hugh. I may have done you a great wrong, a great wrong."

"You have done me only good," Hugh insisted fiercely.

Thurstan only shook his head again, thinking back. "I told myself that I had no time to seek your father or even more particulars about your mother, but I fear that was not my real reason. Did I not in my secret heart wish to keep you for myself? What ill could have befallen if I were a day or two late in finishing my visitations? Yet the next day I flew from Durham, carrying you with me—"

"Father," Hugh said gently, taking Thurstan's hand in his

and squeezing it to gain the old man's attention, "you did not hide your name. You *did* speak to the sisters. You know that if any person had come asking for my mother, the sisters would have sent him to you. And you were not so far away, only in York. That means no one came to ask and that your desire to keep me—for which I thank God most sincerely—cannot have done me harm. It is most likely the nurse's tale is the true story."

Thurstan sighed. "Perhaps it is so—I mean you may have been born outside the holy state of wedlock, although even that is not sure. The sisters said your mother spoke of her husband coming for her."

"But no one did come, and perhaps her use of the word 'husband' was no more than an easy way to save herself from the expostulations of the sisters, who would not want her to fall into sin again."

This time Thurstan smiled. "If you had come into the Church, you would have made a fine devil's advocate. It is true that no inquiries were made up until the time I left for France, and so it may also be true that your poor mother had been deceived. If so, by God's mercy she never knew she had been abandoned. Still, I do not think your father was of common blood. Your mother had money with which to pay the sisters, real coins of silver. Also she was trying with her dying breath to tell me something, something very important. I know you have often been plagued by the name Licorne, but I am sure it has some meaning. She struggled so—I have never seen so desperate a struggle. I wished to give her the rites for the dying, but she would not listen until, in parts, she uttered forth first 'li' and then 'corne.'"

"She sounds a gallant lady," Hugh said, rather pleased. He could feel no grief for a person he had never known, but he could be proud of his mother's courage. "I am sorry I never asked about her before, but I felt such questions would not be welcome. She had sinned—"

"Hugh! It is not our place to judge, but God's. Did not Christ stand before the woman taken in adultery and say that only the sinless might stone her?" Then he patted Hugh's hand.

"Sit down, my son, and finish your meal." And when Hugh obeyed, he said, "I was mistaken in this matter also. I thought you were not curious because you did not ask—or, perhaps, I did not offer information because I did not wish to stir your curiosity—but what is important is that so great a struggle as your mother's must have had a purpose. This, perhaps even more than the word 'husband,' makes me believe there is a chance you are not a bastard and that somewhere there is a family to which you belong."

"Somehow I doubt I would be very welcome to them," Hugh remarked dryly.

"*Mea culpa.*" Thurstan sighed. "Perhaps if I had sought them out when you were an infant—"

"Father," Hugh said harshly, "*no one came.*"

"Do not judge, Hugh," Thurstan warned. "There might be reasons you could not guess for a seeming neglect. However that may be, I am glad we have at last touched on this subject. Before you go, I will give you a parchment on which I have written out all the circumstances and all that I have learned and sealed it with my seal, having as witness the bishop of Durham, the abbess of the convent—although she is now dead and there have been two abbesses since then—and others, so that none can doubt of whom you were born or when. There is a copy with the charters and muniments in the safekeeping of the Church. You may do what you will with your copy, but if you wish to learn more, I will assist you in any way I can."

"I am not sure," Hugh said uneasily.

"There is time enough to consider what will be best for you." Thurstan's tone dismissed the subject, and Hugh was not surprised when he continued, "Now, let us come to the reason I would like to have your service for a time. After certain letters passed between me and Scotland, it became clear that the only hope for keeping the peace is for me to meet with King David in Roxburgh—"

"You!" Hugh exploded. "You cannot go so far. You will kill yourself."

Chapter 10

HAD HUGH FELT LESS GUILTY, HE WOULD HAVE SAVED HIS breath, for once Thurstan conceived some act to be his duty, he was inflexible. He had withstood both the king and the archbishop of Canterbury for years on a matter of principle, and Hugh did not really expect his own arguments, which depended on Thurstan's physical well-being—a matter to which his foster father gave no consideration at all—to have any effect. Nonetheless, because involving Thurstan in the effort to stop King David from invading England had been his idea, Hugh argued and pleaded. The end result was as he had foreseen. Thurstan kissed him fondly and said he was glad to be so highly valued, but he laughed at Hugh's fears and brushed them away.

One thing only did Hugh's reasoning accomplish. When he pointed out that Thurstan's ability to make and enforce an agreement might be greatly lessened if he were seen to be ill and exhausted, the archbishop agreed to leave sooner than he had intended so that they could travel slowly and he could break his journey and rest for several days or a week if necessary.

Once Thurstan mentioned the journey he intended to make, Hugh needed no further explanation of what use his foster father had for him. Hugh's duty was, of course, to captain the troop of men-at-arms that would protect Thurstan and the extensive baggage train that would accompany him. Thurstan might privately eat and drink little, wear a hair shirt, mortify his flesh, and practice other asceticisms, but he did not ever confuse the humility necessary in a man with the majesty necessary for an archbishop of the Church. Thus, the contents of the baggage train—the rich vestments, jeweled ornaments, precious plate, even a reliquary of gold and gems containing a saint's fingerbone to be given as a gift to King David—were very valuable indeed.

Theoretically, a holy man like the archbishop and his belongings should be safe from any threat; unfortunately, theory and practice were far apart. The wretched outlaws who preyed upon travelers in some of the areas Thurstan's party must pass were mostly too far gone in sin to concern themselves with who their victim was. Excommunicated already, they had nothing to fear for their souls and would be deterred only by sure knowledge of failure.

In addition, it was not unknown for a king who was being thwarted by a churchman to seize that person and apply forcible inducements to gain his silence. No one expected King David, who was a good man of strong faith, to act in such a barbaric manner. Nonetheless, considering that the pressures on the king of the Scots were great and that there might be other powerful men around him who were not as bound by conscience, it was foolish to offer the temptation of being helpless. Thus, fifty mounted men-at-arms were to accompany Thurstan, fifty men handpicked by Hugh for their strength, skill, and steadiness of character.

Once they were on the road, Hugh was pleasantly surprised by Thurstan's stamina. They had with them the luxurious traveling cart of Sir Walter's wife, Adelina, but the archbishop preferred to ride on horseback, insisting that he would be less tired by that exercise than by being bumped over the rutted roads in the traveling cart. Hugh did not argue—aside from extracting a promise that Thurstan would ride in the cart if it rained—because he knew the pace would be so slow for the baggage wagons over the gluey mud of the roads in the spring that the horsemen would have long rest periods. But there was little rain, the roads were better than Hugh had expected, and they took only five days to cover about seventy miles to

Durham, arriving early in the afternoon. When Thurstan had settled into the luxurious guest quarters in the bishop's palace, Hugh suggested that the archbishop stop and rest for a few days in Durham. The quicker pace was telling on Thurstan, who was beginning to look tired. The archbishop did not deny that a rest would be welcome, but he said he would prefer to stay at Hexham abbey.

"Hexham abbey?" Hugh repeated blankly.

"Yes, I can rest there for a week to recruit my strength for the rest of the journey. It is past Hexham that the roads become very bad…"

Thurstan went on explaining why he preferred to break his journey at Hexham rather than Durham, but Hugh hardly heard. The mention of Hexham had brought back, as vividly as if he were reliving the incidents, the day he had spent with Audris. He was caught up in a storm of conflicting emotions, a violent desire to see her, fear of the pain he knew being with her would cause him, an aching need for her to have remembered him as he remembered her, and a stabbing guilt over that wish because he did not want her to suffer.

"Why do you object to Hexham?" Thurstan asked in amazement, responding to Hugh's expression.

The tone of surprise finally pierced Hugh's self-absorption. "There will be no room to quarter the men," he replied.

It was the first thing that came into his head, and as he said it, he became aware that it was true. Hexham was not one of the great abbeys. It had been long established, founded by Saint Wilfrith in the seventh century, but it had declined after William the Bastard's scourging of the north. Like the area itself, Hexham abbey was recovering; a beautiful new church was being built to replace the old Saxon church of Saint Andrews, which, like Jernaeve, was built of Roman stones. Hugh's insides did an odd flip-flop when he thought of it. He and Audris had listened to mass in that old church and had watched the work on the new one for a while.

"True, true," Thurstan was saying, his brow creased with thought. "There is not so much traffic through Hexham that they need overlarge guesthouses. And the abbey has no rich patron nearby. There is a lord... yes, yes, I recall the name—Fermain. They pay their tithes faithfully—I cannot fault the lord on that, but the Fermains are not given to making gifts to the Church." Suddenly Thurstan smiled mischievously. "So, mayhap I have found a way to take just a little over the tithe. Tomorrow you will ride ahead and ask for lodging for my men from Fermain."

Thurstan's insistence that he go to Jernaeve seemed to Hugh like a kind of divine intervention, as if God had given His permission and told him there was no wrong in his desire to see Audris. A wave of longing for her swept over him, a need so immediate that like great hunger it knotted his bowels and caused a trembling inside him.

"I can ride over before dark today," Hugh said, "and return early enough to be with you on tomorrow's journey. It is only a little over twenty miles to Jernaeve, and less if I ride cross-country."

"*Now* what imprudence do you expect me to commit?" Thurstan asked, half exasperated, half laughing. "If you will name it, I will promise not to do it. That will save you a long ride in the dark."

Of course, this time it was not Hugh's concern for his foster father but his eagerness to see Audris that was driving him. He felt ashamed of grasping so greedily at what had been offered him, and opened his mouth to agree to go the next day, but the words that came out were, "Oh, no. How can I tell what you will take into your head to do? I would be up all night anyway, worrying about what promise I had forgotten to ask for."

Thurstan stared at him, then shook his head. "Was I such a plague to you as a child? Did I hang over you and constantly forbid you to do this and that?"

Hugh could feel himself flush and laughed uneasily, knowing he should give up the expedition, but he was unable to do it. "No, of course you were not," he said ruefully. "I am only restless and—"

"My dear son!" Thurstan exclaimed. "How stupid I am, thinking only of how riding makes my old bones ache. I had forgotten what a trial it must be for you to plod along at a pace suitable to me. By all means, go."

"Father, I did not mean—"

"That you are tired of me," Thurstan interrupted again, smiling. "No, I know you too well to think that, Hugh. You are young, that is all. And you know I will not miss you or lack for company." The smile turned wry. "I will have visitors enough. Each will have a problem or a favor to ask—which is why, as I said, I prefer Hexham for a rest. My lodgings will be less elegant, but I will mostly be left in peace."

"I will stop at the abbey and tell them you will stay with them for a week," Hugh offered. "Or have you written to them already?"

"No, I did not write," Thurstan admitted. "I was not sure how traveling would affect me and feared I might need to stop before we got so far. Then, of course, I could not have spared the time. It is a good thought to give the abbot warning, but tell him also, Hugh, that I wish no special provision made for me. I have been so busy since this journey was decided upon that I have had no time really to pray. My soul must rest as well as my body, and it will rest better if I am one with the good brothers in all things. But do not stop if it will cause you to ride back in the dark."

"I do not think I will ride back tonight at all," Hugh assured him. "Sir Oliver will give me shelter at Jernaeve, or I can stay at Hexham. I will come back at dawn tomorrow. I am sure I will arrive before you start, but I will explain to Drogo. If I should be late, he will start the cortege, and I will meet you on the road."

"Then I am content. Go with God, my son."

Hugh knelt to kiss Thurstan's ring and then rose and hurried out. He was quivering with impatience, mentally thanking God that he had not yet unarmed. He had only to snatch up his shield and helmet from his quarters and rush off to the stable. There, he bellowed at the grooms for not saddling Rufus quickly enough, and when it was done spurred the destrier so that he leapt ahead, scattering the servants in the courtyard. One poor woman tripped and fell. She was in no danger, for Rufus had both room and time enough to turn aside, but she cried out in fear as the steel-shod hooves flashed past her, and Hugh slowed his pace guiltily.

He had intended to go directly to Jernaeve and stop at Hexham at dawn on the way back to Durham, but the near-accident seemed to be another warning against grabbing greedily at a few extra minutes with Audris. I will have a whole week, he told himself. Let me not be foolish and show myself unworthy of the favor granted. Besides, he knew he must talk to the prior as well as give Thurstan's message to the abbot.

There was nothing Hugh could do to stop his foster father from rising twice in the night to attend Matins and Lauds if he wished. And Thurstan might actually eat more of the plain food served the brothers than he did of the elaborate dishes usually presented to him. Those aspects of being "one with the brothers" could not be altered. On the other hand, Hugh wanted to make sure that the prior would arrange to set up Thurstan's own bed in the guest chamber or, if he insisted on sleeping in a cell and his bed would not fit, that a good mattress and thick feather quilts would be provided. The days were warming, but the nights were still cold, and Thurstan felt the cold.

Although Hugh tried to keep his mind on the problem of saving Thurstan from himself and what other hints he might give the prior without seeming to tell the man his business, he was aware of a churning eagerness that urged him to forget his duty for a little while and go first to Jernaeve as he had originally intended. But Hugh feared the hot, sick eagerness was an evil temptation. If it was, the "permission" to be with Audris would be withdrawn when he showed himself unworthy by lack of control. He made a real effort, therefore, to subdue his impatience, both in answering the abbot's excited questions and when, far from being annoyed by his interference, the prior wanted the most minute details about how the archbishop should be attended and served.

As Hugh spoke to both men, patiently assuring them over and over that the archbishop desired only peace and time to rest and pray, he was rewarded. The unpleasant grinding in his bowels diminished, and after both abbot and prior were satisfied, he was able to ride the last few miles from Hexham to Jernaeve at a moderate pace. When he came to the ford, he felt no need to splash across it at once; he could pause to look up at old Iron Fist, to seek Audris's window in the south tower and savor his joy. A minute later, a harsh call demanding his identity came from the guard on the wall. There was a brief delay while Hugh pulled his eyes from the dark opening of the window.

"I am Hugh Licorne, Sir Walter Espec's man," he bellowed back, then asked formally, "May I enter and be welcome?"

Inside the tower, Audris had just removed her working dress, stained and muddy from the garden. She felt restless and irritable because most of what she had been doing could easily have been left to the gardeners. She should really have been out in the hills checking on the nests she had marked to see if eggs had been laid and how many, but after the rumors began that King David was gathering an army, her uncle had made her promise that she would not go out alone.

Audris understood. No Scottish army could come south without warning, but single men or small troops could be out spying out the land, where the herds were, and other such matters. If they came upon her and took her prisoner, it would be a disaster. Oliver would have to yield Jernaeve. But understanding and knowing that her uncle was right made her confinement no easier to bear.

Audris looked at the gown Fritha had laid out for her to wear, trying to decide whether she should put it on and eat the evening meal with her family or indulge her bad temper by remaining in her chamber. She heard the guard's challenge and went toward the window, idly curious. Since the guards had been alerted about the rumors of a new Scottish invasion, they challenged everyone. The visitor might be one of her cousins or a yeoman from a bound farm, none of whom would change her half-made decision to send Fritha for food and eat alone. A second thought quickened her step. Perhaps it was a messenger from Bruno. They had heard nothing from him since the letter announcing the king's departure for Normandy.

Hugh's voice made Audris cover the last few feet to the window in a leap. She stared out incredulously, drinking in the sight of his destrier and his hair flaming in the ruddy light of the setting sun. She heard the guard shouting something, but the words were lost on her as Hugh turned and she saw the unicorn on his shield. Later she realized that the guard must have warned him that he had passed the shallowest point of the ford, but at the time it seemed to Audris that he had turned to reassure her, for there were other red-haired men who rode chestnut horses. Impulsively, she held out her arms toward him from the window, then snatched them back and looked down at them, her cheeks reddening as she realized what she had done.

That heedless action saved Audris from several other actions that might have had more serious consequences. It made her reconsider her next impulse, which was to rush out to greet Hugh as he was riding in, and her desire to don her finest gown and wear her richest jewels. When she noticed that Fritha was staring at her with round-eyed astonishment, she realized that she had been making little dashes about the room—first toward the stairs, then toward the clothes chests—and uttering soft, senseless cries of "My unicorn, my unicorn."

Audris blushed again and plumped herself firmly down on her chair, closing her eyes and folding her hands in her lap in the posture Father Anselm had insisted she assume when he wanted her to think over some unconsidered act. His grave, kind voice sounded in her memory, not scolding but urging her to consider the consequences of what she did.

She remembered when she had said impatiently, "Then tell me why what I desire is wrong and let me go!" he had shaken his head and replied that it was her nature to observe and react, seemingly without the intervention of conscious thought—which was why she was quick enough to snatch a young hawk from its nest. Most of the time, he assured her, smiling at her distress, the results were not bad because her heart was kind and her nature sweet. But, the warm voice warned, inconsiderate kindness could sometimes do more harm than deliberate cruelty. She *must* learn to think.

The enforced blindness and stillness had always brought order to Audris's thoughts—if thoughts they were. Invariably, images of what had inspired her action and what she desired to accomplish moved in orderly progression past her mind's eye, followed usually by a variety of "could be" pictures. Most often when Father Anselm had bidden her sit and think, all those "could be" images were dreadful.

This time, however, the pictures did not appear in order. First Audris saw her uncle's reaction to her racing half-naked out of the keep to greet a man with whom she had once spent a day. A gasp of laughter ended in a shudder of horror, but before the chill had finished running down her spine, a new picture flooded into her mind, erasing all else. The unicorn, whiter than lilies, was walking in the dappled shade of a new-leafed wood, his blue eyes turned to the maiden, who walked beside him with an arm around his neck. The image was so compelling that Audris went at once to her loom, but it was empty—and then she remembered Hugh riding into the keep. Eagerness stirred in her again, but the image of the unicorn in the wood was like a promise of better things if she would be patient.

She looked at the bliaut on the bed, a soft yellow, to be worn over a gray undergown. Both were very plain, and Audris glanced toward the chest of finer gowns. But Hugh was poor; it would be unkind to mark the difference between them. Then she smiled as she remembered that he had looked at her with interest from the first, when she had been wearing a work gown all speckled with the threads of her weaving.

"I will go down," Audris said to Fritha. "Help me to dress, have your dinner, and then string my loom. Use white warp threads, and only the finest."

She did not respond to the new surprise in Fritha's face. Audris rarely wove from the time of early planting in spring until the rains of autumn, but Fritha's surprise at her order to ready the loom reminded Audris of the maid's earlier astonishment. Audris was relieved that she did not need to explain her earlier unusual behavior when Hugh answered the guard, nor did she need to warn Fritha to silence lest she mention it to anyone. Mute and illiterate, the maid had no way of communicating anything beyond the simplest needs. Audris had acted, as usual, impulsively, and taken Fritha into her personal service out of pity when she came upon the girl being beaten for not being able to explain something, and the act of pity had been rewarded many, many times over in different ways.

When Audris reached the hall, Hugh had already been greeted by Lady Eadyth and was in one of the wall chambers being unarmed. Although he was not sufficiently important to merit his hostess's personal attention, a man in Sir Walter Espec's service would almost certainly have news to tell, and his dinner conversation could not be wasted on upper servants. Thus, Eadyth went to arrange that an extra place be laid on the high table—and it was Audris who rose from the fireside and ran to greet Hugh when he entered the hall.

"Unicorn, unicorn," she whispered, seizing his hands in hers. "I could not believe it when I heard you call your name. Good news or ill, you are welcome to me."

"I hardly dared hope you would remember me," Hugh replied, and before he could recall his promise to himself that he would not trouble Audris with his hopeless desires, he had raised her hands and pressed his mouth to them.

The kisses were scarcely a polite greeting, and Audris almost leaned forward and kissed his bent head. Only a more urgent need saved her from that imprudence, for she needed her mouth to ask, "How long? How long can you stay?"

The anxiety in her voice changed the direction of Hugh's emotion. The uprush of passion, which in another moment would have led him to wrench his hands from hers and pull her into his arms, was checked. In its place rushed a recurrence of his earliest feeling about Audris, a sense of her fragility and helplessness, which engendered a protectiveness more over-whelming than passion.

"Is your need desperate?" he asked. "Can it wait two days?"

The sensations Hugh's lips had wakened in Audris were purely sensual, so it was not surprising that her interpretation of his question shocked her. She uttered a small outraged gasp, but could not find words to repudiate so conceited an assumption.

"Has the king sent more suitors to badger you?" Hugh asked next.

Audris uttered another gasp and then burst out laughing as the context of his first two questions became clear and she realized how innocent they were and how she had twisted his meaning. Simultaneously, under the laughter, she was aware of an odd dissatisfaction. She had been offended when she felt Hugh believed her to be so hot for him that she could not wait two days, but that he should only think of her as needing his protection was equally unsatisfactory. Then both amusement at her own stupidity and pique were swallowed up by the hurt she saw her unexplained laughter had dealt him.

"No, do not be angry," she cried. "You do not know what I thought you meant when you spoke of my need. It was my own silliness at which I laughed, not at you."

The pain of Audris's contemptuous rejection, which Hugh had read into her sudden burst of hilarity, was too sharp to permit him to make sense of what she had said. He could only retreat into stiff formality.

"I have no cause for anger," he said, releasing her hands and bowing. "It is no wonder you laughed. I was indeed presumptuous, forgetting how staunch a protector you have in your uncle."

"That was not why I laughed!" Audris exclaimed. "I swear it was not." But Hugh started to turn away, and in her fear and remorse for hurting him, Audris gasped, "I thought you meant *need* like a mare in heat—a mare cannot wait two days—and then I understood and—and…"

Hugh had stopped when she explained, and as what she said penetrated, he turned a dull red. "Demoiselle!" he protested.

"I am very sorry if I have shocked you," Audris offered, but her lips were already twitching upward into a mischievous smile. "It is the season. It is all my uncle talks about." Then the smile faded. "Except the chance that there will be war."

"Of that I bring good news," Hugh said quickly, glad to leave a topic that he could not discuss without consequences that were bound to be embarrassing. "I have come to beg lodging from your uncle for fifty men-at-arms and their horses."

"Foreriders of an army?" Sir Oliver asked.

Both Hugh and Audris started, having been so intent on their conversation that they had not noticed Sir Oliver approach. From the tone of his question, it was clear that he had heard nothing except the last few words Hugh said and was unaware of the intensity of their first meeting. Hugh turned toward him.

"No," he replied, "we are escort for Archbishop Thurstan, who goes to Roxburgh to convince King David to keep the peace."

"That *is* good news," Oliver said. "Is the archbishop far behind? It is almost dark."

"He is settled for the night at Durham."

Hugh then began to explain Thurstan's desire to rest at Hexham before beginning the last and most grueling part of his journey. He was not looking at Audris, but she was at the edge of Hugh's vision, and his sensitivity to her was so high that he was able to feel her tension relax when he asked for a week's lodging for the archbishop's troop.

"Certainly." Sir Oliver nodded. "I will welcome his lordship's men and keep them until the archbishop is ready to go, even if he should feel the need to remain at Hexham another week or two."

"That is very generous," Hugh said, trying to hide his surprise. He had heard enough from Sir Walter and from Bruno to know Sir Oliver was a man careful of cost, and the price of feeding fifty men and fifty horses was not negligible.

Sir Oliver's lips twisted wryly. "Every day that his lordship keeps the Scots from descending on us is a gain. In another month, we will take in the spring hay, which means, in case we must bring our stock in from the pastures to protect them behind our walls, that we need slaughter a few less cows, sheep, and horses. And if the archbishop can hold King David until the crops are in, we will be saved grievous loss."

It was Hugh's turn to nod. "I am sure he is aware of it, but I will remind him on the road of the need to draw out the discussions, particularly if there seems no hope of convincing King David to keep the peace."

"I hoped you would say that." Oliver smiled. "I would not wish to intrude on Archbishop Thurstan's needed rest, but if you think it would help for me to go to Hexham and speak to him, I would be willing to do it."

"Perhaps he would wish to speak to you," Hugh answered. "I must ride back to Durham tomorrow to join the escort, and I will ask him."

"You have easy access to the archbishop?" Sir Oliver sounded surprised, the tone making it clear that he thought Hugh no more than a common messenger.

"Yes," Hugh replied, his lips thinning.

Sir Oliver misunderstood and shook his head. "I have no favors to beg," he remarked with a cynical smile. "I had forgotten for the moment how devout Sir Walter is and his many gifts to the Church. I was curious about how you came into his lordship's service, but I suppose you are lent to the archbishop, and he is courteous for Sir Walter's sake."

The inference Sir Oliver made was natural, and under ordinary circumstances it would have roused no more than mild resentment in Hugh, which he would have swallowed. Audris had moved slightly so that Hugh could no longer see her at all, but he felt her presence, and that she should hear him dismissed as a nothing, a simple messenger who could be passed around for use with no more thought or regret than an old cloak, wakened a fury in Hugh. The need to be a person of consequence in Audris's eyes made him ignore the probability that mention of his relationship to the archbishop would produce the usual obscene snicker. Hugh was so angry that he hoped Sir Oliver would impugn Thurstan's honor; then he could challenge Oliver and make him eat his words.

"I am Thurstan's foster son," Hugh snarled. "It was the archbishop who placed me in Sir Walter's household, and I serve Thurstan out of love, because *I* was asked to lead his escort, and because it gives me great joy to serve the man I hold dearest in the world."

"Sir Hugh." Audris's hand caught his. "I am sure my uncle meant no insult."

"No, I did not," Sir Oliver said, clearly astonished by Hugh's reaction. "My wife sent a man to say someone had come from Sir Walter. I had no way to know you had been knighted and were no longer bound to Espec. Even so, I cannot see anything in what I said to make you fly up into the trees."

As Hugh's flare of temper died, he felt like a fool. He could not explain that he had not been angry because Sir Oliver had not accorded him the honors of knighthood. In fact, it was far better for Sir Oliver to believe him a puffed-up popinjay than that he guess Audris to be the cause of his guest's overreaction. Then, too, he was all too aware that to attack Sir Oliver could scarcely endear him to Audris, who clearly loved her uncle.

Hugh laughed uneasily. "I am sorry for sounding discourteous, Sir Oliver. I am angry at the world, I fear. I love Thurstan, and he is old and not strong. To make such a journey is dangerous for him."

"Ah, I understand." Sir Oliver nodded. "Well, well, I can see why you are worried. In addition to the hardships of the road, I have no doubt there are those who take advantage of the archbishop's arrival to press him to grant favors or solve their problems. You need not fear that we of Jernaeve will trouble him in that way, but I see, too, that you might not welcome my suggestion that he continue the negotiations with King David as long as he can. Still, it is not Jernaeve alone that will benefit."

"I know that." Hugh sighed. "I do not hold anyone to blame—except myself. I was the one who asked him to intervene with King David."

"But I am sure you never expected that he would go himself," Audris said softly. Her hand was still on his, and she squeezed it comfortingly.

"Put it aside," Sir Oliver remarked with rough kindness. "God looks to His own, and Archbishop Thurstan is surely under His care. Come and sit."

He gestured toward the fireplace, settling himself on a bench and patting the other end to indicate that Hugh should sit beside him. Hugh smothered his impulse to grin. His outburst of temper seemed to have had some good effect. Ordinarily, he suspected, Sir Oliver would not have been so polite, and it was soothing to be treated with honor when Audris was there to see.

"You are Sir Hugh Licorne," Sir Oliver went on. "I recall now that you are Bruno's friend and that he mentioned your bold work at the siege of Exeter. I knew your face, but at first I could only connect you with Sir Walter. Tell me, how serious is the trouble with the earl of Gloucester and the western lords?"

"More serious than I like—and Sir Walter feels the same. King Stephen should never have pardoned Redvers after he refused the lady's pleas—you know of that?"

Oliver nodded, but it was Audris who asked, "Then why did he? Was it out of kindness?"

Audris had fetched a stool and set it at Hugh's end of the bench, close by his knee, as she spoke. He wondered whether Sir Oliver would object and then realized the idea had occurred to him only because of his guilty conscience. There was nothing unusual in what Audris had done. Everyone who could clustered close to a new guest, all agog not to miss a word of whatever tidbits of news he brought.

Relieved, Hugh smiled at her. "Partly, I think, but still it was all wrong to yield to the importunities of Gloucester's party when it was clear that Redvers must open Exeter without terms or die of thirst within a few days. Yet I think—although I know the king did not wish to anger Gloucester—that what made Stephen agree *was* his kindness. I think the lady's tears, her utter despair at his harshness, preyed on the king's mind and weighed on his heart so that he welcomed Gloucester's interference. He thought too little about giving the impression that he was weak and could not resist any demand Gloucester chose to make so that he would go to any length to pacify the earl's party. And I think they pressed their case at that time rather than earlier for just that purpose."

"That bodes ill for us here also," Oliver said bleakly. "If Stephen is held in Normandy and the south by war, he will be unable to help us against the Scots."

Hugh shrugged. "I fear we will need to look to our own defense. That was why Sir Walter returned to Helmsley soon after Prince Henry was called back to Scotland by his father and sent me to Exeter instead of going himself. The excuse for King David calling Henry home was so weak that it was clear from that moment that the king would not keep the truce."

"Then you think Archbishop Thurstan's mission is hopeless?" Audris asked.

"Not hopeless." Hugh turned to her and suddenly had trouble remembering what he was about to say. She was not beautiful, but to see her face nearly stopped his heart. He swallowed and went on, "King David is a man of honor and deep faith. He does want land, and his wife has a claim to Northumbria, but he also fears he is forsworn in the oath he took to support Matilda. If Thurstan can convince King David that breaking the truce is equally faithless—and that he will look like a coward, too—to attack when Stephen is gone out of his kingdom—"

"By God's hangers that is clever!" Oliver exclaimed with enthusiasm. "I begin to have hope that I will harvest my fields before war comes."

"God willing," Lady Eadyth sighed, coming up to her husband. "Will you wash, my lord?" she asked. "The tables will soon be placed for the evening meal."

Oliver rose. "I will," he said, beckoning Eadyth to come with him, for he was not sure she had arranged for Hugh to sit with them, and he did not wish to ask in Hugh's presence lest he prick the new-made knight's pride again.

"My aunt will come back in a moment," Audris murmured, "and we will have no time to talk alone later because my uncle will want to extract every piece of news you have. But when you return to Jernaeve, he will not have so much to ask. Will you come riding with me then?"

"It will be my honor and my pleasure to accompany you to ride, to walk, to sit, or for any purpose at all," Hugh replied, his voice also low.

His words were formal—Hugh was too shaken by the passion her soft request roused to find words of his own—and the last phrase had no special meaning when he said it, but as soon as it was spoken, a very specific purpose leapt into both their minds. Audris's misinterpretation of his offer of help had brought the fact of their sexual desire for each other into the open. Now any exchange between them that was not diluted by the presence of other people brought that desire to the fore. Audris blushed and lowered her eyes, and then raised them to his again.

"I do not know my purpose," she said honestly.

Hugh was struck mute and did not dare continue to look at her, so that when Lady Eadyth returned a few minutes later, as Audris said she would, she found both Hugh and Audris staring into the flames on the hearth in what seemed to be companionable silence. Audris was equally accurate in her prediction of the rest of the events of the evening. Sir Oliver monopolized Hugh completely. He began at the table, hardly giving Hugh time to chew and swallow. In fact, if Audris had not pushed chunks of cold roast onto Hugh's knife and now and again popped into his mouth some of the meat and vegetables from the bowl they were sharing, he would have got little to eat. Actually, it was the gentleman's duty to pick out the choicest bits of food to give the lady, but it was a custom that Sir Oliver, who did not believe in pampering his wife, ignored unless they were in very high company. Oliver even nodded brusque approval of Audris's attention to Hugh because it saved him from being distracted from the conversation by choosing his own meal.

When Oliver had wrung his guest dry of public news, he began to question him about the events of the siege of Exeter, asking about the weapons and tactics used, in case there should be some new wrinkle in the making of war that he had missed hearing. And when that subject was exhausted, he started on Hugh's own activities, demanding almost blow-by-blow descriptions of the attacks Hugh had led and the sorties he had turned back. His interest was so technical that Hugh answered easily, never wondering whether he would be accused of boasting.

Oddly, rather than feeling unhappy or impatient at Sir Oliver's intervention, Hugh and Audris were enjoying themselves immensely. Audris felt a tingle of warmth and a quiver of excitement each time her fingers slipped between Hugh's lips with a tasty tidbit. The sensation was thrilling, and intensified when her breast or shoulder came in contact with Hugh's arm as she leaned across to feed him.

Hugh found her activity equally titillating and amusing, for he had noticed Sir Oliver's approval. Nor did he feel guilty, even though the hot, engorged sensations of physical arousal made him grateful to be sitting with a tablecloth over his lap and grateful, too, that he did not need to lift it to wipe his hands. The excitement was a clean pleasure. Hugh felt no lustful urge to seize Audris and satisfy himself. He was having no trouble keeping his mind on Oliver's questions or answering them. His only difficulty was to keep from laughing aloud because he was so full of pure joy.

Audris and Hugh parted without regret soon after the meal was over. A single meeting of their eyes before Hugh lifted Audris's hand to kiss it with formal gallantry was sufficient to say all that was needed. A promise of joy without haste or fear was given and received by each. They would have a week, a whole precious week.

Chapter 11

Naturally enough, over the next two days while Hugh moved Thurstan and his cortege from Durham to Hexham, the glow faded. It rained both days, which made for slow, miserable traveling, and Hugh had time enough to fret himself sleepless over whether he had misunderstood, understood too well, or deliberately deceived himself. Each time he came back to Audris's remark about the mare and her later statement that she did not know her purpose, he felt the response surge up in his body and wondered what he was to do if her purpose should become that of the mare. He was less sure when he was away from her that his desire was clean.

Audris had none of these troubles. She had gone up from the hall to find her loom strung as ordered and had begun to weave. The rich border of blue and silver, a perfect match for that on the first panel, was finished before she sought her bed that night. By the time Hugh arrived in the late afternoon of the second day, the grass and bases of the tree trunks of the forest glade, the feet and lower part of the maiden's gown, and the cloven silver hooves of the unicorn were finished. When the hail of the wall guard was answered by Hugh's voice, she did not run to the window as she had two days before, only smiled and finished the pass with her spindle before she tied off the thread.

Still, what was in her face was final confirmation to Fritha that the red-haired knight with the strange face had become the center of her lady's existence. Fritha was mute but neither deaf nor stupid, nor did she ever forget anything that Audris ever said. She remembered very well the talk between her lady and the half brother Bruno when Audris had spoken of Jacob and his long labor to win the wife of his choice. She had understood then what her lady wanted from a man. She looked at the joy that blazed in her mistress's face as Audris hammered down the woof with the comb, a joy so overwhelming, so complete, so inevitable that there was no need to rush to grab it.

Fritha had been told by her lady that she would not take a husband while Sir Oliver lived, and she wondered if Audris had changed her mind. Despite all signs, Fritha did not think so. In any case she knew that Sir Oliver would not accept the redhead, knighted or not, as a husband for the heiress of Jernaeve. Did that mean her lady's joy would be crushed out?

Sir Oliver was startled when he saw Audris emerge from the doorway of her tower and come flying across the hall in her customary light-footed rush—and he was greatly relieved, too. He had heard that she was weaving, and he had been sick with worry that she would emerge from her chamber with terror-filled eyes days hence to show him a completed tapestry of a land devastated by war. That she had broken off her weaving before it could possibly be finished was a good sign. Usually she did that only when the picture had no special meaning.

"Uncle!" she cried, coming to a sudden stop as soon as she saw him, and then coming closer more slowly. "I heard from my window that Archbishop Thurstan's men have arrived."

"So they have," he agreed, raising his brows. "But what has that to do with you?"

"Nothing," she admitted, laughing. "It was only that their coming reminded me of what I had no chance to ask you the day the unicorn was here."

"The unicorn!" Oliver exclaimed. "Whatever are you talking about, Audris?"

"Hugh Licorne, uncle. The unicorn."

Oliver began to laugh. "Call him Sir Hugh, Audris. I thought you had gone mad—or really seen a unicorn." The last words were very soft, not meant for his niece's ears, but Oliver believed that if any mortal woman saw a unicorn, it would, in truth, be Audris.

"Sir Hugh, then," Audris said obediently. "That day he was here, you were so busy with him that I never had a chance to talk to you myself. If King David has agreed to meet with the archbishop, those plans must have been made some weeks ago at least. Would not the king recall any men sent to spy out our flocks and whether we had patrols? All would be changed long before the talks were over, so watching us now would be to no purpose. And even if any were about, surely they would not try to seize me. That would be a great shame to King David if it happened while he was talking about the truce."

Oliver nodded. "Yes, I suppose that danger is past for the time." Then, thinking of the two days he had spent worrying over her new weaving project, he said sharply, "You could have asked to go out the next day. Why the devil did you start to weave instead?"

Audris's eyes opened wide. "But uncle, the rain was pouring down. I had nothing else to do. I could not work in the garden. I would have been drowned. And there was no purpose to going into the hills. The birds would not be flying, so I could not see into the nests anyway."

Oliver grunted, which was as close as he would come to acknowledging that his question had been unreasonable. Then he considered what she had said in another context and shook his head. "Well, you are not going to see the nests tomorrow either, even if the change in the weather holds. I will not have you climbing the cliffs so soon after heavy rain, especially where the hawks nest. That rock is all rotten, and the wet seeps into the cracks. No climbing, Audris. I forbid it. A piece of rock could break away…" He fell silent and shook his head again.

Audris touched his hand lovingly, moved by his constant care for her. "I am not so foolish," she assured him. "There are other nests, not on the cliffs. A short-winged hawk or two would not be amiss in the mews, and they nest in trees."

Her uncle sighed heavily. "It is neither fitting nor safe for you to climb trees either, Audris. I—"

"But think how pleased the king was with the falcon you gave him last year," Audris interrupted, chuckling. "In admiring your gift, he forgot completely that he had not accomplished his purpose and got me married."

Oliver grunted unhappily. This was not the first of these discussions, although usually Audris avoided the subject of how the hawks got into the mews because she knew it made her uncle uncomfortable. The numerous and well-trained inhabitants of the mews had been of great value over the years. They had played a major part in pacifying the late king's rapacity, in soothing bellicose neighbors, and in convincing judges that Fermain's claims were more valid than an opponent's. Oliver knew that Audris's repeated visits to the nests had an effect that made the birds easier to train and less likely to pine in captivity. Nonetheless, both conscience and propriety argued that he should forbid so unusual and dangerous a practice.

"It gives me so much pleasure to take them and train them." Audris patted her uncle's arm and then went on persuasively, "I will take someone with me. Fritha—and Sir Hugh." She laughed suddenly, a delighted trill of amusement. "Yes, I will take Sir Hugh, and then I can go up on the cliffs with a rope. He is so strong, uncle."

"You could still be hurt," Oliver said uncertainly.

"A scrape and a scratch at the very worst," Audris assured him. "He would not let me fall, so I could not be broken anywhere. And what will you do with him all day if I do not take him away? In this season you are too busy to entertain a guest."

Since Oliver did not trouble himself much about being polite unless his guests were very powerful men and an advantage could be gained from arranging hunts and other activities to entertain them, he had not even considered that aspect of Hugh's presence in Jernaeve. Guests were usually passing through and only remained a night or two at the most. Now that Audris had reminded him that Hugh would be with them for a week, he realized that boredom would probably soon cause the young man to follow him around if he was not otherwise occupied. There could be no harm in that, since Oliver's tasks at this season were all agricultural, not military, but he was not a person who enjoyed making conversation.

"You are a good girl, Audris," he said. "If he will go, take him."

A happy thought had occurred to Sir Oliver. He did not believe Sir Hugh could know about Audris's habit of climbing trees and cliffs. Doubtless he would express such horror at her behavior that she would forgo the activity. At that moment, Hugh entered the hall, and the notion regarding him pleased Oliver so much that he went forward with a broad smile to greet his guest.

"You are very well come," Oliver said. "Are your men settled below?"

"Yes, I thank you," Hugh replied, somewhat taken aback by his host's warmth, for Oliver was known for his reserve. "It was most kind of you to clear a barracks for them. The weather is so uncertain, and they have already had two nights out in the wet."

"There is room enough in Jernaeve." Oliver waved away the thanks. "But I am glad you are content, for I have a favor to ask of you."

"If it is in *my* power to do, I will be happy to serve you," Hugh said cautiously.

"It is nothing to do with the archbishop," Oliver assured him. "Merely, my niece has been confined to the keep since we first heard rumors that David would not abide by the truce. I would be grateful if you would ride out with her."

"Ride out... with Demoiselle Audris?" Hugh's voice cracked between the phrases, and he choked and cleared his throat before he could get out, "Of course. The favor is to me."

Eadyth, who had come forward to greet Hugh also, frowned. She wondered whether it was only surprise at her husband's precipitate proposal that had brought their guest so close to strangulation. Audris was no beauty, but she had winning ways. Eadyth recalled how companionably Audris and Hugh had been sitting, like old friends, by the fire. Audris must have put him at ease at once, and then she had been so attentive in feeding him when Oliver kept him talking. Of course, Audris would have done the same for any person; she was a sweet, kind girl. But if this young knight had misunderstood her attentions to him and felt he was in some way special to her, was it kind to push him into Audris's company?

Eadyth had no fears for Audris; Hugh was poor and ugly, and Audris could have her choice of men. Many richer and better-favored suitors had already been turned away; yet, it did puzzle her why Audris had come down each time Sir Hugh arrived. Usually Audris kept to her chamber when there were guests in the keep.

As Audris flitted around Oliver's back, took Hugh's hand, and laughed up into his face as she thanked him for being willing to assume the burden of her company, Eadyth saw the young knight lower his eyes and swallow. He was clearly unable to reply to this mischievous sally, and Eadyth felt sorry for him. She was reasonably sure Oliver had suggested the arrangement because he did not want Hugh around to bother him. Audris had ridden out alone for years. Eadyth would not dare protest or even urge her husband to change his mind, but she could warn Audris, for Audris would not willingly cause anyone pain; she was just innocent and heedless.

Stepping forward, Eadyth said sharply, "Audris, stop your nonsense. You are too playful. Do you not see that Sir Hugh has not had a chance to be unarmed? He is tired and wet, too. Go your way and let me see to our guest's comfort."

Oliver looked at his wife, slightly surprised by her sharpness, and then dismissed it. Women were forever finding finicky "manners" to impose on each other—and on men, too, when they could. It was nothing to him. He nodded at Hugh and said, "I will leave you in my wife's care, then," and walked away.

"Can I not help, aunt?" Audris asked. "After all," she added merrily, "I think I have a debt to Sir Hugh for agreeing so graciously to bear with me for a whole week. Most men—"

"Audris!" Eadyth snapped. "Do not try my patience. Sir

Hugh has been on the road for many days, and between the dust and mud, he will want a bath. It is ready, and the servants are waiting for him. Go your way, I said."

Color flew up into Audris's cheeks. She cast one glance at Hugh, then turned and fled. Eadyth stared after her, startled at her reactions, for most criticism flowed off her niece as gracefully and with as little effect as raindrops flowed off a swan. By the time Eadyth faced him again, Hugh had his own expression under control.

He had been still reeling under the shock of having Sir Oliver virtually order him to go riding with Audris, which he felt her uncle would try to prevent, when she herself delivered two more shocks. First, her teasing about his acceptance of the duty of being her escort indicated no surprise. She *knew* what Sir Oliver was going to say, and Hugh was convinced that she had somehow induced her uncle to say it. Then there was the look Audris had given him as she blushed and ran away—so did a young mare nip or nudge a stallion and then flee.

Lady Eadyth gestured him forward, and Hugh moved with her, dimly hearing her speak of Audris's playfulness and heedlessness. He was mostly aware that she was talking more than usual and in a higher-pitched voice. "She is very childish in some ways," Eadyth concluded as she brought him to the doorway of the chamber prepared for him, "for she has not had to bear the burden of man, children, and household. I hope you will not think she means more than to be kind."

"I do not mistake Demoiselle Audris's meaning, my lady," Hugh assured her, keeping his face expressionless. "Bruno has told me a great deal about her."

"Ah!" Eadyth exclaimed, feeling that everything had been explained. "If Audris knows that Bruno is your friend, she will hang on you as though you were her dearest possession, for she prizes Bruno above all others living."

Hugh made no reply to that beyond a bow. He never lied. The statements he had made to Eadyth might have misled her, but both were true, whereas to agree to what she had said would have been lying. Although Lady Eadyth's explanations of Audris's behavior should have convinced Hugh that his fears of having misunderstood Audris were true, actually her manner had conveyed a meaning quite opposite to her words. Hugh was now sure that it was *not* because he was Bruno's friend that Audris favored him.

At this moment all Hugh wanted was to be away from any person to whom he owed courtesy so he would not have to talk. Nor did he want to think what to do about Audris. In the muddled state of his mind it could do no good, for he had been thinking about little else, without coming to any conclusion, for two days and nights. Thus, he breathed a deep sigh of relief when Lady Eadyth did not follow him into the wall chamber, where a tub of steaming water was set before the small hearth. There was no reason for Lady Eadyth to accompany him. He was no earl or great baron, whom she would have bathed with her own hands as an act of courtesy. For a simple knight, the offer of a bath and the specific attentions of servants was already honorable treatment, but Sir Oliver's unnaturally effusive welcome had made Hugh wonder.

Pushing all his problems to the back of his mind, Hugh looked with pleasure at the chamber that would be his for a week. He had never had a room to himself before, except for having slept in this same room on his previous visit to Jernaeve—only that night his eyes had been blind to outward things. He was familiar, of course, with the small rooms hollowed out inside the thick stone walls of a keep. This one was no different from others, lit only by what light came in from the open doorway to the antechamber, where a window was let into the wall facing the bailey, and by several pitch-headed torches in holders fixed to the walls.

A broad bench had been moved into the chamber and was covered with doubled fleeces to serve as a mattress. It stood back against the wall opposite the door, a chest with a stool beside it was placed before the wall dividing the little room from the hall, and there was a hearth on the side wall facing the bailey, with a slit above it that served to carry away some of the smoke. A small fire burned brightly on the flat slabs of stone in a hollow of the wall provided for the hearth.

Such luxury! Hugh sighed and moved farther into the

room. Compared with the hall itself, this chamber was warm, cozy, and well lit. Moreover, Hugh had never had a private bath. In Helmsley he had bathed in the communal outbuilding reserved for the purpose, where he and a friend or two sloshed one another with water from a bucket. Looking at the size of the tub, Hugh had a moment's doubt that he would fit, but the rising steam, showing the water was warm, and the clean, thick drying cloths warming by the fire convinced him that this was a luxury he must taste.

Having delivered her warning to Hugh and felt from his manner that he understood her, Eadyth went to find Audris. She had seen her niece leave by the door that led to the bailey, and the first servant she accosted told her with an intonation of awe reserved only for Audris that the Demoiselle had gone into the kitchen area. Eadyth smiled wryly. Although she managed Jernaeve, she might not be noticed as she passed through the keep, but there was never any difficulty finding Audris. Every person stopped work to watch Audris pass, to touch her gown or cloak if possible.

Eadyth found her niece, as she expected, in the outbuilding used to dry and store herbs, soap, and other household necessities. It was ordinary enough, too, to see her sniffing at an aromatic bundle. Part of Audris's duty in caring for the castle garden was to decide what quantity of any particular plant to grow, and to do that, she had to examine the quantity and condition of the herbs that were stored. Glad to catch her niece alone, Eadyth combined a form of apology, saying she had not meant to hurt or embarrass Audris before a friend of Bruno's, with a lecture on how her behavior toward Hugh might have been misinterpreted and caused the young man much pain.

Audris listened quietly and then said, "I will be more careful, aunt, I promise you."

Eadyth was well content with that, knowing that Audris hated to hurt anyone. She dismissed the matter from her mind, turning her thoughts while she was in the kitchen area to checking on the cooks' preparations to feed the fifty extra mouths. In the building behind her, Audris continued to choose herbs for a few minutes more and then silently left. With her she took a small parcel of herbs in a clean linen cloth, which she rhythmically twisted and bent and rubbed between her hands so that the dry, brittle stems and leaves were broken into a coarse powder. A delightful odor wafted from the bag, not sweet, but clean and spicy.

A small smile curved Audris's lips as she climbed the dark, steep stair of the forebuilding. She had been more fortunate than she deserved, for her aunt had totally misunderstood her. She had not run away because she had been scolded but because when Eadyth said Hugh was to have a bath, an image of him naked had risen in her mind. The instant response of her body—a flood of warmth, a tightening in her groin, and a strange pleasurable throbbing between her legs—had startled her into retreat. She had found herself in the storeroom with no idea what she was doing there until the sharp aromatic scents reminded her that Eadyth often asked her for herbs to sweeten the bath water of noble guests. Then she had known why she had run to the storeroom.

As she entered the hall, Audris paused, wondering whether it was wise to enter Hugh's chamber. Would the servants tell Eadyth? And would her aunt think her action strange after she had been warned not to lead Hugh astray with signs of favor? Common sense bade her go back to her tower until she was called for the evening meal, but her desire prodded her forward, her feet carried her lightly ahead, and the smile that had faded with her doubts came back to her lips. Probably the servants would say nothing about her to her aunt, and even if they did, she could say she had just stepped in for a moment to bring the herbs. Eadyth would think it another mark of her heedless nature.

❧

Hugh had not realized until he was immersed in the warm water and being scrubbed with a rough cloth how tired he was. The combined stress of worrying about Thurstan and his desire for Audris—a desire that he feared bordered on the dishonorable—had worn him down more than violent physical activity could. Now he simply leaned back against the staves of the tub with his eyes closed and let himself be soothed by the servants' ministrations. He was only dimly aware of their low-voiced conversation, too indifferent to make the effort to understand what they were saying in their own guttural language, although he could comprehend some English when he tried. The murmur of talk added to his comfort, though, and when it stopped abruptly, Hugh opened his eyes—and choked.

Audris stood in the doorway, a small linen bag held forward as if she were about to offer it to the servants, but she did not speak, and her eyes, Hugh saw, were fixed on him. He was aware, too, that the servants had drawn back as if surprised or frightened and were watching Audris intently, but he had no time to wonder at *their* odd behavior. Audris's was sending cold chills—and hot thrills—up and down his spine. Her failure to speak or shift her eyes, which might have been natural had she hesitated only briefly, had lasted far too long. She seemed dumbstruck by the sight of his body.

"Is there something you desire of me, Lady Audris?" Hugh had been desperate to break the silence, and his voice came out forced and harsh—but the words! He choked again as he realized what he had said.

Shocked by the harsh, angry-sounding voice, Audris breathed in sharply and lifted her eyes from Hugh's body to his face. She saw at once that he was not angry—horrified would be a better description of his expression—and she wondered if she had again acted differently from other people. But simultaneously with the thought, the sense of what Hugh had said became clear. Irrepressible mischief brightened Audris's eyes, and a giggle followed the intake of breath.

"Only to give you pleasure," she said sweetly, as if she had no idea what her reply could mean in the context of his question, and advanced toward him.

Hugh was crammed so tightly into the tub, which was designed for smaller people than he, that it was impossible for him to move, except to get to his feet—and that would scarcely have helped. Nonetheless, instinctively he pressed back, away from Audris's approach, his muscles rippling with the effort. Audris paused, her eyes slipping down over the broad shoulders, thick-muscled arms, and wide chest, all shining with water so that the uneven light from the torches gleamed and glittered as frustrated motion lifted or lowered bands of flesh under the skin. A last glance flicked farther down still, to the corded muscles of his powerful thighs. Her lips parted, and quick as a snake's her tongue flicked across them.

Hugh very nearly did erupt from the water, but her expression of greedy avidity was gone, and she was coming forward again. He had one flash of doubt whether the girl was sane before she opened the cloth and sprinkled the powdered herbs into the bathwater. The warmth and moisture released the scent even more powerfully, and the room filled with the sharp, clean odor. Everyone breathed in deeply, even Hugh.

"There," Audris said, chuckling. "Does that not give you pleasure? Good herbs add much enjoyment to a bath and a sweetness to the body afterward."

"Little witch," Hugh breathed, too softly for the ears of the servants to catch the words, and then, more loudly, "Wait until tomorrow, Demoiselle. I will show you then how grateful I am."

Audris laughed, acknowledging the hidden, playful threat, cast one more lingering glance over Hugh's body—and saw the head of his shaft rearing upward between his thighs. She turned and fled, this time to the safety of her tower, where she stood staring at her loom, seeing the completed picture. Was it foretelling? If so, Hugh was only teasing her as she had teased him—or did that swollen shaft speak the truth hidden under playful words? Then there was no foretelling in the picture, and… and what? A vivid image of Hugh rose in her mind. He was very fair where sun and wind had not tanned his skin and not at all hairy. Only a narrow, inverted triangle of curly hair, as red as that on his head, spread across his chest at the base of his throat and ran down his breastbone nearly to his navel. Below that she had seen only dimly because of the bathwater, but it seemed that a thinner band of hair grew from the navel to the thick pubic bush—from which that straining shaft had risen.

Slowly Audris moved away from the loom and sat in her chair. If her picture were not foretelling, on the morrow she would no longer be a maiden. The pulsing in her groin grew more insistent. Audris shifted in her chair and sighed. She knew now that she wanted Hugh as the mare desired the stallion or the doe the buck. Strong sexual images flowed through her mind, and she trembled with need, hugging her arms across her body and hunching her shoulders to free her sensitized nipples from the inflaming touches of her shift. But she was not a mare or a doe. Even as her mind insinuated Hugh and his roused manhood into the male role of her images and she bit her lips with longing, she was aware that for her there must be more than the mating and the parting. Was her unicorn no more than a white bull? Did she want a white bull who moved from cow to cow without thought or regret? Yet if her unicorn were pure, must not her desire remain unfulfilled?

Her thoughts went round and round until they were broken by a gentle touch on her arm. Audris started. The candles were alight in her chamber, and Fritha was making the gestures for food and a query—meaning did Audris want her to fetch food or did she prefer to go down herself? Audris hesitated and then rose and straightened her gown. She was no coward, and she was unused to indecision and doubt—she wanted an answer.

She did not obtain one. Although Hugh was formally courteous, choosing the best of the food for her and cutting or breaking it into the small pieces deemed suitable for a fine lady, his conversation was directed almost exclusively to her uncle. There were a few new pieces of news, gleaned from Thurstan and from their host in the place they had lodged the past night. Beyond that, Hugh confined himself to general talk of male interest.

Tense as a bowstring when she sat down beside him, Audris was soon ready to laugh at herself. Unicorn or bull, she had good reason to believe the man behind the symbol clever. No matter what Hugh's intention for the following day, he would not betray himself to her aunt and uncle. They, Audris could see, were well satisfied. She could not help smiling when her aunt nodded approvingly at her, but the smile was not actually in recognition of Eadyth's approval. Audris had realized that Hugh not only had himself been a model of propriety but, without a look or a word, had forced *her* to behave just as she should.

Only after the meal was ended and the washing water and towels brought to clean their hands, did Hugh mention their proposed ride the next day. He rose and bowed to Oliver and Eadyth. "If you will pardon me, I will seek my bed, for I am weary." And when both had expressed polite concern and approval, he turned fully to Audris, which made his face invisible to her aunt and uncle. Bowing again, he said, "I will be ready to attend you after Mass, Demoiselle, if the weather permits." And brought his lid down over his right eye with a slow deliberation that was as challenging as a laugh.

Chapter 12

THERE WAS A TENDER MIST STILL HANGING OVER THE RIVER and spreading across the hills when Audris, Hugh, and Fritha rode out of Jernaeve. The mist was not so dense, however, as to obscure the sun or the fact that the sky beyond it was all but cloudless. It only lent enchantment to the landscape, softening the stark shapes of protruding rocks, giving a pearly opalescence to the fresh, pale green of the new leaves on the trees, and making the morning twittering of birds into unearthly music.

Struck by the beauty of the scene, Hugh and Audris were silent as they rode out of the keep and across the demesne meadows where the Fermain cattle grazed on the lush grass of spring. They had not said much to each other yet, for Hugh had come up from attending Mass in the tiny church in the bailey to find Audris, dressed for riding, breaking her fast with her uncle and aunt. He wore only hunting garb, a short homespun wool tunic that came to the middle of his thighs over chausses of the same material and a bright red wool cloak. Before they left, Hugh had fetched his sword and his shield from his chamber, and Sir Oliver shrugged. Clearly he did not think weapons would be needed, but did not object either.

Fritha was waiting at the door, laden with blankets and bags, and Hugh cast a glance at her and raised a brow. He said nothing until they were in the stable, but while the horses and Fritha's mule were being saddled, he had asked, "Why did you bring her?"

And Audris had said, "For convenience and my uncle's ease of mind. Do not consider her, she is loyal to me—and she is mute."

An odd expression crossed Hugh's face, and he had looked as if he were going to say something; if so, he thought better of it, and went to fasten the sword and shield to appropriate places on his saddle. He had not spoken again until, halfway across the pasture, with the hills silver and sparkling in the sunlit mist rising before them, he drew a deep breath and said, "I love this land."

"Jernaeve?" Audris asked, surprised.

Hugh turned his head to smile at her. "No, I meant this northland. The Southrons say it is poor and barren, and I have seen that to be true, but I do not care. This is my place, and I am content with it. Do you love only Jernaeve?"

"I love the hills and fields," Audris replied after a slight hesitation, for once thinking before she spoke. "Jernaeve is the only place I know, so I cannot say for certain, but I think so long as there were forests and high, bare cliffs and I were free to wander about them, I would not care whether the place were named Jernaeve or otherwise. I am not like my uncle or Bruno. Jernaeve is Uncle Oliver's life—his reason for living. And Bruno's heart is in Jernaeve."

"It is his homeplace," Hugh said somberly. "He has nothing else to cling to."

Audris knew it was not only Bruno of whom he was speaking. "And you?" she asked so softly that only the pure, clear quality of her voice permitted the question to be heard above the dull sounds of the horses' hooves.

"I have Sir Walter, who loves me, and my foster father, Thurstan."

His answer was firm, but in it Audris sensed fear and uncertainty. To probe further would hurt him, but to change the subject completely would hurt also. "How did you come into Thurstan's care?" she asked, feeling that he must have told that tale many times and whatever hurt was in it would be dulled by familiarity.

It was a less painful subject than she realized, because, unlike many foundlings, Hugh knew his mother had not willingly abandoned him. The poor woman could not help dying, and she had, from what Thurstan said, struggled to her very last breath to do her best for her child. Hugh cheerfully related what Thurstan had told him.

"But was there no hint at all of who your mother was in what was said by the sisters who attended her?" Audris asked when he had outlined the events.

Hugh laughed. "To speak the truth, I have been so busy and concerned with other things that I have not once looked at the parchment Thurstan gave me. Can it matter?"

"Of course it matters!" Audris cried. "What if there is an old mother or a sister or brother who loved your mother and has feared and wept for all these years, never knowing what had become of her? I am sorry enough that Bruno cannot make his home here with me, but I have never had to fear that he was suffering or dead and I did not know."

"Mea culpa," Hugh breathed. "In my selfishness I never thought of that. God forgive me, for I have sinned out of pride, thinking I would not humble myself to those who did not care enough to come or send a message to the convent where I was born—but perhaps they did not know. If my mother hid herself for shame—"

"Why shame?" Audris asked sharply. "There might be many reasons for a woman to hide herself. If her keep were taken or her husband a rebel, innocent as she herself was, she might hide. You must examine the parchment closely when you can and not think—"

"I have it here in my saddlebag," Hugh interrupted, smiling again at her vehemence. "I forgot all about it." Having said that, he frowned and then sighed. "Perhaps I wanted to forget. Perhaps I fear to find that my father was some low-bred churl—"

"And will that make you less you? You talk as silly as Bruno does." Audris nudged her horse closer to Hugh's and held out her hand to him. When he took it in his, she squeezed gently. "There is a place on the east side of the hill where the sunlight comes first. The grass will be nearly dry there, and we can wait until the mist clears. Shall we look at your parchment?"

"If you wish," Hugh agreed, partly because he could say nothing else but also because there was comfort to be found in sympathetic companionship, but he was still uneasy, and changed the subject by asking, "And what will we do after the mist clears—no, before you answer that, tell me how you wheedled Sir Oliver into virtually ordering me to accompany you."

"That needed no wheedling." Audris laughed. "I only had to remind him that you would soon be bored, having nothing to do in the keep, and would doubtless like to accompany him as he rode the lands. My uncle is not a man who cares much for company."

"I would not have guessed that from his questions at the meals we shared," Hugh remarked.

"Questions to obtain information are different. It is idle chatter, such as comment on the good or bad points of the stock or the weather or the possibilities for a good harvest—suchlike talk bores him."

"Very practical."

Hugh chuckled, but he looked sidelong at Audris, remembering how silent her aunt had been and thinking that it was no wonder Audris valued Bruno and wished for him. She must be starved for a friend, for someone to talk with, and that confirmed the solution to Audris's behavior that had finally occurred to him after she had run away. He knew that she had seen his physical arousal and fled from it, not because she was ignorant or innocent in the sense of lacking understanding of what the arousal meant—that was impossible for a woman of her age, especially one who spoke so familiarly about mares and stallions. Nor did Hugh believe she was frightened, for he had seen the desire in her face when she looked at his naked body.

Audris, he had come to understand, acted first and thought later. It was that conclusion that had prompted him to behave so calmly at the evening meal; he knew it must be his responsibility to think ahead for both of them. Not that she lacked the ability to think—her management of her uncle proved that—but sheltered as she was, she had never had a real reason to curb her openness and impulsiveness. Hugh also knew what would happen if he offered a suggestive word or gesture when they dismounted as Audris planned. She would offer herself to him as openly and innocently as a young doe, with no more thought for what might follow her action than a doe's. He could not permit that, no matter how his body raged with desire. He must *make* her think. After that...

"You are right about one thing, though," Audris said, breaking the little silence that had fallen. "It was very odd that my uncle nearly fell into your arms and pressed you so straitly to come with me. It was not like him at all."

"Perhaps he thought my presence would prevent you from going somewhere or doing something he disapproved?" For just an instant jealousy reared its leering head, and Hugh wondered whether the hunger betrayed by the swift flick of Audris's tongue over her parted lips could be felt by one utterly innocent.

"But he knew what I wished to do," Audris assured Hugh. "He did forbid me to climb to the falcon's nest on the cliffs for fear some rock, loosened by the rain, might fall, but after I said that you would hold me on a rope, he—he did not approve, but he did not forbid me." She saw the look of horror on Hugh's face, and fearing he believed that she was forcing him into the difficult position of secretly helping her commit an act of disobedience, she added hastily, "I would not disobey my uncle in what he straitly forbade."

Hugh scarcely heard the last sentence. "Hold you on a rope," he repeated incredulously, even more horrified than if she *had* admitted she usually met a lover when she rode out alone. "You cannot mean what you say."

Audris's apparent fragility had become familiar enough that Hugh was no longer constantly aware of it, but her casual talk of hanging over a cliff on a rope brought into vivid focus the translucent skin over the fine, light bones of her face and the narrow, long-fingered hands, seemingly as delicate and frangible as the limbs of a songbird.

"But Uncle Oliver told you—" Audris began, and then began to laugh as revelation came to her. She recalled that her uncle had said nothing about hawk nests, only suggested that Hugh ride out with his niece. Now Audris knew why Oliver had been so cordial and so urgent; he had *expected* Hugh to be horrified and refuse her.

The joyous trills of laughter woke memories in Hugh also. He saw the expression on Bruno's face more than a year past and heard him curse himself for teaching Audris to climb. Audris had laughed then, too, cozening her half brother, calling him dearling, and distracting them— No, she had not. That greedy pig Lusors had interrupted them, and the subject of climbing had been buried under more immediate tensions. Now Audris was shaking her head.

"I have been taken in my own snare," she said merrily. "I thought I had been so clever and maneuvered my uncle into agreeing that I could go on the cliffs, for he did not say a word against it after I told him you would hold me and not let me fall, and instead he put you in as his champion—all unknowing, too." She laughed again and then, still smiling, shrugged. "Ah, well, let it be. I will just check the nests in the lower forest."

"And how do you do that?" Hugh asked.

Audris's eyes sparkled with mischief. "I climb the trees. Uncle does not think it proper, but he knows it is not dangerous, so—" She stopped speaking suddenly and stopped her mare, gesturing for Hugh to stop also, and then whispered, "Oh, look, is that not like the land of faerie?"

They had come to the crest of the rather low ridge, which fell away in a gentle slope to the east, much like the rise they had climbed. To the north, the spine of the ridge continued to rise more and more steeply until it culminated in a sheer but broken face of rock. If one looked eastward, though, ignoring the wild and threatening jumble to the north, one saw only the beauty of the small valley created by a minor tributary of the river. The mist was so thin now that the sparkling stream, the slender saplings that bordered it, and the single buck drinking at its edge were all clearly visible. Nonetheless, all seemed to be swathed in the most delicate of veils, which gave an aura of unreality and mysterious loveliness to the scene. Hugh did not dare speak lest his deeper voice carry and betray them, but soon his stallion stamped and snorted. The buck lifted his wide-horned head, silver streams of water raining from his muzzle. One moment more he stood, then turned and fled.

Audris breathed a tremulous sigh and looked up at Hugh's face, but his eyes were still on the misty valley; they were luminous with love, and his lips were relaxed and soft, his whole expression one of peace and contentment, Then he blinked, drew a sharp breath, and looked with practical attention at the area.

Audris noted the change. "Do you think to hunt him tomorrow?" she asked neutrally.

Hugh turned his head, looking startled. "God forbid! He has given me such pleasure, I only wish he could be marked somehow to make him safe. If I hunt by your uncle's invitation, I will go south and west. Not here. I could not spill blood here." Then his lips twisted. "I daresay you think me a fool. I am sure many hunts have passed over this valley."

"I cannot say whether others might think you a fool," Audris said softly, "for I do not always think as others do. To me, you are not. I do not think it foolish to be grateful for a gift that brings so much delight or to wish to keep the bringer safe in the hope the gift will be renewed." She smiled at him. "There is no hunting in this valley, except with hawks. I begged my uncle to spare it many years ago, and so far he has done so."

Hugh nodded without answering. He thought it kind of Sir Oliver to leave Audris's valley untouched, but knew it was not a great sacrifice, for it was small and the deer could escape easily up slopes and into woodlands with much low growth that would make pursuit on horseback unpleasant and frustrating. Audris had prodded her mare forward gently, and Hugh followed, but she did not go far. Perhaps some fifty yards from the top the slope flattened in a rough semicircle. On either side of the level patch the decline was regular, but a huge boulder or an intrusion of harder rock had not worn away as quickly as the rest of the hillside. Over the years, soil wearing from the crest above had packed down on the firm base so that now the lip of the semicircular table ended in a sharp dropoff. It was not more than fifteen or twenty feet high, but from below they would be invisible if they sat or lay a few feet back from the edge, yet sitting they would be able to look down into the valley.

A slithering sound made Hugh turn, his sword half drawn, but it was only Fritha coming on foot with the rolled blankets in her arms. Without instruction she undid the blankets' lashings and spread them. Hugh dismounted quickly, but before he could come to Audris's aid she had slid down herself and handed her rein to the maid.

"Will Rufus go with Fritha?" she asked. "I like to tie the horses on the other side of the ridge so they will not frighten whatever creature might come into the valley."

"I would rather see him settled myself," Hugh said. Rufus was calm now, not changed out of a horse's proper nature into a crazed killer by the scent of blood and the sounds of battle, but the stallion was always high-strung, and Hugh wanted no accidents.

"Do not forget to bring Thurstan's parchment back with you," Audris urged, "and if you are hungry, ask Fritha for the basket with the cheese and wine."

He returned alone, carrying the basket in one hand and a somewhat crumpled roll of parchment in the other. Audris was surprised when Fritha did not come with him, for she had not instructed her maid to stay behind. She blushed faintly, assuming that Hugh had told her to stay with the animals and wondered whether it was only Hugh's concern for his fine stallion being out of sight or whether it was a device to be alone with her. Both ideas disturbed her in different ways, but what disturbed her most of all was that she did not know which she wanted to be his reason.

"I am sure there will be some clue in the parchment that you can follow," Audris said hastily and in a rather breathless voice.

Hugh smiled at her, set the basket down, sat down himself, and unrolled the parchment, holding it so that Audris could also read. She sat stiffly for a few minutes, but soon she was absorbed in the tale Thurstan had recorded and leaned confidingly against Hugh without realizing it.

"How sad. How very sad," Audris murmured. "I wonder why she left the nuns? It is clear that she was well provided. See here what Thurstan says of the furnishing of her chamber—her own sheets and her gowns, though few, of the best cloth, and fine swaddling for the babe—" She broke off and looked up at him. "You were that babe. It is very strange to think of you as a babe, Hugh. You are so big."

"Perhaps that killed her," he said, frowning.

He had thought as little as possible about his parentage over the years of his youth, and even when Thurstan had introduced the subject, he had not felt much, except for a flicker of gladness and pride that he had meant enough to his mother to spark her desperate struggle to place him in safety. Now he felt a sharp pang of grief and guilt, and he looked at Audris's small body and shuddered.

"I should not think so," Audris replied thoughtfully. "I have seen large babes born of small women with ease and small ones that could not be born at all. The fault seems to be in the woman, although sometimes it is needful to turn the babe. In any case, Hugh, it is not something you had any choice about. There can be neither guilt nor sin when free will is absent. What happened was in God's hands, not in yours. And it is long, long over now. What interests me is why she fled the convent."

Hugh was very willing to leave the unpleasant idea that had occurred to him and admitted there did not seem to be any reason for his mother's action. It was clear that she had gone willingly to the nuns. A small troop of men had escorted her there, but none had entered the convent with her, and all the nuns knew was that the men rode away at once. After that, she could have left at any time, for she had the wherewithal to pay new protectors and to find other lodging if she wished. They pored over the parchment, but could find no other fact of significance except the list of nuns who had at one time or another attended Hugh's mother.

"You will have to go back to the convent and speak to those who are still alive yourself," she said.

"They will remember nothing at all after all this time," Hugh replied. "Why are you so set on my finding out my mother's people? Audris, I hope you will not think me a coxcomb, but I have seen that you favor me. I cannot guess why. God knows I am no beauty—"

"Your eyes are beautiful," Audris said, smiling, "and your mouth is gentle and tender, but I would not care even if you had no feature at all with charm. You do not look at land only to see if it is fit for sheep or for the plow or for the hunt. You see that sometimes a place may be of value for itself, for its beauty alone. And you do not see me as a key that will unlock a box of property. You looked at *me*, at *me* as Bruno looks at me. I told you that when we first rode out together more than a year ago."

"I do not look at you as Bruno looks at you," Hugh said deliberately. "You must understand that, Audris. I do not feel as a brother feels."

Color stained her cheeks as memory brought back the image of that raised shaft with the foreskin drawn back from its reaching red head. "I know that," she whispered, looking down at her fingers twining restlessly in her lap.

"And you must know also that finding my mother's people—and perhaps even my father's, if he was not some common churl—probably still would not make me a fit suitor for you."

Audris lifted her head. "I never thought about that," she said earnestly. "It was for your sake—and for any who remembered your mother with love, if there be any—that I urge you to follow the trail. Hugh, you must answer the doubts in your own heart." She put her hand over his. "It is better to know—even a bad thing—than to doubt. But truly, I am sure you need have no doubts about your father's blood. Remember the troop of men who came with your mother and the rich furnishings. And remember that the nuns said she spoke with confidence of her husband returning for her."

"He did not return, nor was there any other who came to ask about her," Hugh pointed out, but there was no longer force or bitterness behind the remark. It was more a warning to himself, for a faint hope was beginning to stir in Hugh.

The points he and Audris were discussing were all significant, and Hugh found that he was less doubtful about his ancestry. Audris had suggested that his mother hid her name because her husband had been a rebel. Hugh had been born in 1114, in the first third of the late King Henry's reign, just about the time the king felt strong enough to make demands on his vassals and expect instant obedience. Henry could be very vindictive and also liked to provide a few horrible examples as warnings. Say his father had been imprisoned and died in prison or executed outright, Hugh thought; he would never have betrayed his wife's hiding place. She had been heavy with child. If the babe were a boy, as it had been, his father would not want his wife and his heir in the king's hands too. Could an estate have been forfeit—possibly to the king himself? Crown lands could be returned to a disseised man's heir! Hugh knew he already had Stephen's favor, and if Sir Walter would use his influence…

Dreams! All dreams because he desired a woman. "So if you do not care whether I am suitable as a husband," Hugh went on, his voice suddenly harsh, "what do you want of me?"

"I want a man who does not scorn me as a pale nothing that he *must* take to get Jernaeve," she said bitterly and shook her head as Hugh tried to protest. "And you are beautiful to me," she went on, blushing but meeting his eyes. "I love your face, which is so different, and your body… is very beautiful."

Hugh started to bend his head to kiss her, remembered his promise to himself, and pulled back. "Audris, you must not leap at each idea that comes into your head. I assure you that my body is much like that of other men. There is nothing special in it. And if you would talk to others as you talk to me, many men would look at you with desire."

"Is that true?" Audris asked.

"What, that all men's bodies are the same or that you are a desirable woman?" Hugh countered.

"I have seen other bodies," Audris said. "They are not all the same, but I know what you mean."

"Then, in the same way," Hugh snapped angrily, "I cannot swear that *every* man would desire you, but many would."

"I am glad of that." Audris smiled brilliantly. "I would not want you to be cheated."

"What?" Hugh exclaimed, startled.

"Why should you be satisfied with what no other man would want?" Audris teased. "Do you have such poor taste? Or, if you desire me out of pity, thus taking only half a loaf or a quarter, would you not be deprived—or still hungry? So I am glad you think others would want me too."

The smiling face turned up to his was irresistible. Hugh caught the back of her head with one hand, her chin with the other, and pressed his mouth on hers. Initially the kiss was as much a mark of his irritation as of his desire, but when Audris's arms went around him and her lips answered eagerly to his, he forgot he had been angry. He let go of her chin, knowing there was no need to hold her, that she would not pull away, and used that arm to press her against him.

In the circle of his arm, she was so slight, so pliant, that he did not dare take his support from her head lest the force of his kiss break her neck. It was a silly idea, but still, fear began to mingle with Hugh's passion. And he had sworn to himself he would not take her, not unless… Hugh did not permit himself to complete that thought. He drew back his head, turned his face away, and slackened his grip on her.

"For pity's sake, Audris," he whispered. "Say me nay. Help me. I am only a man, and what we are doing is wrong."

Unicorn, Audris thought triumphantly, not an uncaring bull but a pure, fierce unicorn, gentle only to the maiden. The word brought a faint chill of doubt. For the unicorn, the maiden was a trap; she held him and subdued his ferocity so the hunters could kill him. Audris's arms tightened convulsively around Hugh for an instant; then she told herself it was the maiden's choice. If the maiden were faithful to the unicorn instead of to the hunters, no harm would come to him. She unlocked her arms from his neck and cupped his face in her hands, turning it toward her again.

"Do you feel sinful?" she asked.

Hugh looked into her pale, clear, pool-deep eyes. For once there was no laughter, no light teasing there; her expression was solemn, even sad. "No!" he exclaimed passionately. "For you are my woman, and the only woman in the world to me. Whatever comes after, I shall cleave to you, forsaking all others."

Audris knew the last few words were part of what the priest said to a bride and groom. She clasped Hugh's hand and said firmly, "And I to you, in sickness and in health, until death—"

Hugh wrenched his hand free and covered her mouth, knowing he could have and should have stopped her sooner. He had been paralyzed by the joy of hearing her give herself to him, but he could not let her finish making what she might believe a binding oath.

"Audris, dear and beloved Demoiselle," he murmured, taking his hand away and barely touching her lips with his in recompense for his seeming rejection. "You must not promise what circumstances might make impossible for you to perform."

"*You* swore," she said.

"My case is different," Hugh pointed out. "I am my own master, and it matters not at all whether or not there is issue of my body. Whatever I am, it is not a king's son or a great earl's, which would make my marriage a matter of state. I am free to swear my life and my soul to you, but you are not free. If your uncle ordered your marriage—"

"He will not," Audris broke in. "He would never force me. And what difference can it make whether or not I say the words aloud for you to hear? You can stop my tongue, but what is in my heart and mind is there already. I will never marry until—until I can have you, unicorn."

She had been about to say "until my uncle dies," but she could not force out those words. Up to this moment she had thought them often, and said them sometimes, with ease and freedom—because her uncle's life had been her protection, and she truly wished that he should live long, even outlive her. Now, suddenly, Oliver's life was an obstruction, a firm wall between her and Hugh. But Oliver had *given* her her life—only a little neglect would have disposed of the babe that had come into his hands—and he had cared for her for over twenty-three years. Could she wish him dead now, just because she had found a man she desired?

"You must not say such things. There is *no* chance that I would be acceptable to your uncle."

But Hugh was only saying words demanded by his strong conscience. Inside him was a growing determination to have this woman who set him afire body and soul. Others had won great estates by the strength of their arms. He knew his ability as a fighter. What he had lacked had been a reason to fight. Fortunately, he had taken the first step; he was Sir Hugh. The next must be to establish himself as nobly born, if possible. Hugh did not doubt that there would be lands and honors enough changing hands in England and elsewhere. Rebellion was brewing all over. If Audris was right about her uncle—and she might be, Hugh thought, for he was not unaware that Audris's husband must supplant Sir Oliver—he might win enough land to make him a suitable match. He could sweeten the pot, too, by offering to take Audris to *his* lands and letting Oliver remain in Jernaeve. It was Audris he wanted, not the castle.

The grim expression that had formed on Hugh's face as he made his decision alarmed Audris. "I will say nothing to my uncle of how I feel, and he will not ask," she assured him, but then she added passionately, "And I will never marry. I want you and none other. Hugh, please…"

She was not sure for what she was pleading, only that Hugh's face had become hard, the brilliant blue of his eyes suddenly seemed as cold as the blue of deep ice, and he seemed to be slipping away. But when she spoke, his expression changed at once to concern and tenderness, and he took her in his arms.

"You need not say 'please' to me," he murmured. "You have only to tell me what you want, and you will have it."

Relief brought Audris's lighthearted mischief bubbling up. "Even if I ask for the moon?"

But Hugh did not laugh as she expected. He loosened his grip and drew back just enough so she could see his face and he hers. "I would try, Audris," he said very soberly. "I would die trying, even though I knew what you asked was impossible to achieve."

He had meant to reassure her, to say without actually saying the words that he would strive up to and including the giving of his life to make himself fit to ask for her in marriage. But Audris shuddered and pulled herself tight against him, burying her face in his chest.

"I want you, only you," she cried.

"Yes, beloved Demoiselle." He tightened his arms, trying to give her comfort. "I hear and understand."

Instead of comfort the words sent a chill of terror through Audris, and she lifted her head, her eyes wide with fear. Hugh answered in the only way he could; since his words seemed only to add to her unhappiness, he offered his lips. He had intended a brief touch, but Audris locked her arms around his neck and clung to him.

Hugh was torn apart between guilt and desire. He realized that he had done a grave wrong in showing his admiration so openly when they had first met, but he had thought then that he was unlikely to see Audris again for many years, perhaps never. It had not occurred to him at the time that she would even remember him, except dimly as Bruno's friend. What had passed between them when he came to beg lodging for Thurstan's men had been more to blame, perhaps, but it was as if he were being carried along by an irresistible force. In any case, it was too late, he thought, as his tongue stole out between his lips to invade Audris's mouth. She had remembered, as vividly as he had, and longed and desired as he had.

Carefully, with his mouth still bound to hers, Hugh eased them down on the blanket so that they lay side by side but with Audris almost atop him. He pillowed her head on one upper arm, bending his elbow so that he could touch her ear and throat. His free hand stroked her body from breast to hip. Although she shivered from time to time, little by little the frantic grip around his neck relaxed. Audris's lips had parted when his tongue came seeking, had closed around it, parted again; now Hugh's tongue touched her teeth and slipped between them. She shivered more violently, and suddenly let go of his neck completely to slide her hand down his body. She found what she sought unerringly, laid her hand quietly over it, and then stroked upward. Hugh had to free his mouth to gasp air. He caught her hand and held it away from him.

"It is too dangerous, Audris," he said thickly, pressing quick kisses to her chin and cheeks between the words.

"Dangerous?" She sounded as if she had never heard the word before.

"Think, beloved," Hugh said. "What if you were to get with child? Think!"

She drew back and stared, then her fair brows drew together. "Why do you speak as if that were a dreadful thing? To me it would be a great joy, the greatest joy. To have your child—"

"Out of wedlock!" Hugh interrupted bitterly. "Do you think I could bear that my son live as I have? As Bruno has?"

"But he would not!" Audris cried. "I think if I had a child, my uncle would agree to my marriage with the father."

She said it only to soothe Hugh. Although she felt sure her uncle would yield and let her marry the man who fathered her child, she was not sure she could ask it of him—even for Hugh. But the thought of having a child, Hugh's child, was a joy that drove her more forcefully than the demands of her body. Her only regret about the decision never to marry while her uncle lived was that she might be too old to have a child by the time she was free to marry.

"More likely he would kill me for so dishonorable an act," Hugh muttered. "And I would not blame him nor raise a hand to defend myself."

Audris stroked his face. "Uncle Oliver would know it was my doing as much as yours."

"Audris, you are mad! Even if what you say is true, we cannot take such a chance. What if some ill befell me before I could return?"

"In wedlock or out of wedlock, there could be no doubt the child was mine," Audris said stubbornly. "My child could not suffer the same fate as Bruno. My father did not recognize him, would not accept him, because his mother was a whore. My uncle could not deny my child—and who is to say it would be a son? Perhaps I would have a girl-child—"

"Audris!" Hugh interrupted again, rather despairingly, for her whole face had lit with joy.

"Uncle Oliver would not like it," she went on as if Hugh had not spoken, "but he would protect my child, and if—if he grew too old or—or died, I would call Bruno back, and he would stand by me."

Hugh pulled away from her completely. "No, Audris. No. I cannot—"

"Am I to have nothing?" she cried. "Do you think I did not understand you when you warned me that ill might befall you and said you would struggle to the death to get me the moon?" Tears rose in her eyes and spilled over. "I desire you! I desire your child! We harm no one by what we do, no one!"

It was true, Hugh thought, surprised. He had been thinking of Audris as he had been trained to think of any nobleman's daughter—as her father's possession to be used in marriage to make an advantageous alliance. To make such a girl desire him so that she would resist her father's will, to take her maidenhead so that she would be less valuable as a marriage prize, would be stealing from her father as literally as taking his purse. But Sir Oliver had no such purpose for Audris and probably would prefer that she did not marry. If Oliver had wanted her married, he would have arranged for a husband years ago. And there was only a small chance she would conceive a child. Some women tried and prayed for years without success. Her words "Am I to have nothing?" rang in his own heart, too. When he left Jernaeve he would complete his duty to Thurstan and then set out to win an estate. If he should die in that attempt, his memories and Audris's would be bitter and incomplete.

Hugh did not answer in words, but sat up and undid his cloak and laid it aside, then pulled off his tunic and shirt. The air was chilly for a moment because he had been too warm without realizing it, and his body was damp with sweat. The mist had cleared while he and Audris were talking, the sun struck full into the sheltered hollow, and he was soon adjusted. Hugh was aware of movement beside him, but did not dare look to see what Audris was doing until cloth brushed his arm and her riding dress fell half over his lap in a crumpled heap. Then he turned.

She was standing, reaching down to grip her shift so she could pull it off, but her eyes were on him and she seemed to have forgotten what she was about. Hugh smiled at her, took one of her hands and set it on his shoulder, then lifted first one foot and then another to pull off her shoes and stockings. He stroked her legs, shapely and hard muscled from climbing, then sighed deeply and bent down to kiss her feet.

When Hugh sat up without replying to her plea, Audris had closed her eyes over her tears, but when she opened them again it was to see his tunic being pulled over his head. A spurt of joy lifted her to her feet and lent her fingers agility in undoing laces, but by the time she had dropped her riding dress, Hugh's upper body was bare. It drew her eyes, and they caressed the swelling muscles of shoulder and arm, the flat, powerful bands across chest and back. Warmth stirred in her, laced by spikes of cold, for here and there were scars—ugly, puckered lines of dead white tissue and a few still angry pink, which stood out boldly against Hugh's fair skin. The cold spikes of fear only added urgency to the growing heat of passion until Audris was bemused by the turmoil in her body.

Placing her hand on his shoulder made the sensations more intense, and the removal of her shoes and stockings sent pulsing waves, like cramps but exquisitely pleasurable, across her thighs and belly. Then Hugh bent down and kissed her feet, taking away the support that had held her upright. Her knees gave way; she would have fallen except that her hand, elbow locked, still gripped Hugh's shoulder. As he bent, she began to tip forward, but his head came up, and his hands gripped her waist and eased her down so she was on her knees before him. Then slowly, as if he wished to give her time to stop him, Hugh lifted off her shift. He did not turn his head as he laid it aside but bent forward and took her nipple in his mouth.

Audris uttered a choked, wordless cry, and her fingers tightened on his shoulder until her nails bit into his flesh. Her other hand came up to press his head closer, but what she felt was already perfect. She needed more. There seemed to be a hungry emptiness between her thighs, and memory displayed the image of what she needed. Her hand fluttered away from Hugh's head, touched his arm, then slid across to his chest, where her fingers stroked his skin, reaching steadily lower until they came to the tie of his chausses. She plucked at it blindly, and Hugh sighed and released her breast. Crying out softly again, this time in protest, Audris brought both hands to his head to redirect his attention.

"Hush, hush," he murmured, and lifted her bodily so he could lay her down.

She clutched at him, fearing in her unreasoning need that he would leave her unsatisfied, but he kissed first one breast and then the other, and dimly she realized that he was struggling to undress himself. Although she still held him with one arm, the other followed his hand as he pushed the chausses down over his hips. Her fingers struck the curly hair and then the hot flesh of his shaft. Hugh shuddered and groaned softly as she slid her hand down and then up. He seized on a nipple again, simultaneously laying his hand over her mount of Venus and probing inward. Audris would have screamed with excitement, except that her breath was caught in her throat. Without realizing what she was doing, she tried to close her legs over his hand and drive it deeper. It was wrong. It was not enough. Audris was far beyond any capacity to think, but she knew what she wanted. She used the arm she had wrapped around his back to pull him over her, even pulling gently with the other hand.

For only a moment Hugh resisted. He had never in his life been so intensely excited nor handled a woman as he was doing with Audris, and he did not want to stop. His past couplings had nothing to do with the woman he used, being solely a result of a need to relieve his sexual tension; he had desired only to satisfy the animal urge, to be rid of it as quickly as possible, and then confess his sin and cleanse himself. His total commitment to Audris had wiped out the guilt and shame that had been mingled with his earlier sexual experiences, resulting in an intensity of pleasure he had never imagined possible. Moreover, Hugh had never seen a body so much his notion of perfection as Audris's. More than he wanted to take her, he wanted to caress—to touch, kiss, fondle—that perfect beauty.

Not only perfect, but pure, for to Hugh, Audris looked virginal. Her skin was white without any hint of sickliness in its pallor, for it was so delicate that a faint rosy flush from the flesh beneath tinted it, and here and there a pale-blue network of thin veins marked it like lace. Her breasts were full but not large, with small nipples and aureoles a light, rich pink. And the curls that peeped from under her arms and crowned her mound of Venus were pure, pale gold. He felt her pull, but he had not yet kissed those golden curls or the moist lips they hid. Insanely, Hugh felt he wanted a dozen heads and a hundred hands with which to kiss and suck and touch.

Then Audris pulled at him again, thrusting her hips upward toward his hand, and the sensuous movement brought an urgent peak to his desire. He turned and lifted himself over her, placing his hand over hers to position himself to thrust. But her hand was so small in his grasp, and she almost seemed to have disappeared under his bulk; Hugh hesitated, but Audris lifted herself toward him, and the head of his shaft, swollen to bursting, slid between her thighs and into the moist opening ready to receive it. Still, fear for her had tempered Hugh's driving need, and he pressed forward gently. Audris gasped. He stopped and began to pull back, but her arms slid around his back, and her legs came up around his thighs and held him.

"More," she gasped.

"I will hurt you," he whispered.

"I do not care!" she cried.

He had hurt her already, but Audris was wild with excitement, and the pain mingled with the pulsing heat and need and seemed to increase it. There was a gaping hollow in her that must be filled, whatever the cost, and she tensed her legs and lifted her hips to drive him down into her. Hugh plunged.

Audris felt she would tear apart, but at the same time there was a blessed fulfillment, and then as he pulled back he tilted to one side, took her breast in his hand, and ran his thumb back and forth over the nipple. The sensation flooded over, down into the hollow that ached and throbbed with pleasure. Audris heaved again, and the pain/pleasure grew and grew and grew, making her thrust up harder and faster each time Hugh drew back, until a convulsion of joyful agony burst so violently that she had to scream aloud.

Hugh heard her, but he had reached a point at which all outer awareness had no meaning. His rod felt large as a tree trunk and as if it had been filled with burning pitch—and each thrust pumped more and more, hotter and hotter substance into him. He had to burst—he had to, and yet he knew there was some compelling reason why he must not, and he fought to hold back that bursting. A moment or two after she cried out, Audris's body relaxed under him. There was no place for thought in the maelstrom that was Hugh's mind and body, but her stillness *was* the signal he had awaited. With a groan of release, he thrust once more, his seed springing from him in a hot torrent, and then again and again, sobbing softly with pleasure as he emptied himself.

Release brought Hugh back to rationality, and in a moment terror had replaced passion; Audris was lying too still under him. The fear lent strength to his trembling arms, for he felt weaker than after a hard battle in which he had been wounded. Desperately, he pushed himself up and to the side. Audris's eyes were closed. Holding his breath, Hugh laid his hand on her breast to feel for her heart. Instantly, her eyes snapped open.

"Just give me time to catch my breath, Hugh."

He flopped over on his back, breathing out in a long sigh of mingled relief and exhaustion; nonetheless, it came to him that Audris's remark was very peculiar.

"What do you mean, give you time to catch your breath?" he asked. "Do you think I want to run races?"

"I thought you wished to couple again," she said, turning to look at him. "I am very willing, but—"

"Couple again!" Hugh exclaimed weakly. "I can barely lift a finger, let alone that part of me necessary for coupling."

"I am afraid I am very ignorant," Audris admitted, smiling. "I was never interested before, so I did not ask. And when you put your hand on my breast, I thought—"

"I was feeling for your heart," Hugh interrupted. "I thought I had *killed* you—crushed you or smothered you. I heard you scream but—"

Audris laughed. "I am not nearly so fragile as you think, but you are not far wrong at that. I felt as if I were passing through purgatory and then reached heaven."

"What?"

"Have I shocked you?" Audris asked. "I am sorry. I often have strange thoughts. I assure you I did not mean to be blasphemous, but once I asked Father Anselm about the pain of purgatory and why it was different from hell. He explained that pain in purgatory was mingled with great pleasure because it lifted one into blessedness. I know the joy of the body is only a pale echo of the joy of the spirit—but I am in the body now."

"And the joy of the body is transient, and that of the spirit everlasting," Hugh said, making an effort and propping himself up on his elbow. Audris was beginning to regret that she had brought up the religious analogy when suddenly he winked and added, "But transient joys may be renewed—as often as one pleases."

Chapter 13

AUDRIS CLIMBED NO TREES OR CLIFFS THAT DAY, AND OLIVER assumed from her silence on the subject of hawks that his plan had been successful; doubtless Sir Hugh had expressed his shock at the idea, and Audris, sweet-tempered as she was, had given up the notion rather than distress her guest. He said nothing to Audris—it was not his way to compliment a woman on her obedience, because he expected obedience—but when she had gone up to her chamber, he said he hoped Hugh would continue to ride out with her.

Fortunately it was very dim in the hall, for dusk was falling and the torches and candelabra had not been lit. It seemed a useless waste to Oliver to light candles or torches on spring or summer evenings, since it was time for those who rose at dawn to be abed as soon as it was too dark to see by daylight. He found sufficient illumination in the light of the fire, still necessary because the thick stone walls of the keep held winter within all year. Thus, he did not see the flush that came up in Hugh's face, and he accepted without surprise the silent nod that answered him.

Oliver had never cared much for the company of women, and he would not have been enthusiastic either if he had been condemned by his host to a week of a woman's chatter. Audris was more amusing than most girls, but all day for a whole week! Oliver clapped a sympathetic hand on Hugh's shoulder and spoke somewhat apologetically about the tasks that kept him busy. He felt a little guilty, but what was important to him was that Audris be kept off the cliffs until the rocks loosened by winter's freezing had fallen or resettled firmly. Hugh would have to endure his boredom as best he could. But in compensation, Oliver did try to provide some entertaining conversation, raising questions about hunting and fighting he thought would interest Hugh.

Eadyth felt even sorrier for Hugh, for she interpreted his silence as pain. It seemed cruel to force him into Audris's company, but she had warned him and Audris and could do no more. And from what she had seen that morning and this evening, Audris had taken the warning to heart. The girl had shown none of her light playfulness, and her early retreat to her own chamber was an overt sign that she did not seek more of her guest's company than politeness demanded.

Oddly, neither Hugh's nor Audris's behavior had been planned in advance. They had spent the whole day in Audris's valley and in the wooded areas of the low hills that hedged it in. Fritha had been summoned from beyond the ridge and settled near the stream with the horses while Hugh and Audris wandered about afoot. Sometimes both had sat silent, watching some small animal go about its simple life; more often they talked—about great matters of state and about small ones of their own lives. At all times, both were utterly content. They had an urge to touch, but walking hand in hand or sitting close was sufficient to satisfy the desire; beneath it, both were aware, lay a wilder, stronger passion, and that gave richness to every other thing they said and did, but passion did not torment them—not yet.

The one subject they did not discuss was what they would say and do when they returned to Jernaeve. Although for different reasons, neither could bear to lie to Oliver, and both had privately decided on silence as the only possible defense. Thus, Hugh was not at all surprised when Audris retreated to her tower; he was very grateful to her. And though ordinarily Audris was sharply perceptive about people—and more perceptive about Hugh than others because of her feeling for him—this time she had not been consciously aware of how he felt. She had responded solely to the urge to weave. She knew she had to complete the second tapestry before Hugh left.

It was fortunate that the soft thud of the comb beating down the woof could not carry through the tower walls; Oliver and Eadyth would have been worried sick if they had heard, because Audris wove far into the night. Fritha watched and smiled, for peace and joy were in her lady's face, her dear lady, who was now a woman. Fritha was right. The need to be Hugh's woman came even before the need to weave, so each day was spent with Hugh.

On the next day Audris did climb the cliff, Hugh's horror conquered by her laughter and assurances that if he would not help her, she would do it alone as soon as he was gone. At least she would be safe from serious harm if he was above holding a rope—but watching her go down was a strange experience. Hugh was ravished by the dichotomy between Audris's delicacy of appearance and her real strength as, skirts bound up out of her way, her face no longer pale and translucent but vibrant and bright pink with exertion and excitement, she crept down the face of jagged broken rock.

The falcon, having left the nest when Audris started down, circled above, screaming and diving to drive away the invader. Audris ignored her, leaned perilously sideways to peer into the nest, straightened, and began to climb up again, Her hands and legs must be as strong as steel, Hugh thought, and a memory of those legs embracing him as they coupled made him hard and ready.

So they made love as soon as she climbed back up, and if Audris was surprised by the way Hugh seized on her, still she did not suffer for it. He was eager to begin, not eager to end, and took time to kiss her golden curls and nether lips as well as most of the rest of her body before, remembering how he feared he had crushed her, he made her mount him.

Both were curious and eager to please the other, so the act of love became easier and more precious each day as they learned each other's body. But every evening Audris went eagerly to her weaving, and between Audris's need to finish her tapestry and Oliver's wish to make up to Hugh for a day of a woman's talk about nonsense, no suspicion of the love affair troubled Audris's guardians. All was perfect—except the march of time; the week came to an end.

That parting was hard and bitter. Hugh knew he would not be able to seem indifferent on the last evening, so he told Sir Oliver that he would leave in the morning to give him time to talk with Thurstan and discover if there had been changes in the plans and to buy supplies and attend to any other details. Rather than leave his host in doubt about when or whether he would return, Hugh said, he would sleep at the abbey. Oliver nodded without comment, thinking Hugh had had all he could take of female company. Oliver did not care; he had gained his purpose anyway. He had reports that the cliffs were as safe as they ever could be.

Neither Oliver nor Eadyth gave Hugh another thought beyond the brief surprise each felt on learning that he had departed at first light, as soon as there were servants awake to close the keep door behind him. They did not even notice that Audris had left Jernaeve; it was a gray day, threatening rain, and both thought she had kept to her chamber, as she often did, particularly as each caught a glimpse of Fritha carrying food to the tower. But this time Audris and Hugh had made a plan to have their last few precious hours all to themselves.

When Hugh left, he took his baggage mule, which carried not only his clothing and armor but his small, weatherworn tent. This he had set up by the time Audris arrived in the little flat area above her valley, and he had brought Rufus and the mule down to the stream, unsaddled Rufus and unloaded the mule, and tethered them there. When Audris came, Hugh unsaddled her mare and tethered her with the others. Then he turned to Audris, and they clung together for a moment without words and then, hand in hand, climbed up the slope to the shelter Hugh had provided.

Altogether it was a silent day, given over to the physical expressions of love. Over the past week they had mostly made love like playing, according to place and mood but, except for that first time, with no great sense of urgency. There had been equal joy in finding so many interests in common and in speaking freely of the deepest feelings each had. This last day both feared to speak at all lest their pain be magnified by words.

Once Audris began to beg Hugh not to put himself at risk to win a heritage, and he had stopped her. Later he had started to explain that his plan was not inspired by greed but because he wanted and needed to be with her, as only a husband could be, all the time. He could not bear, he said, to steal a little love for a day or two once or twice a year.

She had stopped him then, stricken to the heart because all his struggle—even if he was successful—would be useless; she could never marry and drive her uncle out of Jernaeve. So they made love and then lay silent in one another's arms, clinging together for comfort until the gentle kisses and caresses turned fiercer and they made love again.

It was Audris who needed comfort most. Not that Hugh suffered less at the idea of their parting, but he had hope. He was confident of his strength and his ability, and he was sure that some chance would arise for him to distinguish himself enough to earn an estate. He now knew, too, that Audris did not need or crave the luxury in which she lived. For all her diminutive size and fragile appearance, Hugh had come to realize she was strong and hardy. Nor was she bound to Jernaeve as a special place. Give her a loom, a garden, and a wild countryside, and she would be happy. Thus, he was sure he could win permission to marry Audris by offering Oliver the rule of Jernaeve until he died or desired to be relieved of the burden.

Because Audris had not let him speak of the hopes that she feared would cost him his life, she was denied the comfort of his plan to take her and leave Jernaeve to her uncle. Such a notion had never occurred to her. She had for so many years associated her marriage with the transfer of power over Jernaeve that it had become as fixed into her mind as the keep was to its hill. Thus, the future was bleak indeed to her, at best a choice of refusing her lover or destroying her uncle; at worst the knowledge that Hugh had died trying to win her and that she had lost him forever. The agony of those thoughts came in waves, and when one hit, Audris hardly let Hugh breathe for smothering him with kisses, and she clutched him so close that, as strong as he was, he grunted with surprise and discomfort.

No matter that the cloudy sky and intermittent rain hid the sun and that Audris insisted they keep the tent tightly closed to further obscure the waning of the day, the time still passed. Audris pleaded to stay the night, but Hugh would not permit it. He knew Audris claimed she had no cause to fear her uncle, but Hugh believed Oliver's seeming gentleness was because Audris had never given him cause to use her harshly. And even if Oliver were more forbearing to Audris than Hugh judged to be usual for his nature, any forbearance would be strained by a confession of where she had been and what she had done. But Hugh was too wise to give that reason.

"No, beloved," he said. "For this one night might cost us all other meetings. What will you say to your uncle when he asks where you were? You cannot lie, and to tell the truth would seal Jernaeve against me. Come, dress yourself, dearling—and do not weep, breath of my life. Let me not bear the pain of having tears be my last memory of you."

That stopped her pleading, and she hastily wiped away the drops that had begun to course down her cheeks, childishly, with the heel of her hand.

Hugh smiled at her. "In any case, my silly angel, it is too soon for tears. Thurstan will return by this same road, I believe. It is true that he may not wish to rest at Hexham again, but we will surely spend one night in the abbey. Do you think I would fail to pay your uncle the courtesy of riding to Jernaeve and telling him of King David's decision? So, you see, we will not be parted for long. Perhaps I will not hold you in my arms again that day, but great as that joy is to me, it is greater joy only to look on you and hear your voice and know within my heart that you are mine."

"True, true," Audris cried, smiling, although tears still stood in her eyes. "And I have just thought that we may speak together even though our bodies are parted."

"Speak—how?"

Hugh was startled. Audris had told him about the seeming

foreseeing of her tapestries and how Father Anselm had explained what she did. He had accepted the explanation more easily than others would because, being much interested in animals, he had himself noted some of the signs she described. But he had also noted how the common folk with whom they came in contact gazed at her with superstitious awe, and this sudden mention of speaking to each other while physically separated sent a chill through him.

"We can both read and write—" Audris began, and Hugh burst out laughing and caught her into his arms.

Only Audris would have described an exchange of letters as "speaking together when parted." It must be more than half her trouble, he thought, that people did not understand her.

"Why do you laugh?" Audris asked. "You can write to me and I to you, and my uncle will not think it strange, for I will tell him I asked you to send us the news of what happened between King David and the archbishop and also how you judge the temper of the Scots and all such matters." She hesitated, but Hugh's face was buried in her hair as he kissed her neck and ear and lower jaw, and she asked anxiously, "Is that not a good notion?"

"It is the best notion I have heard since your uncle bade me ride with you," Hugh assured her, still holding her and kissing her between words. "I was only laughing because you say simple things in strange ways, and you startled me." He pulled away enough to look at her face for a long moment, then leaned forward and kissed her lips, long and gently. When he freed his mouth, he sighed and released her. "I will go down and saddle your mare, Audris, and bring her up to you. Dress now, dearling. You must be home before dusk."

This time Audris nodded obediently and let him go so he could dress. A great weight of fear had been lifted from her. She would see Hugh again, even if only briefly, but far more important, she would not be left in ignorance for months and years at a time of what was happening to him. That fear had hung over her like a black pall, knowing that Hugh could die and she might not know of it for years or, worse, that he could be lying ill and she would be unaware of it. When

Hugh came back with her mare, Audris was standing on the easy slope of the hill beyond the flat area, ready to leave, and though she was sad, the agony that made her cling to him with the strength of a madwoman was gone.

"This letter writing," she said, "I have thought how it may be most easily done. You have no servant. I will provide one for you. He will go to Hexham with your men in the morning."

"I cannot afford a servant," Hugh said, frowning. "Do not trouble yourself. I can send one of Thurstan's men with the letters."

"The servant will cost nothing beyond food for him and fodder for his horse," Audris replied softly. "Is that too much?" She put her hand on his arm. "I do not wish the letters to stop when you have brought Thurstan back to York. I must know what you discovered about your mother at Durham and how you fare in all things." She saw he was about to protest and shook her head. "Remember what I said to you about your mother's kin—that someone who cared for her, not knowing she was at rest, might have feared and wept all these years, either thinking that a fate worse than death might have overtaken her or that she had forgotten the poor, grieving heart left behind."

"You *cannot* think I would forget you," Hugh said, pulling her close. "By God and His Holy Mother and by all His saints, you are wife to me and the only woman I will ever desire or touch from this time forward. But it is true that, reasonable or not, if you care for me you will worry about me, and a servant from Jernaeve will best know the way home. But what will you say to your uncle?"

"The man in my mind is not a household serf. Morel is a yeoman who has served several times as a man-at-arms in my uncle's troop when he was called by the king to war. Now his sons are grown and married, there are too many in the house, and his wife died, leaving him restless. I know him through his wife. She did the finest spinning of any woman near Jernaeve and spun yarn for my weaving. When she sickened, I tried to help her, but I could only ease her pain. It was then I came to know Morel. He is a good man, Hugh. He was patient and gentle with his woman all the months that she was helpless and useless—which is not so common among those where a useless mouth to feed is a burden. But since she is gone and his sons do not need him, he longs for freedom."

Hugh nodded. The man sounded ideal, for he had enough knowledge of arms that he could care for Hugh's weapons and armor and would not need protection. Better still, he was not an adventuresome boy who would get into trouble nor, like most older men, did he have a wife and children to whom he was eager to return. He could not be too old, either; when Audris had time to think, she thought very keenly.

"Thank you," Hugh said simply. "As to pay—"

"Morel believes he owes me a debt, and I am letting him pay by doing something he wishes to do. I will see that he has a good cloak and extra clothes, suitable to a knight's servant. You will provide food and shelter, and pay what you can when you can. He will be content, I promise you."

Hugh nodded, stood staring at her for a moment longer, and then abruptly bent and cupped his hands to help her mount. When she was seated, Audris leaned down from the saddle for one last kiss, then loosened her reins and touched the mare with her heel. At the crest of the hill she turned to look back. Hugh was standing where she left him, watching her. Audris's heart cried out to turn back for one more kiss, one last word, but she had thought that through while dressing and seen that the indulgence would only pile pain on pain. So she went down the hill, crying bitterly now that Hugh could not see her. At the foot of the hill she turned again, only to look at the land that hid her love—but Hugh was there. He had climbed to the crest and now stood there, still watching her.

Feeling her rider's uncertainty, the mare stopped, and Audris looked longingly at the tall figure on the hill, hoping, despite the knowledge of more pain, that he would call or beckon. He only watched, and at last Audris turned the mare's head toward Jernaeve again, tasting the salt as tears ran down and wet her lips. One last time she turned before a copse of trees that would hide the hill from her altogether.

It was almost too far to make out any distinct feature clearly, but a low-lying bank of clouds in the west opened a rift that showed the sun, and it seemed to Audris there was a flicker of red, bright as a jewel, on the crest of the hill. So Hugh still watched. She waited, looking back at that small fleck of color until the clouds closed in again. Then she rode on.

By the time she came to the village where Morel lived, Audris had composed herself. She had expected him to be out in the fields, since the spring was a busy time for those who tilled the soil, and most men worked until it was too dark to see well. So she called at the door of the house for his daughter-by-marriage to fetch him home. The woman came out and told her Morel was in the shed at the back with his horse, and though she bowed to the ground and could scarcely get out the words for fear of offending Audris, there were bitter lines around her mouth when she said "horse," and she did not offer to call him herself.

Somewhat surprised, Audris rode her mare around and saw Morel currying his mount, which did not need the attention, for the beast's coat already gleamed with combing. Audris's sadness lifted a little as she realized that her need and Morel's were so well matched. She needed a trusty man with no home ties; Morel needed to leave his home, at least for a time. The horse was Morel's pride, a prize of the last campaign he had fought in her uncle's troop. He was the only man in his village to own a horse; that much Audris knew. What she suspected was that Morel refused to put the horse to the plow since they had a cow that could be used, and thus the horse, which was expensive to feed, had become a bone of contention in the family. And when Audris spoke his name, he was so buried in his thoughts that he did not look before he growled, "Let me be," as he turned around with a hand raised threateningly as if to strike. He saw Audris, and his eyes went wide; then he dropped the comb and went down on his knees.

"Forgive me, Demoiselle."

"I have taken no hurt," she answered soothingly, "but I see that all is not well with you."

Morel looked up at her with frightened eyes. How could

she know, he wondered. Because he was a brave man, he did not shiver, and he had seen how kind she could be, troubling to come each day to bring medicine for his wife toward the end. The Demoiselle was good, but it was still a fearful thing that she could see into men's hearts. But he did not speak, and Audris continued.

"I have a task for you that will solve your trouble, I think." And though she was still too sad to smile, it did her good to see the fear die out of Morel's face and the man's eyes light as she told him who Hugh was and the service Morel would be expected to give.

"I will serve him faithfully, I swear to you," Morel promised fervently.

"I am sure you will," Audris said, "but there is one thing you must do for *me*. If Sir Hugh should fall ill or be wounded, you must somehow send me word and a guide to come to him. Only if he is in safe hands may you come yourself. And this you must do even if your master orders you *not* to tell me of his hurt or illness."

"I understand, Demoiselle." Morel bowed deeply.

"Come to the keep with what you need before the gates are closed. The soldiers will leave at dawn. Sometime tonight Fritha will bring you clothes suitable to the service of a knight. She will also give you a purse with fifteen shillings. Of this, ten is your pay. The other five must be kept close to use in case *you* need to hire a messenger or provide for your master's comfort."

Morel only bowed again, mingled joy and fear making him afraid even to acknowledge his charge. He could have left the village at any time, since he was a free man, not bound to the soil like a serf. But to be a lordless man, a wanderer without purpose, was a blood-chilling prospect. Such a person, harmless or not, was always the scapegoat for any crime or trouble in any place he stopped, and even if there were no trouble, would always be suspect or unwelcome. To be a knight's servant, on the other hand, was an honorable state. Thus, Morel was filled with joy, being granted what his heart ached for. However, that the knight was so valuable in the Demoiselle's eyes was frightening. True, she had not charged him with Sir Hugh's health and safety, but would she blame him all the same if ill befell his master?

Audris saw both joy and fear and was content. She felt that Hugh and Morel would agree well and that Morel would soon serve Hugh as much because of his own fondness for his master as because of her orders, but his devotion would be all the deeper for that little spice of fear. Satisfied that Hugh would not go all alone when he left Thurstan's company, she rode back to Jernaeve, stabled her mare, and slipped up to her tower.

Fritha greeted her with frantic signals of relief, but Audris hardly attended. She permitted the maid to remove her cloak, then ate the food Fritha had brought for her earlier. Finally, biting her lip, she went to the back of her loom and looked at the finished tapestry that hung there. For one moment she stared before beginning to sob with a combination of sorrow and relief.

There were no ugly surprises in her work. Serene and beautiful, the unicorn walked through a sunlit wood of graceful saplings with the arm of the maiden around his neck. Little white flowers, like stars, showed where the silver hooves had pressed the earth, and brilliantly colored birds perched in the branches of the trees. The maiden's face was turned toward that of the beast, who was looking at her also; only the curve of the maiden's cheek showed, but her hair was silver gilt under her veil, and the lambent blue of the unicorn's eyes was the same as those of his namesake.

Mechanically, Audris went about the task of freeing the tapestry from the loom. She knew the value of the work. It was so lovely that it pulled her eyes to it, but she could not yet pair it with the other picture—that of the unicorn greeting the maiden—and part with them. Audris frowned. It was not the beauty of the pieces or even the fact that in her mind the unicorn represented Hugh that held her back. There were more pictures to come. Audris shivered. There should be no more. There was no maiden to put in the picture. She who had been maiden was a full woman now.

Audris finished eating, quite unaware of the food or her own motions in consuming it. She could not keep her eyes from her empty loom, and the compulsion to bid Fritha string it finally became irresistible. Once she gave the order, Audris felt more at ease, although she was still troubled because she felt the paired panels were complete. She *wanted* the story to be ended with her and the unicorn together and at peace. Something plucked at what Audris thought of as a drawn curtain in her mind, but she did not want to see it, and she pushed away her food and went down to her aunt.

"I need a suit or two of clothes," Audris said. "I promised them to Sir Hugh for his servant."

Eadyth nodded; she was not surprised either by the request or that Audris had delayed until almost the last hour to mention it. No doubt something had reminded her niece that the men were about to depart in the morning, and that recalled her promise to her mind. As for making the promise, Eadyth knew Sir Hugh was only recently knighted and had no patrimony, and she was sure that Audris knew it too. It was like her niece to find some small way to help that would not give offense, so she merely asked about the servant's size.

"I have seen him," Audris replied. "It will be easier for me to choose the clothes myself."

That did not surprise Eadyth either. Audris was very erratic in the way her charity was distributed, though she was perfectly consistent in giving only to individuals rather than to the Church. Sometimes she would simply tell her aunt what she wanted done; sometimes she would attend to the giving herself with minute attention. Without asking why—Audris always answered her questions, but Eadyth seldom found herself the wiser and was often made uneasy by her niece's reply—Eadyth unhooked the keys to the clothes chest from her bunch and handed them over. For all her good nature and seeming carelessness, Audris was neither foolish nor overgenerous in her charities. Father Anselm had trained her carefully not only to judge the worth of the object but to understand that too much was almost worse than none at all.

Candles were alight when Audris returned to her chamber

with three pairs of chausses, two of undyed homespun and one of good dark-blue woolen cloth, and two tunics, one homespun and the other a rich maroon, all topped by a heavy, hooded woolen cloak. She saw that Fritha had made a good beginning on the warp, but was now peering close to see in the less adequate light. Stringing the loom could wait, Audris told herself. The weather promised fair for the next day, and she must spend it working in the garden, for she had lost a full week of the busy spring season.

A very faint smile touched her lips as memories of how that week had been lost—no, gained forever, with Hugh—flicked through her mind. But the smile faded as her eyes focused again on her maid. Fritha could finish warping tomorrow. Audris fought down the surge of discomfort the thought of delay roused in her. It was as senseless as the need to finish the second panel. That had shown no imminent tragedy that could be averted by timely action.

"Leave that for daylight, Fritha," she said, and became aware suddenly that her legs were trembling.

First, she was almost seized by panic, associating the tremors with her order to her maid, but the answering image that came into her mind was not of weaving; she saw herself locked in Hugh's embrace, coupling. A pang, as if she had been stabbed in the chest, stopped her breath at the vivid picture, but despite that, she was amused. It was no wonder her legs trembled; she was simply tired out. How often had she and Hugh joined their bodies? Was it five times? Six? She could not even remember, but did not doubt it was often enough to tire the sturdiest. Relief swept over her. She would go to sleep. Surely in the morning the strange fancy that she must begin a new tapestry would have departed with her fatigue.

"You may make me ready for bed," she said to the maid, who was putting away the materials with which she had been working. "Then go down to the lower bailey and look for Morel—you remember, the man whose wife I brought medicines until she died, the spinning woman." Fritha nodded. "Give him these clothes. I have bidden him go to serve Sir Hugh so that we may have a trusty messenger."

But the next morning, as soon as she woke, before she even got out of bed to relieve her bladder and bowels, Audris reminded Fritha that the loom had to be strung that day, and she ran up to her chamber again after breaking her fast to check that she had enough silver yarn. There would be enough blue, for blue was a color that appeared in almost every picture; but the silver, rare and costly, she used seldom and sparingly, usually to give a glint of life and light to eyes or to simulate moonlight.

Never before had she expended it so extravagantly as in the unicorn tapestries. Yet, when she opened the chest, she discovered a surprising store of it, pale gray strands of shining silk twisted together with a real metal thread to give the needed glitter. With a troubled frown Audris lifted several hanks from the chest. The silver yarn could not be spun locally; silk came from some unknown land far, far to the east and it traveled all across Europe before it reached England. Why had she bought so much? And when had she bought it?

The cost did not trouble her. Over the years there had been so much gain in the finished tapestries that her uncle never questioned how she came by the yarn she used, whether she ordered the women of the keep or villages to dye and spin thread for her or even went to market to buy it. He paid what she had promised—grain or cattle or wool or even coined money.

Then Audris remembered. A few years past, a merchant on his way to the court in Scotland had stopped in Jernaeve. He knew of the hawks in Sir Oliver's mews and wished to buy one. The silver yarn and other silks had been the price. The memory stilled the chill that had been rising in her. It would have been terrible indeed if she had been driven by a foreseeing she had not even recognized to buy the silver yarn. And then she closed her eyes and hugged herself as gooseflesh raised the hairs all over her body. This seeking out of the silver yarn was proof that the unicorn tapestries were not yet finished.

Chapter 14

HUGH WATCHED AUDRIS RIDE AWAY UNTIL SHE ENTERED THE wood and he knew he would see her no more. Then he turned and went back to the little ledge above the valley, sighing softly. The light seemed to fade from his life as he trudged down to his tent. The practical knowledge that the hill cut off what little light was left in the cloudy western sky had no effect at all on his emotional reaction to the increasing dimness. He almost wished the sun had not come out for those few minutes. The ray of light that slipped through the break in the clouds had caught Audris and enclosed her in a brilliant nimbus. That was a memory to treasure, but though it was too far to see Audris clearly, Hugh had seen from her mare's position that Audris was looking back and that she continued to look back until the sunlight was gone.

Her longing woke mixed emotions in him, all of them violent: a fierce if puzzled gladness that she, who could have any man she chose, should want him; a wrenching sorrow for her because he could not bear that she should be sad, even for him; and a determination, even fiercer than his gladness and stronger than his sorrow, that he would somehow make himself fit to marry her.

In the end the determination, and the exhaustion that followed much strong emotion and a full day of almost uninterrupted love play, overcame all other emotions. Since he could do nothing to forward the purpose of his determination, he thought with wry humor, it would be best to satisfy his other need. He would go to sleep. Hugh walked to the very edge of the flat area, turned his back to what wind there was, and urinated, looking contemplatively into the valley. Just below, his horse and mule grazed quietly; better still, at the far end of the valley, deer had come into the open. He shook the last drops free, went into his tent, rolled himself in his blanket, rested his head on his saddle, and was asleep before he had time to realize he had not eaten.

❧

Hugh was waiting, armed and ready for the road, at the abbey gate when his men rode up, and once he had determined that they were all there and all properly equipped—an easy task with this troop—he told them to dismount. As he turned Rufus toward the abbey gate, one rider came forward, hailed him respectfully, and introduced himself in soldier's argot as Morel, his servant. Hugh smiled at him, as much because the man was exactly what he had expected as to make him welcome.

Keen eyes, an indeterminate gray, but bright with interest, were examining Hugh, and, though Morel's hair was grizzled and his leather-skinned face lined, his arms, shoulders, and thighs were still rounded with muscles that had none of the stringiness of aging. And when Hugh smiled at him, the joy and enthusiasm of Morel's answering grin made Hugh glad he had agreed to Audris's plan. Clearly the man had embraced her order as a gift rather than a duty. Still, there was one doubt in Hugh's mind. Often Audris said things in a way that led to misunderstanding. Hugh wished to be sure Morel knew his service was likely to be unrewarded, except by gratitude.

"You are very welcome to me," Hugh said, "but I hope Demoiselle Audris warned you that I may not be able to pay you for your service."

"There be no need," Morel said, looking surprised. "I be paid already."

Hugh thought the man was referring to Audris's efforts to save his wife. "I understand, but I will give you what I can, and of course, table and bed are mine to supply." He saw that Morel was about to protest and gestured him to silence, adding, "I have one question more. Would you prefer to ride with the servants or the men-at-arms?"

"The men-at-arms, my lord," Morel replied, ducking his head in a kind of bow of thanks. "I be more used to their kind." He looked at Hugh hopefully. "I brought my arms with me. Be you willing for me to wear them?"

"Please yourself." Hugh had to laugh at the new light of pleasure in his servant's eyes. "I fear you are an old warhorse, Morel, more eager for a fight than for the pasture."

"Aye, my lord, it be true. While my wife lived and the young ones be little, I been afeared what would come to them if I died. I burned angry when Sir Oliver called me to arms. But now that fear be gone, and my seeming be that be the only time I *lived*—when I marched to war with Sir Oliver. It be not so much the fighting, though I minded it not, but seeing of new places and strange sights."

"You will see enough of those with me, I think."

But Hugh's grin was rather wry as he raised a hand in dismissal. He was rather the opposite of Morel. He had seen enough strange things and desired nothing so much as to settle in one place with Audris. But for the time being he was sure Audris was right; he and Morel would suit each other very well, and so strong and self-reliant a man would be the perfect messenger.

As he entered the abbey himself, Hugh was well content and thinking happily about writing Audris to tell her how much he liked her man. It then occurred to him that he could not say too much nor send Morel to Jernaeve too soon lest Oliver's suspicions be roused, but it was a shame that his first enthusiasm not be transmitted. And then he thought, why not? He could write a little each day—there could be two letters, one inside the other—so that Audris would live each day with him. The decision made him so happy that he was smiling from ear to ear when the lay brother conducted him into Thurstan's chamber.

"You look well, my son, and happy," Thurstan said.

"And I thank God that you look well and rested," Hugh replied, not actually responding to his foster father's remark.

Since Thurstan was accustomed to Hugh's constant concern about his health, he did not see anything unusual in his answer and merely asked if Hugh wished to eat.

"I thank you, Father, no. I have eaten already," Hugh replied.

He lowered his eyes as he spoke, the innocent question having sent a wave of longing for Audris through him, for he had broken his fast on the basket of food she had brought with her and which they had barely touched. The emotion, though brief, was so powerful that Hugh did not hear his own voice nor realize how his expression had changed. Thurstan looked at his foster son and then away, not wanting Hugh to know he had betrayed himself. He remembered that Hugh had said he had set his desire on a woman far above him. And because Thurstan had not wished to be thought prying—was that not a sin of pride?—he had not questioned Hugh further.

Although he made no sound, Thurstan groaned in spirit. The girl in question must live close—perhaps even in Jernaeve! And he had brought Hugh here, and... The self-accusatory thoughts hesitated. He had sinned, true, Thurstan thought, but that all things should fall together in such a way must be a God-guided event. Did He not know the fall of every sparrow? There was a reason, there must be! The guilt Thurstan felt magnified an earlier guilt. He was sure now that he had not *really* tried to discover who Hugh's mother was. He had not wanted to give Hugh up. And now it was too late—or was it? Could he feel God's purpose so strongly if there *was* no purpose?

Hugh's own emotion made him less aware that Thurstan had not replied, but as the silence stretched, he asked, "Are you ready to leave, my lord?"

"I have a short letter to write," the archbishop answered. "I will be ready by the time the wagons are loaded, but I will need a man to ride with the message."

Hugh nodded and went out, and Thurstan followed him but turned to the scriptorium, where he could borrow a quill and ink and some parchment. He did not want to waste time to order his own equipment unpacked. A desk was quickly vacated for his use, and Thurstan wrote to the abbess of the convent where Hugh had been born. He described the date and events of Hugh's birth and ordered that every nun who was alive and had been in the convent during the week that preceded Hugh's birth and the week that followed it be questioned and requestioned until every fact, no matter how minute, was uncovered.

The mother abbess, he added, was not to stop with her own convent but to write to any nun who had been there and who had moved to a daughter house or even to another convent and request a careful recounting. Restraining tears with difficulty, he now remembered that he had not asked what had happened to the woman's clothing and other possessions. How *could* he have failed to follow so obvious a clue? *Mea culpa,* he thought with a sigh as he added that a careful search should be made for any article of hers that might have been saved.

He wrote to the bishop of Durham, too, not explaining in such detail, but requesting his efforts to spur on the mother abbess's investigation. And oddly, once he had handed the letters over to the messenger, he found his guilt sat lightly on him. He recognized his sin intellectually, but "his heart knew it not." He would not scant confession nor expiation, but there was a growing conviction inside Thurstan that the sin was already forgiven because he had been meant to commit it.

In the courtyard, Hugh had no more time to regret his lost love. After the quiet days with Audris, the bedlam of packing was a strident call to duty. He stood for a moment, half stunned by the noise and rush, watching the servants run to and fro, picking and choosing from the piles of bags, bundles, and odd bits of furniture. The archbishop's great bed was already disassembled and in the lead cart, with his tall, exquisitely carven chair. Around the wooden pieces were the mattress, the cushions, and the featherbeds and, buffered by those, the chests of plate and other valuables.

Hugh saw a servant, mounted on the tail of the cart, ram a three-legged stool down and scream at a boy, who was trying to hand him another, to bring some of the lesser bundles instead. The boy shouted some reply that Hugh could not make out since it was in English, but it must have been impertinent because the man seized the second stool by one leg and flourished it threateningly. Thereupon the boy ran off and picked up a number of untidy blanket rolls and scurried back, but he was laughing, and though the man shook the stool at him, he took good care not to strike the boy with it.

Because it was expected of him, Hugh walked to the cart and prodded the larger pieces within reach, testing how much free movement they had. None shifted at all, and he spoke a few halting English words of praise for work well done. Unless the cart overturned, Hugh was sure that nothing would be shaken loose and fall by the wayside. The screeching and scolding and darting from one pile of stuff to another made the loading seem haphazard, but the archbishop's servants were experienced and efficient. Some had been with Thurstan for many years and had loaded and unloaded his goods thousands of times.

When Thurstan came out and was assisted into his saddle, Hugh led the baggage train out of the abbey gates and back toward Newcastle. They would meet the Roman road south of Corbridge. That road crossed the Tyne over a bridge, and Hugh estimated that the time lost in retracing their path would be more than compensated by the ease of passing the river and the superiority of the Roman road.

It was true that if they went due north from Hexham, they would save some three leagues, half a day's travel, but the archbishop and the baggage wains would have to cross the dangerous ford under Jernaeve. It was too likely there would be an accident—that was no ford for heavy carts, and Thurstan would be soaked—and Hugh did not think he could bear to pass Jernaeve. Audris, too, would suffer if she looked out from her tower when he went by. Or would she be watching for him and worry when she did not see the cortege?

In his mind, Hugh began to explain, as if he were writing to her, why he had to take the Roman road. He found comfort in it and recalled Audris's strange concept of talking together while they were parted. Perhaps it was not so strange after all. When he thought in terms of what he would write, he did not feel so far from her. It was then that he realized he had not the wherewithal to write. He had no reason to carry a supply of parchment and ink. If he wished to send a note to Sir Walter, he needed only to ask Thurstan for materials, but to need more parchment every few days would call for explanations Hugh did not wish to make.

He told Thurstan, who was riding silently beside him, that he had forgotten to ask about something and had to go back to Hexham and was away before his foster father could ask a question. Before the cortege had traveled a mile, Hugh was back with a thick roll of parchment and a dozen quills rolled in his blanket and a stoppered horn of ink in one saddlebag. He had also asked whether the monks had any news of traveling conditions or outlaws on the northern road. Thus, when Thurstan wanted to know what had sent Hugh galloping back, he repeated what he had been told—that the Roman road called Dere Street was sound as far as Byrness and a little beyond. Farther north, the road grew worse, but it was certainly passable as far as Jedburgh. And as for outlaws, they were fewer than usual, by report, because of the rumors that the Scottish army would be sweeping through that area.

Thurstan looked at him and asked dryly, "Do you think I am growing addled in my old age?"

"Of course not," Hugh replied.

"Then why did you ride back to ask questions that, unless I was in my dotage, I must have asked already?"

Hugh had the grace to drop his eyes, but he only said, "Father, it is my responsibility to know these things, and… ah… sometimes your attention is directed to more important matters than the condition of the roads—"

"There are certainly matters more important than the condition of the roads—but not when one is about to travel them," Thurstan interrupted, laughing. But he said no more. Whether Hugh had been trying to save him from embarrassment, as he had implied, or whether he had some private purpose he did not wish to divulge, Thurstan felt no need to pry. There could be nothing evil in anything Hugh did; and if he had a secret he wished to keep, Thurstan judged from Hugh's expression that it was a happy one.

They made a good distance that day, halting to eat just south of where the road breached the Roman wall, then going another eight miles, despite the rising ground, before the sun set and Hugh felt it was necessary to stop. The whole area seemed uninhabited, although one could see sheep on the hillsides and, when the woods grew close to the road, sometimes hear the gruntings of hogs in the shelter of the trees. Sheep and pigs notwithstanding, there was not a village or manor house anywhere close enough to seek shelter for the night. Thurstan brushed away Hugh's concern.

"I have slept in a tent before," he pointed out, "and to tell the truth, I think I would rather have my tent than a village inn's best bed." He smiled teasingly. "I have always preferred to sleep alone."

Hugh could not help laughing. "I must admit that I prefer the company I take to bed to be invited—and to have two legs."

That was the end of Hugh's protest. He was not much worried. They were still too near Corbridge to be in danger from outlaws, for the town would send out men to scour the area if the merchants coming and going made complaint of being robbed this close. Besides, the weather was warm, and although there had been a shower in the late afternoon, the clouds were now gone. Still, settling the archbishop safely in a campsite in the open was more work for Hugh than settling him in a keep or walled manor or even in a village inn. In a keep or manor he had no more to do than make polite conversation with his host if Thurstan were tired; in a village he had only to set a roster of guards to watch the valuables. Here, he was responsible for each detail of the camp. He chose a slight valley through which a lively stream ran and where the upward slopes were not heavily wooded.

The archbishop's tent must be in the safest and most defensible spot, for it would contain all they carried that was most precious—Thurstan himself and the chests of plate and treasure. Hugh marked the place as the center of the camp and had the wains drawn in to surround it. If necessary, the men could make a defensive stand behind them. His own tent would go outside the ring of carts and near the opening that permitted passage between them. The horses and mules needed protection, too. It was actually far more likely that a single thief or two would attempt to steal a few animals than that any large group would attack the camp.

Hugh chose a spot for the animals that would be open and easy to observe and was also down the slope from Thurstan's tent so that there was no chance their urine would run down and offend him. Normally, that was not a large consideration, for the wet just soaked into the ground, but the surface here was already moist—possibly only from the afternoon shower, but also possibly from a layer of damp peaty ground or rock below the topsoil, which would absorb little or nothing more.

Then there were the men's details: a group to cut fodder for the horses to supplement the grain that was carried for just such a situation, a group to fetch firewood, a group to start fires, a group to get water, cooks to be chosen and assigned, supplies to be distributed. Now and again an altercation that Hugh had to settle broke out between the servants, who felt their duties to be confined to the archbishop's comfort, and the men-at-arms, who deemed certain tasks demeaning—particularly when there were servants who could be made to do them.

Last of all, having seen the archbishop kneeling to say his evening prayers while his dinner cooked, Hugh went to set up his own tent. He would not have minded sleeping in the open, as most of the men and servants would, but he felt he should maintain a difference as the leader. To his delight, the tent was already up, his baggage stowed neatly in one corner, his saddle ready to serve as his pillow, his blankets laid out. He had forgotten Morel!

"Thank you," he said.

Morel looked surprised; after all, he had been paid to perform such services, and then he looked worried. "I would have started your dinner, my lord," he said hesitantly, "but there were no supplies, and—"

Hugh shook his head. "Just as well you did not. I forgot to tell you that I eat with the archbishop." He gestured toward Thurstan's tent. "You will take your meals with the men." He detected an expression of relief on Morel's face, and laughed. "You are not much of a cook, I suppose."

"No, my lord, I am not."

"Ah, well," Hugh sighed, still smiling, "one cannot have perfection. It will not matter on this journey, and we can hope that there will be inns along the way when we are parted from the archbishop's servants. In any case, I am prepared. Help me unarm, then light this candle for me—" Hugh took a thick wax candle from one of the saddlebags. "After that, you are free."

As soon as Morel was gone, Hugh extracted his writing materials and, after some difficulty in finding a flat, firm surface to write on, began to "talk" to Audris. He had not expected the keen pleasure he found in describing his day's duties and, more especially, his thoughts. For many years he had written to Thurstan because he knew his foster father cared about him and wished to know what he was doing—but somehow this was different. There was no constraint in what he could tell Audris—unless he were to write that he did not love her, and that would be impossible—because nothing he said would shock or disappoint her. To write to Audris was a pure joy—pleasure in the doing and a sure knowledge that he would delight the recipient. So each evening while they traveled slowly northwest, Hugh continued his letter.

When they arrived at Roxburgh, Hugh started a new sheet, on which he recorded the public events, and he added only a few lines to his private talks with Audris. "It is fortunate," he explained in the private letter after he had described the meeting between King David and Archbishop Thurstan in the one for Sir Oliver, "that most of my time is occupied. Had I been free to write as much as I desired to write to you, I would have needed to beg or buy more parchment at every religious house and town, and then to obtain a second baggage mule to carry the scrolls. Even now I am stealing time to write to you from judging how the house the king has assigned to us may best be defended. But you must not think much ill of me for it. Truly I feel that the archbishop is regarded by the king with veneration and even with love and that Thurstan is perfectly safe here."

It was true that the archbishop was safe; no one would dare harm him directly, but he was not loved equally by all. Some of the Scots gentlemen who had come with King David were poor and resented the settlement made in King Henry's time; they were eager for war. If Cumbria and Northumbria became subject to King David, it would be Scotsmen who would be granted land there. At worst, an invasion would bring them some riches in loot.

Thus, some barons objected to the meeting at first, but they did not raise strong arguments against it because they were sure Thurstan would come thundering denunciations and issuing orders backed by threats of excommunication. They did not fear threats, for they knew that David, although deeply and sincerely religious, had a strong sense of what belonged to Caesar and what belonged to God. In the king's opinion war was definitely a secular subject.

Denunciations would be equally useless because David had strong and, in his and his barons' opinions, valid reasons for what he proposed to do. If the archbishop ordered David to give up his intention of invading England and demanded obedience on the grounds of faith, the Scots barons knew, it would only infuriate the king and make him more intent on his purpose.

They were less certain of David's ability to resist other types of argument. Hugh recorded with some amusement the hurried conferences and sense of dismay among the Scots courtiers when Thurstan greeted the king with expressions of affection and respect and praised him for his forbearance and understanding. It soon became apparent, however, that the archbishop was making little headway. Hugh found he could tell how the discussions were going whether he was present at them or not. The more firmly David resisted any argument that precluded war, the more condescendingly cordial certain Scots barons were toward Hugh.

The resistance to his pleas and reasonings did not make

Thurstan lose hope or patience, for each day he spent in nego-
tiation brought the English crops a day nearer ripeness and
provided another day in which the defense of Northumbria
and Cumbria could be strengthened. Thurstan retained his
temperate tone all through the discussions, expressing his
sympathy for the quandary in which David found himself
regarding his oath to Empress Matilda, but arguing that the
acceptance and crowning of Stephen by the archbishop of
Canterbury must surely lift any possibility of sin from those
who accepted Canterbury's decision. He spoke of his own
doubts, which had kept him from attending Stephen's corona-
tion, and the resolution of those doubts, which had permitted
him to send proxies to Stephen's Easter court.

With equal courtesy but stubborn resistance to all Thurstan's
reasoning and pleas, David maintained that an oath of fealty
was not solely a religious act. His honor was involved, even if
there should be no sin in accepting Stephen as king of England.
His homage had been pledged to King Henry and to Lady
Matilda personally, not to an anonymous "ruler of England."

The archbishop could not argue that subject, although he
protested against a point of honor that would spill much blood
in both nations and cause much misery among the innocent.
Eventually, however, when Thurstan saw that David would
not—or could not, owing to the pressures on him—be
brought to swear he would keep the truce he had made with
King Stephen, the archbishop himself raised a point of honor.

First Thurstan reminded David that King Stephen had been
generous to him when he could have pursued him with a
great army and ravaged Scotland. David had been willing to
acknowledge that Stephen had the right, as England's king,
to cede Doncaster and Carlisle, for David had accepted the
keeps from Stephen when he signed the truce. Since he was
so troubled that his honor would be smirched by keeping
the truce, would he return the keeps? Stephen trusted David,
Thurstan pointed out. Was not David his wife's uncle and thus
bound to him in blood? Was it honorable to violate Stephen's
trust? Could there be greater dishonor, the archbishop asked
caustically, if David restrained his ardor for Matilda's cause

than if he broke a truce made in good faith and attacked a kingdom when its defender was absent in Normandy? For the first time in the fortnight the discussions had lasted, David looked uncomfortable and truly unhappy.

The meeting the king called with his barons the next day was stormy and bitter, and the passions outlasted the end of the conference. The arguments continued in the alehouses long after the decision was made, so that Hugh, sitting in a shadowy corner, had the news before it was carried officially to Thurstan. David would not attack that spring. In fact, he would keep the truce until he could break it with honor when Stephen returned to England.

Some men shouting and banging their leather cups on the tables felt it utterly foolish to let a fine point of honor take precedence over a strong military advantage. Others, and they were in the majority, sided with the king. Even this group was divided over the reasons for accepting David's decision. The proud northern thanes, although they had little use or respect for any agreement made outside their own group and discounted the truce, were insulted by the notion that they feared Stephen or his army. It would give them greater satisfaction to wait until the king of England returned and then defeat him. Hugh was more interested in the argument put forward by a quieter group, the French and Norman men who had been granted Scottish lands by David. They had supported the king's decision because they believed the situation in England would worsen.

Ranulf de Soules, lord of Liddesdale, said he was sure open rebellion would break out in support of Matilda as soon as Stephen was back in England. Not only would the English king be unable to bring his army to help the northern shires, Robert Avenel added, nodding agreement to de Soules's remarks, but Stephen might call away such men as Walter Espec, who would otherwise be capable of organizing a dangerous defense with or without Stephen's help.

Put together with what he had seen during the siege of Exeter—the way Robert of Gloucester had slyly aided the rebels—Hugh could not discount what they said. He knew that Thurstan's hope in getting David to delay his invasion was that once Stephen came back he would be able to negotiate a stable peace. That did not seem very likely, considering the attitude of David's barons; not once had Hugh heard a man suggest that peace would be better than war.

Even so, Hugh's predominant emotion on hearing of David's decision was joy. It meant that there was nothing more Thurstan could do here and after a day or two of oath-taking and ceremonial farewells, they would be on their way... home. The word surprised Hugh as it came into his mind. It occurred to him that he had never used it before. Although he had lived so long with Sir Walter, Helmsley had never become his home. Was he thinking of Jernaeve? No, not Jernaeve. Audris. Hugh smiled, relishing the sharp pang of longing. Where Audris was, that was home.

Chapter 15

HUGH HAD SUFFERED THE MOST IN THEIR FIRST PARTING, WHEN he thought his desire for Audris was hopeless. Now it was Audris's turn. Despair lay heavy on her—not so much because of their parting, although she began to bleed only three days after he left and knew she had not conceived the child she desired, but because of the compulsion she felt to weave. She denied it as much as she could, busying herself with her duties in the garden and going into the woods and onto the cliffs to visit the nests she had marked, where she watched for the young to hatch. Then, when the old birds were off hunting, she would feed the new hatchlings to make them less shy of her.

She tried to write to Hugh also, knowing her uncle and aunt would not ask what she wrote—they never did. Oddly, both would ask her to read a letter or a message to them and even write one in return if the chaplain was not available, but when Audris read or wrote to please herself, Oliver and Eadyth would look aside as if taking book or quill in hand for such a purpose were indecent.

A shadow of a smile touched her lips as she remembered the reaction, but it did not linger. Usually when Oliver and Eadyth pretended not to see her, Audris had to turn her face and stifle giggles to hide her amusement. Surely if writing was decent for holy men and women, it could not be wrong for anyone—and Father Anselm, who was very holy, had said there was no wrong in it and taught her. But the laughter would not come, for her spirit sank ever deeper in despair.

Audris had thought she would find relief in writing to Hugh, in "talking together while parted," but she found she had nothing to say. The pleasure that Hugh had in describing his daily activities could not serve for Audris. A woman's daily round was, to an outsider, dull and repetitive, however interesting and fulfilling (or painful and frustrating) to her. Audris could not believe Hugh would be interested in the height reached by the seedlings in the garden or what decisions had been made about the later plantings. No doubt he would be interested in the hawks' progress, but she feared to write about that lest he worry about her climbing. She would climb whether he worried or not, but why be cruel and bring it to his mind? Perhaps he would forget. Worst of all, she had no interest in relating these matters. Nor could she mention the picture that was forcing her to weave it thread by thread. All she wanted to do was fill her page with "Take care, my love, take care."

She need not have feared Oliver and Eadyth's notice. Her uncle and aunt were totally involved in their desperate efforts to ready Jernaeve for the war they feared was coming. Their conversation was reserved for each other and concerned with what had been stored, what could be expected in the keep for storage within the next few days, how much space there was still to be filled, how many mouths there would be to feed in the lower keep when the serfs and yeomen were called in to defend it, and how many in the upper keep.

There was no panic; Jernaeve had withstood many attacks and several sieges during the time Oliver and Eadyth had held it, but neither had any attention to spare for any outside subject. For them it was enough that Audris was there, engaged in her usual occupations. They did not wonder why her trilling laugh was stilled and her merry mischief ended. Audris was grateful for their indifference.

Because they did not ask anxious questions, she could force herself to take her meals in the great hall instead of in her tower, where her loom summoned her, silently, seductively.

Still, when it rained hard and the light failed and her uncle and aunt dragged their weary bones to bed, the loom was there, waiting for her, and the picture she blocked from her mind formed inexorably under her hands. She would not look at it. She would not let herself "see" it, but she could not always avoid Fritha's eyes, and there was trouble in them. Fritha's duties took her to the back of the loom where the picture was clear—Audris could only be glad the girl was mute and that there were no hand signs for what she might have said if she could.

There was no source of comfort. When she left Hugh, Audris had been soothed by the knowledge that she would see him again, that she could call to her mind images of their pleasure together. Even that failed her. During their first separation, she had feared for Bruno but never for Hugh, although she knew he took part in the fighting. She had never consciously thought of the legend of the unicorn and the maiden at that time, but she had a buried conviction that the unicorn could not be harmed until he was trapped by the maiden. Now every memory of him brought terror with it because she was no longer a maiden.

She called herself a fool; Hugh was a man, not an enchanted beast. She had summoned no hunters to kill or capture him while she held him. If she were to be concerned with the legend, she should fear that the unicorn would reject her because of her lost virginity—but she never feared that. Knowing it was against all reason, she felt she *had* trapped Hugh, that their coupling, which she had urged on him, had stripped him of his invulnerability, and that the destruction of her maidenhead implied the destruction of the unicorn.

The most acute agony eased when Morel came with his first message, two days after Thurstan had settled at Roxburgh. He carried a letter for Sir Oliver—Hugh had decided after some thought that it might be a good notion to ingratiate himself with Audris's uncle by sending him information directly—and to Demoiselle Audris, Morel said, he brought special thanks for her company and entertainment, which his master had asked him to deliver in person. Sir Oliver nodded with little interest and said he believed Audris was in the garden, where Morel found her and gave his real message: there was a large packet waiting for her in the care of his daughter-by-marriage. Audris could send Fritha for it at anytime.

He told her, too, how happy he was in his service to Sir Hugh and thanked her with tears in his eyes for finding him so perfect a master. It was a relief to Audris to hear that Hugh was in excellent health and spirits and that there was no danger at all of any fighting. Under other circumstances, a quick tourney or other, more casual contests in arms might have been arranged for the amusement of David's noblemen, but the Church disapproved of that kind of battle play, and in deference to Thurstan's presence, no fighting at all was permitted. It was not reasonable to be relieved, for there were many ways to die that did not entail violence, but Audris only feared the sword and lance.

Hugh's letter to Sir Oliver, which Audris read aloud to her uncle, described how kindly Thurstan had been received and the extraordinary effort David had made to please the archbishop—in all matters except the most important. Hugh offered little hope that Thurstan's mission would be even partly successful—his letter having been written and sent a week before the archbishop began to harp on the dishonor of a sneak attack. Oliver growled over David's intransigence, but not with real anger. He had not expected Thurstan to be able to deflect the king from his purpose and was grateful for the extra weeks to prepare.

There was a kind of comfort for Audris in Oliver's curt nod of approval and his comment, "He has eyes and ears, that Hugh," as she handed back the parchment. Audris found even more comfort in the long, long private letter she received, which detailed the day-by-day events of the journey and recounted Hugh's amused comments about the different men who had accompanied David. She laughed and wept as she read, leaning on the wall by the window for light, for she truly heard every word in Hugh's voice and could imagine the glint of his brilliant eyes as he wrote.

She went herself to Morel's house late in the day to give him her letter for Hugh and a verbal apology for sending so

little in return when she had received so much. It was pleasant
to see the change in the household. Before they noticed
her approach, Audris saw Morel seated on a stool, leaning
back against the wall beside the front door as he worked in
a contented manner on some item she could not see. His
daughter-by-marriage, Mary, stood beside him, smiling down
at him and talking. He turned his head to smile at her in turn,
saw Audris, jumped to his feet, and bowed.

"I have brought my answer," Audris said, holding out
her letter.

Morel looked down at his hands, which were covered
with grease, and nudged Mary forward. She bowed and
came toward Audris, raising a hand wrapped in the cloth that
protected her skirt so that her hands would not soil the parchment. The raised cloth showed her swelling belly. So that
was why she was not out in the fields with the men, Audris
thought, and most likely that was also the reason she wanted
to be rid of the horse. Perhaps she feared that Morel would
stint her child to feed the animal. Audris smiled and thanked
her, and when the woman timidly reached out to touch her
skirt, she did not pull it away, even though she disapproved of
being touched for luck, like some talisman.

Instead she sighed and said, "You tell the midwife that
if she has need of me for your birthing, she should send a
messenger to Jernaeve and I will come." Then, before either
Morel or Mary could thank her, she asked again about the
possibility of violence at Roxburgh.

"There be some loud talk between the men," Morel
replied. "Them Scots strut like cocks on a dunghill and crow
like cocks too, but my master's troop, they be old at the work
and steady—and he be bidding them hold their hands and
their tongues or he be keeping them housebound. It could be
a few have black eyes and twisted noses—on both sides—but
King David, he be just as firm there be no quarrels, so the
knives stay in the belts."

"And among the knights?" Audris asked anxiously.

"Ah, there be no trouble there. They all talk low and
sweet. The king's own eye be on them—and they think they

be having chance enough to drink Northumbrian blood in a week or two."

"Thank God for that," Audris said, thinking only of the double reassurance that Hugh would not be involved in any fighting.

Morel, however, assumed she had referred to his final sentence, and he smiled grimly. The Demoiselle loved them all—he knew that—and she would *not* thank God for the Scots doing them any harm. Thus, the Demoiselle meant that they would beat the Scots and gain an advantage over them. Sometimes she was hard to understand when she gave advice or warning, but this time he was sure what she meant. He looked up past Audris's head to where one could just make out Jernaeve's bulk, rearing up against the sky, the west face lit with hazy reddish light. His lips twisted.

"They be like to drink deep here, Demoiselle—cold river water and hot oil. Old Iron Fist be a good lesson to a cock that crows too loud and far from home."

"Yes, Jernaeve is safe, very safe."

Audris was not certain why Morel had said what he did, but it came home to her that it was true. Jernaeve was safe. If Hugh were in Jernaeve… With the thought, the compulsion to weave washed over her in a flood so strong that she started to turn her mare's head before she knew her hands had responded. This time she did not fight it; she let the mare carry her away, for the end of Morel's sentence had come back to her like an echo. In a week or two, he had said. The Scots believed they would invade in a week or two, and there was nothing in either of Hugh's letters that made their belief unlikely. Was that why she had felt so driven to weave this picture? With a sob of fear, Audris kicked her mare into a gallop. Perhaps the danger to Hugh was *in* Jernaeve, and if she did not have the work done in time, the unicorn would die for lack of warning.

But that was nonsense! Her tapestries were not real fore-telling, as a prophet foretold. Father Anselm had explained to her how what she noticed while she watched the birds and beasts and what he had taught her about God and nature came together to make the pictures she "saw" and then wove. It could not be foretelling; only witches could foretell. But the people, all the people, believed she was a witch. Audris shuddered with terror. Father Anselm loved her. Had he lied to her—to everyone—to protect her? "Thou shall not suffer a witch to live." Those were the words in Exodus. Had Father Anselm loved her enough to damn his own soul?

It was a horrible notion, but it calmed Audris, and she slowed her mount's headlong gallop. Possibly Father Anselm *had* loved her enough to lie for her sake, but he was a truly good, truly holy man, and he would not have loved her if she were evil. And her tapestries had never brought evil, so why should it matter if they were foretellings? She touched the mare with her heel to speed her pace just a trifle.

I am a fool, Audris thought. Father Anselm told me it was a gift—a special gift—and that I must use it as it comes. Because Hugh is dear to me, I have forgotten all I ever learned. I *know* that hiding from the truth cannot help, cannot change the future. That will come, as the flood and the drought came. The thing itself cannot be stopped, but the worst results can often be averted with care if one has warning.

Over the next few days, as she finished the work on her loom, Audris often repeated to herself what she had thought on that ride home. She needed whatever comfort she could draw from memories of her beloved teacher, for the sense of doom still hung over her. Audris had hoped that when she no longer struggled against the impulse to weave, she would feel pleasantly detached, simply satisfied with a task she loved, as she always had in the past—even when she wove the pictures that showed Death. But this time her heaviness of heart would not lift, and when at last she bade Fritha turn the loom so she could see the work, she had to clasp her hands and bite her lips to keep them from trembling with fear.

Still, she cried out with horror at what she saw, blinking to clear the tears from her eyes so she could look again and find she had seen wrong. But the image remained. The unicorn was there, grown huge and wild, showing the terrible and fierce part of his nature rather than his enchanted gentleness with the maiden. The beast filled almost the whole tapestry, neck arched, head down as if he were about to thrust his horn through Jernaeve keep to split and break it while his cloven hooves shone silver among the blackened crops and ruined buildings of the lower bailey.

"No, he would not," Audris whispered, but the tears ran down her face, for she knew the fierceness *was* part of Hugh. She had felt it in him all that week, burning under his tenderness, felt the hot eagerness to fight his way to greatness, to destroy anything that blocked the path to her. That was what desire for her had wakened in him! She stood appalled, then shuddered and turned away, sobbing, "Take it down, Fritha! Take it down and hide it away."

The days passed. Audris's loom stood empty, and her eyes slid away from it guiltily each morning when she rose from her bed. Her work lay folded away in the chest with the special yarns, but she could not rid herself of its image in her mind. She tried and tried to find a different meaning in the picture, but her tapestries had never been subtle, and what the work said was that Hugh was a danger to Jernaeve. Yet she could not bring herself to tell her uncle, and more days passed. Then Morel rode into Jernaeve again, and this time he brought good news, though not the best: for this summer, at least, there would be no war with the Scots; King David had yielded so far to Archbishop Thurstan's reasons and pleas that he had agreed not to attack English lands until King Stephen returned from Normandy.

Oliver and Eadyth had been standing tensely, almost expecting to hear that Morel was only a few hours ahead of the invading Scots. The news released them, not only from the fear of immediate attack but from the tension that had driven them, even in their sleep, to *will* everything into readiness. Eadyth sank into a seat, first sighing with relief and then bursting into tears. Oliver put a hand on her shoulder and patted it in a rare gesture of companionship and comfort.

Audris was stunned. If there was no war, what danger could Hugh be to Jernaeve? Either she had read the picture amiss, she thought, or it was *not* a foretelling but only an image of her own fears. That was a comforting idea, and she eagerly waited for Fritha to return from Morel's house, where she had sent her to fetch Hugh's letter to her. It was much shorter than the last since, as Hugh explained, there was not much new to say. Most of it had been written after Hugh learned that they would soon be leaving Scotland.

"I ache for you," he wrote, "yet I am glad that I will have no more than a brief vision of all that is bright and beautiful to me. I do not wish to be free of the pain of longing for you, especially now when my duty is near over and I will so soon be able to take up my quest. If I were to stay near you, I would be wrapped in a golden dream of contentment—as we were that first day when we walked in your enchanted valley. Ensorcelled by your presence, I would desire nothing and do nothing and thus, perhaps, lose all through having you snatched away from me. The pain of longing will be a spur to me, and so much the sooner, as the pain is greater and drives me harder, will I make myself worthy to be your husband."

The passionate eagerness, the joyful embracing of pain as a spur to fierce purpose, woke all Audris's fears again, and she had to stop reading and blink the tears from her eyes. Hugh had written in plain words what she had felt in him—determination, hot and hard, to win her regardless of the cost. The singleness of purpose terrified Audris; although she loved Hugh and wanted him, she had duties and obligations that she could not violate, even for his sake. Yet neither could she deny him. She craved his desire for her and her alone. She could not reject his need, for it answered a deep need in her. Slowly, she looked back at the letter.

"I hope," he had written, "that we will be able to talk in private for a little time—and I do mean talk, not converse in the cruder meaning of the word—for there are questions I must ask you. Think on this, beloved. For myself, I would like to follow the king to Normandy and take up that service to his person that he offered me when I first met him. I refused it then, for I felt unable to leave my old master, but as long as there is no war with Scotland, Sir Walter does not need me. There is easy advancement for those who serve under the king's eye—but that brings me to the question I must ask. If I am fortunate and win a holding in Normandy, would you go so far, my love? I have asked you before, and you have told me that you would be willing to leave Jernaeve, but is Normandy too distant from the hills and valleys you love?"

Audris looked up from the letter again, but there were no tears this time. Her eyes were wide and amazed and bright with inward joy. One thing was sure; it was she herself that Hugh desired, for it was plain that he intended to leave Jernaeve to her uncle and even wished to take her so far away that Oliver could not feel his management of Jernaeve to be watched. Now she remembered that Hugh had asked more than once whether she was bound in spirit to Jernaeve—yet she had never connected the question with her uncle. "Fool!" she muttered, shaking her head at herself. How could she have overlooked so simple a solution to the problem of wanting to be with Hugh but needing to leave her uncle as master of Jernaeve?

Her eyes fixed on the last few lines of the letter hungrily. "I would not have you say yes for love of me and then yearn for your own land. I have some reason to believe that there will be opportunities for me in England. That might be dangerous to write more clearly, and my hand is slow compared with speech, so I will leave these matters to talk about. It will be soon enough to write more if we can find no chance to be together. I burn for you. I am afire with desire and nothing can quench my agony but your cool, silver hair and pale, graceful hands. Does this sound strange? We were hot enough in our coupling, but that warmth was turned outward toward each other. When we are parted, the heat turns in on itself so that my need for you eats at me within as a fire may eat the heart of a tree. Morel is here. I must finish this. Pray for me, Audris. Pray that I do not forget my duty to the man who stood as father to me when I was a nameless, helpless babe and harm him by urging him to travel faster than is good for his enfeebled age, only to be near you sooner."

So Hugh recognized the danger in his desire, Audris thought as she slowly folded the parchment to put it away.

That was the man, but the beast was there too; the letter disclosed the wild passion struggling within the bonds of duty, and she shivered, torn between fear and longing. What was she to say in answer? Truly she did not think it would matter to her where she lived, but she also did not believe her uncle would agree that Hugh take her across the narrow sea. Nor did she want Hugh to go so far without her. She would rather wait for the opportunity Hugh hinted might come in England, but should she tell him that?

She opened the letter again, reread the end, and closed her eyes, both thrilled and horrified once more by the barely controlled passion. Would the beast throw off the bonds the man had cast over it if she wrote of delay? It was one thing to strive forward despite pain, but to wait, enduring that pain helplessly, was another thing. The picture in the tapestry again rose in her mind. Would her denial make the unicorn wild and dangerous?

Audris went slowly to the foot of her bed, where a small table held Father Anselm's writing desk. She drew a stool up to the table and lifted the cover of the desk to take out a quill and a small slip of parchment. Her eyes were blank with thought as she tested the point on the quill, found it good, and began to work the wax plug out of the small polished inkhorn, fixed into the playful embrace of an exquisitely worked bear cub lying on its back. She caressed the little sculpture absently. Her uncle had brought the ink-horn back from one of his rare attendances at King Henry's court and thrust it at her brusquely, growling, "You and your beasts. I could not get you out of my mind once I saw it. I still think it unseemly for a girl-child to write, but take it. It is for you." At the time she had been more frightened than glad, but now she understood better. Her eyes focused on the little bear for a moment, then she dipped the quill and began to write:

> *From Audris of Jernaeve to Sir Hugh Licorne, greetings. If you are well, I am well also. Beloved, I must first beg pardon again for so few words, but I have been much distressed by a strange thing in my weaving and have had little spirit to*

write. I will say only this. My desire cleaves to you and to
you only. By my own choice, I would follow you and live,
without fear or regret, wheresoever you made a place for me.
But as your life is not only by your choice, and that is right
and good in my eyes, so mine is not only by my choice. You
are wise also in knowing that these matters are better spoken
of than written. When you come, I will find a time and
place for us to be private together. Fare you well, light of my
eyes, until I can see you with my eyes and, God willing,
hold you in my arms.

She read it over twice, folded it, and sealed it with wax,
then told Fritha to carry it to Morel in the lower bailey. There
was enough assurance in the letter not to arouse any desperate
feelings and enough warning, too, to prepare Hugh for
trouble. When he came, she would show him the tapestry and
then they would decide what was best to do. And perhaps, she
thought, caressing his letter as she slid it into the desk before
she put away her quill and restoppered her inkhorn, perhaps
before he comes something will happen that will help me
know what to say.

After another week passed, Audris could hardly bear to
leave the keep, although the hawks were hatched and she
should have been spying on the nests to choose the best of the
hatchlings. Most of her work in the garden was done, except
to point out which early flowers and young leaves should be
culled for drying, so she had little excuse to stay in Jernaeve,
but she expected Hugh to appear at the gate at every moment,
and wherever she was, she listened for the sentry's call. It was
Morel who came, however, not Hugh, and he brought only
a verbal message to Oliver and a note as brief as her own to
Audris, which he slipped into Fritha's hand.

Without greeting or salutation, Hugh had written: "If there
is some danger to you or yours, heart of my heart, tell Morel,
and I will come to you at once to be your shield. But if the
strange thing in your weaving is not a threat, I cannot help
you for a time. My dear father in God, Archbishop Thurstan,
hid from all how greatly he had been tired by these meetings

with King David. Unknowing, for he made no complaint, or perhaps because in my great desire to be with you I was deliberately blind, I brought him as far as Jedburgh. Here, at last, he confessed his weakness, and my eyes were opened. I fear we will be delayed some weeks while Thurstan gathers strength."

The note ended as abruptly as it began. Audris sighed, guessing the violent impatience that had been curbed, and curbed by so thin a margin that Hugh did not dare express his feelings lest they overwhelm him. Still, she told herself, he must be calmer by now; she herself was calmer—the time that had passed had dimmed the first shock of seeing her tapestry—although she still had no answer to the danger it displayed or how to keep Hugh from going to Normandy. So Audris wrote a soothing reply, saying that her picture was more a puzzle than a threat, expressing her concern for Thurstan and her approval of Hugh's decision to stay with him, and ending with the reminder that they were still young and had time for a way to open.

The delay in Jedburgh was more than a few weeks. By mid-August Thurstan was still barely strong enough to move from his chamber to the garden of the manor house in which they stayed. Also in August a long, scribe-written letter came to Jernaeve from Bruno in Normandy. It was a source of much rejoicing to Audris, for not only did it assure her that her half brother was safe and well, but it provided news that made it ridiculous for Hugh to consider going to Normandy. Oliver was far less pleased with the news than Audris. He was glad enough to know that Bruno was well and in high favor with King Stephen, but the other aspects of the letter roused considerable concern in his mind.

By the end of August Thurstan was ready to travel again, but Hugh permitted him to move only in short stages so that they did not reach Jarrow abbey until the beginning of September. There Hugh left Thurstan to rest for two days while he paid off those men-at-arms who had come from Northumbria, leaving some at Newcastle and a few others in Prudhoe. This put him within six leagues of Jernaeve, and he thought that would not be so far a ride to pay a visit of courtesy as to raise doubts in Sir Oliver's mind about why he had bothered to come.

Hugh rode in, apurpose, more than an hour after dinner was over. He had waited in the hot midday sun in agonized impatience just out of sight of the keep for a long time in the hope of missing Sir Oliver. Thus, he was barely able to conceal his relief when he heard that he had won the prize for which he had struggled—his host was in the fields watching the reapers. With a last desperate effort at calm, he asked for the Demoiselle Audris and was told she was in the garden. Licking dry lips and trying to steady his uneven breathing, Hugh walked across the courtyard, around the wall of the small church, and into the most beautiful castle garden he had ever seen. It was so rich of scents—the sharp aromas of herbs, the sweet odors of flowers, and the rich flavor of ripening fruits—so bright with color, that for one brief moment Hugh was distracted from the desire that burned inside him. And then Audris stepped out of a patch of shadow.

They stood quite still, their eyes meeting and holding, knowing they must not run into each other's arms. Then Hugh bowed low, and Audris turned her head and said to the gardener, who was still in the shadow, "Go, and take the others with you. We will finish these tasks tomorrow. My uncle's guest must not be disturbed if he wishes to walk in the garden."

And while the serfs scurried out, Hugh moved slowly toward his lodestone and lifted the hand she held out to him formally to his lips, murmuring, "I am at peace. I see you, and I am at peace." He chuckled, shaking his head in amused wonderment. "If you knew the images in my dreams these last months, you would run from me in horror."

Audris squeezed his hand, which still held hers. "I doubt it," she replied, laughing also.

Then she tugged him forward along the path, which soon divided right and left around a large bed of sweet-smelling roses. Behind the bed was a broad patch of grass, sheltered on all sides; the tall rosebushes divided it from the rest of the garden; fruit trees espaliered against the wall of the keep were to the left, where the western sun would encourage ripening; tall foxgloves stood opposite the roses, and some delicate plants that Hugh did not recognize nodded in beds near the outer wall to the right. There was such a place in the garden at Helmsley also, where on fine days Lady Adelina and her maidens had disported themselves on cushions to sew and talk and breathe the sweet air.

Hugh knew he and Audris could not be seen, but despite her provocative answer and the desires that had tormented him for weeks, Hugh did not seize her. It was she who flung her arms around his neck and pulled his head down until their lips met. Then he pulled her to him and could easily have forgotten time and place, except that as his arms tightened, the rings of his mail bruised her so that she cried out in pain. He released her at once, and in the next moment she was laughing and pushing him back so she could unbuckle his sword belt. She laid the weapon on the bench near the roses, then seated Hugh to untie the neck guard of his mail.

"I have been practicing," she said, glowing with joy and pride in her efficiency. "When Bruno first came back to Jernaeve, I could not undo his hood for him, and I was ashamed." But when she pushed the hood off and saw Hugh's face clearly, her eyes grew large with concern; she stroked back his hair, its normal fiery color dulled by sweat, and bent down to kiss his forehead gently. "You are very tired, dear heart," she murmured.

He uttered a little snort of disgust. "Not for any good reason. God knows I have done nothing for many weeks that could tire the frailest creature in the world."

Audris smiled at him. "You are of an impatient and hasty spirit, dearling. I do not think it sits well with you to pace slowly at the head of a cortege of honor."

"More blame to me," Hugh sighed. "I am greatly ashamed that I could feel impatience in the service of a man who loves me and has showered me with kindness upon kindness over all the years of my life. I am unworthy of his love, and very likely unworthy of yours also—"

Whereupon Audris stopped his mouth with her own, but when he tried to embrace her, she slipped out of the closing circle of his arms. "Let me take off your armor," she said.

His surprise doused the spark of resentment struck by her rejection of his embrace. "You!" he exclaimed, then laughed at her. "One sleeve would weigh you down, and if you overbalanced and the hauberk fell on you, it would squash you flat."

"I am stronger than I look," Audris protested, but Hugh continued to laugh as he stood up, bent forward, and pulled the mail hood up and out so that his head went through the neck opening. "At least let me help," Audris begged, and tugged the sleeves over his hands. When both head and hands were free of the more constricted portions of the hauberk, Hugh bent forward even farther, almost doubling at the waist. Audris lifted the hem of the armor over the curve of his body, and the hauberk slid off of its own weight. As he straightened up, Audris gathered the garment into her arms and lifted it triumphantly, but Hugh was a larger man than most, and his mail shirt was heavier than those Audris had previously handled. As she turned to lay the hauberk on the bench, she did overbalance slightly and staggered. Hugh caught her in one arm, took the armor from her with the other hand, and tossed it blindly toward the bench behind him while he fixed his mouth on hers.

Without a word, they both sank to the ground, each struggling one-handed to undo and lift the clothing out of the way while they continued to clutch each other close. Their union was brief and awkward, but so strong a sexual excitement had been building in them, all the more violent for being consciously repressed and denied as they spoke and touched, that both exploded into climax within moments of coming together. They lay for a few moments longer, stunned by the violence of their release, until Hugh finally drew his head back far enough to see Audris's face.

"Alas, I am a liar, it seems, as well as being unworthy," he whispered huskily, but he was wearing a broad grin. "I remember writing to you that I would be content only to look at you."

Audris giggled, "How fortunate, then, that I never wished to believe you. I am not so high-minded as you, my heart, and want as much of you as I can get when we can be together."

"Which gives me great joy," Hugh replied, kissing her lightly once more as he gently separated himself from her and straightened her skirt.

Sighing, for she loved the feel of him linked to her even after their passion was spent, Audris did not try to hold Hugh. She knew that what they had done was foolish, and it would be dangerous to indulge herself further, so, as Hugh pulled his own clothes into decent order, she pushed herself into a sitting position, her back against the support of the bench. Hugh shook his head at her, moved his armor to the very edge of the bench, and lifted her to the other end, seating himself beside her.

"I will never understand why you chose me," he continued, half in earnest, half jesting. "Still, I submit gladly to God's will—and yours—in this matter. You know that much of my impatience has been because I am so eager to win some land. Have you thought, as I asked you, of whether you could leave this country, Audris?"

"I answered that without need of thought," she said softly, laying her hand on his. "*I* would be willing to live anywhere that we could be together—but there can be no question of going to Normandy."

Hugh's red brows drew together in an angry scowl. "Why? If I am willing to forgo such a place as Jernaeve, what complaint can your uncle—"

Audris took her lover's face between her hands, kissed him on the nose, and laughed at him. "If he saw that scowl, he might fear you would murder me the first time I crossed your will." She laughed again as Hugh drew an outraged breath and, before he could speak, went on, "No, dearling, it is nothing to do with my uncle. I thought perhaps you had heard the news from Normandy. There is nothing to be won there."

"I have heard nothing," Hugh said. "I sent word to York that no business was to be forwarded to Thurstan—not even if the cathedral burnt down—and my messenger must have frightened the wits out of Thurstan's secretary, who then sent no news at all. That meant I have been cut off also. Is the king dead?"

"Oh, no, but he has been accused of plotting to kill or capture Robert of Gloucester by an ambush, and this enraged the Norman barons—although there is another side to the story—"

"Wait," Hugh interrupted. "Tell it from the beginning. From whom did you have this news?"

"From Bruno. You remember that he was taken into the king's service."

Hugh looked at her. "Of course I remember. Did I not tell you that Stephen offered me service at the same time?"

"Perhaps it is as well you did not take it," Audris said, frowning, "for either the king is not as honorable as he should be or—and I do not know which is worse—he is not so strong-minded as he should be. Bruno, who is loyal to a fault, excuses Stephen for everything, but whichever way *I* look at the story, I find the king to blame."

"If you would tell me what happened," Hugh urged, with just a note of impatience creeping into his voice, "perhaps I might judge for myself."

A strong masculine laugh made both Audris and Hugh start with surprise and turn to where the left-hand path around the rose bed entered the grass plot. Hugh's heart leapt into his throat. Sir Oliver was staring at them, still half hidden behind the rosebushes. How long had he been there?

Chapter 16

In the next moment, Hugh realized it was only his own guilt that made him think Audris's uncle was suspicious. Sir Oliver seemed to have paused only to listen to his niece's last remark and Hugh's reply, for he came forward, smiling and uttering a warm welcome.

"My man came down to the fields to tell me you had come, Sir Hugh, and I wished to thank you for sending us news of the meetings with the Scots."

Although his worst fears were set at rest by the friendly words, Hugh was still so shocked at seeing Audris's uncle that he could not speak and only nodded while he offered up wordless but desperately sincere thanks to Mary. It could only have been the gentle Mother's well-known indulgence to the foolish that had shielded them and kept Sir Oliver from arriving a few minutes sooner.

"Will you stay a few days?" Oliver continued, adding with a wry smile, "I promise I will not leave you to Audris's tender mercies again. She is a good girl, but to converse with her might sometimes drive a man mad."

"I must be back in Jarrow abbey tomorrow," Hugh replied, fortunately still too unnerved by their narrow escape to take offense at Oliver's dry criticism of Audris.

"I am not so bad as that, uncle," Audris cried, laughing and pouting deliciously at the same time.

"I have never been able to get a straight tale out of you in my life," Oliver growled. "If Sir Hugh can, I would like to know how he does it."

"He listens more attentively," Audris teased, her eyes sparkling with mischief.

"What is the straight tale, Sir Oliver?" Hugh asked quickly, appalled by the expression on Audris's face and by her remark, which he felt hinted at their relationship.

As he spoke, Audris rose from the bench and settled on the grass, gesturing for her uncle to take her place. He nodded at her and sat, and Audris casually leaned a shoulder against Hugh's legs, ostensibly so that she could look at Oliver while he answered Hugh's question. Hugh stiffened nervously, torn between the delight he felt whenever she touched him and a strong desire to strangle her for her mischief. Sir Oliver looked at her and frowned.

"Audris, you are making Sir Hugh uncomfortable," Oliver remonstrated, gesturing her away.

"No, no," Hugh assured him. "She is light. If you permit, I am happy to serve as the Demoiselle's prop and make her comfortable. But what is this new trouble with Robert of Gloucester of which Bruno writes?" he asked hastily to change the subject, for Audris had uttered a choked chuckle and he feared what she might say next.

"You know that Robert of Gloucester was given Caen to hold by King Henry?" Sir Oliver asked. Hugh nodded and Sir Oliver continued, "Bruno thinks that Matilda's husband, Geoffrey of Anjou, chose to attack Mézidon mostly because it is no more than three leagues from Caen, and he expected Gloucester to open Caen to him. In that, Geoffrey was disappointed, for Gloucester seemed to hold by his oath to Stephen and even sent aid to Stephen, which enabled the king to take back Mézidon."

"But that—"

"Wait," Sir Oliver interrupted. "That was not the end of the matter. Up until then, Stephen had accomplished everything he had set out to do. He had induced Louis of France to recognize him as duke of Normandy as well as king of England, and he had also made peace with his brother, who felt he had an equal claim to the English crown—or a better one, since he was the elder—and resented Stephen's quick taking of it. Resolving then to complete his work, Stephen called out his vassals in Normandy and assembled a large army at Lisieux, intending to drive Geoffrey out of Normandy altogether."

"That was when everything went wrong," Audris said, seeing the eagerness that had come into Hugh's face.

Oliver frowned at her, but nodded agreement. "Bruno said the real cause of the trouble was the jealousy and suspicion the Norman barons felt for Stephen's Flemish mercenaries and their leader, William of Ypres."

"I can understand that," Hugh remarked. "There was feeling against Ypres at Exeter, too. Ypres has been given more than one estate as prize and reward, yet he and his Flemings are *paid* for their service, while the barons must not only serve for nothing but pay their own and their men's expenses."

"Well," Oliver went on, "when men are angry to begin with, a small thing can set them off. What *happened* was that the barons fell on the mercenaries. There was, Bruno says, considerable slaughter on both sides because the mercenaries were not overwhelmed and fought back, and the barons— either because they knew they were in the wrong or because they feared they would get no fair judgment from the king— gathered their men and left the royal camp without warning or asking Stephen's leave."

"That is rebellion!" Hugh exclaimed.

"It is only worthwhile to call it rebellion if a king is strong enough to defeat the rebels and profit by taking their lands," Oliver commented dryly. "And it is only truly rebellion if the cause is petty and dishonorable—but it is about the cause that I have my doubts. Bruno *says* it was, indeed, petty—no more than a pipe of wine wrested from a Norman knight by a companion of Ypres. The knight flew to arms and called his comrades to his aid, and the fight soon spread into a general battle. Then, because they disdained explanation or restitution and feared the king's wrath, the Norman barons fled."

Hugh shrugged. "I have seen men fall on each other for no greater a cause."

"So have I," Oliver agreed, "but Bruno adds to the letter that another tale is current and that he feels he must tell me what is said so that I will not be surprised or believe he wished to hide it. The other tale is not of petty spite. It is said, Bruno writes, that the barons attacked the mercenaries to destroy an ambush set to kill Robert of Gloucester when he came into the camp. And the reason given for the barons' withdrawing without permission was that they had learned the king had agreed to the ambush, conspiring with William of Ypres against Gloucester, despite Gloucester's loyalty in supporting the king against Matilda's husband."

"If this is true, it paints no pretty picture of Stephen," Hugh said. "There were many things the late king did I thought were wrong, but I do not remember that Henry ever connived at murder."

Oliver knew different, but it was Audris who said, "It is weakness, not deliberate evil. By the end of his reign, Henry could give an order and know it would be obeyed—or the man who disobeyed broken. Stephen must win his way to that position." Then she shook her head and half closed her eyes, remembering the king as she had seen him. "But I do not think Stephen will ever be like Henry. I could see in Stephen that he will be pulled this way and that, ever shifting with the strongest will and the last to speak to him—"

"Audris!" Oliver cut her off sharply. "Girls know nothing of such matters. Hold your tongue."

"Yes, uncle," she said meekly, and bowed her head as if contrite. She was contrite, in a sense, because she knew her uncle did not like her to speak about what she saw in people before strangers. She had forgotten that Oliver did not know Hugh and she were one.

Hugh frowned at the reprimand, but Audris squeezed his ankle, and he recalled that he had no right to interfere between Oliver and his niece, so he said, "The mercenaries alone cannot be sufficient to drive Geoffrey of Anjou out of Normandy, and I do not think Robert of Gloucester will help bring the barons back under control."

"Nor does Bruno think so," Oliver agreed. "Bruno says,

in fact, that the whole tale of the ambush was made up by Gloucester, who saw a way to give more help to his half sister Matilda than by yielding Caen and exposing himself as a traitor. This way he could blacken Stephen's name and reputation while keeping his own honor clean."

"I cannot believe that," Hugh said slowly. "I mean that Robert of Gloucester made up the whole tale. I have met him, and I know Sir Walter has a deep respect for him. He is, to my knowledge, an honorable man." Hugh's brows lifted. "Of course, Gloucester is not stupid either. I would guess that the truth lies between—that there *was* an ambush plotted by William of Ypres; he is a man who thinks of results without troubling overmuch about honor. Whether the king did connive in the plan, I am less sure—but once the plot was exposed, Gloucester might well believe Stephen did. And Gloucester would gladly seize on it as an excuse to ruin the king's plan to win back Normandy."

Oliver grimaced. "If that is true, Gloucester will soon break into open rebellion."

"That is what the Scots expect," Hugh reminded his host. "I heard nothing from them of what you have told me, but I think they had the news. Their intention is to wait until Stephen is embroiled with rebellion in the south or in Wales, and then come down on us."

"Well, at least we are forewarned." Oliver sighed. "I do not fear for Jernaeve. The Scots never have patience to sit out a siege of years, and the keep can be held for years. But the lands: They will be despoiled if there is no army to protect us." He rose suddenly. "Bruno's last word was that the king, with the help of the archbishop of Rouen, was trying to reconcile the barons to him, but I fear he is not likely to be persistent—which means he may give up on Normandy and return here. And that means the Scots may be down upon us sooner than I had thought. If so, I must think again about what to store and what to sell. Once more I thank you for sharing with me what you saw and heard in Roxburgh. You are welcome to Jernaeve, Sir Hugh, to stay as long as you will, now and at all times hence."

He left abruptly, and Hugh watched him stride away with a worried frown. Audris turned to rest more fully against her lover, dropping her head to his knees. The warm and open invitation her uncle had offered had brought a brief spurt of joy because it would be possible to meet her lover frequently, and then a dreadful sensation of sinking that made her feel all hollow as the image of her last tapestry filled her mind.

Hugh touched her gently. "I wish your uncle had not said that. His unsuspecting welcome casts a still worse light on my stealing your favor."

Audris lifted her head, and her clear eyes met her lover's. His assumption that he was the prime mover in their relationship—which was untrue and a typically male revision of actuality—annoyed her enough to deflect her anxiety momentarily.

"You did not steal my favor," she pointed out. "I gave it freely to you—and my *favor* is my own to give." She saw his uncomprehending surprise and sighed. "My marriage and my possessions may be in my uncle's ward, but my feelings are in mine, and no man may order what they should be." Then she laughed at herself for trying to explain and reached up to touch Hugh's troubled face. "Never mind, dear heart. It is my physical being and Jernaeve that concern Uncle Oliver. You have taken—or been given—nothing my uncle would think of great value."

"Not even your maidenhead?"

"Since if I cannot marry you, I will not marry at all, I cannot see any way he would ever become aware of my 'loss'—if a loss it is," Audris answered, but the image of the unicorn about to gore Jernaeve and trampling over the ruined lower bailey came into her mind again, and tears came to her eyes.

"Audris!" Hugh exclaimed. "What is it? Heartling, do not weep! I will find a way—"

"No," she whispered, closing her eyes and fighting the tears. "I am afraid. I am afraid of the picture I made. It is so strange."

"The picture?" Hugh repeated blankly.

Over the weeks while he waited for Thurstan to regain his strength, a prey to frustration, anxiety, and guilt, Hugh had forgotten what Audris had written about the tapestry she had made. He did remember her telling him about the woven pictures, which seemed to predict natural disasters, but he had done considerable riding and hunting while in Jedburgh and had seen no signs of an especially hard winter or plague, and it was too late in the season for drought to harm the crops. Besides, this must, he thought, have something to do with him particularly, or Audris would have told her uncle. What had she been frightening herself with? He bent forward and kissed her closed eyes, gently broke the grip with which she was clinging to his thighs, then lifted her to the bench to sit beside him again.

"Tell me," he urged.

Audris wiped away the remains of her tears and opened her eyes, but looked away across the garden to the foxgloves against the wall. She was visualizing the picture, trying to formulate words with which to describe it clearly. Before she spoke, however, she realized that her description could not be accurate. All it would tell Hugh was what *she* saw, and that was already tainted and distorted by her fears. She had never tried to describe or explain her pictures; she had simply showed them and let those who saw them decide what they meant.

"No." Audris shook her head. "I cannot tell you. I have said too much already by admitting my fear. You must see the picture and decide for yourself. I—I have fallen victim to some foolish fancies. I fear you will be hurt in your striving to win a place for me, and yet I can see no other way for us to be together. I fear that even if you offer to take me with nothing, my uncle will not agree… for my sake, my heart, not because he does not honor you. You are so dear to me, I fear everything."

"That is a sweet thing to hear," Hugh said softly. "No woman has ever feared for me. Still, I wish you would believe that there is no need for it, for it grieves me that you should have the smallest pain on my account. Of course God may strike down any man—or any woman also—in the full flower of their strength and pride. We both know that. Yet we must have faith. Look you, dearling, how we have been protected from our own foolishness this very day. Shall I come and look at your picture now?"

Audris stood, and Hugh turned to pick up his sword and hauberk. "I have told no one else about the work," she said as he rose to follow her. "I do not know why, but I need to keep this one and the others by me for a time, so do not speak of them, I beg you."

"I will do in all things as you desire," he assured her, smiling fondly—and with a touch of indulgent condescension for her fancifulness.

Hugh could not take seriously any threat displayed in a woven picture. He saw that Audris was worried, and his heart ached to think that she should carry any burden. She was so small and light, flitting down the garden path, needing to take two steps to his one and hardly turning a piece of gravel as she went. He would find a soothing explanation, he told himself, no matter what the tapestry showed.

He did not get to see the picture that afternoon. On their way out of the garden, they met Lady Eadyth coming in. Sir Oliver had sent word to his wife that Sir Hugh had arrived so she could have a room made ready, but Eadyth had not forgotten that Hugh was too much attracted to Audris. Audris had behaved very well after she had been warned not to add to Hugh's desire, but Eadyth did not trust Audris to remember her warning. So as soon as she had given the necessary orders for a fire to be lit in the chamber and a bench to be brought in and laid with fleeces for a bed, she had come to fetch their guest. It was easy enough to separate him from Audris; she had only to bid Audris go and change her dress, which was all stained from the garden, and suggest to Hugh that she would lend him a gown so he could take off his arming tunic.

Although Eadyth pretended not to see, the glance Hugh cast at Audris and the shake of the head with which Audris replied troubled her; there was a kind of intimacy about the unspoken communication that made her uneasy. It was too ephemeral an exchange, however, for Eadyth even to formulate her doubts. Oliver came into the hall soon after Hugh had changed, and when Eadyth saw how much her husband favored Hugh, she pushed the doubts away altogether. Moreover, there was nothing more to disturb her, even after Audris came down.

The talk was all of politics—whether it would be possible for Stephen to reconcile himself to the Norman barons, with Robert of Gloucester subtly urging them to resist and Geoffrey of Anjou offering a welcome to those who wished to rebel; how long such a reconciliation would take if it were possible; and whether if the king stayed very long in Normandy, there might be open rebellion in England, or whether the Scots would grow impatient and try to force King David to break the agreement he had made with Thurstan. Oliver was so interested in the talk that he had a second pitcher of wine and then a third brought to the table after the evening meal was eaten and ordered candles to be lit when the light failed.

Audris wished the men a good night and went away when her uncle called for lights, realizing that Oliver, although not the most perceptive of men, would certainly wonder at her behavior if she outsat him. She sent Fritha down to watch, with orders that the maid bring Hugh to her chamber as soon as everyone was asleep. Meanwhile she took out the third tapestry and readied it for hanging beside the other two panels.

Eventually the third pitcher was empty, and when Oliver suggested more, Hugh was able to laugh, shake his head, and remind his host that he had to leave very early the next morning. He might have cut the talk shorter, except that he was fascinated by the possibility of rebellion in England. Hugh knew it was easier by far for a faithful follower to obtain a rebel's possessions than to obtain an outright grant of royal property from the king.

It cost the king nothing to give away land that had never paid revenues directly to the crown and had the added benefit of exchanging a faithful vassal for a rebellious one. Hugh went to bed with his head full of hopes inspired by the talk and the wine and dreamed of saving Stephen single-handedly from an ambush and being granted all of Gloucester's lands. He was just kneeling to offer thanks when someone seized his hand and began to draw him away. Furious, he tried to jerk his hand free, but the tugging persisted.

It was fortunate for Fritha that Hugh felt, even in his dream, that it would be highly impolitic to begin a fight in the king's presence. Dimly he recalled that some private quarrel had caused Stephen much harm, and he forbore to strike out at the stupid person who was preventing him from thanking his benefactor. Instead, he made a huge effort and mumbled, "What do you want?" Infuriatingly, the tugging only continued—but the sound of his own voice had half waked Hugh, and he opened his eyes.

Still muddled by sleep and too much wine and half blinded by the light of the candle she held, he stared at Fritha blankly. At first he thought Sir Oliver had sent him a girl to warm his bed, and he shook his head angrily and gestured for her to be gone, but Fritha only pulled at his hand again. Annoyed, he again asked what she wanted, but when she pointed to her mouth with a look of extreme surprise he finally saw the harelip and recognized her as Audris's mute maidservant.

Instantly, thinking that Audris wanted to spend the night with him, desire flooded him, and he leapt out of bed and would have gone at once, naked as he was. Fritha caught at him, shaking her head wildly, and then pointing firmly to the chausses and shirt that lay on the chest. By the time he was dressed, Hugh's drunken notions were gone, his head had cleared, and he remembered Audris's picture.

But the wine was still working in him and he was aware of a weight on his spirits that made him strangely reluctant to go with Fritha. The "strange revelation" in the tapestry, which he had dismissed so lightly in the sunlit garden, became more threatening in the dark chamber, illuminated only by the dim night candle in the corner and the small one Fritha held.

In the deep-shadowed hall, the yellow glimmer of the few night lights was swallowed up in the immensity, leaving the dull, angry red glow of the banked fire. Hugh clenched his jaw; there was light, but one could not see in it, and lack of vision changed the sounds of snores and sleepers' movements on their pallets to strange groans and slitherings. It came to Hugh as he followed the silent maid, who wove a skilled and noiseless path past the sleepers on the rush-strewn floor, that

he had become almost a different person since he had first seen
Audris in her tower window a year and a half ago.

In the past, he had no high desire for land or title; he had
been content to serve a man he loved. Now ambition burned
so hot in him that he had come close to cursing his father
in God for the infirmities of age and holiness. Before he had
laid eyes on Audris, he knew what sin was; he had not been
perfect, but he repented and did penance when he erred. Now
he sinned with joy in his heart, with neither guilt nor desire to
confess. He looked back over his shoulder toward the upper
end of the hall near the hearth. There, before the opening,
lay black heaps, barely visible in the sullen red glow, some
twisting slowly. So would hell look. Was he being warned?
Was Audris what the people thought she was—a witch? Had
she ensorcelled him? He remembered writing just those words
to her.

Hugh stopped, feeling his heart beating slow and heavy, but
Fritha seized his wrist. He almost jerked away, and then he
saw she was lowering the candle in her hand to show him the
step into the stair. The small, prosaic fact of the step and the
stair ahead loosened the web his wine-sodden imagination had
been weaving around him. He felt a new jolt of apprehension
when Fritha darted up the stairs ahead of him, but it was only
to pull open the door to Audris's chamber. A bright glow of
candle and torch light spilled down the stairs toward him,
extending a golden carpet of welcome, and Audris was there,
stretching out her small hand. The weight of oppression lifted;
warmth surged through Hugh's body, and a delicious ache
started in his loins. He took the stairs two at a time, caught
Audris to him with one arm, and pulled the door shut with
the other.

Although she was startled by the way Hugh seized her,
Audris did not resist him. As soon as he pressed her close
and she felt the hard, engorged shaft against her belly, her
own craving woke. She had been eager for him all the time
they sat side by side at the table, strongly stimulated by the
warmth of his thigh against hers and the occasional touches of
his shoulder, arm, and hand. It was the main reason she had

been tempted to outsit her uncle; in her desire she had almost forgotten the tapestry. But her desire had been quenched when she looked again at the third panel of her weaving. Once it was before her eyes, she could no longer comfort herself with the notion that she had misread it; the savage intent of the unicorn was so clear it terrified her.

Audris regretted bitterly that she had ever seen Hugh, ever noticed his desire for her. Until that day, she had lived in contentment. True, sometimes she felt vaguely that she had missed the high joys of life, of possessing and being possessed by a mate and children, but she now knew she had also been almost untouched by the deep agonies of fear and desire. Now both racked her. The passions of the heart were a kind of madness, and in that madness she had invited a fierce and savage destroyer into her safe, small world. As she stared at the wild and threatening beast she had woven, she told herself she would find a cure for her madness; she would show Hugh the panel and send him away forever so he could not break and tear Jernaeve, neither the keep nor herself—for the pain she felt, racked between fear and desire, was like to being rent apart.

Still, the moment she saw him on the stair, his strange face with its wide-set, brilliant eyes illuminated by the light from her chamber, she felt so strong a joy in him that the fear and longing all seemed small pricks in comparison with what filled her, and she stretched out her hand to welcome him. And the rage of wanting that seized her when she felt him hard and ready, the need to be filled with him, made her think of the tapestry only as a thing to be hidden from Hugh until she could complete herself with him. His head was already bending toward her; she had only to lift her lips, and when their mouths were sealed, to turn him so that his shoulder was toward the wall where the panels hung and his face toward the bed.

Hugh dropped his arms to press her tighter against his swollen shaft, to lift her and then set her on her feet again so that her body rubbed against him, moaning softly with plea-sure behind his dammed lips. Audris held his head between her hands, so when he had to pull away to gasp for more air, he should see only the bed. She need not have held him; he did not try to look right or left, but lifted her and strode across the room to the bed, where he laid her down. He had even forgotten Fritha; Audris heard the door open and shut, but Hugh never shifted his eyes from their rapt contemplation of her.

She saw him reach for the tie of his chausses and held out her arms to receive him, but he did not accept that invitation to join himself to her instantly, as he had in the garden. Instead, he took off his clothing entirely, watching her, feeding himself on the hunger with which she looked at his body. Then he undressed her. There was only her bedrobe to remove, but Hugh lingered long over drawing it off, stroking and kissing whatever part of her he bared.

He resisted her and continued to caress her, even when she was so driven by passion that she lifted her hips toward him and twisted half off the bed, reaching for him with her legs to draw him into her. He knelt before her then, to give her ease and drink her nectar, but it was not enough. She cried to be filled, and he came into her at last, both of them crying out with his first thrust but not subsiding, building to a climax so violent that it was closer to agony than pleasure.

They lay quiet afterward for some time. Once Hugh moved as if he would separate them, but Audris's strong legs were locked around his hips, and she would not release him. He sighed and abandoned himself to the warm, sensual delight of being immersed in her without excitement or the pangs of passion. Later, when he felt himself filling again, he turned so that she was above him, leaving her to move on him or not as it pleased her. It took a very long time, for in the beginning Audris did no more than keep him hard while he played with her hair, caressed her pale, silken skin, and twisted himself nearly in two to lip at the pink buds that tipped her breasts. And their climax was like their lovemaking, long, slow, gentle thrills that passed into peace. Oddly, it was the peace that set spurs of eagerness into Hugh, sharp pangs of wanting this woman above all other things in life—above life itself, for if he could not have her, he had no use for life.

"I am afraid of you, Audris," Hugh whispered to her as she rested on him.

She did not answer, but Hugh soon felt his breast wet and realized she was weeping.

"I did not mean to hurt you," he sighed, but she still said nothing, and he did not know how to comfort her.

Slowly, reluctantly, she lifted herself off him and stood beside the bed, her hand stretched out to him. The tears coursed down her cheeks, but she did not speak, and she stepped back when Hugh reached out to take her in his arms, forcing him to sit up and then follow her. He was looking at her as they walked across the room, regretting the words that had hurt her and seeking a way to soothe the pain he had inflicted. Then she reached up and turned his face so that his eyes fell on the first panel of her tapestry.

The beauty of the work made him catch his breath, and he realized instantly that it was the picture that was somehow connected to Audris's tears. He studied it eagerly but could see nothing in the magnificent beast and its salutation to the maiden in the tower to frighten even the most timid. Then he saw it was not the only piece.

He nearly wept himself at the joy and confidence that united the maiden and the unicorn as they walked together in the sunlit woods, but he did not allow his eyes to linger on that happy picture, for he knew this could not be the cause of Audris's distress either. The third panel brought another gasp—of pain this time.

"I would not harm Jernaeve!" Hugh cried and then fell silent, appalled, not having consciously thought of himself as the unicorn until he heard his own words.

"Not by your will," Audris agreed softly.

"Why did you weave that?" Hugh asked, his voice harsh.

Audris shook her head. "Not by *my* will." Then after a pause, while Hugh stepped back and looked at all three panels, she asked, "Do you know what it means?"

"Of course not," Hugh snapped. He wanted to ask sharply why there should be any meaning in a ridiculous picture woven by a silly girl, who even said she did not always know what she

was weaving—but he could not. There was something compelling in the set of panels and a subtle flattery in the exquisite
ferocity of the beast. He tore his eyes away and looked back
at Audris. "I desire you greatly, but I am not fool enough to
consider winning you by taking Jernaeve. Truly, I cannot see
any way I could be a threat to your castle, but I will go and not
return here—"

"Perhaps it does not mean anything," Audris cried, catching
at him. "When I began the work, I only intended to make a
pretty picture, a fairy-tale picture."

Hugh was again staring at the three panels. Audris had said
aloud exactly what he wanted to hear—and he had to reject it
utterly. Whatever she intended, she had produced more than
a fairy tale. But… "It is wrong," he said. "That third one does
not belong—"

"I know. I know," Audris agreed miserably. "I did not
want to do it. The two together—the greeting and the
meeting—that should have been the end."

"No," Hugh said slowly, "that is beauty and joy, but—but
it cannot be the end of the tale, not even of a fairy tale. And
the threat cannot be the end of the tale either. See, the maiden
is not in the window."

"There is no longer any maiden," Audris whispered.

Hugh looked startled, stared at her, and then cupped her
face in his hand, lifted it, and kissed her gently. "Light of
my life, do you fear that I will turn away from you, wish
you harm, because you have given me your body and are no
longer a virgin? That is the legend; but beloved, I am *not* a
unicorn. It is not even my real name." He repeated what the
archbishop had told him about his mother's death.

Audris's tear-drenched eyes stared up into his. "I wish I
could believe that what I have woven is a picture of that fear,
but I have never thought, never had a single doubt, that you
would cease to cherish me."

"The fear might be in your heart, and you not wish to
know it."

Hugh put his arm around her and held her to him gently.
He did not believe it himself, for Audris had no experience

of unfaithfulness or rejection, and it is hard to fear what has never been experienced or even threatened. Every person dear to Audris cherished her; even Bruno, who had been away for years at a time, had been faithful, and never forgot to send a message whenever he could. She had not even seen any examples of abandonment, Hugh thought, at least, not among those of her own class. Sir Oliver might not be an affectionate husband, but if he had any woman other than his wife, she was not in Jernaeve. Hugh doubted Sir Oliver had a mistress at all; he did not seem interested in women—and the tone of Jernaeve was wrong for a lascivious master. Still, if he could comfort Audris by the suggestion that she feared he might stop caring for her, he was willing to support the idea.

"One does not always know what is in one's own heart," Hugh added. "And anyway, it is a mistake to judge an unfinished—" He stopped abruptly as Audris covered her face and sobbed.

"I do not wish to weave another picture." She shivered against him, and he tightened his grip on her. "I am afraid."

"Then do not weave, beloved," he soothed.

"I cannot help it!" she cried. "I am driven. I cannot help it. You do not know how I struggled against this last weaving."

"But why?" Hugh asked gently, although his heart was rather heavy. He knew what Audris feared the final panel would show. "Is it not better to know what you fear? Audris, you told me that your weaving shows what you have seen and heard and learned and put together in some way inside yourself. If that is true, must it not be your fears that are portrayed here?"

She had stopped crying and was standing quietly in his arms, her head resting on his breast. "Nonetheless, you will come to Jernaeve no more—is that not true?"

Hugh hesitated, then said, "I will not come again, true. I do not believe I am any threat to Jernaeve, but warnings are granted us from time to time, and it is stupid to be blind apurpose. That does not mean that I will give you up, Audris." He lifted her face again and smiled at her. "You have made your nose all pink with crying, and that is foolish. We must have been parted in any case while I win the right to offer myself as husband for you."

"But there is nothing to be won in Normandy!" she exclaimed. "Do not go so far from me."

"No, beloved, I will not," he assured her, then frowned. "At least, I will not go unless the king does not return to England—but I think that unlikely. What I will do first is try to discover if I have a right to a name other than Licorne. When I come to your uncle with a proposal of marriage, I would like to have some proof that I am *not* the son of some common churl, which I have always feared might be the reason for my mother's silence about her husband's name. But I have not forgotten what you said about the likelihood that my father was regarded as an enemy by Henry, perhaps even imprisoned to his death or executed. It is worth a few weeks' investigation in any case while I wait for news about what the king will do."

"You will take Morel and write to me?" she asked, her arms tight around his broad chest, her eyes pleading.

He kissed first the pink nose and then, lingeringly, her lips. "Yes. And though I cannot *come* to you, we will not be parted long—I swear it."

Chapter 17

HUGH DID NOT REALIZE HOW MUCH THE GRIM VOICE IN WHICH he uttered those words to Audris frightened her. She "heard" also what he did not say aloud, that he was pledging his life to the purpose of winning her and would die rather than fail. To Hugh there was nothing dreadful in such a pledge, for he had made it in his heart each time he fought beside Sir Walter, and it was an implicit part of his duty in leading Thurstan's guard.

Sir Walter had never needed so desperate a defense as to endanger Hugh, and the archbishop's cortege had not been attacked. But had there been the need, Hugh would have fought to the death to protect Sir Walter or Thurstan. In fact, though his voice was grim with determination, Hugh's statement gave him great pleasure; this time he saw ahead a great prize, a prize far beyond the satisfaction of a duty well done.

What troubled Hugh was the tapestry. He had set himself to comfort Audris that night, burying his own anxieties, but a remnant of the strange fear that had seized him in the dark hall clung to him. Not that Audris had ensorcelled him—beyond the devotion caused by her natural sweetness and charm. He did not think that. A potent sorceress does not weep and tremble with fear at her own work—or have a bright pink nose and sniffle pathetically from crying. But there *was* something different about Audris; she sensed things that others had to learn slowly, like the weakness of the king. So after he left Jernaeve the next day, Hugh vowed he would not so much as speak the name of the keep, lest something he said bring danger to it. The vow was only a sop to Hugh's real fear, though. He knew the only threat he posed to Jernaeve was the possibility he would rip out its heart by taking Audris away. When that notion slipped into Hugh's mind, he pushed it out again and buried it. Months, perhaps years, would pass before he could ask for Audris. Until the time came, he told himself, he did not need to worry about Jernaeve.

Yet so swift a solution came to Hugh's first problem, which was to discover his mother's identity, that he could not help wondering whether Audris's warning picture might be more timely than it seemed.

Having brought Thurstan safely into the comfort of his palace in York and under the careful scrutiny and tender care of servants who loved him, Hugh rode back to Durham and requested a meeting with the abbess of the convent. This was granted at once, and, to Hugh's surprise, a large bundle wrapped in a fine woolen blanket was given to him, in addition to a thick packet of parchment. Hugh had expected to receive the report of the inquisition of the nuns who had been in the convent when his mother was there, since before they parted Thurstan had told Hugh of the letters he had written to the bishop and abbess.

"What is this?" Hugh asked, gazing at the bundle, which was large and heavy.

The abbess smiled. "We were far more successful in carrying out our lord, the archbishop's, orders than we expected. That is everything your mother brought with her to our convent— except the gown she wore when she carried you away—it was so stained with blood as to be unsavable—and the cloth used for the shroud in which she was buried."

Hugh was staring at her in amazement, and she smiled again.

"Yes, it is unusual. Naturally we give away the effects of those who die in our care after we are certain that no relative or other person has a claim on them. But in questioning my daughters about your mother, as the archbishop instructed, I learned that the abbess of that time had saved your mother's belongings in the expectation that the archbishop would send for them or come to collect them. I do not believe she felt any surprise when the archbishop did not do so at once; she must have understood that there were many, many demands on his time in those early months of his tenure. Then the abbess died quite suddenly, and there was a... a period of difficulty."

Hugh nodded without speaking. Probably there had been a nasty conflict about who should be appointed abbess, either among the sisters themselves or between the sisters and their bishop or, possibly, between the bishop and the king. The problem had been compounded, no doubt, by the growing disagreement between Thurstan and the king, which made it impossible for the archbishop to mediate. But whatever it was, Hugh had little interest in the subject.

"Fortunately," the abbess said, nodding at the bundle, "that had not been held in the abbess's house but placed in storage and marked to be kept until Archbishop Thurstan requested it be delivered to him—and so it was kept, shifted from place to place over the years." She smiled at Hugh once more; this time her eyes shone brilliant with faith. "I am sure it is God's will that you have your mother's belongings. I do not believe, even knowing the effects had been kept for a time, we would have found them, except that when I was elected abbess of this community, I had a thorough search and accounting made of all the storerooms. Thus, I was able to put together old Sister Agatha's memory of storing your mother's things and the old parcel marked for Thurstan in the storeroom."

"I thank you, Mother," Hugh said. "I am beginning to hope it is God's will that I discover who I am, but I do not wish to deprive your house of the fruits of your kindness. Is there a place where I could look through this bundle? I have no use for women's garments or even sheets and blankets, and I am sure you have great use for them. If I could separate those personal tokens that might lead me to my family, I will leave the rest in your hands."

Since the sisters could indeed make good use of the items Hugh had mentioned, the abbess was happy to lend him the chamber set apart for priests who visited them. Hugh was glad he did not have to wait to carry the bundle to his lodging, for beneath his calm exterior, he was shaking with eagerness—and with apprehension. The apprehension had always been there, but the eagerness had come on him suddenly, sparked by the light of faith in the abbess's eyes when she said it was God's will that his mother's possessions come into his hands.

Hugh was glad of the privacy also because his hands were shaking as he untied the ropes that held the bundle together. It was natural to think again of Thurstan's description of his mother's struggles to name him. Could Licorne be a clue to something in her belongings? He began to unfold each item carefully, shaking out creases in the hope that he would find among the embroidery some symbol that was repeated frequently enough to be characteristic of her family.

There was nothing helpful in any of her gowns or under-garments or even in the purse he found at the very center of the bundle, which still held a handful of silver coins. He put a tithe of these aside for the sisters and, rather dispiritedly, for his hopes had been raised very high by finding the effects after so many years, lifted and shook out the fine fur-lined winter cloak. It was too small for him, of course, and too valuable to be given to the poor or sold for charity. If the furs had not dried out, he thought, perhaps he could have them remade for Audris. He began to feel and tug—and something crackled. Hugh's heart leapt up again. He felt frantically around the garment and soon enough his hand found an open seam and a hidden pouch, which held a folded parchment.

The first lines answered one of his questions; he knew at once his mother's name and family. He read:

> "From Sister Ursula to Margaret of Ruthsson, sorrowful greetings. Dear sister, I am writing this letter to you, rather than to our father as you asked, and having it delivered to you secretly because I fear for you so greatly. I beg you to repent your sin and part from Sir Kenorn. You must not think of him as a husband, to whom you must cleave, abandoning all others. You must think of him as a devil who has seduced you. Alas, I fear he is truly of that spawn, so strange is his countenance and with hair like the flames

of hell springing from his head and brows. He has seduced
you as the devil seduces many women. Sir Kenorn tells you
that marriage has absolved you of the sin of lust, but this
is not true, my beloved sister. You have married this man
against our father's will because you lust after him. Thus
you sin each time you give yourself to him, even as his wife.
Moreover, I am certain that marriage will not reconcile our
father to your husband. Indeed, I fear that such news will
drive him to violence, even to murder. Nor do I believe that
Sir Kenorn's family will welcome you, especially as you
will come dowerless and with curses. Beloved sister, heed
me—come to me. Cast yourself into the arms of Christ. Let
God save you from the double sin of disobedience and lust.
Written this twelfth day of April in the year of our Lord,
eleven hundred and fourteen."

Hugh sat staring at the letter after he had read it, hardly
believing its reality. But there could be no doubt. The parchment was old, the ink faded, and the nuns could have no
reason to play so foolish and uncertain a trick. He wondered
whether his mother had ever actually known the contents of
the letter. Possibly not, for it was not likely that she herself
could read, and the situation was too dangerous to ask the
castle chaplain or anyone local to read it to her. The very fact
that the letter had been delivered to her in secret, rather than
to her father, must have been a signal that her sister refused
to mediate between them. For a moment Hugh felt bitterly
angry at Sister Ursula, but then he wondered if the refusal
had been to *protect* his mother. *Murder.* Yes, if Margaret had
feared her father would pursue and take vengeance, she might
well have kept her name secret from the nuns. In any case,
Ursula's letter had come far too late. Hugh had been born on
the seventh of September, so his mother had been more than
four months gone with child in April.

The unflattering picture of his father as a devil rather
amused Hugh. From Sister Ursula's description, he must
resemble his father very closely indeed. And Kenorn had *not*
seduced his Margaret—he had married her. Hugh knew that

there were churchmen who preached that to take joy in any pleasure of the flesh was one of the deadly sins, but Thurstan was not of that school. He had taught Hugh that any simple pleasure, moderately indulged, that did no harm to anyone was a joy to God, who wished His children to be happy. Then Hugh sighed. He could hardly blame Kenorn, he thought. He himself had done far worse, for he had seduced Audris without marriage. And his father seemed to deserve Margaret's devotion: he had not abandoned her; Thurstan had been told that the lady came with a male escort and that she said she expected her husband to return soon. *But he had not returned.* Hugh sat staring at the blank wall opposite the cot on which he sat. His father had not returned. Why?

There were so many possible reasons, a number of them ugly and painful, that Hugh shrugged off the question. It was unanswerable at present, and a far more important question was unanswerable also—who was Sir Kenorn? The name was not common, but without some hint of geographical locality, a search was impractical. Hugh would have liked to know, although the answer was no longer of essential importance. Hugh had proof that he was legitimate and that his father had been a knight, which implied noble birth, and that was all he had ever wanted.

Hugh had no expectation of profiting in any way from learning who his parents were. A disobedient daughter could not expect a portion; in fact, he had got more than he should from the coins in her purse. And the probability was very strong that his father had been as penniless as he was, very likely a younger son, selling his sword where he could for his bread, and no doubt desiring a lady whose father, of course, would not accept him as a suitor. Again like father, like son. Hugh's lips twisted wryly, but then he frowned. If Kenorn was poor, where had Margaret come by the silver in her purse? Hugh sighed and smiled wryly again. Very likely the coins had come from her father's strongbox. It was very wrong, but Hugh found himself liking and admiring his mother more and more, regretting that he had never known her. She must have been a strong and daring woman.

That raised still another question. Why had Margaret left the protection of the nuns to carry her child to the cathedral? The answer to that, and possibly a hint as to his father's family, might be in the report the abbess had given him. Perhaps Margaret had said that Kenorn went north or south, which was little, but better than nothing at all. Hugh gathered all the garments—except the fur-lined cloak, the purse, and two very fine silk veils, which he wished to give to Audris to keep for him in memory of his mother—and the sheets and blankets, tied them together again, and left them in a corner of the room. The packet of parchment he took out to read where the light was better, in the tiny separate garden maintained for the priest's pleasure.

Most of the answers given to the abbess's questions were very short. Some of the nuns who had been in the convent at the time had never seen Margaret; others could remember little or nothing about her; but Sister Agatha's response was very long. Sister Agatha had been present when Hugh was born, and the memory of the event was still very clear in her mind, partly because of her exertions to stop Margaret's bleeding and her fury and frustration when, with success within her grasp, Margaret had seized her child and run away. It was the fault of a nun left to sit with the patient while Sister Agatha caught a few hours of rest. The nun, who had more faith than common sense, had urged Margaret to take last rites—thereby implying she was dying—and had urged her also to have her son baptized at once and to dedicate him to the Church before her husband could carry the child into a life of sin.

It was plain from the result what had happened. Weak and fevered, Margaret had feared that if she died, her son would be hidden from Kenorn and forced to become a priest or a monk. So she had pretended to agree, sent the nun to fetch a priest, pulled on a gown, and struggled out to place her babe in safekeeping. Neither her courage nor her devotion to her husband had faltered, even in the face of death. Hugh found his eyes full of tears. The stupid nun was now dead and beyond his vengeance, but he felt an enormous desire to know his mother better.

He also felt an enormous desire to ride directly to Jernaeve to pour his excitement and his newfound love and grief for his mother into Audris's sympathetic ears. Hugh wished, too, to tell Sir Oliver that he was not a nameless brat raised up beyond his station by Thurstan's indulgence but rightfully a gentleman's son. He was on his feet before he remembered the weaving in which the unicorn's horn pointed at Jernaeve. Hugh's lips tightened. He would have to write to Audris instead, but he would send her the cloak, the veils, and the abbess's report for safekeeping.

Hugh then wondered whether he should go back to York and tell Thurstan, but decided he would write to him also. So much business had piled up while the archbishop was in Scotland that it would be his rest periods he would give up to see Hugh, which would do more harm than good, even though his news would assuage Thurstan's guilt about keeping him instead of trying to discover his family and giving him into their care. Likely he would have been killed by his grandfather if Thurstan had brought him to Ruthsson. Nor, Hugh thought, would it be wise to tell Sir Walter yet. His master would probably want to obtain a "daughter's portion" for Hugh by force—and Hugh did not want that.

Having thought of Ruthsson, Hugh wondered whether there was still someone there who had known his mother and could tell him about her. In fact, it was not impossible that his grandfather should still be alive. If he were recognized as Kenorn's son, that might be dangerous—or it might not. His grandfather might have mellowed with age. He might even welcome Margaret's son once he was assured that Hugh would make no demands on him. And it was at Ruthsson, Hugh thought, that he might be able to obtain a hint about his father's family. Yes, he would start for Ruthsson the next day.

In the end, Hugh did not send off his letter to Audris immediately. Before he left the convent, he asked and received permission to thank Sister Agatha personally for her care of his mother, and the old woman, delighted to see him, had more tales to tell. Hugh listened gladly, for Agatha confirmed his opinion of Margaret's steadfastness and mentioned that the man who had brought her had—Then she paused and peered more closely at Hugh.

"He had your face," the old woman said. "I could not forget his face, with the eyes too far apart and the chin too long—and that nose! So *he* was the husband. Poor lady, she did not tell us that."

"Did he come back?" Hugh asked, wondering if Kenorn had some reason for not wanting to identify himself and had found a way to hear the news about Margaret without asking directly. If so, Agatha might have caught a glimpse of him without knowing, then, who he was.

But Sister Agatha shook her head. "I never saw him if he did, and I had asked the abbess's permission to speak with the husband if he came—to tell him I grieved with him, for she was a fine, brave lady."

Actually, Hugh heard most of the stories twice, for the old nun was beyond work and had little to do, and Hugh did not want to deny her the pleasure of talking herself out. So it was too late to send Morel to Jernaeve by the time he had left Sister Agatha and thanked the abbess, who rejoiced at the successful outcome of his search and, when he had made his donations, assured him that she and her daughters would pray for him and for his reconciliation with both his mother's family and his father's when he found them.

He did write to Audris that evening, partly because it was now natural to him to share everything with her. At first he thought he would send Morel to Jernaeve the next day and arrange to meet the man at some well-known keep or market town on the way to Ruthsson. But the letter was somehow incomplete without knowing whether he would be kindly received by his mother's relatives, and he decided to wait until he could add that information.

It was an easy ride the next day to Morpeth, where Hugh decided to spend the night, since he did not wish to arrive at Ruthsson near dark only to discover that he was not welcome. He was surprised to find the town buzzing with excitement and seemingly girding itself for both good business and trouble. Telling Morel to go ahead to Morpeth keep and discover whether he would be welcome that night, Hugh himself dismounted at the alehouse nearest the keep. It was necessary to duck his head and bend his back to clear the lintel of the door, and he stood just inside it for a minute, blinking while his eyes adjusted to the dark room. There was the usual, comfortable odor of such places: smoke, musty wood, and stale beer and food, overlaid by the redolence of some kind of stew and roasting meat.

By then the man of the alehouse had hurried over, but he had greeted Hugh with profuse apologies. The rooms were all bespoke for the tourney, the man said in slow, careful English, looking anxiously at Hugh's face to see if he understood. He could not promise a place… But as he looked up along Hugh's big body and into his eyes, the man's voice faltered.

Hugh smiled and answered in his awkward English, "I come not for that, goodman, only for a draught of your ale. My servant seeks lodging for one night in the castle. Then I go on."

With a heartfelt sigh of relief, the man gestured Hugh toward a massive, rough-hewn table that stood in front of a strong shelf, seat high, which appeared to be part of the wall. Hugh grinned. That was one way to keep guests from using the benches as weapons or from destroying the furnishings if they felt they had been cheated or insulted. The table, too, seemed indestructible. It was made of a huge log, split in half and fastened together, and was far too heavy to lift or damage, except with a good ax. Even so, Hugh thought, as the land-lord hurried away to bring him his drink, that table had taken considerable punishment. There were advantages and disad-vantages to being near the keep. Noble guests could afford to pay more… but some of them objected to paying at all.

There was a second, similar arrangement on the other wall of the room, and before Hugh had seated himself, a man sitting behind that table called out in French, "Will you join me here?"

"I thank you," Hugh replied, walking over and sliding behind the massive table. "My name is Hugh Licorne, and I have been in service with Archbishop Thurstan until a few days ago. What is this about a tourney?"

"I am Sir John of Belsay. It is possible de Merley up at the keep will have a bone to pick with you." He laughed as he said it. "Your archbishop has deprived him of his favorite sport—therefore, the tourney. Having prepared and armed against the Scots and heartened us all to fight, he was disappointed that there would be no war after all."

"I can comfort him on that account," Hugh said dryly. "He will not lack a chance to fight the Scots." He went on to give a brief summary of what he had seen and heard in Roxburgh, refreshing himself from time to time with swallows from the leather jack the alewife had brought to the table.

Sir John shrugged. "There is little profit in a war fought on one's own land. Had King Stephen pursued the Scots last year instead of compounding with them and rewarding them with Carlisle and Doncaster for attacking us, we would have been the richer and not needed to send an old man to plead for peace."

Although he was essentially in agreement with what Sir John said, Hugh was not about to voice his sentiments. For one thing, he could not help wondering whether Sir John was not one of those who had yielded tamely to the Scots when they came in 1136; Morpeth had yielded and now had a new castellan. In the second place, Hugh was not one to cry over spilt milk (not one to tumble milkmaids and spill milk either, but he used the phrase like everyone else), so what Stephen had done or left undone in the past was over, unless a lesson could be learned from it. Most important of all at this moment was that Hugh did not want to speak out against the king, whose service he hoped to join.

"We would not have been *much* richer," Hugh said, laughing and knowing he had chosen the right bad scent. "There is not much worth looting in Scotland."

"You are right about that," Sir John agreed, also laughing. "And do you find a single trinket worth bringing back—like as not your neighbor will cry that it is his, stolen from him in the last Scottish raid! Ah, well, there is more profit in a tourney. Not that de Merley will profit, except so far as the artisans will pay extra taxes, which comes to nothing." Then Sir John's expression, which had been merry all the while he was complaining, changed and became solemn and uneasy. "There is another reason, too, a quarrel *à outrance*."

"De Merley could not settle the quarrel without a trial by combat?" Hugh asked.

"It is not de Merley's right to settle it," Sir John replied. "He is castellan of Morpeth, no more. It is King David's son Henry who should mediate, but Henry of Huntington would probably not mind seeing a private war going on in Northumbria, and even if he wished to help rather than harm, he does not dare come into England just now. De Merley was glad enough to sanction a judicial combat. Better to have one man dead—or even two if they are closely matched—than let a war start that might draw in others and set the whole province aflame."

Hugh nodded but made a neutral reply. What Sir John said about de Merley's desire to avoid any chance of war was reasonable, but Hugh was uncertain of his feelings on the subject of trial by combat. He knew the archbishop opposed such battles, regarding as blasphemous the notion that God would judge the right by the shedding of one Christian's blood by another.

In fact, Hugh knew of several cases of judicial combat in which might, rather than right, had triumphed. On the other hand, he had also seen a few in which the obviously weaker party had been victorious—and it was part of his faith that no man, no matter how insignificant, and no act or thought of any man, was unknown to God.

That God was aware of the battle was certain in Hugh's opinion; that God was obligated to give victory to the righteous was, on the other hand, not certain at all. Men had free will; if they wished, they could engage in actions that were foolish and destructive... or even evil. If God intervened to prevent sin, there would be no purpose to free will. It was possible, on the other hand, that faith in being right could add to a man's strength and endurance, and that fear of guilt could drain a man's strength and dull his ability.

Meanwhile, Hugh's cheerful and friendly companion was urging him to return for the tournament, which was to be held on the day after All Hallows, and remarking that Hugh looked to be a strong fighter.

"I might come back," Hugh temporized, "but I have some private affairs to attend to first. I am not sure how long that will take, and All Hallows is only a little more than a fortnight hence. But if— Ah, here is my man. Well, Morel?"

"You be welcome in the keep, my lord, and be asked to come so soon as you be able."

Hugh drained his jack, felt for a silver farthing in his purse, and tossed that to the alewife, who had come in from the back when she heard Morel's voice. He lifted a hand in farewell to Sir John, who nodded, then smiled and said, "If you come for the tourney, ask for me. We will find a way to cram you into our lodging. All Hallows is a poor eve to be cold and alone." Hugh thanked him warmly and promised he would find him if he came to the tourney. Then he made his way up the rise to the keep, which overlooked the town.

He was welcome, indeed, both for his firsthand account of the events in Scotland and for the news from Normandy conveyed in Bruno's letter. There had been rumors of a grave disaster, the worst of which reported a counterambush to avenge Robert of Gloucester in which the king was killed. Fortunately Bruno's letter was dated after that news had come, so Hugh could deny it with authority.

His host, who had been appointed by Stephen to replace a castellan with waverings toward Matilda, was relieved of his worries, at least temporarily, and could hardly do enough for Hugh, urging him to come to the tourney and assuring him of a place in the castle. Hugh repeated his plea of private business and asked directions to Ruthsson. He was surprised by the shadow that crossed his host's face, but the directions were freely given, and a guide was even offered, since the distance was only about six leagues. Out of courtesy, Hugh asked no more questions and assured de Merley that he would find the place.

The next day, Hugh doubted the wisdom of refusing the

guide. He and Morel had ridden northwest on a road that very soon became little more than a rough track and led into increasingly thick forest. One could see areas where the trees were smaller and thinner, indicating that once—before the ravaging of William the Bastard some fifty years earlier—there had been cultivation. But no effort had been made to resettle the land. Perhaps William had not had enough loyal friends—or did not want to send his friends to so barbarous a place where the Scots threatened to descend to rape and burn. After about two hours Hugh began to wonder whether he had mistaken the direction, but the track did go on, and then he detected a few signs of life. There were animal droppings on the road, and in the forest, a thin column of smoke rose.

Pointing to that, Hugh told Morel to take heart. "At worst," he remarked, "the smoke marks an outlaw camp, and, after all, outlaws must prey on something."

Morel laughed. "If so, they be more stupid than most outlaws, who be stupid enough. This be a place to starve better than to steal." He looked at the column of smoke. "Charcoal burners more like, my lord."

"Well, then," Hugh said, "we must be coming to some place where people burn charcoal."

And, in fact, it was not long after that they saw some wild-looking hogs rooting near the edge of the track, which then opened out into rough fields where sheep and goats grazed, and finally, when they could see the river glinting in the distance, they came to a miserable village. Hugh's heart sank when he saw the dreadful hovels and the filthy clothing made of patches of rag over rag. Whoever ruled at Ruthsson, for this was surely Ruthsson land by now, must be a monster, he thought. But then he realized that the women and children had all come out to the road to gape at him, rather than run away to hide. Usually the extreme poverty that was evident here was caused by a cruel or rapacious landlord, but since the people were not afraid, there must be some other reason.

Beyond the village were more fields, in which the stubble looked somewhat richer, and beyond the fields… Hugh pulled his horse to a stop and stared. The track itself went almost straight down to the river, where it divided right and left, there seeming to be no ford. It was not possible to see where the left fork went, but the right climbed up a steep hill to a plateau a hundred feet or more above the river, ending at a formidable gate in a massive stone wall that ran for about thirty feet and culminated, ridiculously, in a log palisade that curved away beyond Hugh's sight. Hugh frowned. The condition of the wall implied that Ruthsson had changed hands during Hugh's lifetime and that the present holder was either a fool or indifferent to the current political situation.

The gate and about twenty feet of the wall, the part Hugh could see at least, was older than he was; the stones showed growth of lichen and moss, and the end of the wall was obvious. Attached to the old wall was an additional section of ten feet or so that had been built within the last five years. The new section could not be older than that, for the stone was rough from fresh cuts and marked with streaks from the mortar. But this new section also ended in a cross wall, and there was no sign that further construction was intended.

Hugh had, of course, seen other cases of unfinished walls, where the cost had outrun the builder's ability to continue or the king had grown suspicious and interfered by imprisoning, executing, or exiling the builder—or, in less extreme cases, by simply ordering that construction stop. But then there were signs of the interruption: blocks of stone lying ready and piles of earth and stones for filling. In any case, the normal way to build was to raise the entire wall inside the palisade so that it served as an extra defense while it was being built. This system weakened the defenses.

It was a discouraging prospect, but having come so far, Hugh decided that he would at least ask about the family that had held Ruthsson when he was born. Sometimes the documents relating to a property passed with it to the new holder, and if he was not curious, such writings might lie undisturbed for many years. Hugh was assured of a glad welcome the moment he and Morel turned on the upward track. He heard a call from the tower that flanked the open gate, but no portcullis shrieked its way down, nor did the huge doors begin to swing shut; and by the time he rode through the gate and into a large bailey containing many buildings, the master of the keep was striding forward to greet him.

"You are well come," the elderly man called. "What brings you so far from the beaten track? Are you lost?"

Hugh dismounted, and a groom came forward to lead Rufus away, but he shook his head at the man. "No, I am not lost. If this is Ruthsson keep, I have come here apurpose. I thank you for your welcome, too, but I think I had better answer your first question before I accept it."

The smile disappeared, and the man stiffened. "You are from Heugh?"

"Hugh?" Hugh echoed. "That is my name—Sir Hugh Licorne, but I do not know what you mean by 'from Hugh.' If I am from anywhere—"

"You are not a messenger from Sir Lionel of Heugh?"

Hugh shook his head. "No, I never heard of the man or of the place either."

The smile returned. "If you are not from Heugh, then whatever your reason for coming to Ruthsson, you are welcome. I am Lord Ruthsson, baron of all you survey." He laughed and waved a hand meant to encompass the untilled, forested hills and miserable village. "Come within and let my servants make you comfortable."

Hugh accepted that. He had issued a warning, but apparently Lord Ruthsson was so glad of company that he was not prepared to listen to it. Besides, Hugh doubted Lord Ruthsson would be affected by his purpose. He did not seem the kind of man to murder his daughter for marrying without his approval, so Hugh nodded permission to the groom to take Rufus, signaled Morel to dismount, and followed his host toward the main hall.

The building was a surprise, too. It was large and high, and Hugh could see that the sharply peaked roof had recently been repaired, but the style was very old. Actually, Hugh could not remember seeing a whole building of the same type, only ruins left from the days when the Norsemen had come into Northumbria and some had settled there.

"Are you newly seisened of this land?" Hugh asked.

Lord Ruthsson looked astonished. "Newly seisened? No! I am, in fact, in direct male line from that Hrolf Ruth's son who carved the holding out of the forest. What made you think I was new blood here?"

"Forgive me." Hugh felt awkward and confused. This must be his grandfather, and yet he could not conceive of this man being the "father" of Sister Ursula's letter. "You spoke as if you were not accustomed to the isolation of this keep, so I thought—"

"You thought aright," Lord Ruthsson interrupted. "I am not accustomed to these barbaric surroundings, nor do I enjoy them," he added bitterly. "Until he died, I was a friend of the heart to King Henry—truly a friend to the man, not a courtier to the king. I asked nothing and desired nothing, only to share my thoughts, my wonderment, my learning... The late king was not called Beauclerk for nothing. Henry loved learning. He... But I forget myself and become a barbarian, too. First you must be made comfortable—at least as comfortable as one can be in Ruthsson. Then we can talk."

Hugh felt even more confused and said nothing as his host raised his voice in a shout, and a manservant came from the shadows at the side of the hall. He led Hugh to a stair that went up to a gallery where wide benches fixed to the wall and covered with mattresses were designed to serve as beds. Hugh's hauberk, with the sleeves folded in, went into the space under the bench, which also provided room for his sword and helmet. Morel came up the stairs with the saddle-bags as the servant took the shield Hugh had laid on the bed and hung it from a peg in the wall so that its point rested on a narrow ledge. The shield, Hugh realized, marked the head of his bed and identified him, and that thought made him notice that the unicorn was growing very battered.

Jealous of his prerogatives, Morel had sent the servant away and helped Hugh out of his padded arming tunic and into a fine, dark red garment that, surprisingly, did not clash with Hugh's flaming hair. Hugh murmured his thanks absently. He was still looking at the worn device on his shield, hoping that Stephen would return to England before he had to have the shield repainted to remind the king of who he was. Once he was established, Hugh's thoughts continued, perhaps he could abandon the unicorn device. And he could not help wondering whether it would be safe to go back to Jernaeve—to Audris—if he found a new name for himself and a new device for his shield.

Hugh put that enticing thought aside for consideration when he had found a name and device to which he might lay claim. The first step in that direction, he hoped, was below, and he went down to the main floor of the hall. The shutters of the large windows stood wide open, and the sunlight of a bright October day poured in so that Hugh did not have to peer through the dimness. He found Lord Ruthsson seated in the traditional place, with his back to the north wall, facing the large, open, central firepit, where cheerful flames leapt and crackled and the smoke rose up to the high peaked roof to blacken further beams thick with the soot of centuries and finally to escape through hidden openings.

Lord Ruthsson was not so traditional, however, as to place his guest on the other side of the firepit, with his back to the south wall. In the old, wild days, perhaps, that was a necessary safety device, giving the host time to leap back to the wall and seize his sword and shield, which hung there, to protect himself. Actually, although there were a sword and shield hung on the wall, they were obviously relics of time past, and a bench was drawn up close to Lord Ruthsson's chair with a handsome cup and a pitcher of wine already standing on it.

Gesturing for Hugh to sit, he said, "As I told you, we are an old family, and we have always kept the old customs. You are welcome here, to food and to fire, for three days, though you be my worst enemy."

"I am not that, my lord," Hugh replied, remaining uneasily on his feet, "but I might be your grandson."

Chapter 18

FOR A MOMENT AFTER HUGH SAID HE MIGHT BE HIS GRANDSON, Lord Ruthsson gaped at him. Then he shook his head and laughed aloud. "Not *my* grandson, Sir Hugh, unless you are older than you look."

"I am three and twenty years of age, born seventh of September in the year eleven hundred and fourteen to Lady Margaret of Ruthsson."

"Margaret!" Lord Ruthsson exclaimed. "But Eric—who *was* your grandfather—wrote she died..." He got up suddenly and embraced Hugh, then stepped back to look at him, as if seeking some resemblance to his niece. And, though he shook his head at finding nothing of his family in Hugh's face, he kept a hand on the young man's shoulder, almost as if he feared Hugh would disappear, and said in a voice that trembled, "You are my grandnephew, not my grandson, but my dear Hugh, why did you imply when you rode in that I might regret my welcome to you. Why would I *not* welcome you?"

"I think this will best explain," Hugh said, reaching under his tunic and his shirt to pull out the letter Sister Ursula had written, which he was carrying tucked into his chausses, protected by wrappings of oiled silk.

Lord Ruthsson took the parchment and went back to his chair. He read it quickly, then looked up at Hugh and gestured again for him to sit. This time, Hugh did so gladly.

"They were two of a kind, Eric and Margaret," he said. "Both as stubborn and hotheaded as old Hrolf, who defied his king and came to settle here. And Eric might have killed her for defying him—he almost killed me when I would not agree to his plans for me. But who the devil is this Sir Kenorn that Margaret married?"

"I hoped you would know," Hugh said. "I have no doubt he was a younger son and penniless, which would be reason enough for your brother to object to the marriage, of course. But the name is not common, and I hoped he might be remembered, even though it was more than twenty years ago. He must have been a guest, and for some time, to have won my mother's trust and affection."

"As to that, I am not so sure," Ruthsson replied. "I mentioned that Margaret was hotheaded. It is all too possible that she conceived a desire for Kenorn all of a sudden and, having conceived it, clung like a limpet to her opinion for pure stubbornness. As to Eric's objection, I will tell you plainly that I do not understand why Ursula was so certain and so frantic. You see, if Kenorn brought nothing, Eric would not need to find a dowry."

"But my grandfather might have had some alliance in mind—" Hugh stopped when Lord Ruthsson shook his head.

"For that, he had sons—and then the dowries came to him. But if you resemble your father in body as well as in looks, I do not believe Eric *would* have objected. You see, he would have obtained a prime fighting man for nothing but his daughter's favors, which to him would have been nothing at all. Well, perhaps Margaret did not approach him right, or he had quarreled with Kenorn—Eric did not forgive—or taken a dislike to him for some reason. In any case, *I* have no objections. I am very, very glad you came here. I thought I was the last of the family."

"The last?" Hugh echoed.

But Ruthsson had looked back at the letter he was still holding and frowned. "I cannot see why Ursula would not even agree to write to Eric about the marriage. It is strange, for it would have cost her nothing, and I know she was fond of

Margaret. Nor do I understand why she was so violent against
your father—or how she could have seen him. Unless… Once
Margaret spoke to me of ending the long-standing quarrel we
had with Sir Lionel of Heugh by making a bond of blood with
them, but she could not have been so mad. I told her that
even *I* would not accept that solution."

Hugh, however, had lost interest for the moment in his
father's family. If Lord Ruthsson was the last male, the property would pass to heirs general—which would make him, as
daughter's son, the heir! "My lord," he said, "do not, I beg
you, take what I ask amiss. I assure you I mean no offense,
but—but am I your heir? What of my cousins, the children of
my grandfather's sons? I think they come before me, even if
they are only daughters."

"No children survived. Four strong sons Eric had, and
three daughters—and not one grandchild lived, except you,
of whom he knew nothing." As he spoke, Lord Ruthsson had
been again examining Hugh's face feature by feature. At last
he sighed and shook his head. "You are big enough," he said.
"The men of Heugh are giants, but you have no look of them.
I have never seen this Sir Lionel, but his father was a small-
eyed, mean-mouthed man with a face like a pudding. I cannot
believe you are Heugh get."

"But am I—"

"My heir?" He laughed bitterly. "Yes, you are. Heir to
nothing."

"Ruthsson is not nothing," Hugh said. "I do not know
what has happened here—"

"Despair and neglect." Lord Ruthsson sighed. "Eric and I
share the blame for it. Eric lost heart when the last of the boys
died, for he did not think I deserved to inherit Ruthsson. He
was right about that, for I never cared for Ruthsson or any
land. I cared only for my liege lord and my books. I was ten
years older than King Henry. I never dreamed that he would
die before me. I thought the lands would go back to the
crown, and I was glad to be able to bring such a gift to my
lord and my friend." Tears rose in his eyes, "Now it will all
go to Lionel Heugh! To Lionel Heugh!"

"Why should Ruthsson go to Sir Lionel?" Hugh asked, utterly amazed. "Did you not say I was your heir?"

"It goes to Sir Lionel because he claims it by judicial combat, and—"

"At Morpeth?" Hugh asked, thinking it was no wonder de Merley had looked at him strangely when he said he had personal business to attend to and then asked directions to Ruthsson.

"Yes, in two weeks' time," Lord Ruthsson replied dully, almost as if he had lost interest in the subject.

"What claim has Sir Lionel to Ruthsson?" Hugh prodded.

His great-uncle sighed. "Oh, the claim goes back to my grandfather's time. It rests on the old Danelaw claim of sister's son's rights. My father was a second son's second son. His eldest sister had married Lionel's grandfather. Heugh's daughter—who brought the manor and farms of Trewick with her—married my uncle, the eldest son. But when he died, they were still childless. My grandfather put his daughter-by-marriage into a convent—it was her wish—and because he paid her dowry to the Church, he kept Trewick. Heugh demanded Trewick back; my grandfather refused. But when he died, Heugh claimed Ruthsson by sister's son's rights for his son, according to Danelaw."

"But that is ridiculous!" Hugh exclaimed. "I mean, it is ridiculous now. I know nothing about Danelaw, but once William became king, Danelaw could not have any force. The Heugh family might have a claim on Trewick—the land of a childless widow should go back with her to her family—but if *she* joined the Church instead of returning to Heugh... I am not sure about that, but I *am* sure the claim against Ruthsson is nonsense."

"Of course it is," Lord Ruthsson agreed, but his voice was still dull. "Sister's son's rights had long been abandoned by Danelaw. Then they tried force, but we beat them, so Heugh brought the case before the new king—I mean William the First—and lost. But they never give up, and old Heugh's son renewed the plea when William Rufus became king. Fortunately, Rufus died before giving judgment, and when Henry came to the throne, I was already his close friend, and even Heugh was not stupid enough to threaten us."

"But then Sir Lionel has *no* claim," Hugh pointed out, "not even to Trewick, if judgment went against him in William the Bastard's time."

Lord Ruthsson uttered a bark of bitter laughter. "No, he has no claim, but who is there to dispute him in a trial by combat?"

"I!" Hugh exclaimed, struggling to keep himself from trembling with joy. "Lord Ruthsson, *I* will dispute him."

Ruthsson, who had been sitting slumped in his chair looking at nothing, sat up and stared at Hugh, then slumped again and shook his head. "No, no, do not. He will only kill you, and the end will be the same, except I will have your death on my soul."

"I have not yet met a man who could best me," Hugh remarked softly, but his lips drew back from his teeth. "My master Sir Walter could in his prime, but I was a stripling then. Have you seen Sir Lionel fight?"

"I saw his father—and I could not find a champion to fight for me against him."

"You have one now," Hugh insisted. "Should I ride back to Morpeth and tell de Merley?"

"Hotheaded and stubborn." Ruthsson sighed, looking troubled. "You are surely Margaret's son."

Hugh laughed at that, and though the old man had not yet completely accepted Hugh's offer, Hugh knew the further protests Ruthsson made were for the sake of his conscience. By the time the newfound relatives sat down to dinner together, Hugh had been ordered to call his great-uncle Uncle Ralph, and they had exchanged much information on both sides, particularly any item that might affect the attitude of Sir Lionel.

Hugh had explained that he was not friendless and would have the support of Sir Walter Espec and Archbishop Thurstan if he needed it. In return, Hugh had been told more about Heugh than about his own family, except that two of his mother's brothers had died in battle, and the other two, with their whole families and his youngest aunt—as well as more than half the village—had been swept away by the pox. Only his grandfather had lived. He learned, too, that the ennoblement of the family, which unfortunately was not matched by its wealth or power, was very new. Because Ralph had never been knighted, King Henry had given his friend a patent as baron so he would have some title after his brother died.

When they were finished eating, they settled down beside the hearth again and progressed to discussing the details of the challenge. One item of information was very welcome to Hugh: his uncle had taken the top floor of one of the merchant's houses in the town for the entire period of the tourney. Since Hugh had no idea how either Sir John of Belsay or de Merley felt about Lionel Heugh, he had felt reluctant to accept either invitation for lodging. He remarked with satisfaction on this fact, only to discover that his uncle was not listening.

"I shall go to Morpeth tomorrow and announce that my nephew, who was knighted by King Stephen, has come to do battle for me," Ralph said, his eyes brightening. "And I will say nothing of poor Margaret's dying in childbirth, so everyone will think it likely you have brothers and come from an influential family. If Heugh thinks you have relations who will try to avenge you and complain to the king about this ridiculous challenge, he may withdraw it."

"But I do not want the challenge withdrawn," Hugh protested vehemently. "Did you not tell me before that Sir Lionel has no children and that the property will go to a female cousin?"

"Yes, but I do not see—"

"I doubt the guardian of this girl-child would push Heugh's claim once Sir Lionel is dead," Hugh pointed out. "On the other hand, if he withdraws the challenge, acknowledging that his point of law is worthless, there is not a thing to prevent him from bringing an army against us. Just now, there is no overlord at all in Northumbria to say him nay, and the king is in Normandy. Nor can Ruthsson be defended in its present state. Forgive me, uncle, but this is a time for the truth. It would be overwhelmed in the first assault. I can fight one man, but not an army, so both of us would be dead, and Heugh would own Ruthsson by right of conquest with no one to contest him. In fact, I cannot understand why he did not march on Ruthsson as soon as he knew of Henry's death."

"I think he feared my influence with Matilda, for she knows and loves me well. And when Stephen was made king, I suppose Sir Lionel waited to see whether I would find favor with him." Lord Ruthsson laughed. "I did not even try. Stephen is a good man, but he has no more use for a book than to set it afire to keep himself warm. Sir Lionel's head is just as thick, or he would have known that. Besides, the challenge was cheaper than bringing an army, and perhaps he expected to win by default. He is well known in these parts for his ferocity and may have assumed I could not pay high enough to get a champion—which was true. Not that he is afraid to fight."

"Good," Hugh said, "I am glad to hear it, for his death will rid us not only of a single enemy but of the entire quarrel. I would like to keep our relationship a secret entirely. I am afraid Sir Lionel might try to void the challenge or perhaps spoil the effect of my victory by claiming that you bribed me to fight for you with a false name of nephew. In fact, let Sir Lionel believe that he *will* win by default. Then my entry in the lists will be an unpleasant surprise."

Lord Ruthsson looked doubtful, but after a moment he nodded. "I will do as you say. It is your risk, and you must do as you think best in all things. Once Heugh is gone, no one will wish to contest your claim to be my heir." Then he smiled wryly. "Not that there is much to contest about. Tomorrow I will ask the bailiff to take you over the farms, and mayhap you will change your mind about fighting over this scrap heap."

Hugh made no direct reply to his uncle's remark, only saying mildly that he would be glad to do anything his uncle wished him to do. He was fighting desperately to conceal his real feelings, afraid the wild joy that filled him at being heir to anything at all would alarm the old man. After all, Lord Ruthsson did not know him. He seemed to think that Hugh had large expectations from Thurstan and Sir Walter and that the property meant little to him. If he realized that it was all and everything, that it was not only a livelihood but the path to the woman Hugh desired more than he desired to live, might not the old man begin to fear that Hugh would do away with him to have immediate access to his lands? He would be wrong; a living uncle to acknowledge him, to name him nephew and heir, was far more valuable to Hugh, who had never had a relative, than the immediate possession of anything. Heir was good enough.

Hugh would have liked to excuse himself so he could write to Audris of the wonder that had dropped into his hand, but he could not deny his uncle the pleasure of having someone with whom to talk. In a way it was interesting, especially since Hugh kept having rosy visions of Audris listening, replying, and arguing. Hugh was not so caught up in games of the mind as she, but he had received the best education available while he was in Thurstan's care and was therefore not completely ignorant of the subjects his uncle touched. Much that had lain dormant in his retentive memory stirred under Lord Ruthsson's prodding, and though Hugh made no pretense of being a scholar, he had enough learning to ask sensible questions.

It was very late by the time he convinced his uncle to go to bed, but Hugh could not resist writing to Audris. He told himself it was because he might find difficulty getting away from Uncle Ralph the next day, but it was really because he was too excited to sleep. He was bursting with joy and needed to "talk" to his "wife" so that she could rejoice with him. Fortunately, he had already written about the information he had obtained at the convent, so he was free to pour out his joy at having found a welcome, a family—even if it consisted of one old man—and an inheritance, all at once. Without thinking that Audris could feel differently on any subject than he felt, Hugh continued to describe his pleasure at having arrived in time to fight Lionel Heugh:

> *Wishing to make conditions as easy as he could for his champion, my uncle took lodgings in the town as soon as the challenge was issued. Thus, I will be in Morpeth town at the house of Uhtred the Mercer from All Hallows Eve.*

I do not know which day of the tourney de Merley has set for this trial by combat, but I look forward to killing so inveterate an enemy of my family. I am surprised at my rage toward him and my thirst for his blood, for although I have killed men, I cannot remember ever desiring to kill a man. My desire to rid the world of Lionel Heugh is not only for my own sake, because to be heir to Ruthsson and Trewick without any contest or threat marring my claim will make it possible for me to ask for you in marriage. You know that is a prize greater than any other could be to me. But I think, truly, my rage and hatred toward Sir Lionel are because he has acted with such cruelty toward my uncle, who is an old man and—as far as Heugh knows—the last of Ruthsson blood. Could he not have let the old man die in peace and end the quarrel thus? Not that my uncle seems like to die. He is hale and spry and a man of such an inquiring nature that you, light of my life, would find him perfect company. Although he is worldly and cynical and not in the least holy, in other ways he reminds me of what you have told me of your Father Anselm.

I should hate to think of such a man cast out to starve, for he does not seem to have asked for or received anything from King Henry except the wherewithal to live from day to day at the court. If he were deprived of Ruthsson, I do not believe he would have anywhere to go for a roof over his head. Each time I think you would never have met my uncle had I not come in time to take up arms in his behalf, a great hunger wakes anew in me to cut down the fool that would destroy a man worth ten of any other. Beloved, I could write and write, but I am come to the end of this sheet, my candle is guttering, and I must end this letter so that Morel can carry it to you tomorrow. I am so filled with joy that I can hardly contain myself.

❧

Morel arrived in Jernaeve on 23 October, not much more than a month after Hugh had departed. It had been a very long month for Audris. The promise Hugh had made to her that they would not be parted long hung over her like a threat. She had been frozen by fear of the grim purpose in his face and voice, and when he let her go and moved away, her arms slid along his body, powerless to clutch at him to hold him near. She stood where he had left her long after he was gone, until Fritha, who had led Hugh back to his chamber, returned and found her and took her to her bed. Fritha wept in sympathy, gently patting and stroking her mistress and regretting her muteness because it prevented her from offering more comfort.

The maid was so distressed by Audris's frozen silence that she did not go to her own bed but sat on the floor beside Audris's, listening. Fritha hoped to hear the slow rhythm of breathing and the small shiftings of a sleeper; she feared to hear weeping; worse, however, was that she heard nothing at all for a long time, until at last a tired voice urged, "Go to bed, Fritha. You can do nothing for me now. Tomorrow… tomorrow you must set a new warp on my loom."

In the weeks that followed, Audris did not fight the compulsion to weave, as she had in the past. She did not scant her other autumn duties—she saw to the gathering and storage of herbs for seasoning and for medication, to the proper mixing of dried flower petals for sweetening the air and laying between the light summer garments to keep pests and foul odors away, to the steeping of roots and leaves for elixirs, the compounding of lotions and salves. She watched the young falcons begin to hunt and marked the nests to which the best of them returned, and she set ready the devices she would use to take them, letting the birds grow accustomed and lose their fear. But when the weather was wet or she could not sleep, she wove.

The picture that was forming was the last she would ever make that showed a unicorn. Sometimes, as her hands guided the threads, she thought how different a person she had been when she began the first panel—a fantasy, she had called it and had lightly thanked Hugh for giving her the idea. And that had been only a few weeks after she had told Bruno that what she desired was to be to a man what Rachel was to Jacob.

How ignorant she had been; it had never occurred to her that there must be a price to pay for the joy of being the central core of another person's life. She knew now that one could have either a dull, even plain of simple contentment or the great beauty of high mountains of pleasure and happiness mingled with the bitter, dark valleys of grief and pain. There could be no peaks of joy without valleys of fear.

Audris thought, too, of her childish resentment of the pain Hugh had brought her, of her angry wish to be rid of him. That was gone, together with her ignorance. As she watched the hawks or worked in garden and stillroom or wove at her loom, images of the two sorts of life—the even plain of small fondnesses and the rough, hard terrain of human love—had flowed back and forth in her mind. Long before the tapestry was finished she had made her decision. She did not fear to climb the cliffs for hawks nor fear the pain of falling—she loved the forest and the cliffs best, not the tame, plowed fields—and so she would not fear to love, nor the pain of weeping.

And on the day she told Fritha to turn the loom so she could see what she had wrought, she only sighed. She had known what the picture would be: in a garden bright with flowers the unicorn lay on his side, eyes closed, head pillowed on a woman's skirt. The woman's hands tenderly held the great head with its single shining horn, and she was bowed over the beast so deeply that one could see only the top of her head and the waterfall of silver-gilt hair mingling with the pure white of the unicorn's lustrous mane. The beast might have been asleep; there was no mark or wound on the glossy hide—but Audris's heavy heart could find no comfort in that false hope.

Then her eyes caught something else, a subtle shadow... When she "saw" it, her glance flew away from the picture, and she stared out the window, fighting cold waves of terror. The shadow lay across the flower beds, one arm outstretched toward the bent form of the woman.

One part of Audris marveled at her own skill in depicting so subtle an image by the use of darker hues for the flowers, leaves, and grasses where the shadow fell. Another part of her shuddered with horror, fearing that Death had shown himself again in her work. Before she could bring her eyes back to her tapestry Audris had to remind herself fiercely that hiding from the truth is always more dangerous than knowing it. More careful inspection revealed nothing more than she had seen when the shadow first caught her eye. There was no clue as to who, or what, darkened the bright garden.

Nonetheless, Audris was comforted by her study of the image. To her, there seemed to be a kind of tenderness in the way the shadow hand reached out. There was no sign of the pointing, accusing finger of the Deaths shown in most memento mori. And then she remembered Father Anselm saying, "Death is always kinder than life, for God and His Mother are infinitely merciful and will pardon any sin sincerely repented. It is life that is unforgiving and makes us pay dearly for our mistakes."

True enough, Audris thought, almost smiling. Did not the priests say there was no love, except for God, no marrying nor giving in marriage in heaven? Without human love, there could be little pain—and many fewer mistakes. All the while, Audris's eyes were fixed on her work, and suddenly she shook her head. True, the shadow might be that of Death, but she did not believe it. The tapestries that warned were *never* subtle. Death stood out plain and clear, showing his scythe and his fleshless grin. A sense she had felt before, that she was misreading her last two pieces, grew more insistent.

"Take it from the loom, Fritha," she said calmly, "and hang it next to the third piece. And lay a new warp on the loom. It is time to do something for my uncle."

The new work, a gay harvest scene, took shape quickly under Audris's skilled fingers. October was a quiet month for her, though a busy time for Eadyth and Oliver. Ale was brewed in October and the slaughtering of cattle and hogs with the concomitant salting and smoking of the meat begun, though that would not reach its height until all the grazing in the stubble fields was gone. Audris took no part in these activities, and Eadyth had long since given up trying to teach her. Now, Audris rather regretted that, for the harvest tapestry was soon finished and weaving left her too much time for thinking. She craved activities that would keep her head as busy as her hands and tire her so much that she would drop asleep as soon as the need for her attention was gone.

Thus, although it was rather early in the season, Audris summoned the falconer and his boys and went out to take the hawks she had marked. She explained the early trapping by saying that she feared a turning of the weather, which had been so fine for several weeks—everyone else was saying the same, so her remarks were harmless—but her reason was that she expected Morel any day, and each moment that was not fully filled was becoming a torment.

Although she knew it was unwise to set times because limits of days always made waiting harder, Audris had counted the days and leagues from Jedburgh to Jarrow and, assuming the same rate of travel, calculated when Hugh would arrive in York. Judging by his impatience, she guessed he would leave York at once for Durham to seek traces of his mother. She hoped fervently he would find some information, for she feared if he did not, he would go to the king in Normandy for lack of some more fruitful action.

Audris did not want Hugh to go so far from her. She knew her desire to keep him in England—and in the north of England—was selfish and perhaps even stupid. After all, the tapestries showed the unicorn threatening Jernaeve and also dead in Jernaeve's garden. Perhaps the best solution for them all was for Hugh to go far away. But still Audris could not bear the thought of his being so unreachable.

Thus, Audris was more than willing to give the training of the young hawks over to the falconer when Morel came into the mews. The news in Hugh's long letter nearly stunned her. Actually she had had as little expectation as Hugh of his finding any trace of his family, and she had far less hope than he that he would obtain a heritage through service to the king. What she had feared was that he would be hurt or killed, not that he might appear in a few weeks' time demanding her as a wife. Oliver would never agree, Audris feared, not even if Hugh offered to take her to Ruthsson and make no demand on Jernaeve. She had let herself dream a little when Hugh had first made that offer, because she wanted an easy solution so much—and because she had had so little hope that Hugh would succeed.

Audris knew her uncle's pride. From his point of view, she and Jernaeve were worth more than Hugh, and it would be useless to say she wished to marry Hugh rather than any other man. Oliver would consider such a desire a form of madness—or sin. Her uncle would laugh at her, insisting that if she wished to marry, she had suitors of great power and large property and that he would not waste her on a powerless young knight with one poor manor. And Hugh would not accept that. He would—Audris's eyes flew to the third panel, and she felt she understood it at last. It was Uncle Oliver whom she had always thought of as most closely one with Jernaeve. It was not the keep but her uncle that Hugh threatened. The tapestry was *not* a foretelling, but a mirror of her fear, as she had long suspected.

In the flood of anxieties that beset Audris, that was an island of relief. At least she was no witch. And in the light of that ray of reason, the last panel was not a threatening prediction but a natural result of her own anxiety. Unfortunately, it offered no assurance either. Her eyes went back to the letter she still held and flicked down the sheet to the end. For Hugh to fight for Ruthsson so that he could present himself as a suitor was useless, Audris knew. She would write and warn him… But he was not fighting for her alone; there was his own livelihood and his uncle to consider.

Partly because of the tone of easy confidence in Hugh's letter and partly because of her recent rejection of the tapestry showing the unicorn dead, Audris did not consider the actual trial by combat. She simply accepted that Hugh would win his battle and be unscathed. Her mind leapt forward to the next step and pictured Hugh asking for her and being rejected. Hugh's reaction might take many forms, but whether he used reason or rage, the result would remain the same. He might even challenge her uncle, but there was no danger to Oliver in that; her uncle would just laugh.

That would not be the end. A small thrill of mixed pleasure

and sadness passed through Audris. Whatever her uncle said, Hugh would not give up. The third panel might not be fore-telling, but it depicted Hugh's nature well. He would fight for what he wanted—and for what he believed she wanted. But what could he do? And as the question formed, the answer came. Hugh would take his complaint to the king, and he would not need to travel to Normandy to do it.

Only two days before they had had another letter from Bruno, warning them that King Stephen would soon come back to England. The king had appointed William de Roumare, earl of Lincoln, and others as justiciars to govern Normandy, and Stephen himself, the scribe had written under Bruno's direction, would be sailing for England by the end of November. Bruno hoped that David would not be so literal in his interpretation of keeping the truce until Stephen was back in England as to attack the moment he had news of Stephen's arrival. Probably the difficulties of waging war in winter would cause the Scots to hold off the start of hostilities. But Bruno had felt Oliver should be warned, just in case David decided to ignore the onset of winter to obtain the advantage of a surprise attack when Stephen was not ready to oppose him.

Audris could not be certain that Stephen would favor Hugh's petition, but she knew her uncle had a reputation of regarding his own interests before those of any king. In any case, Hugh's assertion that Audris now did wish to marry and that her uncle was forbidding her her natural right would cause trouble. And if she were summoned and the question put to her whether she wished to be married... Audris shud-dered. No matter what she said, she would be doing mortal hurt either to the man she desired or to the man who had given her her life.

Somehow she must explain to Hugh that he must not ask for her. But the thought of the pain she would cause him—and before a desperate battle... Audris looked up at the last panel of her work. *Only* a mirror of her fear? But the fear had a real cause. Again she read the portion of Hugh's letter that dealt with the trial by combat. For the first time she realized how soon the battle would be and realized, too, that Lord Ruthsson had not been able to obtain a champion to fight for him. Hugh might die—or even if he were not killed in the battle, he might be sore wounded and die from lack of good care. For once no pictures formed in Audris's mind. The thoughts came as words, and there was a frightening sense of a black and empty place somewhere behind her eyes. And then that place slowly filled with an image of Morel riding away, but not alone. Behind him Audris saw herself on her own mare and Fritha on her mule.

Audris drew a deep breath and smiled. She would go to Morpeth! How simple a solution to her immediate problems; she could be with Hugh before the battle so that if the very worst came to pass, at least she could have added a few precious hours of joy to her memories—and she could have tried again to conceive his child. If he were wounded, she would be there to attend him. And, in the best case, where Hugh conquered without hurt to himself, she could explain why he must not ask for her in marriage.

Arguments began to form in Audris's mind, but then she shook her head. There would be time enough to consider what she would say to Hugh when she was with him. First she must get to Morpeth. Leaving Jernaeve would be no trouble. Though she did not often travel far, she did occasionally go to Durham or some other market town to buy special yarn for her weaving or fine fabrics for her gowns. Moreover, this was a good time to say she wished to go, for it was in winter that she spent most time at her loom, and just now, she hoped, her uncle would be too busy to offer to accompany her himself.

That hope was fulfilled. After Oliver had come in from one of the southerly farms, where he had been overseeing the culling of cattle, and settled by the fire in the hall, Audris brought down the harvest tapestry. Oliver was delighted. This was the kind of work a merchant would trade for gladly, and Audris had produced it at just the right time. Jernaeve needed salt, and in the light of the news Bruno had sent, sword blades and metal ingots for new war-machine parts and arrowheads would not come amiss. Oliver had thought he would need to pay in silver because, with the threat of the Scots war, he could not barter away surplus grain or meat—if Jernaeve were besieged, they would need the food themselves—but now the woven picture would pay for all.

"You are a good girl, Audris," Oliver said. "It is a pretty piece. I will send word to the merchant—"

"I will carry your message myself, uncle," Audris interrupted. "I need new yarns and especially strong linen for my warp, and this is an idle time for me." She thought of the young hawks she should be training and blushed, but did not take back what she had said.

Oliver frowned, and Audris's heart leapt into her throat. If her uncle forbade her, what would she do? She could go anyway, of course, but she knew Oliver would scour the countryside for her, and there would certainly be men who knew her at Morpeth to send word back to Jernaeve.

"You wish to go now?" Oliver was not actually asking, Audris realized. The question was part of his process of thought. "I cannot go with you now," he added.

"I know that, uncle," Audris assured him. "But the weather is fine in this season, and it will be pleasant to visit the different mercers and give me something to do while you and Aunt Eadyth are so busy. With the extra work that the preparation for war gives you, it will be winter, I fear, before you can spare time for me."

Oliver nodded, although his frown did not clear. What Audris said was true enough. When the harvest was in and stored and the meat salted and smoked, he would turn to building new engines to defend the walls and to increasing their stocks of arms. "Where do you wish to go?" he asked.

Audris blushed again, and her voice shook slightly as she said, "To Newcastle first, uncle. But if I cannot find what I want, I might go farther."

The frown grew in intensity on Oliver's face. His first impulse when he heard the uncertainty in her voice and saw her blush was to say he would send Eadyth with her if she was afraid to go alone. But he could not spare Eadyth to go with the child now, and then it occurred to him that Audris was *not* a child. Women were not good for much, it was true, but Eadyth had borne several children and managed a keep when she was much younger than Audris. If he and Eadyth should be swept away by a plague, what would Audris do? Oliver wondered if perhaps he had oversheltered Audris. It would be best for her to go alone. She would be close enough in Newcastle, or even in Durham, for him to ride over in a few hours and disentangle her from any difficulty. She was shrewd enough in trading, he knew, and could be trusted not to give more than true worth for anything she acquired.

"Very well," Oliver said. "I will send five men with you, and if any trouble should arise, you can send for me, and I will come. You have nothing to fear, Audris, there is no need to weep."

"I am not afraid," she replied, which was the truth since the tears were of relief and, a little, of gratitude mixed with irritation. Oliver's voice was harsh and his words brusque, but Audris was beginning to realize that it was not only as a symbol of Jernaeve that she was dear to him. It was a most unwelcome perception, binding her even more straitly to her decision that her love for Hugh must not be allowed to hurt her uncle.

"Good girl," Oliver approved. He did not believe her denial, but he knew that true courage was the art of mastering fear; not to feel fear was only foolhardiness. "And when do you want to go?"

"Tomorrow. No. I will need time to make ready. The day after tomorrow."

"Make ready what?" Oliver asked.

"Sheets for my bed, a clean pillow or two, and suchlike," Audris replied. "I would not care to sleep in someone else's dirt."

Her voice was steadier; she was finding less difficulty in bringing out the half-truths, comforting herself with the belief that she was doing no one harm by speaking them. And she was not lying. She did intend to bring sheets and pillows as well as the extra clothing and salves and other medications that the bed linens would be used to hide.

Oliver *tchk'd* with indulgent amusement and laughed at her for becoming a fine lady, and Audris protested indignantly that her aunt always carried their own bed linens whenever they traveled, at which Oliver shook his head—for he had never noticed. But he soon tired of the subject and asked about the hawks. Leaning back out of the light so that Oliver should not see her unease, Audris said that the falconer had them well in hand.

"He will be glad to see me go," Audris said—again speaking the truth. "He wishes to give his boys more to do, but they are so afraid of me that they can do nothing right while I am in the mews."

Oliver frowned again because he did not like to be reminded of the awe in which the common folk held Audris, but he said nothing about that, turning the talk to a more general discussion of the hawks in the mews. Then Eadyth came in from the cheese shed, and Oliver abandoned Audris to discuss some matters of storage with his wife, so Audris felt free to slip away. She went first to the mews to tell the falconer that she would not be back to help with the hawks. Then she visited the shed where the herbs were dried and the stillroom, collecting what she felt she might need, though she prayed she would need nothing.

Audris's plan was already clear in her mind. She would send Morel back to Hugh the next day with the information that she was coming to be with him at Morpeth and that she would be at Newcastle for a day or two if he had important word for her. The day after, she would go to Newcastle. On the third day she would tell the merchant who most often took her work that a tapestry was ready and buy warp thread, which she did need, as well as any yarn that she found to be suitable for her work.

Most likely news of the tourney at Morpeth would be related to her at one merchant's stall or another, since some would be going there themselves. The concourse of people brought together for a tourney provided customers, and the mood of excitement made them ripe for buying. In any case, Audris thought, she could say the merchants told her. Then, the morning of the fifth day, she would start out for Morpeth. If the men-at-arms refused to take her without warning her uncle, she would send a man back to Jernaeve. Otherwise, she would stretch the time out until the tourney began before sending word of where she was. She did not think her uncle would mind; Oliver might be surprised, but he was used to what he called Audris's fits and starts and probably would accept her desire to see the tourney as natural.

Not only did Audris's plans run smoothly, but Morel found Audris's party in Newcastle on the evening of the day she had spent with various merchants. Hugh had sent Morel, with a short note full of incredulous joy about the possibility of her coming, a hint that all was not so perfect as his last letter implied, and a warning that he might be a day or two behind her in coming to Morpeth. Morel was also instructed to guide Audris's party and to settle them into Uhtred's house, where Lord Ruthsson had arranged lodging.

Audris had further reason to be glad she had chosen Morel to be Hugh's servant, for he was no fool; he had long since guessed that the affair between his master and the Demoiselle was a secret. He made no judgment; the lords did not live as commoners did, and in any case the Demoiselle was a law unto herself—to Morel's mind she was above and beyond any ordinary rule. Thus, to the men-at-arms, some of whom he knew from past service, he pretended that he had come to Newcastle on his master's business. Having found them "by accident," he asked to speak to the Demoiselle to beg lodging for the night with his friends.

Audris greeted him with glee, not only for the sake of Hugh's note but because he provided an easy way to introduce the subject of the tourney to her men. Between them, they prepared a plan that would account for Morel's accompanying them to Morpeth and almost ensure that none of the men would protest against going. Returning to the men, Morel spoke with great enthusiasm of the tournament to be held, whetting their appetites for a spectacle they seldom were allowed to enjoy because Sir Oliver rarely attended such events. Thus, when Audris sent for the captain of the small troop and said various merchants had mentioned the tourney to her and she wished to see it, there was no protest against going without warning Sir Oliver. The captain had been ordered to accompany and protect Audris; he had not been told where to take her.

Chapter 19

WHEN MOREL RETURNED TO RUTHSSON WITH THE NEWS THAT Audris intended to come to Morpeth, Hugh could scarcely believe his good fortune. Not only did he long to see her and crave her physically, but he had some explanations to make that would be much, much easier to say than to write. She would be less angry, he thought, about the false hopes he had raised when she saw the grief they caused him. By the evening of the day he sent Morel off with his letter to Audris, he had regretted writing it. His regret had nothing to do with what he had told her about the trial by combat—it had not yet occurred to him that Audris might regard a battle to the death with less enthusiasm than he did. What worried Hugh was the strong impression he remembered giving that he would come directly from his victory in battle to propose himself as a husband for her.

A day of riding around Ruthsson had driven home the truth of his uncle's remark that he would be heir to "nothing." Having seen the condition of the people and property, Hugh realized that he could not suggest bringing Audris to Ruthsson to live. She might not mind the lack of some of the luxuries she had in Jernaeve, but it would not be right to inflict on her the active discomfort of life in Ruthsson. Moreover, from what he knew of Audris, she was not fit to pick up the burden of rebuilding what was the woman's share of a manor's workings. Hugh wished for no change in Audris; she was perfect as she was, an inestimable asset. Her work—the tapestries and the hawks—was worth more than a knowledge of baking and brewing, but she herself would be deprived if someone did not do the lesser tasks.

Thus, despite his eagerness, Hugh's step was heavy and slow as he mounted the stairs to the solar of Uhtred's house on the afternoon of All Hallows Eve, and though he caught the slight figure that flew into his arms and held her close, he did not smile.

"Oh, God! Oh, God!" Audris cried, beginning to cry. "You have learned you will be overmatched in this combat. Do not fight, Hugh. Let me take your uncle back to Jernaeve. I will—"

"Overmatched?" Hugh echoed. He had been about to protest against Fritha's slipping out of the room as he entered it, since he thought it unwise that Uhtred should know he was alone with Audris, but indignation momentarily replaced all other emotions. "I am not overmatched! Who told you such a thing? Whatever are you crying about, Audris?"

"No one told me. I fear for you," she sobbed.

"You will make your nose all pink again," he warned, laughing now. "I have told you more than once that you are a goose. What do you know of combat?"

"Very little," Audris admitted, sniffing and blinking the tears from her eyes as she allowed Hugh to lead her toward the bench by the side of the hearth. "But I have seen war, Hugh. Jernaeve has been attacked more than once, and my uncle has gone out many, many times to drive away outlaws and raiders. I have mended the wounds—and been unable to mend them and watched men die."

"Wounds you may need to mend," Hugh said, "and if so, I will be glad of your skill, but you will not need to watch me die. Now listen, Audris. I do not tell you when or how to weave; that is your skill. Do not tell me when or how to fight; that is my skill."

"One is not likely to be hurt or killed while weaving," Audris replied sharply.

Hugh laughed. "I chose the wrong skill. Let me say instead that I do not tell you when and how to climb for hawks."

"But you *did* tell me," Audris protested. "You argued and protested and called me wild and mad—"

"But you climbed the cliff anyway," Hugh pointed out, his brilliant eyes sparkling with amusement. "So now we are even. You have protested my desire to fight—and I have listened to you no more than you listened to me."

Audris sat silent for a moment, examining his face. She could see that Hugh was speaking the truth about the coming battle—at least, as much of the truth as he could possibly know, for he was describing his own confidence. She had an impulse to offer to give up her climbing if he would give up this battle, but for once thought preceded speech. Partly she held her tongue because she suspected the offer would be useless, but there were other, more compelling reasons for Audris's silence. She realized how much her own spirit would chafe under the restriction of keeping her promise once her immediate fear was over. So much more would Hugh suffer self-hatred if by any chance she could force him to go back on his word to fight for Ruthsson. Her desire for Hugh did not give her the right to destroy him. Nor did the suffering his death would cause her excuse inflicting suffering on him.

The decision made, Audris's nature shied away from the anticipation of pain. She was here in Hugh's arms and would not be so silly as to lose her present joy through grieving over a horror that might never happen. But then she remembered Hugh's unhappy expression, and she said, "But if you are so certain of your battle, why did you look so sad when you came in?"

"Because I fear it will not be possible for me to claim you so soon as I first thought," he replied, relaxing his grip on her so he would not seem to restrain her if she was angry. "Ruthsson is nearly a ruin. I cannot bring you there until I have improved the land at least enough to feed and clothe you."

Audris pulled away from him in surprise, staring wide-eyed, unable to believe that all her worries had been for nothing.

"Dear heart, do not be angry," Hugh begged, touching her cheek gently. "It is not that I want you less, but that I cannot bear that you should suffer the poor life that would be all I could offer you."

"I am not angry, dearling," she cried, throwing her arms around his neck. "And I would not care how hard the life, but my uncle—" Audris stopped abruptly, cursing the tongue that always wagged before thought caught up with it.

But Hugh had not taken offense; indeed, he was nodding agreement. "Sir Oliver would not hear of such a marriage, and I would think less of him if he would agree to it." He leaned forward to kiss her and, when their lips parted, sighed. "He is right, but that does not make it easier to bear. I want you, Audris."

"And I am here," she said, reaching up to undo the fastening of his mail hood.

There was a great joy and a great wonder in Audris. Before she had known Hugh, she had not truly realized what she was capable of doing. It simply had not occurred to her that there was no need to wait passively for events to take place. A small smile just barely turned up the corners of her lips. In the spring, because of her driving need to be with Hugh, she had instinctively set into her uncle's mind the notion of letting her entertain his guest. That her uncle had his own reasons for yielding so quickly did not matter; Audris knew she would have managed to get Hugh to escort her even if Oliver had resisted. And this time she had been driven to devise this plan to come to Morpeth because she feared a conflict between Hugh and her uncle. Her fears were unnecessary, but she had learned a most interesting lesson: when the need was great, she could take action on her own.

Her thoughts were interrupted by Hugh uttering a soft groan and catching her to him for a hard kiss, which he broke as abruptly as he had initiated it. "You are here, and that is nearly a miracle—but it is not what I meant, Audris. I want you for always."

Audris dropped her eyes. "Come," she said softly, "take off your armor and let us rejoice in being together. It is wrong, I think, to spoil present happiness with dark thoughts. I cannot remember now where I read it, but in some ancient work there was the line, 'While we live, let us live,' and I think it an excellent precept."

She stood up, holding out an inviting hand, and Hugh took it, but he did not rise. He turned the hand so he could kiss the palm and then the wrist. Audris sighed and stroked his hair, but held him off when he began to pull her toward him.

"Take off your armor," she insisted. "I do not want to have chain-shaped bruises all over me."

He shook his head. "Uhtred saw me come up. I must not stay long. Fritha should not have gone out."

"Uhtred will not know Fritha is not here," Audris replied, and began to lift her gown in preparation to pulling it off. "I am not a fool. She is just outside the door to warn us if someone comes."

Hugh bit his lips and shifted on the bench as heat rose in his loins and the swelling of his shaft moved its sensitive head against the rough wool of his chausses. "What good will a warning do if we are rolling around on the floor naked?" he muttered, his words somewhat obscured by his need to swallow as Audris let her gown go and frowned thoughtfully.

"You are right about that," she said. "I gave my men leave to go about the town, but they are too faithful, and one or two stay always below, either in the shop or in the shed where they are sleeping."

"No one was in the shop except Uhtred," Hugh said, getting carefully to his feet. "But—"

"Oh, good!" Audris exclaimed, her eyes alight with a demonic mixture of laughter and desire. "Then I need not be cheated of my first sup of you."

"What?"

Audris did not answer in words, but bent swiftly and grasped Hugh's arming tunic, lifting the garment so that the front split of his hauberk folded back, away from his thighs. He gasped with surprise as she levered the tunic up until she could pull open the tie of his chausses and bare his lower body.

"Sit!" she ordered, choking with laughter over his stunned expression as she pushed him backward toward the bench. "No, silly, astride. Sit astride."

Astonished as he had been by Audris's action, Hugh understood quickly enough what she intended. A spike of conscience told him he should be more sensible, that he should curb Audris's wild, heedless mischief—for he felt it was as much mischief as desire that had given her this notion. But the thin thread of good sense attached to the spike of conscience was poor mooring against the huge wave of erotic impulse that swept him back onto the bench, and it frayed to nothingness as, lifting her skirts, Audris came astride him and took the tip of his straining shaft between her nether lips.

Hugh tried to heave upward, but could hardly move, and Audris was laughing, her hair coming undone, her skin glowing from within, her eyes closing as she lost herself in sensual sensation. The position was horribly awkward; the bunched clothing between them prevented them from coming together completely. Still, Hugh found that the frustration only added to his excitement, as did his helplessness to remedy the situation. Not only could he not lift upward to impale Audris more firmly, but he could not pull her down onto him either, because he had to lean back and support himself with his arms behind him to make union possible at all.

What constrained Hugh freed Audris. She was not certain why her hunger for Hugh was so intense this day that she could not forgo coupling for the few hours until night. She always enjoyed their lovemaking, but this time she did not need to be aroused; she could barely wait to take him into her, without kisses or touches. She had started the love play in fun, but once begun, she had to have him.

Still, remnants of the pure mischief that had made her lift Hugh's tunic mingled with a thrill at being the aggressor and burst out in laughter and playfulness. She giggled and squirmed, never leaving Hugh, but not trying to engulf him or establish a rhythm either. The irregular motion was building her excitement higher and higher, and when she heard Hugh gasp, "Audris, stop!" it was too late. She thrust herself down on him as far as she could, shaking and sobbing in fulfillment.

Hugh's protest had come too late for him, too. The edge frustration had lent to the physical sensations generated by

Audris's play had built Hugh's passion even faster than the normal movements of coupling. He had tried to free one arm to hold her still for a moment to give him a chance to control the explosion building within him, but he almost fell off the bench and could not grasp her. By then he was too swamped by the oncoming waves of his climax to realize he could lie down and free his arms. It was only in the actual convulsion of orgasm, as his weakened arms gave way under him, that he fell slowly backward and came to rest.

There was a brief silence while both caught their breath, as the roaring of blood in their ears diminished until the snapping and hissing of the flames in the hearth became audible. Then Audris began to laugh again, and Hugh put a hand behind him and levered himself upright. Audris put her arms around his neck, but he seized her by the waist, lifted her off him, and shook her.

"I am not honeyed wine to be picked up and sipped and put down again as you please," he growled. "Your 'first sup' of me! Audris, are you not ashamed?"

"No," she said defiantly, eyes alight, and still laughing as she shook her skirts into order. "Are you ashamed of your desire for me?"

He looked at her helplessly while he pulled up and tied his chausses. He had been shocked by the violence of his response, which he felt must be sinful lust, but the sense of wrongdoing dissipated before Audris's merriment and delight. Her pleasure was so open, so free of the darkness of hidden evil, there could be no wrong in it.

"No, of course I am not ashamed of wanting you, but—" A vivid image of his initial astonishment not only at what Audris had done but at her remark about the "first sup" of him made his lips twitch. But he could not allow her to escape totally unscathed for her naughtiness, so he pulled his mouth down into an expression of severity and said, "There must be a modicum of decorum between a married pair, Audris. It is nowise proper to be—to be…" And then, as an expression of utter consternation appeared on Audris's face, he bit his lip hard.

"You do not mean it, do you?" she asked. "When we are married by a priest, you will not always insist on—on plain fare?"

Hugh burst into laughter. "Will you stop talking of me as if I were part of your dinner? Plain fare! Do you take me for a boiled cod?"

"No, indeed!" Audris cried, smiling brilliantly as her joy bubbled up in relief. "You are a sweet subtlety—honeyed violets for eyes, whipped cream skin, and sweet, ripe strawberries for hair. I could eat you whole."

"You are mad!" Hugh exclaimed, laughing harder. He knew that by common judgment he was ugly, and here was Audris, using for him the terms in which a man spoke of a beautiful woman.

Audris chuckled. "No, I am hungry. I have just remembered that I decided to wait for you before I had dinner. Let us go out and see what is offered in the food stalls, and perhaps I will stop seeing you as a tasty dish."

When they came down, with Fritha trailing behind them carrying bowls and dishes and clean white napkins in which to bring back their dinner, Hugh was relieved to see Uhtred nod at them without sly looks or sidelong glances. That reminded Hugh, however, of another piece of information that Audris might not be pleased to hear. In view of what the landlord of the inn had told him when he first came to Morpeth, Hugh had not even tried to find separate lodging for his uncle; he had told Lord Ruthsson about Audris, and now he explained to Audris that his uncle would be coming to Morpeth the next day and would be sharing Uhtred's solar with her.

"I cannot complain," she said, "since it is his lodging and I am eager to meet him, but—but what of us?"

"Us?" Hugh repeated.

"Will Lord Ruthsson be… ah… uneasy if you share my bed?"

"I would not come to you in any case the night before a combat, Audris." Hugh grinned down at her. "If 'sharing your bed' means what I think it means, it would be fatal. I would be too tired to lift my sword to strike or my shield to defend myself."

Audris raised wide, frightened eyes to him. "Did I do wrong?" she whispered. "Have I done you harm in my heedless eagerness to love you? Was that why you were angry—"

"No, beloved, no," Hugh assured her. "I was only jesting." But he could see that she was troubled, and he added, "I was more concerned that having had your 'sup,' you would be the less eager for me to come to you this night. Although I cannot see how that can be managed, so I am glad after all that—"

Delight replaced the anxiety in her face. "There will be no trouble in your coming to me. You need only find a place to stay until it is dark, and then come quietly to the door of the shop. In the time I have been here Uhtred has not slept in the shop. He goes to his father-by-marriage, where his wife and children are staying. By then, my men will either be abed, or if they are abroad, they will not be at all eager for me to know, so Fritha can let you in."

Having settled what was important and come back to Uhtred's house with a selection of savory dishes, Hugh asked Uhtred to help him unarm and left his mail and sword in the shopkeeper's care, where he had earlier left his helm and shield. He and Audris then sat down to eat on a cloth laid in the mercer's small garden. They spoke eagerly of what had passed during the time they were parted, most particularly of Ruthsson and Hugh's history.

Many other topics were touched, both small matters and large—every subject except the trial by combat, which would precede the tourney. Hugh did not speak of it because he did not think of it; he was too confident of his ability to need assurance, particularly from a girl totally ignorant of the techniques of fighting. Had he met a man who knew Lionel Heugh, there were questions it would have served him well to have answered. Hugh knew there must be such men in Morpeth, but it was far more important to him to be with Audris than to seek them out.

Audris did not mention the battle because she did not wish to think about it. There were those who believed in rushing to meet trouble; Audris thought them fools. She knew one could not hide from the truth, but trouble was another matter entirely. Very often if one hid, ran away, or turned one's back on trouble, it disappeared. It was soon enough to meet trouble, Audris felt, when it was upon her and unavoidable.

They parted at dusk, Hugh stopping to ask Uhtred to have his armor carried up to the solar and reminding the mercer that his uncle and he would share Demoiselle Audris's quarters for the next two nights. The shopkeeper nodded without surprise; it was ordinary for several parties to share a lodging, and Lord Ruthsson had paid him too generously for him to cavil, even if the lady were to pay for her bed.

In any case Uhtred would not have complained; he was glad to have the Demoiselle and her armed men in his house. The tourney had brought crowds of people into the town; many wished to buy Uhtred's expensive cloth—but a few wished to take. Uhtred had already been saved losses by shouting for help, which brought one of Audris's men-at-arms running with drawn sword, thus ending the threat. Still, Uhtred did not like to stay open after dark, and he locked his door soon after Hugh had gone out, served those already in the shop, and closed for the night.

Hugh was back inside no more than a quarter hour after the mercer was gone, and he and Audris felt entirely like a true-married pair, for they were neither bound by time nor looking uneasily over their shoulders. They had a cozy evening meal in front of the fire, served by Fritha, who was all smiles, and talked mostly—as a husband and wife would have done—about day-to-day details of Hugh's estate. Hugh learned that although it was true Audris herself had not the faintest idea how to cook or make cheese or cut out a gown, she had several clever suggestions for finding people with such skills and inducing them to work well without knowledge-able supervision. Hugh began to shorten his time estimate for bringing Audris to Ruthsson. She would be even more of an asset than he had realized.

Both were very glad of the "sup" they had had of each other in the late morning. It had taken away the urgency of their need for coupling and left a warm, easy desire that caused no discomfort. They finished their meal, their wine, and their talk and went peacefully to bed, where they had "plain fare" according, as Audris said with teasing laughter, to Hugh's notion of what was decorous for a married pair. She admitted, as she was drifting off to sleep, that she had enjoyed her plain fare enormously, but she woke Hugh in the middle of the night and provided a much sharper, spicier meal, which they topped off with a very sweet dessert in the predawn, when Hugh had to leave before Uhtred opened his shop.

It had begun to rain not long before, so Hugh was, fortunately, able to return to the shop soon after Uhtred arrived and say this was no morning for sleeping out and he had come to take shelter. He seemed barely able to stagger up the stairs, which led the mercer to the right conclusion—although he was off target both when he wondered which town whore had been skilled enough to drain so strong a man so thoroughly and when he assumed the reason for Hugh's excess to be the coming battle. He was correct, however, in his conviction that Hugh was no danger to Audris in his present condition. In fact, although Hugh got into bed with her, she hardly stirred, and they both slept soundly until Fritha woke her mistress because it was nearly time for dinner. Audris then woke Hugh.

That day passed just as pleasantly, for Lord Ruthsson arrived soon after Hugh, Audris, and the chamber had been put to rights, and Hugh had been absolutely correct when he said that Audris and his uncle would be enamored of each other. Since it rained all day, the three spent their time talking and playing games before the fire. The only inconvenience they suffered was that Hugh had to go with Fritha to buy food; mute maids have advantages and disadvantages, and Hugh went cheerfully enough since a wetting was nothing compared with always wondering whether a maid could have let a hint of their love affair slip to the wrong person. The talk among the three that afternoon ranged far and wide, for the "unseemly" education that Father Anselm had given Audris was more precious than gold to Ralph of Ruthsson. But in all the talk, not one word was said about the battle to be fought on the morrow, though none of the three could completely block out all thought of it.

For Audris and Ralph of Ruthsson it was a dark shadow that came and went, making the warmth and joy they were sharing more precious and more poignant. Hugh alone welcomed the occasional reminders, as when his uncle said something about the tie that binds and Hugh recalled a fraying tie on the closure of his mail hood. But it was not important, not a danger, and he did not think of mending it. His heart was too full to bother with mundane leather ties; he was full to bursting with joy. He had never had a place and people of his own. Both Thurstan and Sir Walter loved him, but to Thurstan he was a son to be prayed for and guided, to Sir Walter he was a beloved ward. And he could not be at home with either because Thurstan's home was the Church, which did not beckon Hugh, and he was unwelcome to too many who had a rightful place in Sir Walter's Helmsley.

Here in this room, where the cheerful fire crackled and spat and Audris's sweet voice and trilling laugh blended with his uncle's light tenor and deeper chuckle, Hugh had a true vision of what life could be in Ruthsson. Here, he knew he was more than loved, more than welcome; he was necessary. Though he spoke less often than the others, he was the linchpin that held everything together, the hub around which the wheel of life turned. All he had to do to make the vision into a reality was kill Lionel Heugh the next day.

Chapter 20

HUGH WOKE FROM A SOUND AND PEACEFUL SLEEP WITH A HEART as light as a feather. Of the three, he was the only one who was perfectly rested and happy; however, if neither Ralph nor Audris was quite as bright-eyed or ate quite the quantity of bread, cheese, and cold pasty that Hugh did in breaking his fast, both did manage to smile and eat. Ralph put on a face of good cheer partly because he knew it to be necessary. It would do his nephew no good if he shook Hugh's confidence. Also, he kept assuring himself that Hugh had given good evidence of knowing his own abilities; Hugh was *not* a simpleminded, boastful coxcomb, and if he said he could win against Lionel Heugh, he could.

Audris's calm came from another source. She knew nothing of Hugh's opponent. To her it was frightening enough that he should fight at all, but each time she had awakened in the night she reminded herself that the picture she had woven of the unicorn showed him dead in a real garden, like that of Jernaeve, not a patch like Uhtred's, and, more important, the unicorn bore no wound. With a fine lack of logic, she did not now question whether or not her tapestry was a true foretelling. She clung fiercely to the knowledge that there was no garden here in Morpeth and there was no wound on the unicorn. Hugh would win.

This specious reasoning upheld her until they all had ridden to the tourney field. Below Morpeth keep, a flat field of the common had been cleared of grazing animals and marked out along two sides with rough lines of stakes. On the south side, where the sun—if it shone—would warm the noble spectators, boards had been fixed to the stakes to make a low fence, which, hopefully, would keep the horses of the contestants from crashing into the watchers. The north side, which would not get the benefit of the sun except near noon, was for the lesser folk and had only the stakes; it was not particularly important if the horses rode down a few of the common people.

Well behind the low fence were a few rows of benches. De Merley and his lady already occupied a portion of the central bench, and highborn guests from neighboring keeps were selecting places on others. For the trial by combat in which only two men and two horses were involved, all would prefer to sit. Many would prefer to stand for the melee that would follow, since one could more easily move around to follow an exciting piece of action—or run for safety if the battle overflowed into the spectator area. To east and west there were no limits to the field; in theory the defeated party in the melee were free to flee—and their opponents to follow them in an attempt to take more prisoners, of course—to the east or west.

Hugh had not bothered to explain any of this to Audris. He was awake long before her, since he had slept much better, and by the time he had gone to the latrine, looked at the tie on his hood, and decided it would last this one more time, he had decided to tell her nothing. He knew that Lord Ruthsson, although no fighter, was an old hand at tourneys, having attended many with the king, and would keep her safe. For the rest, he thought it was better for her to have new things to look at and to question. Perhaps then she would have little time to be afraid. He had not forgotten her weeping and saying she feared for him. He had then emptied his mind of everything concerning the battle while he sought out the priest of the nearby church and confessed.

At first Hugh's idea seemed to have been right, for Audris stared around with some surprise as they rode onto the field. "Are we not going to the keep?" she asked. "My uncle took me to a tourney at Prudhoe, and it was held in the large bailey. This is a great space for a joust."

Hugh and Lord Ruthsson both began to talk at once, and, of course, instantly stopped. Ralph smiled. "You tell her. I will ride ahead and speak to de Merley."

Smiling too, Hugh said, "Your uncle took you only to the 'ladies' meeting,' where pairs of men contest with each other with blunted lances. Here, after I have done with Sir Lionel, a small war will be fought. That needs more space..." His eyes clouded. "It can be dangerous, too. I mean for the watchers. Stay by my uncle, and if he tells you to run—run."

"Will they try to kill each other as in war?" Audris asked, eyes wide.

"No, not at all." Hugh was amused. "The purpose is to take opponents prisoner and charge them ransom—and a dead man can pay no ransom. To avoid quarrels, the price is set at a fair valuation of the defeated man's horse and armor. Thus, the rich and vain pay more than the poor and the modest."

Audris was about to ask another question when her horse slowed and stopped at the fence. Hugh jumped down and lifted her from her saddle, placing her on the bench side of the fence. He stepped over himself and led Audris to de Merley, where his uncle waited.

"My grandnephew, Sir Hugh," Lord Ruthsson said, "and Demoiselle Audris."

Hugh bowed slightly, and Audris smiled.

De Merley stared at Hugh for a moment, gave a brief nod to acknowledge Audris, and looked at Hugh again. "So you *were* Ruthsson's champion," he said with a slight twist to his lips.

"No," Hugh replied. "Why should I have tried to hide it? I had no idea my uncle was involved in the trial by combat when I was in Morpeth."

"Hugh's coming was surely an act of God," Ralph said. "He came to patch up an old family quarrel and offered himself as my champion as soon as he heard of Heugh's threat. God, I think, has already shown His favor to Ruthsson."

De Merley made no reply to that, but his lips were set in a thin line. He simply got to his feet and said he would see them to the herald, who would make the formal declaration that Hugh was Lord Ruthsson's champion. He started off, and Lord Ruthsson followed. Hugh looked down at Audris and caught the hand she put out to detain him. He bent to bring it to his lips and smiled at her.

"Not long now, Demoiselle," he murmured. "It will not take me long. Do not fret—or make your nose pink."

"Unicorn," she whispered.

But Hugh had already turned away, striding after de Merley and his uncle, catching Rufus's rein as he went and saying something to the great horse as he looped the reins around his arm. Audris watched him take his helmet from the strap that held it to the saddle and seat it on his head. He lifted it and wriggled it back and forth until the band was settled comfortably above his brows and the noseguard, which extended down from the band, just barely touched his nose without pressing against it. Then he looked back over his shoulder for a last glimpse of Audris.

She forced her lips to curve, but at the moment she was more startled than sad or frightened. She had never seen Hugh in a helmet before, only with his mail hood up. The change in his appearance was so great she hardly recognized him, for the noseguard hid the shape of his nose and disguised the odd wide spacing of his eyes.

She watched him join a group of men on the western side of the field and saw that there was an argument going on. Very faintly she heard Uncle Ralph's high tenor and knew he was angry. Then Hugh put a hand on his shoulder; she could not hear Hugh's deeper voice, but what he said seemed to have calmed his uncle. There was some coming and going that puzzled her, but then several men in handsome armor gathered, and a priest came and began to speak, raising a cross and a jeweled box that must contain relics. Audris's eyes stung with tears, and she shivered with fear. Was the priest giving Hugh last rites?

Before the tears could fall, however, the lord of Prudhoe accosted her, expressing surprise at her presence at the tournament and asking for her uncle. In her need to answer lightly and convince him that curiosity alone had brought her to Morpeth from Newcastle, where she had been buying yarn for her weaving, her rising panic about Hugh receded.

When Hugh looked back and saw Audris staring after him, so small and pale, all forlorn, he suffered his first pang of regret that she had come to Morpeth. He wished that he had said something more to reassure her and regretted that he had not explained the battle, explained that she must not fear every sword stroke, for what might look dreadful to her was an accustomed thing to him. He saw her smile, at last, and turned his head quickly, for he feared tears would follow that tremulous curving of her lips. His uncle would comfort her, Hugh told himself, and after the tourney, if she was still so fearful, he would make certain that she was not again exposed to seeing him fight. But despite his concern for her, her fear was precious to him, and he felt all the more determined to possess her.

On that high note Hugh reached de Merley and his uncle, who were speaking to the herald. To his surprise, he saw that de Merley was both angry and embarrassed, and his uncle blazingly furious. "He is my heir!" Ralph was shouting. "How can he swear not to claim the lands? He *must* claim them!"

"But I cannot be a party to alienating lands that might be claimed by the crown," de Merley said uneasily.

Ralph broke into another angry tirade, and Hugh realized that de Merley did not believe he *was* Ralph's nephew. De Merley thought that Ralph could not pay enough to induce a champion to risk his life against Lionel Heugh and had added the reversion of Ruthsson to the price. He put a calming hand on his uncle's shoulder.

"I *am* Lord Ruthsson's grandnephew," he said calmly. "I can prove it by documents, and Archbishop Thurstan, as well as the sisters in the convent where I was born, will swear that my mother was Margaret of Ruthsson. What I am willing to do is to take oath that I am daughter's son to the late Eric of Ruthsson, and the eldest male of the blood of Ralph of Ruthsson. And I will swear also to present to the king my claim to be heir to Ralph, lord of Ruthsson, and have it confirmed."

Under Hugh's hand, Ralph stirred angrily, but Hugh

tightened his grip, and his uncle subsided. De Merley nodded brusquely, not completely satisfied, but knowing he could obtain no more. If Hugh was Ruthsson's nephew, he had a right to the land—although the king might not be pleased; if he was not, de Merley had witnesses to Hugh's swearing falsely. He sent one of his squires, who had been assisting the herald, to find the priest, who was not far off. The Church officially disapproved of tourneys, but a priest need have no fear of being reprimanded for attending. Was it not his duty to give last rites to any who might be fatally wounded? And in any case, for a trial by combat, which nearly always ended in death, he must attend the loser—or both, if both contestants died—and invoke God's attention to the contest so that all would accept the outcome as His will.

By the time the more important men who had come to the tourney had been summoned as witnesses and Hugh had sworn his oath, both sides of the field behind the marking posts were crowded with spectators. Hugh looked around at the busy crowd, all dressed in their best, many seated and breaking their fasts with food brought from home or beckoning to the vendors who threaded through the crowd hawking their wares. He smiled to himself, thinking that their desires and his were directly opposed—not that the spectators cared who won or lost, but that they anticipated a long, bloody contest, whereas he would be delighted if Sir Lionel were unseated and broke his neck on the first pass with lances. His attention was drawn from the crowd by the herald, who mounted his horse and rode to the other end of the field. Hugh presumed it was to determine whether Sir Lionel was ready, and he watched closely, hoping to catch sight of his opponent.

The herald was a local man, and although he did not particularly like Sir Lionel, who had a hot temper and a quarrelsome disposition, he still felt a certain loyalty to another local magnate. Thus, he intended to pass along the surprising news that Lord Ruthsson, who all had thought the last of his blood, had discovered a long-lost nephew. He got only as far as "Lord Ruthsson has found a champion at last—"

"Do you think I fear that?" Lionel Heugh snapped angrily.

"I am not blind. I saw the conclave that went to greet him. I know what you think, too. But my quarrel is just, and I do not fear the judgment of men or God."

The herald was annoyed by Sir Lionel's attitude. He had spoken with the intention of doing Sir Lionel good, for after seeing Hugh, he was not so certain as he had been originally that Sir Lionel would win. In fact, he had intended to warn Sir Lionel that Ruthsson had found blood relations who would doubtless contest Sir Lionel's claim, whether or not he was successful in the battle, because the king had not actually sanctioned the challenge. Now irritation led to the realization that his news could serve no purpose. For Sir Lionel to back down as soon as a champion appeared to support the aged and unwarlike Ralph Ruthsson would make him the laughing-stock of the entire shire.

Irritation also reminded the herald that although there was some justice in Sir Lionel's claim—custom did decree that the dowry of a childless widow be returned to her family—he, like most others, had been disgusted by the challenge to Ruthsson, who was old and without friends since the death of King Henry. No one had been disgusted enough to risk his life for Ruthsson—and that, of course, had made all of them even angrier at Sir Lionel. So he said no more and was very grateful that, at that moment, the sound of bells rose faintly above the noise of the crowd. The herald glanced to the east and judged from the height of the pale sun that the bells had sounded for the hour of prime.

"It is time," he said with relief, and turned his horse abruptly toward the center of the field. Once at his goal, he began to call out the parties and the terms of the quarrel.

Hugh had watched the herald cross the field and looked with considerable interest at the man to whom he spoke, who must be Sir Lionel. Judging from a comparison with the herald, Sir Lionel was as tall as Hugh and might be heavier. The distance was too great to see small details, but Sir Lionel's armor looked well worn. There might, Hugh thought, be more to his uncle's warnings than he had first credited, and he turned to Ralph, who was still protesting against de

Merley's suspicions, and asked him to return to Audris. Both men looked around. De Merley, seeing the herald coming to the center of the field, hurried off to assume his position as judge. Ralph seemed about to say something, but instead embraced Hugh, pulled his head down to kiss him, embraced him again, and hurried away.

As the herald began to speak, Hugh walked to the squire who was holding a bundle of lances and examined them carefully, choosing three, which he named in order of use to the squire, and then another three in case Sir Lionel wished to extend the number of passes of jousting. He then mounted Rufus and took the first lance in hand, resting the shaft easily on his right foot while he waited and turning his destrier so that he could watch his opponent.

Sir Lionel had already tucked the shaft of his spear under his arm. A flicker of satisfaction passed through Hugh, although his face remained expressionless. Despite the difference in their ages, Hugh was reasonably certain that Sir Lionel was a less experienced jouster than he was. Hugh knew enough not to tire his arm holding a lance while a herald called the challenge; they were usually long-winded beasts, heralds.

In this case, Hugh was only partly right. He had plenty of time to loop his reins around his saddle pommel, so that his right hand would be free to manage the lance and his left to hold his shield, because the charge, which was complicated, took time to recite. Unlike other jousts, the herald actually added no flourishes of his own, nor had either contestant hired a pursuivant to cry up his ancestry and prowess. The priest who had taken Hugh's oath, however, followed the herald onto the field to call on God and the saint with whose relics he symbolically consecrated the field to judge the battle.

Hugh added his own devout prayers to Mary to protect and uphold him. He was diverted by the memory of a legend that told of the Holy Mother taking the place in the jousts of a knight who had been particularly devoted to her when he was unable to come to the field as promised, and Hugh murmured, "I need not ask so much of you, Domina, only to cast an eye in my direction and lend strength to my arms." He had closed his eyes to concentrate on his prayers and did not see the priest retire to a seat beside de Merley's lady.

Thus, the herald's bellow, "In God's name, do your battle!" took Hugh by surprise. His eyes snapped open in the middle of an Ave Maria to see the herald spur his horse off the field, out of the way.

Reflexively, Hugh flipped two loops of the rein off the pommel to give Rufus his head, swung his lance into position, drove his spurs into Rufus's sides, and shouted loudly to incite his horse to its greatest effort. Over the edge of his shield, his eyes watched his oncoming opponent narrowly. They were headed directly toward each other; Hugh's knees gripped the destrier firmly, exerting an equal pressure but ready instantly to prod hard right or left to follow Sir Lionel if he swerved or to swerve himself to avoid a collision. In the moments in which he closed with his opponent, he could perceive no weakness in Sir Lionel's riding style, but he hardly had time for a flash of disappointment before they came together.

The shock was hard, both horses checked in their stride momentarily, but Hugh had withstood much harder, and he twisted and lifted his shield, urging Rufus leftward into Sir Lionel's horse as he drove his own body forward as hard as he could. His hope flared high as he slatted off Sir Lionel's lance and saw the man bend back in his saddle, but in the next instant he fell forward himself as Sir Lionel forced his shield upward and Hugh's lance slipped off over his opponent's head. He gasped as his chest hit the pommel of his saddle, but the blow was a mercy because Sir Lionel brought his spear around in a vicious arc that could have broken Hugh's arm had it hit him. As it was, it passed harmlessly over his back, and Rufus plunged on out of range.

Hugh was infuriated by what Sir Lionel had done, mostly because it made him realize how foolish he had been to think a battle *à outrance* would be fought according to the courteous rules of tourney jousting. This was war, he reminded himself, and his purpose was to kill Lionel of Heugh. He swung Rufus around, yelling and spurring, grinning with vicious joy when he saw that his opponent was only just starting his turn, his lance all out of balance. Sir Lionel made a desperate effort to aim and steady his weapon, and although it was too late to save him, the wild swing of his lance caught Hugh on the side of the head. The blow was not severe, but as Hugh struck and Lionel toppled back off his horse, instinctively clinging to his weapon, the lance flew upward, catching on the ornamental rim of Hugh's helmet and pushing if off. By the time Hugh's own lance had done its work and he was able to cast it away, it was too late to catch his helmet or even see where it had gone.

The crowd was roaring, some shouting praise of Hugh's blow, others imprecations because they thought the battle was over too soon. Hugh was too busy to hear more than a vague noise, to which he paid no attention. Lionel's horse had veered in toward Rufus because his rider struck him hard on the right flank as he fell. Rufus instinctively veered away, and at the speed he was going, he was well past where Lionel had fallen before Hugh could check him or turn him. Hugh was aware of a change in the sound the crowd was making, so he was not surprised when he got Rufus around to see Lionel already on his knees with his sword drawn.

Hugh had checked Rufus and had his leg over the saddle to dismount before he recalled that in a judicial combat there would have been no shame in riding Lionel down. His hesitation was so brief that no one noticed, and his courtesy was marked by another great roar of approval from the spectators. But Hugh was not concerned with displaying either his courage or his courtesy; he was only thinking of Rufus. In a tournament, his horse would have been safe; no man who expected ever to show his face again would have struck at the stallion. In a combat that would end with death for one of the adversaries, Rufus would be merely a bigger and better target, and no one would blame Lionel for killing the horse to even conditions between himself and the rider.

As Hugh dismounted and drove Rufus away with a gentle blow and a word of command, Lionel climbed to his feet. Hugh ran forward, drawing his sword, hoping to find his opponent still dazed from his fall, but the blow he launched was readily met, and Lionel skillfully twisted his long, kite-shaped shield to catch Hugh's sword and hold it. He was not successful, but he pushed the weapon down far enough to get in a shrewd blow of his own. Hugh caught it on his shield and was most unpleasantly surprised by the man's power. He felt the shock to his shoulder, but what was far worse, he could feel the shield pull outward from both elbow strap and handgrip. Seemingly, the frame had weakened somewhere.

Hugh responded with a flurry of cuts, an attempt to prevent Lionel from exploiting his advantage and, if he were lucky, to end the struggle. He succeeded only in turning Lionel around and driving him back, but he could see the attack was accomplishing nothing. Hugh even caught the ghost of a grin on his opponent's hard mouth, and he was infuriated again. Heugh was no jouster, but he *was* a fighter, and he was plainly expecting Hugh to wear himself out in wild, fruitless attacks and then fall an easy victim to the "wiser man" who had defended himself without expending much effort.

This flash of rage was brief, however, for Hugh saw a way to turn his opponent's contempt to his own advantage. He would do his best to make Sir Lionel think he had less stamina than strength by easing off and renewing his attack several times, each time making the period during which he attacked shorter and the strokes feebler. Then, when Heugh thought he was nearly exhausted, he would pretend to trip or use some other device to draw Lionel to attack him—and then he would take him. In accordance with this plan, Hugh slowed his slashing strikes, which did rest his arm, while he seemed to search for another opening. Lionel reacted immediately by attacking in turn, with the clear intention of keeping Hugh too active to recover the strength he had expended in his first fruitless onslaught. And Hugh had to admire his adversary's skill and cleverness. Rather than give mighty blows, he poked and prodded, implying with his gestures that Hugh was not worth great strokes.

Even though he knew Lionel's purpose, Hugh was angered and felt a strong urge to renew his violent assault and crush his sneering enemy. Sound training held him back from instant response—and saved his life. Lionel made one more jab at Hugh's right thigh, which Hugh parried, and just when Hugh would have rushed him (had he lost control of his temper), he brought his sword into a huge overhead stroke that would have cleaved Hugh's helmetless skull or his broken shield and his arm if he had caught the full force of the blow. Because Hugh had not swung his sword to the side to slash and had not rushed forward, it was only the tip of Lionel's weapon that he had to ward away. Still his shield creaked protestingly, and Hugh had a sudden cold doubt that he could, after all, triumph.

He could think of no better plan than the one he had decided upon, however, and thrust Sir Lionel's sword violently back at him with his shield while he swung his own—and connected. His enemy, who had been too sure of how he would react, had been slow to respond to the unexpected, and he howled; but he jumped back lightly, showing he was not much hurt. Still a surge of triumph rose in Hugh, only to be abruptly checked when another violent stroke fell on his shield.

That time Hugh gasped in pain, for his arm was actually hit by Lionel's blade and was only saved from being cut and broken by the thickness of the tough hide. The shield frame was shattered; it no longer bowed slightly out from the arm that held it to distribute the force of any blow over a wide surface. Now, each time Lionel struck the shield, it would bend, so the force would concentrate in a small area and do great damage. Hugh knew he could not endure many more strokes on that arm.

Lionel knew it too and slashed at the same spot again, obviously hoping to cut through the hide and destroy Hugh's shield completely—but that time Hugh was ready. He twisted the shield so that the sword blow fell on the right edge, which was supported directly by his hand; at the same time, he himself struck a vicious overhand blow at Lionel's left shoulder and hit him. Lionel roared again—this time, Hugh judged, more with rage than pain, for Hugh's sword had needed to push down the upper edge of his opponent's shield before it could touch his shoulder and the stroke could have had little force remaining. Hugh himself made no sound, although he had had to bite back a cry. He had managed to ward off Lionel's stroke, but his hand throbbed with pain and felt desperately weak; the pain was nothing, but if he could not grip his shield at all, he would be in desperate straits.

A slash at his helmetless head, which he barely parried because he expected it to curve toward his shield, reminded Hugh of another danger he had almost forgotten. To protect himself, he launched another offensive, again driving Sir Lionel back. Hugh could take little pleasure in his enemy's retreat, however, since he was sure it was tactical rather than necessary. But his assault was so furious that he did manage to land two more blows, the second of which drew a cry of pain. He paid for that small success by himself being struck on the left hip— another result of the failure of his shield, because its shape had warped and sagged away from a part of his body he thought was protected. There was an instant sensation of warmth, and Hugh muttered a curse, knowing he was losing blood. He no longer had all the time he needed to tire his enemy; unless Sir Lionel was also bleeding—and if he was, he was concealing his wound under his shield—Hugh would lose strength faster.

There was no help for that. All Hugh could do was to press his attack as fiercely as possible, and he swung and hammered, keeping Lionel's sword as busy as he could. But the older man was a sly fighter, and he got in a shrewd blow or two, once making Hugh yell in sheer agony as a side slash caught his shield at an odd angle and wrenched his cut and bruised hand. Hugh knew he was pushing this attack too long, yet a compulsion drove him to strike and strike again, even though he was tiring. One more, he thought, only one more, and lashed out at Lionel's sword with his shield, simultaneously bringing his own sword around in a ferocious sweep at his enemy's neck.

The shield, which ordinarily would have moved as a solid piece, bent—thrust harder on the left by Hugh's elbow than on the right by his painful hand—and the edge caught Lionel's sword and pushed it in toward his own body. To free his weapon, Lionel stepped back and ducked while lifting his shield to ward off Hugh's sword blow, but his foot landed on Hugh's lost helmet, which rolled, and his ankle bent, sending him toppling sideways. His elbow struck—not the soft ground but the hard metal helmet—and he screamed as the stabbing agony and semiparalysis caused by a blow on the elbow loosened his grip on his sword.

Hugh cried out too, but in triumph, and rushed forward. Hearing Lionel scream and seeing the sword drop from his hand, Hugh believed him more hurt than he was. But a powerful thrust of Lionel's legs sent him staggering back. Instinctively, Hugh flung his arms wide to regain his balance, but before he could steady himself, he was struck a glancing blow on the head by the helmet, which Lionel had thrown at him. The weight of shield and sword added to the impetus of his stagger. Hugh fell backward. Desperately, in the few seconds granted him while Lionel snatched up his sword, Hugh brought his shield across his body and lifted his own weapon so Lionel could not put a foot on his arm and have him completely helpless. He rolled a little sideways, praying he could push himself up while Lionel got to his feet—but he never had the chance.

Instead of trying to stand up, Lionel only got to his knees, scrambled forward, and flung himself atop Hugh, thrusting Hugh's sword aside with his own and hitting him in the face with the edge of his shield as he freed his hand to tear at Hugh's hood so the mail would not protect either throat or head.

The worn tie gave way, and the hood slid off, but Hugh was not beaten yet. He had struck twice at Lionel's unprotected back with his sword. The blows were not very effective, but they kept Lionel's sword hand busy blocking them. And utter desperation lent Hugh unnatural strength, permitting him to thrust the heavier man off him and strike at him once more.

As Lionel fell away, Hugh heard him scream and took another desperate chance—rolling over so he could get to his knees. Hugh knew he should have died in that instant. Encumbered by his sword and shield, he could not roll fast enough to get out of reach. Lionel should have swung his sword at Hugh's back or at his unprotected head. But the stroke did not come, and Hugh did not take time to wonder how he had escaped or even to look for Lionel. He only scrambled to his feet gasping for breath and spun around, swinging his sword in a wild arc.

He hit Lionel before he saw him, heard him cry, "No! Kenorn, Kenorn! No!" and struck again before the words or the passive stance could penetrate to his battle-dazed mind. Both strikes were deadly, the first shearing through Lionel's mail to cut deeply into his back and sword arm, the second also cutting deeply, this time into the left shoulder, breaking the collarbone.

Lionel's sword dropped from his hand, and his shield hung limply down, but he did not fall. He stood staring at Hugh as if he were looking into the mouth of hell, sobbing, "Kenorn? Kenorn?"

Hugh had already lifted his sword high for the killing stroke, but he could not bring it down. He had not yet made any sense of the word Lionel was repeating; he simply could not kill a man who stood helplessly before him with tears pouring down his face, not even lifting his shield to protect himself. Now he heard the crowd again, a rhythmic ululation demanding the death stroke; he smelled the muddy earth, churned up by the battle, overlaid with the stink of blood and sweat. Slowly he brought his sword down, mesmerized by the utter terror in his enemy's eyes—a terror he did not understand because it did not change when he lowered his weapon.

Had Hugh been certain this was not another sly trick aimed at snatching victory out of the jaws of defeat, he would simply have walked away. But he did not dare leave the field while his opponent was still standing, lest later Sir Lionel claim he had forfeited the battle. He hardly dared look away from his enemy. In desperation he began to lift his sword again, but in that moment Lionel sighed, uttered "Kenorn," one last time, and toppled to the ground.

Puzzled about what next to do, Hugh dropped his useless shield to the ground and picked up Sir Lionel's sword. He lifted both weapons in the air, and cried aloud, "I claim the victory! Sir Lionel cannot yield, but I scorn to kill a man who cannot protect himself any longer."

❧

Hugh never remembered the next period of time very clearly. Events seemed to mingle and run into each other.

One moment de Merley was kneeling beside Sir Lionel and shouting; the next the field seemed to be full of people. Hugh braced himself to repel what he feared might be either de Merley's treachery or a mob outraged because he had not given it what it craved, but they did not approach him. It was not until much later that he realized he had been half dazed and the "crowd" was only retainers come to carry Sir Lionel away. He would have understood that sooner, except that Ralph reached him before the others lifted Sir Lionel, and embraced him, kissing him and weeping.

He tried to think of words to reassure his uncle, but no words would form in his mind, and then he saw a strange thing—he saw Audris, lifting up and embracing the broken shield he had dropped. She turned her head toward him, and her lips formed words that he could not hear or read. Then a man loomed up and took the shield from her. Hugh was about to call out to her—her name sprang readily to his lips, although he still could not think in words—when de Merley passed between them, blocking Audris from his sight, and tried to take Sir Lionel's sword from him. Hugh snarled, closed his hand on it tighter, and pulled it away with a force that sent the castellan of Morpeth staggering back—and words came to him, suddenly and clearly.

"Bear witness all!" he cried, lifting the weapon again. "In mercy I did not kill Sir Lionel of Heugh, but I have vanquished him in judicial combat. His claim is false. Ralph, Lord Ruthsson, is by God judged the true holder of Ruthsson and Trewick, and I am judged his true heir. Sir Lionel's sword and shield are my battle prizes—proof of my victory. Will you cry *fiat*?"

And the noblemen stood and shouted, *"Fiat! Fiat!"*

Behind Hugh, de Merley made an irritated moue. He had nothing against Hugh, but his first loyalty was to King Stephen, and for a few minutes he thought he would be able to produce a more ambiguous outcome to the trial by combat—one that would give the king more freedom to act as he saw fit in the matter of Ruthsson. He had chosen judicial combat in preference to a private war, however, and he could not offend all the local magnates by denying the clear result, so he nodded and grunted, "*Fiat!* So be it."

Then he clapped Hugh on the shoulder and smiled. "It was a good fight, and I am glad I was judge and did not wager on it, for I would have lost my money. Will you take part in the melee?"

Five minutes earlier, Hugh would have rejected the suggestion out of hand, but now he was filled with an urge to fight for the joy of it, to clean his heart of the sight of Lionel's horror-filled eyes. Horse and armor ransom meant nothing to many of the men who would be on the field, and the money—or stock and produce—would help revitalize Ruthsson.

"If I can find another shield, I think I will," Hugh answered, grinning.

"Hugh!" Ralph protested. "You are hurt."

"Hurt?" Hugh repeated, and then, reminded, he felt the ache and looked down at his hip, but the blood was already dried brown. "It cannot be more than a scratch," he said.

"Go to the leech's tent and let him look," de Merley suggested, gesturing toward a cloth roof that could be seen behind the area where the commoners stood. "And I will see that your horse and a shield are sent to you."

"Hugh—" Ralph began.

But Hugh shook his head at his uncle, who seemed to him in his exalted mood too much like a mother hen. "Do not fear for me. There will be time for me to rest before I ride out again, and no man I will meet will wish me harm. Here, take Heugh's sword and be sure his shield is brought to you also." Then, to soften what seemed like a rejection and a harsh order, he put his arm around Ralph and hugged him.

"Very well, but—" Ralph said, but Hugh had already turned away, and his uncle shrugged and walked off toward a herald to ask about Sir Lionel's shield. He had a message for Hugh, but it would not matter if delivery was delayed until the melee was finished.

Chapter 21

WHEN AUDRIS RAN OUT ON TO THE TOURNEY FIELD, HER emotions were so tangled she could not have said what she felt. She knew she had been fortunate, for Sir Oliver's unexpected arrival, just after Hugh had overthrown his opponent, had startled her so much that the terrifying events of the sword battle, which followed Sir Lionel's fall, were blunted. On the other hand, her great joy when she saw Hugh rise and triumph was dimmed by the knowledge that she dared not allow Hugh and her uncle to meet and would have to find a way to induce Oliver to leave before the tourney was over. Hugh had said he would not ask for her until Ruthsson was in a better condition, but she was not certain he would keep to that decision, flushed as he was with his victory. And would not that triumph make him less patient with her uncle's refusal? Would he not challenge Oliver—and kill him too? She must take her uncle and leave at once, before Hugh could speak to him.

Sir Oliver had scolded her for going to Morpeth alone. Why, he had asked, had she not said she wished to attend the tournament? He would have taken her to one, although he really thought a melee was too dangerous for her to attend and an unfitting sight for a gently reared demoiselle to witness, too. Worse, he pointed out, she had also exposed herself to a different kind of danger; once word got out that the heiress of Jernaeve was present, virtually unprotected, a number of impecunious gentlemen—or even rich, high lords—might feel that to abduct her, marry her out of hand, and hide her away until she was with child would be an easy way to obtain Jernaeve.

The need to listen and respond had distracted Audris just enough that she did not scream or faint when Hugh went down or when he rose up again. And the cries and gasps she could not restrain, and the loss of her train of thought, could be accounted for by her friendship for Hugh. But when she saw Hugh's shield broken and discarded, the thought *the unicorn is dead* rushed into her mind. And though she now recognized a separation between Hugh and the symbol she had used for him, a compulsion seized her to have the shield. She needed to cherish the symbol that had brought them together and was now no longer necessary.

After she had taken up the shield, she could not help caressing it as if it were a living creature that had been killed. But when she saw Hugh's eyes on her, she remembered that she must go without even speaking to him again, and she murmured, "Farewell, beloved. Farewell," although she knew he could not hear her. Perhaps he would be able to read her lips and understand.

She was so intent on the shield and Hugh's face, marred by a red bruise that stretched from his forehead all down across one cheek to his jawbone, that she jumped with shock when her uncle's hand fell on her shoulder. There was no way to tell whether Oliver had heard her; Audris thought not, for it was very noisy with the crowd crying out, de Merley giving orders, the men lifting Sir Lionel cautioning each other, and the heralds calling to one another as they prepared to clear the field for the melee.

Nonetheless, there was a shocked and thoughtful expression on Oliver's face when he took the shield from her and pulled her away, and he seemed to be thinking of something quite different when he told her what a fool she was to run out on a tourney field among busy men. And when she said, shuddering, that she had seen blood enough and did not wish to watch the melee, her uncle did not say she should have thought of that earlier or even send her back to her lodging to wait until he had enjoyed the spectacle. He gave her one intent stare, then agreed that she should be taken back to Uhtred's house to pack up her possessions while he gathered up their men so that they could depart at once.

Nor, when her mare was brought, did her uncle protest by more than a wry twist of the lips when she demanded firmly that he give her the shield he had laid down. She wondered at that, and because he uttered no warnings about the unsuitability of her favorite until, days after they had returned to Jernaeve, she realized that Oliver probably did not really object to her fixing her affections on a totally unlikely suitor. No doubt it had occurred to him that if she loved Hugh, she was even less likely to accept any other proposal for marriage.

Audris had wondered, too, how Oliver knew where to find her, but her uncle explained that during the ride home. The merchant to whom she had offered her tapestry had been so eager to obtain it that he had brought the price to her lodging in Newcastle the day after she left for Morpeth. There her men had freely discussed their pleasure in an unaccustomed treat so that, when the merchant asked for her, he had been told her destination. Since the merchant's desire for Audris's work was undiminished, he had gone on to Jernaeve, where he had innocently passed on the information.

The knowledge that her uncle almost certainly had guessed that she loved Hugh relieved Audris of any need to pretend cheerfulness, and for several days she kept mostly to her chamber. At the end of the week, Fritha came up from an errand on which Audris had sent her with a letter from Hugh concealed in her bosom. Its contents both infuriated Audris and almost reconciled her to her early departure, for Hugh wrote lyrically of his success in the melee. Had she still been at Morpeth, she would have been frightened out of her wits to see him fight again, but the letter itself proved that he had come to no harm. What worried her most was the eagerness with which he wrote of how he would use the ransoms he collected to restore his estate so that he might the sooner propose marriage.

Fearing to deny the possibility of their union so soon after his triumph, Audris confined herself, in her reply, to praise of his prowess, pleas that he would consider her terror and not use that method again to enrich himself, and recapitulations of her fond memories of the time they had spent together. Even so, after she had sent the letter off—a regular system had been established in which Morel's daughter-by-marriage brought Hugh's letters to the keep and waited until she saw Fritha, and Fritha carried Audris's replies to Morel's cottage—Audris felt sad and guilty. Soon, very soon, she would have to tell Hugh that she could not marry him; she could not let him go on believing that she would become his wife. The sons of earls had proposed and been refused; Oliver would never agree to a suitor with so much less rank and property.

Audris fell to weeping because she might never see Hugh again. One result of her uncle's guessing where her affections lay was that he probably would not allow her to travel alone in the future. And she could not, no matter how much she racked her brain, think of any reason—aside from the true one, which she would not use for fear of endangering her uncle—for telling Hugh that he must not propose marriage. She cried herself to sleep that night and woke terribly sick in the morning, frightening Fritha half to death by vomiting and refusing breakfast. By midday she had recovered, but though she went to the mews to oversee the training of the young hawks, she found herself near to weeping several times, even though she had not been thinking about Hugh.

She woke sick in the morning twice more that week and began to worry about her health, which, despite her delicate looks, had always been extremely robust. She dosed herself with betony, chamomile, and pennyroyal, and the symptoms disappeared, but oddly the worry did not. All through November the unreasonable sadness would sweep over her periodically, and she found herself irritably cross with the world so that she could barely keep from angry retorts to innocent questions or conversations.

To be bitter and irritable was so far from natural for Audris that she was frightened by the change in her nature, which only made matters worse. By the third week in November, another letter had come from Hugh, but she had not answered it. She was afraid that the emotional storm inside her would spill out into her reply—and this was the wrong time for a letter full of grief and rage, because her guilt would not allow her to deceive him any longer, and she still had found no reason for refusing to marry him. And to make matters worse, Fritha was acting very strange, pleading by gesture for her to eat more than she wanted and peering at her mistress while pretending to be busy at some piece of work. That, too, added to Audris's guilt because she knew she had been sharp and unreasonable with her maid.

In the end she had ridden down to Morel's cottage herself to tell him to return without an answer. A bitter wind was blowing up the river valley from the east, and Audris had been feeling colder than usual for her, too, so she did not ask Morel to come out but braved the rather fetid interior of the cottage and went in. It was, in fact, smoky from the fire that burned in the middle of the floor, but neater and better furnished than most yeomen's homes. There was a real bed toward the back wall, where a door closed off the shed that protected the animals, and in the opposite corner two smaller beds and a pallet on the floor. Near the fire there were several stools, as well as a chair, from which Morel leapt to his feet when she pushed open the door.

A minute or two was spent in Morel's stammering welcome, and before Audris could give the lame explanation she had devised, a baby, perhaps wakened from his sleep by the voices, wailed lustily from behind the bed. Mary hurried from the fire, where she had been stirring a pot, to quiet the child, taking him into her arms and baring a breast as the best pacifier.

"My grandson," Morel said, pride making him bold enough to volunteer information for which Audris had not asked.

"God keep him as hale and hearty as he sounds to be now," Audris replied, and then, remembering that she had offered to help with the birthing, she turned to Mary and said, "I am glad you had no trouble bearing him. May I look at him?"

Mary crossed the room to display her treasure, who had stopped crying as soon as his mother lifted him, and she glowed with delight when Audris gently touched the infant's cheek. "It be no trouble at all," Mary said, much emboldened by Audris's interest in herself and her child. "And it be right, too, for him to be giving me an easy time. In the beginning he made me that cross while I be carrying him—and that sick!—it be a great wonder that my man and Da here did not beat him out of me."

It was fortunate that Audris was looking at the child, who was crowing softly and reaching toward one of her glittering earrings, which had caught the firelight, for the swift change in her expression—the widening of her eyes and the lips that opened and closed without sound—would have alarmed Mary. In the next instant Audris had burst out laughing and leaned forward to kiss the little boy and cry, "Bless you, baby. Bless you."

The joy in Audris's voice and in her face made Mary happy too, for she misunderstood them totally, believing that Audris had seen a wonderful future for her son. What Audris had seen was her own stupidity; sick in the morning and weeping and irritable, she had seen those symptoms often enough to know them, but had never stopped to think. She was with child!

Having smiled once more at Mary and her child, Audris turned to Morel and said, "I have no letter for your master, but I wish you to return to him lest he fear for you—or for me—because you have been away so long. Tell him that I have not written because the hope of a great joy fills my heart, but I cannot tell him what it is until I am more sure that it will come to pass."

She left quickly, not waiting for Morel's reply because she knew he would ask what his master would want to know—when he was to return. To answer that question might answer another, prematurely, although as she rode back to the keep she became more and more sure that she had not bled since the second week in October, just before she started for Newcastle. Fritha confirmed this memory by holding up her fingers to show how long it had been since she had washed Audris's bleeding cloths, and Audris caught her breath with joy and knelt to give thanks to God and more especially to Hugh's favorite saint, the Virgin.

When the thanksgiving was over and Audris was settled in her favorite chair close beside the small hearth where a bright fire snapped and crackled, occasionally gusting smoke with a rich, piney scent into the room, it was a natural connection to think that *her* conception was not holy and that it would be necessary to explain it to her uncle. Somehow this seemed much less simple now than when she had discussed the matter with Hugh in the early summer.

Nor did she feel as lighthearted now as she had then when she considered the bastardy of her child. Her uncle, she knew, would acknowledge her babe and protect it, but her uncle was growing old—and she did not have the same faith in her cousins that she had in Oliver. His sons had always envied and resented her. When she was a child, until they were sent away for fostering, they had made her life miserable—and might have done worse if Bruno had not protected her.

As Audris considered all the ramifications of being a bastard, she grew more and more uneasy. True, she could summon Bruno if she saw her uncle was failing, and he would come—but could she be sure Bruno would survive the king's wars? Was it fair to draw him out of the king's service and possibly deprive him of the opportunity for advancement that might just be ripening into fruitfulness? And there was an even more dangerous aspect to consider. What if she herself died before her daughter was married or her son reached manhood? Would her cousins respect her will that her child inherit Jernaeve despite its bastardy? Audris doubted that strongly.

Audris was reasonably sure that her cousins had come to terms with the knowledge that Jernaeve was hers and that she would doubtless marry and bear sons who would hold the keep, but a bastard would be too great a temptation. Surely they would run to the king with petitions that the "two bastards"—her child and Bruno—be disseised and driven out and the true, legitimate heirs of the line be seisened of Jernaeve.

Perhaps Bruno's service with the king would protect them… perhaps not. And worse yet might befall, Audris thought. What if she died in bearing the child? There would be no time then for her to summon Bruno, and her babe might only live as long as her uncle. Audris knew that all her worries might be in vain, because only about half the children born survived. But to die of natural causes was the will of God and not a fate from which she could protect her child; being murdered by her cousins was another matter entirely.

As the thoughts moved slowly through Audris's mind—thoughts in words always moved slowly for her, and she did not dare allow herself to make pictures of what she had been thinking—oddly enough she found herself growing more and more joyful. Marriage was the answer! With a child in her belly, marriage to Hugh was no longer simply a satisfaction of her own selfish desire to be with him. Every fear or doubt about her child's condition in life would be solved completely by marriage to Hugh. She had a quick image of his face, overlaid almost at once by a series of pictures of him overthrowing Lionel and saving himself by sheer strength from what looked for an instant like sure death. With Hugh for a father, no child could want a better protector. And now marriage to Hugh no longer meant her uncle would lose Jernaeve; Hugh had an estate of his own—Ruthsson.

Then the light that had been growing brighter and brighter in Audris's eyes dimmed. The solution to her child's problems might be simple, but the method of achieving that solution was not simple at all. A whole host of unpleasant possibilities flashed before Audris's mind's eye—possibilities of conflict and anguish for her uncle and her husband—which led inevitably to a jewel-bright image of herself and Fritha following Morel along a road bordered by trees decked in the delicate green foliage of early spring. Peace flooded Audris's soul. That was right. That was a true foreseeing. She did not *need* her uncle's permission to marry; all she had to do was go to Ruthsson in secret, and then keep Hugh and Oliver apart until her uncle had accepted the inevitable.

From that moment, Audris began to prepare. Now that her own vision was clear, she knew just what she must write to Hugh as soon as she was sure she would not miscarry the child. In a sense she was already sure, but to act on the certainty in her heart seemed like flinging a challenge in the face of fate.

She would wait at least until Morel returned before explaining to Hugh what she intended.

Audris's next thought was for her uncle and aunt, who would be deprived of her weaving and hawking. She could do nothing about the hawks, but the falconer knew her methods and would likely manage very well without her. As to the weaving, if she worked consistently instead of spending half her time reading or dreaming by the fire, she could prepare many tapestries in the months that remained before she must leave. Already several subjects had come into her mind.

"Fritha," she called, her voice as light as her heart. "Fritha, string my loom."

❧

On a bright spring day in the first week of April, Audris mounted her mare and Fritha her mule, and they rode out of Jernaeve. Fritha shook with fear, and Audris shed a few tears at leaving—but not many. In the last few weeks, life had started to become a little complicated, and the joyful expectation of seeing Hugh was intensified for Audris by the relief she felt at no longer needing to hide the increasingly unmistakable signs of her pregnancy. The few tears had been for the grief and hurt she knew her uncle and aunt would feel at her secretiveness and departure. But the tears had been few because she had strong hopes that once she was married and her child born—once her bond to Hugh was irrevocable—she would be a welcome visitor in Jernaeve, as Oliver and Eadyth would be welcome visitors in Ruthsson.

She had left a very long letter, written over the five months she had remained in Jernaeve, explaining what she had done and why. For her aunt's benefit she had detailed such matters as the stores in the stillroom and herb shed, the plan of the garden and which gardeners knew best what to grow and how to grow it, and all the other household chores that were her responsibility. For her uncle, she had praised the falconer and mentioned which of his boys showed the most promise, as well as describing the many tapestries she had prepared and warning him to sell only one or two at a time with several months between sales. At the end of the letter she had come back to more personal matters.

> *I beg you to believe that it was not through any mistrust of you that I departed with such secrecy. Indeed, it is far otherwise. What I feared was the opposite—that you would insist that Hugh become master of Jernaeve. Neither he nor I desire that at this time. The estate to which he is heir has been diminished by neglect and needs his care to be restored. For the love I bear him, I wish to join him and help him in his labor. It is because I know that Jernaeve could be in no safer nor more honest and loyal hands that I feel free to follow my heart. Do not be angry with me, I beg you, but forgive my waywardness as you have always so kindly done. I will not be long gone from you. When my babe is born, I will write again to ask if I have been forgiven, and if I have, I will come with the child to ask your blessing.*

So when the few tears had been shed and wiped away, Audris laughed at Fritha and bade her be of good heart. "I cannot guess why you should cry," she said. "I have been happy here—you were not." Having watched the gestures of Fritha's hands, she laughed again. "It is very silly to be afraid. You have ridden through these hills and woods with me many times. Yes, I know the Scots came down on us in the winter, but King Stephen drove them away and you know that Morel is waiting for us at Hexham and that an armed troop will meet us at Corbridge to take us to Ruthsson."

The fingers flew frantically again, and Audris shook her head and sighed impatiently. "I will come to no harm, and neither will the babe." But she did not continue to attempt to reassure her maid. She was far too tired of this argument, which had been the main subject of letter after letter from Hugh from the time she had proposed her original plan.

Fortunately, she had guessed Hugh's first reaction would be to come racing south from Ruthsson. Her absolute prohibition and the reminder of the tapestry showing the unicorn piercing

Jernaeve had managed to restrain him, but a flood of letters followed, all on the theme of her health and the well-being of her babe—even Ralph had written, urging her to eat, to rest, not to do anything that would strain her. Audris had thought of the peasant women in the fields and her aunt Eadyth, big-bellied with the last of her daughters—the little girl that died in the plague Audris's first Death tapestry had foreseen—all of them working as hard as if they did not carry a babe.

She had answered those first letters with reasonable protests, later ones with meaningless soothing, and then had simply ignored what she felt to be male ignorance, but, she thought with exasperation, it was a wonder Morel's poor horse still had legs. It seemed to her that they should have been worn off short from the frequency and rate at which Morel traveled between Ruthsson and Jernaeve.

However, she had come to realize that Hugh's frantic insistence on a strong troop was not unreasonable. Although the Scots had attacked soon after King Stephen returned from Normandy at the end of November, they had been driven back and the south of Scotland ravaged in revenge. There were rumors that King David's retreat was only temporary, but there was not much chance of an invasion just now, Audris thought, as she rode along. Like everyone else, the Scots were busy with their spring planting. They would get their crops in before they began the war again—if they still intended to come south—but a troop that could fight off a small raiding party was still a good idea, since Ruthsson was much nearer the border than Jernaeve.

Audris shivered and sought a more pleasant subject of contemplation. Her mind came back to Morel, seeking comfort in the many trips he had made without danger, and then she smiled. In another way, too, the results of Morel's many trips had been good. Little by little, most of her clothing, all of her jewelry, one by one the unicorn tapestries, skein by skein and spindle by spindle the supplies for her weaving left unused had all been sent to Ruthsson. She could not take her loom, but that was a minor matter; a new one would be built as she directed. The spinning and dyeing of yarn was a more difficult problem, and it would take her time to find women who spun—or could be taught to spin and dye—suitable yarn.

The sense of satisfaction she felt every time she remembered that she could weave whenever she desired was soon overlaid by a newer sense of puzzlement. Her original plan had been to ride directly north to Ruthsson and meet Morel and the guard troop at some gap in the great wall. Of course the troop, to which Audris had agreed, was not all Hugh and Ralph wanted to send. They had an endless list of additional comforts for her—in order of rejection—a traveling cart complete with featherbed and physician, a horse litter (also with accompanying physician), a man-carried litter (when Audris reasonably pointed out that she would be more jolted and bruised by cart or litter than in riding her own smooth-paced mare), several women of all ages to support and attend her, and... Audris found she had forgotten the rest of the silly suggestions. She almost wished she had saved the parchments to laugh over with Hugh when he saw how strong and well she was—but parchment was precious and had to be scraped and reused.

The new puzzle was why Hugh had, at the last moment when it was too late to answer his letter, changed the plan that had seemed settled. His last instructions had been to meet Morel at Hexham and then to come on to Corbridge, where the troop would await her. But Hexham to Corbridge before turning north would add nearly three leagues to the journey to Ruthsson, which seemed strange after Hugh's objections to her riding at all. Not that Audris minded the extra riding. What exasperated her about Hugh's and Ralph's and even Fritha's anxiety was that she had never felt better. Except for the nausea and ill-temper of the first few weeks, she had been full of energy and bubbling with high spirits. She touched her mare with her heel to increase her pace to a loping canter, keeping her eyes forward so that she would not see Fritha's anguished face or attempts to signal. The sooner she got to Hexham, the sooner she could satisfy her curiosity about the change in plans. No doubt Morel would know.

This assumption, Audris found to her chagrin, was *not* a true foretelling; Morel, who was waiting about half a mile from the monastery, knew nothing. He could tell her no more than that his master begged her to rest herself at Hexham before starting the "arduous" ride to Corbridge. Audris threw up her hands and raised her eyes toward heaven and laughed.

"So that my uncle should know exactly what route I took? I have heard that being with child sometimes gives a woman strange fancies, but it seems to have addled your *master's* wits instead of mine. I hope to come to Ruthsson this very night and to travel so that we meet as few people as possible, not stop to repose myself at every village, abbey, and manor along the way."

With those words, Audris set her heels to her mare's sides again and started off the road across the countryside to avoid Hexham abbey completely. Nor would she enter Corbridge, stopping in a sheltered coppice not far from the town and telling Morel to bring the troop out to her. But Audris was not fated to get to Ruthsson that night. The first sign was only two riders approaching the coppice rather than the whole troop. Audris's lips set hard, losing their normally smiling curve. She was sure that Hugh had told the captain of the troop that he must stop for her to rest and the man had come to insist that she go into Corbridge. Well, she would do no such stupid thing. She would simply ride north alone if she must. And then recognition pierced her exasperation. The big red horse had to be Rufus.

"Hugh!" Audris cried, urging her mare toward him. "You lunatic! Did I not tell you—"

"*I* am a lunatic?" he cried, leaning off his horse to embrace her with tears in his eyes. "How could you believe that I would allow you to ride all that distance—"

"With only Morel, who is as faithful as my own soul, and a full troop of men to guard me?" she retorted, laughing but hugging him back as well as she could in the awkward position and taking one brief kiss before Hugh pushed her back, exclaiming that she must not twist herself about.

The second man was now leaning off his horse to kiss her also, and she realized that it was Ralph, not Morel, who had accompanied Hugh. "Morel is so much in awe of you," he said with scorn, "that if you took it into your head to jump from a cliff, saying you could fly, he would believe you. Hugh and I are the only ones strong-minded enough to argue with you."

"There is nothing strong-minded in leaving a clear trail for my uncle," Audris protested. "I hope he will believe my letter and accept what I have decided, but if he should take it into his head that Hugh seduced me for some evil purpose, or that, finding myself with child, I grew afraid he would be harsh and fled in fear of him, he will pursue me to save me either from my 'evil suitor' or from myself. I do not desire two men I love to confront each other in anger. I wish my uncle to grow accustomed, to see me a happy woman, and to be content with the man I have chosen."

"I am not so much a fool as you think, my love," Hugh soothed. "You are not well known by sight, and I have taken care that no one sees my face, which I know is too easy to remember. My uncle has made arrangements for our lodging, which is why I asked him to undertake the fatigues of this journey—"

"I am not so old that I cannot ride a horse," Ralph interrupted plaintively.

Audris burst into laughter. "*I* am delighted not to be the single sufferer from Hugh's ill-advised conviction that everyone but him is too fragile to breathe without his help. Hugh, what *has* got into you? And what journey are you talking about? Are we not going to Ruthsson? That is not much more than ten leagues, and I assure you I am fit to ride that far today."

Hugh smiled uneasily, knowing there was some truth in Audris's protest—not about herself; she was far too careless of herself and of their child, too—but perhaps he did tend to coddle Ralph when there was no need. It was because of his joy, which increased day by day, rather than diminishing, in the love the old man bore him, in being part of a family with roots and ties to the land. And that feeling had made Audris and the burden she carried more precious. Hugh would not have thought it possible to deepen his feeling for Audris, but belonging to Ruthsson and Ralph had done so. He could find no words to explain, certainly not here and now, with the fickle skies of April clouding over and a sharp breeze beginning to whine through the young leaves on the trees.

"No," he said, "we are not going to Ruthsson. But look, it may rain. Will you not come and rest until the skies clear, Audris?"

"Hugh," she cried, "I am growing sure that you *have* lost your wits. First of all, if we stop each time clouds appear in April, we will never leave this place. I will not melt in a little rain, and I do not need to rest after riding less than three leagues. What is more, you are wrong about my not being known in Corbridge. I have been there often enough that someone might recognize me or my mare. Do not be a fool. Let us ride on now."

Hugh looked doubtful, but Ralph said, "It will do no harm to cross the river, at least. We are well supplied and can set up camp at any time—and Audris is right about not leaving a trail. I will go back and get the men started. We can meet a mile down the road south of the bridge."

"South of the bridge?" Audris echoed as Ralph rode away. "Why south? Where are we going?"

"To Durham, to be married," Hugh replied, starting Rufus toward the road that would take them south of the town to the old Roman bridge that crossed the Tyne. "My uncle pointed out to me," he continued as they rode along, "that in our circumstances it would not be wise to be married by some local priest without substantial witnesses." He grinned at her sudden expression of doubt. "You are not the only one who can make plans. I have been to York to explain the whole matter to Archbishop Thurstan."

Audris's mouth formed a silent O of concern, and Hugh chuckled.

"He was not best pleased with me, but he has known for a long time that I had set my heart on a woman above my station. Still, he is not a man to make an ado after the soup is spilled, and I am no longer a nameless brat. So he wrote to the bishop of Durham, who will marry us in the presence of such highborn priests and deacons as are in his service or visiting the cathedral."

"Did the archbishop think so ill of us that he would not himself bless us?" Audris asked in a stricken voice. For herself, she did not much care, but she knew Hugh loved his foster father and feared he was hiding a deep hurt beneath his smile.

"Of course not, dear heart," Hugh replied, taking her hand and squeezing it comfortingly. "I did need to hear a lecture on impatience and greed, but I know I was forgiven. The reason Thurstan gave for not offering to marry us himself was that he did not wish you to ride all the way to York in your condition. But I am afraid… He is not so well, my heart. I think he fears he will not be with us long to bear witness to the fact that we are truly man and wife."

Audris saw the pain those last words cost Hugh, although he spoke them steadily. "Then we *must* go to York, my husband," she said, shaking her head and holding up the hand he had released to cut off his objections. "No, the ride will not be too much for me. Look at me, Hugh. Am I pinched and pale? Are my eyes bruised with lack of sleep, my hair dull with ill health? I am strong, and our child is well set within me. God knows I have brewed potions enough to help women hold a child; I know the signs of a woman near to miscarrying, and I have none of them. Please, my heart, let us go. I so desire to know the man who raised you up as a child—and I think it would ease his heart to know me."

"Are you sure you are strong enough, Audris?"

She could see in Hugh's anxious face the desire that Thurstan should know her and the fear that if they did not go now it would be too late, and she laughed like a bird singing. "Of course, I am sure. We will stop in Durham and be married and, if you like, rest a day there. Then we will go on to York."

Chapter 22

AUDRIS'S SON WAS BORN ON THE FIRST DAY OF JUNE, A FULL month before his time by, Audris announced, a special dispensation of God and His Holy Mother. Had Eric Thurstan not taken them all by surprise, she pointed out, any number of dreadful consequences might have followed. First, she would certainly have been driven insane by Hugh and Ralph, who, day by day, showed a greater and greater tendency to hang over her and ask how she felt every few minutes. Second, Audris admitted merrily, she might have burst like an overripe fruit if the babe had grown any greater inside her. Third, the early delivery saved her from the attendance of a "great physician" Hugh insisted he would bring from York, who, Audris was certain, would have poisoned her with his cordials or bled her to death. Last, and not least, Eric's sudden and rapid, if violent, advent on the one day in weeks when both Hugh and Ralph were out of Ruthsson rid Audris of the need to reassure two frantic men in the midst of her labor.

"But," Audris said complacently to Hugh, who was sitting beside her in the shade of a broad fruit tree, watching her suckle the child, "it was only to be expected. From the moment I conceived him—or perhaps from a month after that—Eric has shown himself to be sweet-tempered and thoughtful. Think how little trouble he was to me when we went to York."

Hugh's besotted expression as he watched his son feed was not the only thing that made Audris feel complacent.

The garden in which they sat had been a tangled wilderness in April. Now it was ordered and would soon be lovely, actually lovelier than Jernaeve's garden, because it was larger. The fruit tree beneath which they sat would have shaded too much of Jernaeve's limited arable space; here, backed by the south wall of the garden, it merely provided a pleasant spot to sit and look at the spring that spilled over into a tiny sparkling rill, now running over a bed of clean pebbles with a delicate musical tinkle. Watercress would grow in the rill soon, softening its voice, and kingcups would blossom along its edge. A movement along the back of the great hall, which was the north wall of the garden, reminded Audris of a minor drawback—now the gardeners of Ruthsson looked at her with the same awe in their eyes as Jernaeve's gardeners did. And the villagers, too. Perhaps it had been a mistake to heal that child—but how could she, knowing the medicine to cure it, have allowed the little one to suffer, when her own babe lay beneath her heart? Hugh's chuckle broke into her thoughts.

"Diplomatic little fellow, too," he remarked in answer to her praise of her son. "Think how he kicked just when Thurstan laid his hand on your belly to bless him. My foster father was thrilled."

"Oh, Eric has done everything right," Audris said, laughing. "Even to looking so much like you that you could not deny him despite being born a month before his time and the size of a full-term babe."

"Audris!" Hugh leaned over the nursing child and kissed her fondly and tenderly. "You know I would not have doubted you even if he were as dark as your uncle—"

He stopped abruptly as a shadow passed over Audris's face. When they had returned to Ruthsson from York, they had learned that Oliver *had* pursued his niece, hoping, they assumed, to get her back before she could be married. He had demanded and obtained entrance into Ruthsson—not because the place was any longer so vulnerable, but because Hugh had warned the castle guards not to oppose Sir Oliver, which they could have done. In the five months after his battle with Sir Lionel, Hugh had hired a few mercenaries and taken about twenty sturdy yeomen's sons into service. His troop was up to forty, and they were now well trained and well blooded on the local outlaws, who were a much diminished and chastened band, seriously considering going elsewhere.

Unfortunately, the peace offering of free entrance to Ruthsson had, apparently, not compensated Oliver for the loss of his niece. He had not attempted to take her back again—having learned that the marriage was to be celebrated by the bishop of Durham and supported by the archbishop of York, he doubtless recognized that it would be impossible to annul it—but he had not answered Audris's letter announcing Eric's birth, and she had grieved over his continued anger.

"Do you think we did wrong in not naming Eric for your uncle?" Hugh asked, following an uneasy train of thought that had often crossed his mind.

"No," Audris replied, forcefully removing her nipple from her son's mouth, at which he began to emit such shrieks of rage that her following words were drowned, and she made haste to offer him her other breast without trying to drive up any wind. That would have to wait until he was sated, but he sucked so strongly that she had to change breasts midfeeding to keep herself from becoming sore.

"About the sweetness of his temper I have my doubts," Hugh remarked with obvious admiration for the loudness of the noise his son made and the ferocity with which he struck out with his arms and legs in his rage, which burst open the cloth in which he was swaddled. "But he is surely strong."

"He certainly is," Audris agreed, glad and rueful at the same time. "But as to your question, I did not wish to name Eric in my family tradition, neither Oliver nor William, which was my father's name. My lands will go to a daughter or to a second son. It was better to name him in your family line. And speaking of naming, I have long meant to ask you, Hugh, why you did not wish to name him for your father. Kenorn is an unusual name, and I like it, but you seemed so set against it when I asked—"

"Until I am *sure* my father did not desert my poor mother on purpose, I will name no child of mine for him," Hugh said.

"You remember that he did not return to the convent after I was born."

It was clear that he was not really thinking about the answer he had given to Audris's question, however. A somewhat startled expression was on his face, which changed to a slight frown. Audris had a right to leave Jernaeve to whichever of her children she wished, and her intention of using it to provide a rich dower for a daughter or an estate for a second son that would preclude envy between older and younger brothers was not unreasonable. Moreover, Hugh knew that when he had brought Ruthsson and its outlying manors, including the rich farms of Trewick, back into prime condition, his eldest son would be well provided.

Nonetheless, he felt as if the child in Audris's arms were being deprived, and it occurred to him that there might be some property belonging to his father that was now rightfully his and would descend to this son. Perhaps it was not much, but Hugh had a sudden clear memory of the horror in Lionel Heugh's eyes when he gasped "Kenorn," and he began to wonder if the greedy Heugh family had stolen something from his father and then contrived some ill fate for him, as well as trying to steal Ruthsson from his uncle.

"Your speaking of my father reminded me, though, that my likeness to him may have saved my life," Hugh said, and went on to describe the last moments of the trial by combat from his point of view.

"Sir Lionel called you by your father's name," Audris repeated, "and seemed horror-struck, you say? Perhaps they were friends? Or did he know Kenorn to be already dead?"

"Either might be true," Hugh agreed. "In fact, either is more reasonable than my thought that he might have cheated my father as he tried to cheat my uncle. But whatever his reason, Lionel Heugh surely knew my father. The crops are in, Audris, and there is nothing much for me to do here. I think I will ride down to Heugh and ask who Sir Kenorn was and if he had a family here in England."

"No!" Audris cried. "You are mad! He will try to kill you again."

"Why?" Hugh asked. "There could be no profit in it. My death would not win him Ruthsson now."

"Oh, Hugh, might he not hate you for your victory? And I know there is a longtime enmity between your family and Heugh."

"I am not so sure the victory was mine," Hugh said thoughtfully, calling back to mind the details of the last few minutes of that battle. "And I think whatever enmity Sir Lionel has for Ruthsson is overridden by what Kenorn meant to him—whatever that was. Looking back, I am sure that Sir Lionel accepted defeat rather than fight me—or, rather, Kenorn. He could have killed me as I tried to roll away. He *was* close enough. I know because of where I struck him as I turned back."

"How can you know why he did not strike?" Audris asked. "You may have hurt him more than you guessed when you were fighting on the ground. Hugh—"

"I am no novice in battle," he interrupted her, frowning. "I tell you, Audris, I do not think he desires my death at all. He *would* not strike at me after he called me Kenorn. In fact, he would not even raise his shield to protect himself. That was why I could not kill him. I *could* not strike a man who just stood there and watched his deathstroke come."

Audris now wished fervently that Hugh had not had such delicate sensibilities, but it was useless to say so. Instead she turned the conversation, hoping that Hugh would forget the notion that had come into his head. He did not resist the change of subject, cheerfully taking Eric, who was now sated and asleep, so that Audris could adjust her gown, but he did not forget either. Later in the evening Audris found him talking to Ralph about going to Heugh. At first she did not interfere, hoping that Ralph's protests would have more effect than hers, but it was soon clear that opposition was only fixing Hugh's purpose more firmly.

She went early to the women's quarters, a separate building much like the great hall but on a smaller scale. Since the light was almost gone, the women were clustered in small groups talking and laughing. They looked at her as she passed, Fritha carrying Eric, who was sound asleep, behind her. Two half rose, snatching up the yarn they had been spinning to show her, but her eyes were fixed ahead, and both women sank back down with their companions, who were already going back to their talk. Deep in thought, Audris passed the central hearth and stepped up onto the raised dais, thick with fresh rushes. She paused a moment to rest her hand on one of the two chairs with carven arms and backs that faced the fire, not much more than embers on this mild evening. Fritha went around the other side of the chairs, crossing in front of Audris's new, curtained bed to lay Eric in his cradle, which stood beside it. He whimpered, but Fritha rocked him gently, and he quieted.

Sure he would sleep, Audris turned to the right, where, flanking a large open window, two to a side, the unicorn tapestries hung. They had a glowing life, even in the dim light. Audris's eyes flicked to the last two. She had explained them to herself over and over, but she could not help wondering whether there was a garden in Heugh and whether the girl-cousin, who was Sir Lionel's heir, was a silver-blond who lived there. It was hardly likely, but her decision was made before Fritha came to help her out of her gown. Hugh came soon after, anxious because she had slipped away while he was still trying to convince Ralph it would be worthwhile to go to Heugh. She laughed at him and reassured him, and then, while Fritha was brushing her hair, she announced calmly that if Hugh went to speak to Sir Lionel, she would go also.

There was a momentary stunned silence before Hugh exploded, "No! You will not!"

"Why not, dear heart?" Audris asked, stopping Fritha and turning toward her husband with a hurt look of surprise. "You say there is no danger. Why should I not go also? I have no more to do than you at this season, since I am not hawking, and I would like to see new places and new people."

Hugh was immediately flooded with guilt. Ruthsson was a very isolated keep, the river behind it unfordable, and the land covered with steep, thickly forested hills. Therefore, the road from Morpeth ended at Ruthsson, and provided no route to the north. In the months since they had come back from

York, not a single visitor, not even a common wandering juggler with his pipe and crude songs and tricks, had passed their gates. Hugh knew that many guests, high and low, came to Jernaeve, bringing news and fresh opinions and fresh faces to spice the round of dull daily activities.

Because Audris was so much at ease and had so quickly endeared herself to both Ralph and Thurstan, and because she had eagerly sought his company, Hugh had no way of knowing that she actually did not crave variety and had most often secluded herself from Jernaeve's visitors. And, although he and Ralph had scoured not only Ruthsson but every other manor on the estate for any item that could add to the comfort or beauty of her bower, he still felt that she had sacrificed a luxurious home to live in a wood hut. Somehow the fact that Audris never once complained, that she seemed delighted with her quarters in a separate building, only made him more guilty.

"Would you like to go back to Jernaeve?" he asked in a choked voice. "I am sure—"

"Hugh!" Audris exclaimed, getting up from the stool on which she was sitting and hurrying to embrace him. "I am happy here, very happy, but it is just the beginning of summer, a perfect time for riding abroad and seeing new sights, and I am idle." Her eyes began to twinkle with mischief. "Besides, hungry as you must be by now, I am not willing to let you out of my sight."

He could not help laughing. Audris was not a jealous woman—and she had no cause to be; it had been one thing to sin with a whore when his heart was empty and he felt the need. Now when a little patience would renew for him the exquisite joys to be found with his pure and lawful love, he would sooner castrate himself than touch another woman. Besides, she contrived—at the price of a small sin—to ease him. That reminder—that Audris would gladly and cheerfully share even sin with him—only renewed the pang of guilt that her teasing had soothed a trifle, and Hugh began to reconsider his first refusal. Then he frowned.

"But Audris, your nonsense aside, you cannot ride while you are still bleeding," he pointed out. "And what will you do about Eric? You cannot leave him, unless you choose a wet nurse for him. He must eat."

"Leave Eric?" she repeated. "I would not think of it. Why should I not take him? I will carry him as the common women do, in a cloth against my breast, which will make it easy for him to take suck. And if I tire, Fritha can hold him for me. You know she can be trusted. As to my bleeding, it is hardly anything now." She took his hands in hers and looked up into his face with bright, hopeful eyes. "If we stay only one week longer—and you should, truly, to see the first hay cut and ricked—I will be clean. I do not wish to be parted from you just when we may love again."

"I will certainly stay the week," Hugh said immediately. "As to your coming with me—well, we will see."

But Audris laughed and pulled down his head to kiss his nose, and after a moment Hugh laughed also. Why should she not go, Hugh thought. We can ride in slow stages and stop any place that catches our fancy—and I can leave her and Eric in Trewick, which is less than two leagues from Heugh, where they will be perfectly safe if I am wrong in my guesses about Lionel Heugh's feeling for Kenorn.

The week stretched to a month, Audris devising first one and then another innocent delay, but she saw in the end that Hugh *needed* to learn as much about his father as he could. Still, when they came to Trewick after an easy ride that had taken them first to Morpeth, where they stayed a night, Audris did not want to remain behind. At first she threatened to follow him, alone if necessary—and Hugh knew that the men-at-arms, primed by Morel, were too much in awe of her "powers" to contest any order she gave. But Hugh finally convinced her to stay by pointing out that her presence would increase the danger for him, if there was any, by offering Sir Lionel the temptation of wiping out all of Lord Ruthsson's heirs in one stroke. He almost gave up the idea entirely, because her eyes were too large and swimming with tears, but she sighed and bade him go, knowing he would never be content until he followed the first real clue he had found concerning his father to its conclusion.

As he rode away, Hugh resolved only to enter the castle, make himself known to Sir Lionel, and say he would come again the next day. He would be able, thus, to judge his erstwhile enemy's attitude, and it seemed to him that if he were allowed to come and go freely, Audris would be reassured about his safety. He was annoyed both with her and with himself for the uneasiness her fear generated, and when he had ridden across the drawbridge that spanned the deep outer dry moat and passed through the gate, he gave his name, defiantly, as Sir Hugh of Ruthsson, lifting off his helmet and pushing back his hood.

A single voice cried out, "Sir Kenorn—my lord!" and immediately, "No, it cannot be."

Hugh turned quickly, asking, "Who calls Kenorn?" but there was no answer, and he could not see anyone who might have spoken, although one or two men near him had also turned and looked curiously in the same direction, then turned back to stare at him. Hugh was now certain the answer to his father's identity lay in this keep. He did not try to find the man right then, because he hoped that Sir Lionel would answer his questions willingly, but he was determined to have an answer.

Looking about as he rode through the outer bailey, across the second drawbridge, and into the inner bailey brought other things to Hugh's notice. Heugh was a standing testimony to the violent energy and fierce purpose of its holder within the last decade—brutally strong and raw with newness. The stone of the walls was bright and glittering with recent cutting, and the mortar of the top floor of the great, square stone keep in the center of the inner bailey was still oozing in places.

Yet there was a certain impression of disorganization about the activity in the bailey; two smiths seemed to be quarreling about whether they should prepare horseshoes or get on with some other task, and a number of projects—one of them the building of a handsome new mews, the other, even more puzzling, the completion of the forebuilding to shelter the outer stair that rose to the keep entrance—seemed to have been abandoned half done. And it was a careless abandonment at that, with planks left exposed to rain and sun and the piles of sand for mortar disintegrated into wide patches.

When Hugh dismounted, he had to hail a groom to take Rufus's rein, which no noble guest should need to do; and when he climbed the stair and entered the door to the great hall, the servant he accosted to ask whether Sir Lionel was within looked frightened. Hugh put out a hand to hold him, wondering whether he, too, had mistaken him for his father, but he was not quick enough. The man ran off toward a doorway at the back of the hall, which Hugh thought must be a stairway, and the other servants rapidly began to disappear. Hugh tensed, wondering whether he had walked into a trap after all, but when he went back to the door and looked out, there was no sign of men gathering to prevent his departure or of any suspicious activity or sound. He stood there, unde-cided, one hand on his sword hilt and the other reaching back to pull his shield forward to defend himself, trying to watch the hall and the bailey at the same time.

But only the lack of normal activity threatened him in the hall, and he swung his head to look outside again. By then, the hall had become so quiet that he heard the rustling of the rushes as someone approached, and he turned with his sword half drawn to find himself confronting a sad-looking middle-aged gentlewoman followed by an elderly maidservant. The gentlewoman swallowed hard and shuddered as they drew close enough to see him clearly, then lowered her eyes, and the maid took one look at him, put her hands to her face, and wailed aloud.

"I beg your pardon," Hugh exclaimed, flushing with embarrassment as he thrust his sword back into its scabbard. "I mean you no harm. I—"

"So you have come," the gentlewoman said. "After so many months I began to think Lionel was only raving."

"Raving?" Hugh repeated. "About seeing Kenorn? I would like to speak to Sir Lionel about that."

"Lionel is dead." She sighed, still not looking at him, then shrugged. "He died of the wounds you gave him—or perhaps of fear, or guilt, or even grief."

Hugh frowned, disappointed, but not as disheartened as he would have been earlier. He was certain that both the lady to whom he was speaking and her maidservant knew his father as well as the man who had called out in the outer bailey, and he suspected that there might be others in the keep or on the nearby estates who also knew Sir Kenorn.

One thing was revealing: the voice of the man in the bailey had held surprise and joy equally before fear had shaded his final sentence; on the other hand, the maidservant, who was weeping softly now, had been terrified—and so had the lady. Hugh was now relatively certain that some wrong had been done his father, possibly right here in Heugh keep, a wrong that the lady and her maid were aware of but the man in the bailey was not. He wondered whether hate, because he had killed Lionel Heugh, or guilt, because of what had happened to his father, was the main reason she would not look at him.

"I am sorry for you, madam," Hugh said, more coldly than he would have under other circumstances, "but the challenge was Sir Lionel's, not mine, and I am not to blame for the outcome. I say again that I mean you no harm. All I desire is to discover what I can about Sir Kenorn, who was my father. I wish to know, for example, why he did not return, as he said he would, to my mother."

"He was dead," the gentlewoman whispered, and her maid wailed aloud again.

"He was murdered by Sir Lionel?" Hugh's voice was harsh, only a hint of rise indicating uncertainty.

"No!" the woman cried. "No! Lionel did not kill Kenorn—I swear it! It was the old man, his father."

Hugh blinked, then roared in incredulous fury, "Sir Kenorn's father—my grandfather—was here and murdered his son in front of Sir Lionel?"

"And me," the woman sighed, and crumpled to the floor in a dead faint.

The maid began to scream, and servants' faces peeped timorously from various entrances into the hall, but not one ran out to help or protect the lady. Hugh stood paralyzed, appalled at having unintentionally frightened the poor woman so much and frightened out of his own wits because he had no idea what to do. She began to stir in a moment, and Hugh knelt down beside her. The maid shrieked even louder, and he turned on her.

"Stop that caterwauling," he snarled. "I mean your mistress no harm. If you know what to do to help her, do it or fetch someone who can help." Then he leaned down and spoke as softly as he could, "Madam, forgive me. I was not angry at you. Please do not fear me."

The maid had clapped her hands over her mouth when Hugh scolded her and then knelt down, too, and lifted her mistress so that she was half sitting, resting against the older woman's shoulder. This time, once she opened her eyes, the lady had never taken them from Hugh's face. At first she looked dazed, but when he spoke to her softly and comfortingly, tears filled her eyes and she sighed. "Kenorn, oh, Kenorn."

Hugh swallowed nervously. The longing in those three words had implications he did not want to consider. "I am not Kenorn, I am his son," he said gently, watching her nervously, for fear she would faint again. She did not do that, but she began to cry bitterly, and Hugh was torn between pity and exasperation. "I see that you are not well, madam," he continued quickly, wanting desperately to get away before she became completely hysterical, "so I will not trouble you further now. May I come again on the morrow to learn more about my father's death? If—"

"Why do you ask me if you can come?" the woman interrupted passionately, the tears still streaming down her face. "You know Heugh is yours! I am nothing."

Chapter 23

HUGH KNELT WITH HIS MOUTH OPEN ON AN EXCLAMATION OF disbelief, too stunned to speak or try to stop her as she began to struggle to get to her feet. Now the weeping maid called for assistance, and two women came to help support their mistress. Hugh still had not recovered from the shock of what she had said to him, and he watched her go without a move or a question before he climbed numbly to his feet. The servants, who seemed to have been reassured by Hugh's gentleness to the lady, had been inching back into the hall, all agog to see the new lord—for Sir Lionel's ravings had swiftly sifted from his deathbed to the inner servants. Hugh's eyes roved over them blankly for a few minutes, then he took a deep breath and beckoned to the nearest manservant.

"Where is the steward?" he asked.

"The lord was his own steward, my lord," the man replied submissively, eager to make a good impression.

I should have known that, Hugh thought. When Sir Lionel died, all authority died, too. That is why the building was left unfinished, the smiths are at odds about what is most important, and why the men-at-arms are slack. A steward would have kept them to their work. But that meant there was no one he could ask to confirm what he thought he had heard. He glanced toward the end of the hall where the lady had disappeared. No one would stop him—he had evidence that the servants would not attempt to protect her—but his courage failed when he thought of pursuing her and asking her to repeat what she had said. In fact, when he thought of her expression as she called him Kenorn and of her fainting and tears, he had a strong desire to forget he had ever entered Heugh, to go back to Audris.

"Audris!" he exclaimed, realizing that he did not need to confront the hysterical woman. Audris would know what to do, how to question her; meanwhile, he could find out what the men in the place knew.

The servant, who was still standing near him, cringed when Hugh turned toward him. "I do not know who 'Audris' is," the man gasped. "Please, my lord—"

The small amount of pity Hugh had felt for Sir Lionel disappeared. "Never mind," he said to the terrified man. "I was not speaking to you. What I want you to do is to make ready a chamber for me, my wife, and a babe. Or, if you are not responsible for such matters, give my word to one who is responsible. Oh, and send a message to the stable for a groom to bring my horse."

Almost before the words were out, a boy had detached himself from the fringes of a group watching Hugh at a discreet distance and run through the outer door to carry the message. Hugh looked dazedly around the hall. His? To have built such a place meant wealth, power... Hugh remembered that his uncle had not been able to find a champion to fight Lionel Heugh. Perhaps it was not only the man himself but his influence in the area that had been feared. By the moment, Hugh found himself feeling more and more depressed. He had been filled with joy when he learned he was the heir of Ruthsson; he had gone to do battle with Sir Lionel eagerly because that battle would give him the right to call Ruthsson his, to restore it to a productive estate, to bring his beloved to his home. Here, all he wanted was to be out of the place, never to see it again.

He arrived in Trewick in such a state that Fritha, who was the first to notice him when he came into the garden where Audris was playing with her baby, pulled Audris around and pointed urgently. "Hugh!" Audris cried, thrusting Eric into her maid's arms and running to her husband. "Hugh, are you hurt? What is wrong?"

"I think I am the lord of Heugh," he said, and shuddered.

Audris put up her hands and cupped his face, drew down his head, and kissed his forehead—but he had no fever. "You are lord of yourself, my heart? I do not understand."

"Not I, not that Hugh," he tried to explain. "Heugh—oh, God, they sound alike, do they not? I mean Sir Lionel's estate."

"Sir Lionel's estate?" Audris echoed. "How can you be Sir Lionel's heir?"

"I do not know," Hugh said. "Perhaps the lady was mad, but—"

"What lady?" Audris asked. "I thought you went to see Sir Lionel."

"He is dead—and just as well, too." Hugh's voice became brisk over those words; he found to his relief that he did not like Sir Lionel any better dead than alive. But then he frowned and repeated, "What lady? Truly, I do not know. She never said her name, and she spoke so strangely from the first words we exchanged, that I never asked…" He began to look dazed and unhappy again.

"Come," Audris said, abandoning the topic for the moment. "Let Fritha pull off your hauberk. Then sit down and tell me the whole. Perhaps—"

"No," he interrupted as Audris turned and put out her arms to take Eric so the maid could attend to Hugh. Audris faced him again, looking troubled. "I do not wish to unarm," he explained. "I told the servants in Heugh to ready a chamber for us." He put out a hand. "I am sorry. I did not think that you might be too tired to go farther. I—I *must* know, Audris."

"I am not tired at all, dear heart," she assured him, her mind racing. It was impossible for Hugh to be Sir Lionel's heir as well as Ralph's. Margaret Ruthsson *had* been his mother, and Lionel Heugh could not be his father. But there were many drugs that could make a man see and hear what was not real—and die of it, too. "Did you eat anything or drink anything there?" she asked, taking Hugh's hands.

"Eat or drink? No. I did not even sit down. I hardly walked ten feet from the outer door. Why——" Then Hugh's eyes cleared, and he laughed. "I am not poisoned, beloved, and I am sure there is no threat against us in Heugh. No matter what my need, you cannot think I would take you or Eric into any danger. You did not see the people. There is no man or woman—except the lady, mayhap, and I am not so sure of that—who would avenge Sir Lionel. They feared him, perhaps hated him, yet they are all... lost. They were *eager* to take my orders."

Audris nodded acceptance, her face clearing. Hugh's color was good, his hands were warm and dry, his breathing was right, his eyes clear—if vague and troubled. She had only been worried by that vague, distressed look, and that disappeared as he spoke of what he had seen and experienced. It was something about the "lady" that was bothering him, and the news that he was lord of Heugh had come from her. Perhaps the poor creature was mad or had been driven mad by Sir Lionel's death, Audris thought. In that case, she herself would be best able to deal with her.

"You go and tell the men to make ready," she said, "and I will see to packing up what little I unpacked."

But actually she sent Fritha to pack while she summoned the bailiff's wife, and they went together to where the dried herbs hung. Audris regretted that they were so old, but she took Saint John's wort, betony, hemlock, willow bark, and several others. As they rode toward Heugh keep, however, and she heard the story in chronological order, Audris began to think there must be more than a madwoman's raving behind the statement that Heugh belonged to her husband. And when they arrived and Audris took the measure of how the servants looked at and welcomed Hugh, she realized that they, at least, believed him to be the new master.

There was only one unpleasant incident when Audris, in her usual gentle, smiling manner, beckoned a manservant who was passing and told him to bring more wood for the fire. The man turned his shoulder and said, "Later." Hugh promptly hit him so hard that he knocked him almost the full width of the hall, which was some twenty feet wide.

"My wife is myself!" he roared. "You will all come to kissing her feet, and if she says to put your hand in the fire, you will put it there, or I will do to you what will make that seem a pleasure."

A soft moan went up from the terrified men and women in the hall, and they literally abased themselves and began to crawl forward to kiss Audris's feet. She put a hand on Hugh's arm. He was shaking. She had hardly been more startled by his violence than by the servant's rudeness—for no one except her male cousins had ever been rude to her—but then she recalled Hugh's disgust at the servants' indifference toward the gentlewoman who had greeted him, leaving her to his mercy and not coming forward to help when she fainted. His outburst was a natural result of that disgust and his general uncertainty and unhappiness.

The next minute, Audris knew, he would have said he had not meant them actually to kiss Audris's feet and gone to help the man he had struck down, but she held him fast and murmured, "Let it be, Hugh. They only understand fear. If they do belong to us, we can teach them better in time." But she herself recoiled from the notion of them crawling to her and kissing her feet. "Stop," she said, raising her voice. "You are not worthy yet to touch me," and they crouched where they were, trembling. "You may rise," she added, "and see to the man who was hurt. And one of you, bring more wood and mend the fire."

"Where is the chamber I said should be made ready for my wife?" Hugh growled.

A manservant tottered a little forward, his eyes filled with fear. Hugh recognized him as the servant to whom he had spoken on his first visit. "The lady's chamber is made ready," the man faltered.

"Very good," Audris said calmly. "Where is it?"

The servant gestured to one of the women, who scuttled forward to the stair that went up to the third floor, usually given over to the women's quarters. When Hugh saw where the maid was going, he balked. Audris smiled at him and patted his hand.

"If you think it safe, dear heart," she murmured, "get Morel to unarm you. I will see to this strange lady and try to discover why she says these lands are yours."

"But if she is mad, she might be dangerous," Hugh protested uncertainly. "She looked at me in such a way when she called me Kenorn that I fear she might attack you for being my wife."

"Do not concern yourself," Audris assured him. "Fritha will protect me—and the other women servants, too, I think, out of fear of you."

Hugh watched Audris walk away, her quick, light step not a whit slower or heavier for the babe she carried, and Eric was no feather, for he was large and strong-boned, growing apace. Hugh felt guilty and uneasy, wondering if he should have so easily accepted her assurances. Audris was afraid of nothing, he thought, because she had never had cause to be afraid. But Fritha was strong, and the maid who scurried ahead would remember what had befallen the man who had only been rude to her and make sure Audris was safe.

Still, he could not bid Morel, who had followed them into the hall carrying changes for the baby and a basket Hugh thought had some clothes for himself and Audris, to unarm him as Audris suggested. His uneasiness made him want to make *something* secure, and he told his man to stay with the baggage in case Audris wanted something from it. He would go out and see to the quartering of the troop.

They had taken a substantial troop—twenty men-at-arms—because Hugh had heard on a trip to Morpeth about a week before they left that King David was besieging Norham Castle and there was news of heavy raiding by the Scots near Chillingham. That was well north and east, and he and Audris were traveling south and west, but Hugh was taking no chances on being caught by a raiding party that had traveled down the Jedwater to the Rede, or, for that matter, on being attacked by the many outlaws who laired in Redesdale.

He did not see his men when he came down into the inner bailey, and a chill passed over him, but the captain of the troop popped out of the stable the moment Hugh shouted for him and hurried over.

"My lord," he said, "this place is almost empty."

"Empty?" Hugh repeated, looking around.

There was a great clanging from the smithy now, and men hurried from one end of the bailey to another, entering and leaving the various outbuildings with expressions of great intensity. Hugh suspected that there might not be much purpose to the movement—aside from an attempt to convince him they were busy and industrious—but he was indifferent to that problem at this moment.

"Yes, my lord, empty," Louis Barbedenoir replied. "There are two fine destriers in the stable—both too fat from lack of exercise—and a pair of handsome palfreys, also in need of exercise, but the stable was built to hold many more horses, and the groom told me that at year-time, all but about fifteen of the old men-at-arms rode away."

"You mean there are no more than fifteen men-at-arms in the keep!" Hugh exclaimed.

"Aye, so said the groom," Louis said, nodding emphatically to add conviction to his statement. "And the ones who remained were mostly too old to hope for employment elsewhere."

"I see." Hugh's lips twisted wryly. "Lionel died some time before the men were to be paid, and either they did not like the place or they did not expect the new lord to retain them. They were not local men, I take it?"

"That I cannot tell you, my lord," Louis answered. "I did not think to ask."

That was natural enough, Hugh thought, since Louis was a Flemish mercenary himself. For reasons he did not specify, Louis had decided to remain in England and had taken service with Hugh for the customary year and a day. Actually, Hugh was reasonably sure Louis, because he was no longer young, had decided to settle down with a master who did not plan to go to war, but Hugh had found him to be a good swordsman and bowman with a steady temper—ideal for leading a small troop and for teaching raw plowboys to be armsmen.

"No matter," Hugh said. "I can ask the men who did stay. In any case, there cannot be any problem about housing our men."

"No, indeed, my lord." Louis gestured with his head in the

direction of a long stone building nestled against the wall of the inner bailey. "A fine new barracks, all empty. I was only waiting for your word to settle the men in."

"Empty, is it?" Hugh remarked. "Then where are the men who stayed?"

"In the guardroom down near the outer bailey gate." Louis looked approving. "The headman may be old, but he has some sense. There was plenty of room for the fifteen of them in the lower guardroom, and they're more needed at the lower gate."

"True enough," Hugh agreed. "Very well, tell the men to move into the barracks, but set up a guard on the inner wall with men ready to raise the drawbridge and drop the port-cullis. I'll ride down and speak to the captain, and you might as well tell a groom to saddle one of Sir Lionel's destriers."

"Shall I ride down with you, my lord?" Louis asked.

"No need for that." Hugh smiled. "I do not suspect the Heugh men-at-arms, and I have some private business with one of them. But a gate should never be unguarded. And it has occurred to me that if news of Sir Lionel's death should somehow come to the ears of the Scots raiders near Chillingham, they might think it worth the miles to come here and see what they could pick up from a lordless keep."

Louis frowned. "Can we hold this place with no more than thirty-five men, my lord? It is strong, but—"

"I would not try to hold it," Hugh assured him, "at least not if the raiding party were of any size, but there is no need to invite them in by leaving the bridges down and the gates open. The Scots are not known for their patience. If we can drive them away, they may look for easier pickings. It is just a precaution, Louis. I do not expect trouble."

"Yes, my lord. I will—"

A clip-clop of hooves made Louis stop and turn. He and Hugh were both surprised to see a groom leading a tall black destrier wearing a worn fighting saddle out of the stables. Hugh did not know whether to smile or shudder. It was clear that everyone who could was listening, and the groom had heard him tell Louis he wanted a horse. The eagerness of the servants to please him was almost funny, but the significance of their desire to please was not. Hugh sighed.

Perhaps they were only basing their conviction that he was the new master on what the madwoman had said to him in the hall—but that would imply that the servants did not think her mad, even though they scorned her. And if she was *not* mad… But that only took him round in a circle, implicitly confirming that he *was* master of Heugh. Still, it was *impossible,* so… He had better stop thinking about it, Hugh told himself. Before he knew it, he would become accustomed to the idea and be bitterly disappointed when he discovered Heugh was not his.

With a nod of dismissal to Louis and a word of thanks to the groom, Hugh mounted and rode across the drawbridge into the outer bailey. Here there were signs he had not noticed when he first rode in. The exercise ground was empty; the grass was long in the paddock where extra horses were kept; in fact, grass was growing around the doors of many of the outbuildings. However, there were men on the walls—too few, Hugh realized, but enough so that the keep did not look abandoned. He dismounted near the guardroom, and a middle-aged man, who had obviously been watching at the door to see if he would stop, came out at once and bowed.

"I am Odard, my lord, captain here. Are you—"

"How many men do you have, Odard?" Hugh asked hastily, afraid that the man would ask whether he was the new lord.

"Myself and fourteen others, my lord."

The prompt answer, which should certainly not have been given to a stranger with no authority, sent the same uneasy mixture of doubt and half acceptance through Hugh. Again he dismissed the problem; there remained a simple duty he must perform as a man of goodwill: no matter to whom Heugh belonged, he must put the keep into the best defensive posture possible.

"My man Louis says he was told the others left."

"The lord was dead, and the lady said she had no right to pay them," Odard replied, then he frowned. "We have had no pay either, my lord, but most of us have been at Heugh since the old lord's time, and we have families here"

"I will see that you are paid, one way or another," Hugh promised promptly. It was only fair. Whatever their reasons, the few who had stayed had kept to their duty.

Odard's eyes lit with relief. "I thank you, my lord. And will you—"

But Hugh was even more wary of questions. Having committed himself to an act for which he probably had no authority, he was afraid of being asked how he would fulfill his promise. He therefore promptly asked a question of his own about the departed troop, and then another about obtaining fighting men from the area if they were needed, more to forestall being questioned himself than because he wanted to know. Just as Odard told him that the local yeomen, like most Northumbrian farmers, could fight if called on, a hail came around the wall from the north that a man riding hard was on his way to the gate.

Odard frowned, and Hugh said, "I do not like this. Tell half a dozen of your men to make ready to ride out."

Odard went off at once without argument, which left Hugh wondering whether his prompt obedience was to the "new lord" or because he also feared trouble. "I hope I have not summoned the devil to us by telling Louis that if the Scots who were raiding around Chillingham heard of a keep without a lord…" Hugh muttered to himself as he walked the short distance to the gate. He heard Odard calling out men and telling them to make ready to ride, but before the horses were saddled, he heard the clatter of a horse on the drawbridge and a man shouting his name. Hugh had little time in which to be surprised, for he answered instinctively and as instinctively caught at the horse, which tried to rear and neighed shrilly. The big stallion shouldered it hard, and it quieted, but then Hugh saw it was not only lathered but showed bright streaks of blood.

"My lord!" the man cried as he tumbled off his mount. "The Scots are upon us! They struck at Trewick not an hour after you left. We fought them off, and I and five others rode out to give warning to you and to Belsay. We were too late for Belsay. The village is in flames and… I think they are in the outer bailey of the keep also. I saw smoke… My lord, they are killing and burning everyone and everything. Killing and burning!"

Hugh caught the man as he staggered, noticing only when he slumped over that there was an arrow in his back. Hugh turned his head and bellowed, "Odard, get those men out to warn the farms and villages. And send out the huntsmen and the foresters, too, whoever is in the keep that knows the countryside, to watch for the Scots and give us warning. Bid the people come in to Heugh, bringing their goods and cattle and whatever food they have in store. When the men are out, get the bridge up and the portcullis down. I will send my men down to help guard the walls." Then he turned to the messenger he was supporting. "You have done right well," he said. "Can you ride up to the keep if I lift you to your horse and a man leads it, or shall I have you carried? Lady Audris will have that bolt out of you and ease you well."

"I can ride," the man gasped. "I think it is only in the flesh, but I could not…"

Hugh did not wait for him to finish, but helped him to mount, calling for someone to hold him steady and lead his horse. A man ran forward, and Hugh mounted the black destrier, riding ahead, bellowing for a groom and for Louis as soon as he was in the inner bailey. He jumped down, shouting orders at Louis as he ran toward the stairs of the keep, hesitating only until his captain shouted back that he understood and turned toward the barracks, ordering out the men who were not already on guard. Then Hugh ran up and, ignoring the servants, who scattered before him, ran across the hall and up again to the women's quarters calling out for Audris as he climbed the stairs.

❧

When Audris told Hugh she was not afraid, she had spoken the exact truth. To soothe him, she had taken Eric from Fritha and slung the baby in the carrying cloth, but she did not expect to be attacked—and she was quite right. In the solar, she found a weeping, dazed woman, sitting on a stool and clinging to a trembling elderly maid, surrounded by garments and a few toilet articles carelessly cast down on the floor. Audris stopped and stared, then uttered a cry of distress. The servants had apparently put the poor woman out of her room to make it ready for the new lord's wife. Hurriedly, she handed Eric back to Fritha and ran forward to kneel beside the weeping lady.

"What will you do with me?" the woman sobbed.

"First beg your pardon," Audris said softly. "I do assure you, madam, my husband had no idea that such an insult would be dealt you. He only asked the servant to make a chamber ready for us. He expected one of the wall chambers would be prepared, not that you would be put out."

Brown eyes, dim with years of weeping, gazed at her. "Kenorn is your husband?"

Audris felt a chill, but she smiled and said, "My husband's name is Hugh. Kenorn is dead."

"Oh, yes, he told me." The woman relaxed her frantic clutch on the old maidservant, raised a hand, and wiped wearily at the tears on her cheeks with the edge of her sleeve. Then she said softly, "I am not mad. It was only for a moment that I forgot. I have never seen so strong a resemblance. I was supposed to be betrothed to Kenorn, but after… after, the old man forced me to marry Lionel. I did not wish to, but once I knew—" Her voice faltered, and she began to sob again, wringing her hands in her lap.

"What is your name, madam?" Audris asked hurriedly, guessing that if she did not change the subject, hysterics would follow.

"My name?" she repeated, but the question seemed to steady her, and she said, "Maud is my name, though Lionel always called me Mold in the old style." She shuddered. "I hated that, but he did not care."

"My name is Audris, Lady Maud," Audris said, "and now we must restore you to your chamber."

"No," Maud gasped. "No. Your husband ordered—"

"Hugh ordered no such thing," Audris assured her, taking her hand and squeezing it gently. "It was a stupid mistake. The servant did not understand what he meant. You must believe me. And you must also believe that Hugh wishes you no harm and will do his best to protect you—"

"No," Maud wailed, "no! He *must* hate me. You do not understand. We sinned against him, Lionel and I. We sinned greatly, we... I... we..."

Tears choked her, and Audris embraced her and tried to comfort her, but the more assurances she offered, the more distressed Lady Maud became. At last she desisted, sitting back on her heels and gently patting the older woman's shoulder for a moment. Audris realized that a cause deeper than simple fear was at the root of Lady Maud's agony, and kindness was only making her pain worse. For now, what she needed was to forget and to rest. Later she might find ease in confession.

"Comfort her if you can," Audris said to the old maid, who had stopped trembling and was watching Audris with grateful wonder. "I will make her a draft that will calm her and help her to sleep."

Then she rose and approached the women servants, who were huddled together as far from Lady Maud as they could get. They all rose as Audris drew near, and she saw among them the woman who had led her up the stairs. Taking the rising as a symbol of respect, Audris asked for the stillroom maid and after a few questions sent her running for steepings from willow bark, betony, hemlock, thornapple, and some honey. Then she sent another to make up Lady Maud's bed anew and to restore the room as much as possible to its old appearance.

When the stillroom maid returned, Audris mixed the steepings—a base of willow bark, a good dose of betony, a spoonful of hemlock (always to be used sparingly because too much would kill), and a few drops of thornapple, which was a fine strengthener but, if used too freely, could cause delirium. A measure of honey to hide, at least a little, the bitterness of the other ingredients, and Audris carried the cup to Lady Maud. She feared she might have difficulty in persuading her to drink it, but Lady Maud took the cup eagerly and drained it at once.

The difficulty rose in convincing her to return to her chamber and lie down, and Audris realized that Lady Maud *wanted* to be put out, she wanted to suffer at Hugh's hands. This left Audris in a quandary. She certainly did not wish to add to Lady Maud's sufferings, but she could not have her sitting forever on a stool in the middle of the room with her clothes strewn around her. She was considering the alternatives of insisting she go back to her own chamber or going down to the hall and ordering a place to be prepared for her there when Hugh came bounding up the stair calling her name.

"What is it?" she cried, running forward.

"The Scots," Hugh replied, taking her in his arms. "They attacked Trewick and were driven away, but seemingly they caught Belsay unprepared. They fired the village and somehow got into the outer bailey—at least, the man from Trewick said he thought the sheds were afire there."

Audris looked up trustingly and asked with perfect calm, "What would you have us do, my lord? Can the women help in the defense?"

"Not you, my love," he said, catching her to him harder, grateful for her calm, even though he was sure it was owing to ignorance. "I am not quite certain yet what choices we have. I have sent out men to warn the people beholden to Heugh to come in to the keep, and others to watch for the Scots. I will know better what to do when some news comes. But the man who brought the message was hurt. Could you—" He stopped abruptly. Audris was skilled with herbs. He had seen her dose the servants and villagers, and even his uncle, when they were ill, but wounds were something else again.

But Audris, thinking the abrupt ending was because his mind had already jumped to his own duties, was already beckoning the stillroom maid toward her as she answered him. "Yes, I will come down to attend him at once. And do you go where you are needed, Hugh. Do not fear for me. I am not unused to war. Jernaeve has never been broken, but it has been assaulted. Go, my heart. See to your men."

Glad that he had not made a promise that could not be kept and glad, too, that Audris did not know that Heugh was so indefensible in its present state, Hugh went down the stairs again. Audris began to ask the maid about supplies but was interrupted by Lady Maud, who had risen from her stool as soon as Hugh disappeared.

"I will gather what is necessary and do what I can for your man," she said. "You must go to your husband and tell him to take you and flee. There are no men-at-arms to defend Heugh. I—I was afraid to pay them. I thought—"

But Audris did not wait to hear what Lady Maud had thought. She flew down the stairs and caught Hugh halfway across the hall. Considering the totally indefensible condition of the keep, he actually had little to do beyond worry, and thus had not been hurrying. When she relayed the information, he was furious.

"That accursed woman," he snarled, "whatever she does— for good or ill—turns to ill. Oh, I knew about the men leaving. I hoped *you* would not need to know."

As he spoke, a flicker of movement caught Audris's eye. It was a manservant, trying to inch closer to hear what Hugh was saying. He was carrying a large platter, and when Audris's head turned toward him and caught him in what he feared was wrong, he held the platter up as if to hide behind it. But Audris's picture-prone imagination saw the round metal as a shield. For an instant she was frozen with fear, leaping to the conclusion that the enemy was already within; in the next instant she saw reality—a servant holding a platter—as if superimposed on her fear, and her mind bound the two together into a hope.

"Hugh," she gasped, "the menservants! If there is an armory here, can you not dress them in some pretense of armor and let them walk or stand on the walls? At least it would *appear* to the Scots that there were men enough to defend Heugh."

He had started to shake his head when she mentioned the menservants. In Sir Walter's keeps the servants fought when necessary, not with swords and bows, which took many years of practice, but by helping push away scaling ladders or dropping stones, boiling oil, or excrement on the enemy. Hugh had thought these men too cowed to help even in such simple ways, but by the time Audris had finished what she was saying, he was grinning.

"You are a prize beyond diamonds," he cried, flinging his arms around her and hugging her so tight in his enthusiasm that she squeaked as her ribs gave. "That much they *will* do, for I can set the men-at-arms to watch that they do not run away." His eyes narrowed. "And I can set them to cocking extra crossbows, too, so that the bowmen we have can run along on the wall behind them, firing as they go, which will make it seem we have many bowmen. Audris, you may have saved us all."

He kissed her hard and then rushed away, leaving Audris smiling despite the gravity of their situation. And she was busy enough herself in the next few hours to drive out fear. When she turned to go up to the women's floor again, she found Lady Maud in the doorway to the stairs, staring at Hugh's retreating back. She did not respond to Audris's questions until he had disappeared, and then she only wanted to know when they were leaving. Audris had to insist quite sharply on obtaining the medications for the wounded man. Then Maud offered again to care for him, but Audris, now realizing that Maud was half dazed from the draft she had taken, ignored her and told the maid what she needed. Despite Audris's urging Maud to go to bed, she accompanied her down into the bailey, standing by Audris as she spoke gently to the wounded messenger, looked at his hurt, and assured him he would recover easily.

She seemed amazed when Audris herself cut the shortbow bolt out of the man, sewed him up, and plastered the wound with an ointment of powdered betony, lemon balm, and the juice of houseleek. Maud kept protesting about something, but Audris did not listen. She was thinking about the limited power of the shortbow. A crossbow bolt would have broken the messenger's rib and pierced his chest, in which case he might well have died on the road before he could warn them, and they would have been taken by surprise, like Belsay, and overpowered. Instead the arrow had been deflected along the rib and done no more harm than tunneling under the skin. Audris smiled and said a few more comforting words, much comforted herself. Surely the messenger's arrival and her vision of the servants dressed as men-at-arms was for the purpose of saving them.

Patting her patient once more, she rose, barely in time to steady Lady Maud, who was wavering on her feet. Audris realized that Maud was almost completely under the drugs; her eyes were glazed, and her mind seemed to have fixed on the danger from the Scots, for she was insisting that Hugh, whom she called Kenorn, "flee and save himself." Audris patiently explained, several times, that it was not possible to flee Heugh with the Scots less than two leagues away. They were as likely, she pointed out, to run right into the enemy as to escape them.

When raising her voice and even shaking Maud made no impression, Audris realized she would not be able to pierce the drug-induced fixation. Maud had to be put to bed, where, hopefully, she would sleep until she became more rational, but when Audris caught one of Hugh's men-at-arms, who had entered the barracks to pick up a few old helmets that had been left, and asked him to support Maud, she screamed and shrank away in terror. Audris was troubled by Maud's reaction, fearing she had given the older woman too large a dose of thornapple. As a result, she hesitated to order the man to seize Maud—and at that moment Fritha came down the steps from the keep with a bellowing Eric in her arms.

As Audris took over her starving son, hurriedly undoing her gown to thrust a nipple into his mouth, she explained Maud's delirious confusion and the remedy. Fritha nodded and half carried, half propelled Maud into the keep and into bed, where, regardless of her protests, she fell asleep almost immediately.

Quieting Maud removed Audris's principal distraction, and by the time Eric was fed and content, fear was creeping into Audris, but she soon found another distraction. She began to wonder if she should do something about the evening meal. She had eaten little of her dinner in Trewick because she was worried about Hugh. Had every male, including the cooks, bakers, and their boys, been herded up on the walls? Audris had not the faintest idea *what* to do. She knew no more about cooking than a bird, but she set out indomitably to determine what Heugh keep could provide to eat.

At the landing of the stair to the bailey, Audris stopped and stared. She had heard some noise as she passed the windows of the hall, strangely empty now that the menservants were all gone, but the thick walls had kept out the volume of sound. Women, children, and animals milled about, crying, calling, lowing, bleating. For a moment, Audris was stunned, and then she realized these must be the wives and children of the serfs, yeomen, and artisans who worked in the small village and on the demesne and the nearby farms. The scene was one of utter chaos, and Audris suffered a spasm of utter panic. She knew that her aunt would have been down among them bringing immediate calm and order and that it was her duty to try—but how? And before she could steel herself to descend into that milling mass and try to exert her authority, the lookout atop the keep tower uttered a long hail.

"They come, my lord! The Scots come!"

Chapter 24

HUGH UTTERED A SINGLE FURIOUS OBSCENITY WHEN HE HEARD the lookout's call. A whole litany of expletives formed in his mind, but he wasted no more time after that first word; he had better uses for his mouth—which were to bellow "Go!" at the messengers ready to stop any more folk from coming to the castle and bid them hide in the woods if they could and, as soon as the messengers were over the drawbridge, to give the order to raise it.

He had hoped for more time, hoped that the Scots would be too busy at Belsay to come on to Heugh before night fell. He had also hoped, of course, that the huntsmen and foresters would return with the news that the attack on Trewick and Belsay had only been a raid and that the raiders had taken their loot and run north. But Hugh had never really believed that. He had known from the beginning that King David intended to attack England again. Even so, he had been too busy on his isolated estate and too happy with his wife and new son to attend much to events in the south, because he had not feared much for Ruthsson. The barren, forested hills, the fordless river, the lack of roads from the north, all made it unlikely that Ruthsson would be attacked merely because it was on the way to somewhere more important. Nor was it likely that an army headed south would retrace its route to assault a small, isolated keep. That would be left for cleanup work after a major victory, and Hugh did not expect the Scots to win a major victory.

On a jaunt to Morpeth, however, Ralph had heard that
Robert, earl of Gloucester, had revoked his fealty to King
Stephen. That was after the Scots had come—although they
did not come near Ruthsson—and had been driven back by
King Stephen's army. Hugh had had patrols out all spring,
but he was not at all surprised when they found nothing. It
was annoying that no information about the Scots could be
obtained from Morpeth on his own or his uncle's journeys
there, but de Merley was Stephen's man, not a local baron,
and he probably had no friends among King David's men who
would be willing to pass news.

What had convinced Hugh there was no danger, even after
he learned that David was besieging Norham, was that Sir
Walter had not sent a messenger. It was largely because Hugh
had not received any warnings from his old master that he
assumed King David would not embark on a major invasion
until Robert of Gloucester arrived in England and embroiled
King Stephen in a serious war in the south so that he could
not again bring an army to protect the northern shires.

Still, as soon as the wounded man from Trewick cried
out that the Scots were attacking, Hugh had been almost
certain that it was no casual raid, that King David had tired
of waiting for Gloucester and decided to move on his own,
hoping Stephen would be busy enough taking first one rebel
keep and then another in England's southwest to ignore the
trouble in the north until it was too late. The hail from the
guard tower changed "almost certain" to absolute certainty
that the attackers were part of a war party. The only question
that remained was how large a part. Hugh ran up into the gate
tower and watched them come.

By his order the men on the wall were silent. Hugh
thought it the best way to avoid the accident of a servant's
crying out something that would give away how undermanned they were. But as the attackers streamed around the
flank of the wall, Odard, who was guarding bridge, gates, and
tower, muttered softly, "This is no army. It is a rabble. And
there cannot be more than a hundred of them. Let us go out
and give them a lesson."

If Odard had not spoken, Hugh might have said the same thing as a first reaction to the kilted warriors with their long, matted hair hanging below hide helmets, their ragged, odd, many-colored cloaks wound around tattered leather jerkins, who poured into the open fields around Heugh in total disorder, shouting threats or curses—since Hugh could not understand the language, he had no idea which. Partly because Odard's remarks had given him time to think, Hugh shook his head.

"How did they get into Belsay?" he asked. The question had been at the back of his mind ever since he had got his men set on the walls and had time to think. Belsay was like Wark, an old-style wooden keep, but even so, its outer wall should not have been overrun so easily. "Is it not likely," he went on, watching the disorderly mass wantonly trample down the sprouting grain and set fire to a shed, "that they came there as they have come here, offering themselves as a temptation. Are there more coming quietly around on the wooded side of the hill? In any case, that rabble out there can do us no harm. Let us wait until morning. Meanwhile, as soon as it is too dark for them to see, train the mangonels on their campfires."

Odard had been frowning a little as Hugh spoke. He seemed surprised at Hugh's caution, but the final sentence cleared his brow, and he chuckled. "Aye, my lord. That will lesson them just as well as a charge."

"Perhaps," Hugh replied dryly, his instincts having been fortified by being put into words. Then he remembered that he would soon have to leave Heugh—if it were possible to leave—and he felt he should try to explain to Odard why he was cautious. "Bid our men be silent and listen closely when the charge of the mangonel strikes. If there are cries, well and good, but I have a feeling the closer campfires will be only decoys—to tempt us out by making us feel we can strike the unprepared men in the dark while they eat or sleep. Then, while we are attacking, the Scots will try to get inside our walls."

"You make them out to be very clever, my lord," Odard said, his voice neutral.

Plainly he did not agree, but Heugh custom did not permit open rejection or even questioning by the tone of voice of a lord's statement. Hugh chuckled. "Better I credit them with too much deviousness than that they enter Heugh because I am too simple. I ask myself, too, why they came here after a day's fighting and looting, just as the light is failing, rather than settling into camp to enjoy the women they have taken, the food and wine…"

Odard's expression changed to surprise and then anger. Clearly Hugh's last remark had got home to him and finally convinced him there was danger of a trap. He had fought in Sir Lionel's service, and it was true that one settled down to enjoy the fruits of victory—unless there was danger of a counterattack or a surprise on the enemy was planned. He promptly assured Hugh with more enthusiasm than he had shown previously that he would strictly obey his orders and make sure his men kept a careful lookout for a night attack.

Hugh nodded, thanked him, and went out on the wall to warn Louis. Odard's casual statement had given Hugh a chill. He leaned forward through a crenel, staring out at the disorderly mass of men making rude gestures and shouting what were now obviously taunts. Hugh had been assuming that the main force of the Scots army was attacking the great castles along the coast, as usual. But what if David had decided to take the interior first, giving himself the advantage of surprise? The whole army would pour down over Heugh to get at Prudhoe and Jernaeve.

An arrow arced upward toward the wall, but Hugh did not draw back. The shortbow was useless against men on the walls. There were tight groups of men among the swirling mass of Scots nearest the edge of the dry moat. Another arrow and then several more followed the first, all fired by men who were part of the running, shouting groups. Hugh heard a man not far from him snort and then mutter an insulting remark. Since Hugh had forbidden vocal reply or firing back, all the man-at-arms could do was stand fully and boldly in the crenel opening to show his contempt for the Scottish weapons. For a few minutes more the hopeless volleys were fired, accomplishing nothing except the loss of numerous arrows in the dry moat and drawing more of Hugh's men to lean into the crenels and make rude gestures. Stupid Scots, Hugh thought—then realizing how ill that thought sat with all his other assumptions about their clever trickery, suddenly drew back himself and shouted for his men to clear the open parts of the wall.

Just as he shouted, the Scots who had been doing the shooting dropped down, and fifteen or twenty swift messengers of death buzzed upward from very small ballistae or very large crossbows. Several shrieks of pain echoed from around the wall, and Hugh strode down the walkway, silently cursing himself for stupidity while he cursed his men aloud for the same sin. They were more fortunate than they deserved, for only one man-at-arms had been hurt. The other injuries had been to servants, emboldened beyond good sense, who had imitated what the supposedly more knowledgeable men-at-arms were doing, and one yeoman's son who had more courage than brains.

More taunts came up from the Scots, but Hugh loudly threatened to break the legs of any man who replied again either by voice or gesture and then prop him up so he could fight anyway. Not that the clear crenels stopped the Scots from shooting. Arrows flew into them or over the walls as fast as the weapons—whatever they were—could be loaded, only now they carried flaming pitch to start fires, or rags soaked in feces and vomit to spread sickness. Hugh sent a servant to the inner bailey to bring down ten or twelve of the stronger women to douse any fire that began and then to gather and burn the filthy rags. His voice was calm and indifferent, but he was sick with hopelessness inside. Fire was a reasonable weapon in the short run, but disease was only useful in terms of weeks or months, which meant a siege, which meant a large army. And if they could waste arrows like that, did it not mean that the full army with supply wagons was nearby?

Hugh leaned back against a merlon and stared across the bailey toward the drawbridge to the inner keep, unwilling for the moment to turn around and look at what the enemy was doing. He saw without making much sense of it a whole procession of women, many more than the dozen he had asked for, coming over the drawbridge with several small carts drawn by asses. That seemed very peculiar; he could not imagine what use asses and carts could be for dousing fires or burning filth, but his mind was not on minor details like that. He was facing the horrible question of whether he dared resist at all once the full army arrived. If he had been alone, the question would never have entered his mind—but there were Audris and Eric. Hugh was aware of a terrible hollow sensation inside himself.

Suddenly a smell, a mouth-watering, delicious smell smote his nostrils. Hugh jerked erect, feverishly sought a stair, and almost fell down it in his haste to get to the nearest little cart, which he could now see was carrying a large caldron full of steaming stew. Simultaneously the explanation for the hollow sensation he felt leapt into his mind. It was not because the Scots were about to attack Heugh; it was because the ravings of that accursed woman had so distracted him that he had missed dinner.

Once his belly was full, Hugh found that the military situation took on an entirely different aspect. In the past the Scots had seldom bothered with sieges. It was true that David's Norman and Anglo-Norman noblemen would most likely be far more conventional in warfare, but the kilted barbarians outside of Heugh could not belong to any of David's polished gentlemen. These were the men of the wild tribes of the north, called by some Picts of Galloway and of Lothian by others. They were not noted for patience—or for getting along well with the more southerly men of David's realm.

Hugh checked that train of thought. This was no time for overconfidence. He climbed to the wall again and went slowly all the way around, straining his eyes to see into the trees in the failing light. He could make out nothing; if there were more troops hidden there, they were either well back or very quiet. But the rain of arrows had virtually stopped, and the Scots were noisily building campfires, seemingly totally ignoring the possibility of missiles launched from the keep.

Hugh considered ordering a mangonel to be loaded, but he suspected that one or more of those seemingly indifferent men were watching the walls with close attention to cry warning if a stone flew in their direction. If they were really stupid and unaware, aiming the mangonels at the campfires after dark would have a far greater effect.

In fact, Hugh's suspicions proved to be correct. The stone balls flew; some, aimed remarkably well, fell right into the campfires, scattering them far and wide—but only a single cry went up into the night. Hugh shrugged. Some poor servant who had been set to keeping the fires alight had been caught, but the troops were no doubt well back. He had the mangonels trained on the farthest fires, but the machines were small and the range was too great. When those stones fell, far short, they got a reaction—jeers and laughter. From then on, Hugh saved his stones and the efforts of the men.

On a second round of the wall, Hugh chose men to take the first watch and bade the others sleep. He did not dare let anyone off the wall. They would have to sleep as best they could where they were, in case a surprise attack at night was attempted. And three times there was a rushing about, a calling and clanging that brought every man near the gate tower on Heugh's walls tensely wide awake.

With each abortive alert, Hugh cursed the Scots wearily, wondering if they knew how thin of manpower Heugh was and were trying to wear the defenders down. But there was another reason for deliberate repeated alarms, and the fourth time, while the calling and clangor went on, on the far side of the dry moat near the gate tower, the invaders quietly put ladders up on the rear walls that faced most closely the woods to the north.

One advantage of being severely undermanned was that the men who guarded Heugh's walls were nervous and more alert than they would have been with a full complement of men-at-arms on call for defense. An ill-placed ladder swayed and scraped; a man gasped in fear of falling, and Hugh's men were calling the alarm. Even so, it was a near thing. Men had to come from a distance around the walls, and knowing the attack at the rear might only be a feint, Hugh dared not empty the rest of the walls of men. He came himself and called the men-at-arms, leaving the less experienced yeomen on guard, and everyone there fought—even the servants poked, prodded, and whacked with their clubs,-rusty swords, and boar spears at the men on the ladders.

They drove them off at last, at the cost of two men-at-arms injured and four servants killed. Hugh thought they had killed or severely injured six or seven Scots, not counting the ones who had been hurt when the ladders were cast down. He praised the men—they had fought well—but he knew that their losses, though fewer, were a disaster, whereas those of the Scots were a minor nuisance.

The Scots tried once more, this time just before the sky began to lighten with dawn, near the gate of the keep, after the usual preliminary of running and banging weapons or pots and shouting. The noise, so often repeated, did not alarm the guards in particular, but it did cover the sounds of the men scrambling down and then up the dry moat and setting the ladders.

This time, however, Hugh's men threw down torches, which he had ordered to be made ready, at regular places all around the walls to make the attackers visible. The men also called out "All safe" along the wall so it was soon clear that there was only one point under attack. And it was easier to drive them off this time, although there were more men and more ladders. Crossbowmen picked climbers off the nearest ladders by shooting through arrow slits and down from the tower roof; dark and moonless though it was, they could make out the moving shadows well enough to aim, and any hit was good enough since it usually toppled the man from his perch.

Still, one of Odard's troop was killed and two more were wounded badly enough to put them out of action, and four yeomen were hurt, although two said they could still fight. Only two servants were killed—one because he was a coward and backed so far from the fighting he fell off the walkway. Hugh sighed, wishing the numbers had been reversed. The yeomen might not be skilled warriors, but at least they knew what to do with a weapon and were unlikely to run away.

Then he shrugged. It scarcely mattered. They might stand off one more attack, or even two, but not more than two, he feared. It was not only a matter of numbers. The men-at-arms, who bore the brunt of the fighting and had to run to whichever place was assaulted, were tiring; he was tiring himself. If the Scots continued these small assaults spaced around the keep, there would come a time when his fighting men simply could not get there soon enough.

Again Hugh started to wonder whether he should surrender—and realized that no one had called on him to give up the keep. He frowned over that, but had not found an answer when suddenly his shoulder was being shaken and Odard was respectfully offering him bread, cheese, and a pot of ale. Hugh blinked stupidly, first at the man, then at the food, and finally, having realized he had fallen asleep, pushed both away with an oath and leapt to his feet to look out over the wall—and blinked even more stupidly. The Scots were gone!

"I was about to tell you, my lord," Odard said. "No one knows when they left. They must have stoked up the fires and slipped away."

Hugh shook his head at the man but said nothing. He walked thoughtfully to the edge of the walkway, lifted his tunic, loosened his chausses, and relieved his bladder. Watching the stream break into sparkling droplets as it fell to the bailey, he considered his next step. What he wanted to do was get Audris and Eric out of Heugh. It was too far back to Ruthsson, and however little chance there was of an attack, that small chance was too dangerous for his wife and son as far as Hugh was concerned. Ruthsson was even less defensible than Heugh. Jernaeve was where Audris and Eric must go. It was nearer than Ruthsson—less than five leagues, Hugh thought—and it was the strongest place he knew. Once inside old Iron Fist, Audris and Eric would be safe—at least, safer than anywhere else.

It was easy to decide that his wife and child would be best off in Jernaeve, Hugh thought as he reordered his clothing and armor. There were a few problems—like whether Sir Oliver would welcome them. Hugh picked up his bread and cheese, rested his ale pot on the wall, and stared out at the countryside. No, Oliver's welcome was the last and least of the problems. Jernaeve was Audris's, when all was said and done; Oliver might not be pleased, but he had to take her in—and Hugh did not intend to enter Jernaeve. Whatever Audris said, he could not rid himself of the image of the unicorn about to break open the keep. Besides, his place was with Sir Walter. Unconsciously Hugh's hand stroked his scabbard and fondled his sword hilt. If Audris and Eric were safe inside Jernaeve, he would be free to enjoy that duty.

The real problem would be getting them to Jernaeve. Did he dare take them out of the keep? Were the Scots gone, or was this just another trick? And what of the land between here and Jernaeve? Would there be parties of Scots roaming about? Would it be better to strip Heugh of every fighting man to make the strongest possible escort for Audris, or would it be best to go with only a few to slip quietly and secretly through the woods? And what if at the end of the road they found Jernaeve was besieged?

One answer came just as Hugh lifted the cheese to his mouth, but it was an answer that only raised more questions. A flicker of color at the edge of the trees drew his eyes, and close attention made out a man moving in a regular pattern just inside the screen of brush. Was he a careless guard who had exposed himself and given away the secret that his Scot companions were hiding in the wood... or was his exposure deliberate, to convince Hugh's men that an army lay in wait for them to open their gates when actually their forces had stolen away?

Later, when the noon sun was cooking him inside his armor as he paced the walls, partly to keep himself awake and partly to keep his men alert, he saw a column of smoke rising like a pillar in the still air not more than half a mile away. A man cried out in anguish, but Hugh did not turn or ask why. Doubtless it was his house and barns that were burning.

At a greater distance a larger pall of smoke rose. That must be a village, Hugh thought bitterly. He was sure the Scots were gone from the woods and were out looting, but there was nothing he could do. He had not enough men to try to drive them off, and he still did not dare take Audris and Eric outside the walls, because there was no way for him to discover how many troops were wreaking havoc in the countryside or how large the troops were.

Aside from the spreading signs of destruction, the land was empty and silent, the trampled fields around the keep shimmering in the heat. Hugh slept most of the afternoon, preparing for a renewal of the night attacks. He woke periodically, drenched in sweat, to drink warm ale, but toward evening a strong breeze tore apart whatever wisps of smoke still marked what had been men's livelihood and mixed them with black thunderheads. Before the storm broke, one of the huntsmen that Hugh had sent out slipped out of the woods and was let in. He had been to Belsay, and it was taken and burnt. He could not say what had become of the people, because he could not get too close.

Scots, not a wild rabble such as had attacked Heugh and Belsay, but a real army, were pouring down the road that came from the Rede valley and heading, he was almost sure, toward Newcastle. But there were no more Scots near Heugh. He had circled the keep working in and out through the woods and fields for about a mile. Every house and stead he had seen had been put to the torch and the fields trampled and torn—but the Scots were gone.

By the end of his report, Hugh could hardly make out what he was saying for the crashes of thunder, and then the rain came in torrents. Hugh came down from the walls and gave permission for most of the men to come down too and take shelter, since the huntsman said the area around the keep was clean, and he bid Louis send guards up only for an hour at a time. He looked out from the door of the guardroom at the heavy drops, already forming puddles and splashing in the bailey, wondering if he could be cruel enough to send the huntsman out again.

The man had been without sleep for two days and a night and was near to falling off his feet, but Hugh was desperate to know if a second Scottish army had come down the Roman road to Corbridge. And then he realized it would be useless.

Tired as he was, the man could never go so far and come back in time for Hugh to use the information. Hugh found a small silver coin in his purse, gave it to the huntsman, and dismissed him. The startled look and stammered thanks reminded Hugh that Sir Lionel had probably not been so generous and made him wonder wryly whether he was spoiling Heugh's servants or teaching them his ways.

He pushed those thoughts aside, knowing he was only letting his mind wander because he was reluctant to decide whether to try to escape Heugh. The thunder was now rolling away, the black clouds laced with lightning were racing into the distance, but the rain, although no longer falling in sheets, was steady, and no break in the clouds showed, even where the storm had passed. Hugh bit his lip. If the rain continued, it might be best to go as soon as it was completely dark. Armies seldom moved at night, and there was little chance of blundering into a large camp, which could be heard and seen at a distance. Even raiding parties were far less likely to roam about at night, especially in the rain. Hugh stood up and shouted for Odard and Louis.

Odard nearly wept when he heard Hugh intended to leave, and it took some time for Hugh to convince him that the keep was now in little danger. "They must take the great places—Newcastle, Prudhoe, Jernaeve—before they make a real effort to break Heugh. They are moving south and will not turn back now, for the land grows richer to the south, and they have already destroyed everything here."

"But we are only twelve now," Odard said, his old voice shaking. "What can twelve men do?"

"I am leaving Louis here, with all but five of my troop, and there will be those who managed to escape the raiders but whose farms have been burned. Take them in and train them as best as you can." He looked at Louis. "Hold the place if you can, but if an army comes, take any terms that will preserve the lives of those within. Also, try to keep your arms and horses if you can. If you must yield the keep, go back to Ruthsson and take with you any servant or yeoman who wishes to go. I do not know whose keep this is, but—"

"My lord," Odard cried, "Heugh is yours. Your—"

"Well, if it is," Hugh interrupted, suppressing the surge of interest he felt, "it can be taken back, so do not die to hold it. Heugh cannot be burnt like Belsay, and I do not think they will try to throw down these walls. King Stephen will drive out the Scots in the end, as he has done before, and the lands will be returned to their rightful holders."

While he spoke, Hugh watched Odard, wondering if the old man would resent his order to abandon Heugh and that he had placed Louis in charge. But while Hugh explained, it became clear that Odard felt only relief. And Louis seemed pleased, which Hugh felt was reasonable, for Louis must know that if he performed well under this burden, he would be rewarded, possibly with a permanent place. Not Heugh itself, but say Trewick; there was room for a "lord" at Trewick. Hugh was tempted to follow that pleasant path of thought, but again checked himself. He had finished one unpleasant task and was reluctant to begin another that might be far worse: telling Audris they had to brave the night, the rain, and the Scots only to part—he to go on to war, she to take refuge in a place where she might not be welcome.

It was almost dark now, and the rain was steady. There was no more time to delay. Hugh made sure that Odard and Louis understood what to do, added a few details, suggesting if they had to yield that they try to turn Heugh over to one of David's Norman or French barons rather than a Gaelic or Pictish chieftain. Then he left them and walked through the bailey toward the inner keep, rehearsing in his mind what he would say to Audris. He was very uneasy; he had not seen Audris since she had run down to warn him that the hired men-at-arms had left Heugh and suggested he dress the menservants up to fool the Scots. What would he do if he found her shivering with fear? Could he force her out to face a greater fear?

He saw her before she saw him—she was sitting on the dais in the large carved chair, looking ridiculously like a little girl playing "princess," or rather "mama," since she was rocking Eric in a cradle with her foot and singing softly. A violent medley of emotions—a sudden enormous hatred for the Scots who threatened the peace and comfort of this most precious of all creatures; an exquisite pang of love, quite literally a pang, for Hugh felt a sharp pain in his chest; an overwhelming desire to protect, to enwrap her in his own body if necessary— stopped him in his tracks. Something made her look up then, and she saw him and leapt to her feet to run to him, crying, "You are safe! You are safe!"

He held her tight, struggling for breath in the aftermath of that violent upsurge of caring, but when she lifted her face to be kissed, he saw that she had been crying, and for a while longer he could say nothing, only cling to her and kiss her, as her eyes pleaded he should. But when he broke the kiss and loosened his embrace, he found that she was smiling, her face illuminated with joy. Hugh drew a deep breath, bracing himself to destroy that joy and bring back fear.

"Beloved, it is true that the Scots are gone, but we are not safe. Heugh has not enough men to defend it. I must take you to Jernaeve."

Audris frowned and the joy dimmed, but she did not seem fearful, and after a moment she nodded. "Very well. I know you are right. Jernaeve will be the safest place. But Hugh, have you not thought that Jernaeve is likely to be under attack also? And are there not likely to be bands of Scots marching here and there?"

Hugh sighed. "You are entirely too clever, my heart. I had hoped you would not have thought of those dangers so you would be saved from fear, but at least it saves me from seeking reasons that would not frighten you for dragging you out in the night and the rain."

"I am not afraid." Audris shook her head. "However reckless you are of your own safety, my soul, you are careful enough of mine and Eric's. I know you would find the safest path for us—and if none is safe, the best of those possible."

"That is just it—the best of those possible," Hugh said. "But none is very good." He went on to explain his reasoning and his arrangements concerning the people now in Heugh, ending, "If Jernaeve is besieged—"

"Let us not consider that for now," Audris interrupted. "Near Jernaeve I know of caves, places in the hills where we can hide until you can decide what is best for us to do. If we are to go tonight, I must tell Lady Maud to make ready."

"Who is Lady Maud?"

But he knew who it must be even as Audris answered, "Sir Lionel's wife. The lady you met here." She hesitated at the expression on Hugh's face, and then went on, "You cannot leave her here."

"No, I suppose I cannot," he replied reluctantly. "But do not let her delay too long in choosing what she will take."

"We can go with nothing if we must," Audris said.

Hugh shook his head. "No, take what you like. There are more than enough horses, for I will not leave Sir Lionel's destriers for the Scots. My men-at-arms can ride them, and we can use their horses and the palfreys to carry the baggage." He pulled her close again with the one arm he had kept around her and kissed her. "Send a woman to the stable when you are ready, and the grooms will come up with the horses."

At the best speed Audris could make, they were not ready until long after Compline. In a sense it was Lady Maud who was the cause of the delay, but not because she cared about her possessions. She made no protesting outcry when Audris told her they must leave Heugh that night, accepting what she was told with quiet resignation. Apparently life in Heugh had been far more uncertain than life in Jernaeve had been, and Maud had fled her home—or prepared to flee it—more than once. She only asked Audris if "her lord," seemingly avoiding saying his name, would not wish to take with him the contents of the strongboxes and what little plate they had. Audris, who had no experience of running from an enemy, had never thought of it, but she agreed at once. Whether the coins and valuables were Hugh's or another's, they should be kept safe, and Maud seemed to know what to do. Audris left her to it and spent the time devising a waterproof covering of leather and oiled silk to keep Eric dry.

In fact, it was only when everything was all ready and they were waiting in what shelter the outside stair provided for the grooms to finish loading the horses, that Maud caused a real problem. The men-at-arms brought the saddle horses around; one of the men raised Fritha to the saddle; Hugh mounted Audris and then turned toward Maud.

"I cannot ride," she whispered, shrinking back from him. "I will delay you. Leave me to my fate."

Hugh's mouth opened, then jammed shut. He spun on his heel and looked at Audris, who turned her hooded head to him. He could not see her face, but he knew what he would have seen in it had there been light enough, and he sighed audibly.

"There must be a pillion saddle in the stable," he growled at a groom, who was holding one of the baggage animals. "Get it and put it on Eadgar's horse." He nodded toward the man-at-arms he meant, and then said to him, "We will switch at each rest stop, using the palfrey meant for Lady Maud as a relief animal."

Hugh told himself he had no right to be annoyed with Lady Maud. Many women could not ride alone and rode pillion behind a husband or brother. Still, the small check made him feel uneasy, although he could not think why it should, since the start of any journey was always full of delays, gasps and wails over things forgotten, and sometimes even turnings back. All things considered, Lady Maud's inability to ride was nothing. There was just something about the woman—perhaps it was only her fear of him, if it was fear—that cast a pall like evil over whatever she took part in.

At first, however, aside from the slow pace made necessary by the rain and darkness, the journey started well. They rode south along a rough track that led to one of the demesne farms, one man well ahead to come back or cry a warning if necessary. The scout was waiting near the edge of what had been planted fields, now a sea of trampled mud that would bear no fruit, to say the way was clear to the river. As they went by, Audris shuddered at the smell of burning that hung in the wet air. She had never gone to look at the remains when raids had passed over Jernaeve lands. When she thought of something that might help or comfort the victims, she ordered it sent to them, but she had no curiosity of that morbid kind that takes a warped pleasure in examining disaster or gazing at grief. In fact, she feared such sights, guessing that they might come out in her weaving.

At the bank of the river they turned west, following another rough track, which led to another farm, also ruined. They went around it, keeping wide of what had been buildings and sheds. Audris felt ashamed, thinking that Hugh had noticed her distress and was reacting to it. She was mistaken; he simply wished to avoid the chance of one of the horses uncovering and treading on a live coal. He saw nothing in the burnt-out ruins to inspire horror; he had fired farms and villages himself when he followed Sir Walter to war. Actually, what thought he gave the devastation was a brief gladness that his messengers had reached these people in time for them to escape and save their stock. The smell of burning was clean; there was no stench of charred flesh hanging in the air.

The track, such as it was, ended at the second farm, and they took to the woods themselves, at first following a little path Audris assumed had been made by the children gathering firewood or, perhaps, by the pigs. The river grew narrower and still narrower as they followed it, mostly by sound, but they rode sometimes nearer, sometimes farther from it as the banks were steeper or more shallow.

They were in wooded land now that showed no sign of cultivation. It was very quiet, for the rain had thinned to a bare drizzle and the horses trod on soft, sodden mulch, which gave back no sound. All one could hear above the very soft gurgle of the river was an occasional snap of a twig and the drip of water from leaf to leaf. Infrequently a horse blew as it cleared its nostrils, and the sound seemed so loud that it made Audris jump each time. The lead man was much nearer, near enough for them to hear when his horse's hoof struck a stone in the turf, because he was watching for side streams or other dangerous irregularities in the ground rather than enemies.

Only once did they find him blocking the way, and as they pulled their mounts to a halt Audris smelled smoke again. The scout and Hugh exchanged some whispered words, then one of the other men-at-arms dismounted, went ahead a little way, and disappeared. It seemed very long, but Audris knew it was really a short time before he reappeared and said aloud, in a quite natural voice, "Woodcutters, my lord. They have seen and heard nothing. I warned them about the Scots."

Hugh turned in his saddle. "Would you like to dry yourself and rest in the woodcutters' hut, Audris?"

"Not now," she replied. "Eric is asleep. If it is safe to stop when he wakes, I would rather stop then for greater ease in suckling him."

"Good, for I would rather stop just before we reach Dere Street. It would be best to rest the horses then, in case there are Scots there and we must go hard and fast to some other breach in the wall."

They did not stop near Dere Street, though. From where they met the woodcutters' trail, the river curved more sharply southward, continuing to narrow as they followed it until it became little more than a wide stream. After about an hour, the woods began to thin and show signs of human use. The rain had stopped completely by then, and the clouds were breaking up, driven by a fickle breeze. In the open areas, their eyes, now accustomed to nearly total blackness, found it light enough to see, which should have raised everyone's spirits.

Audris, however, after an initial spurt of relief, began to feel oppressed. Ugly images formed in her mind of burnt buildings—and worse, of bodies so charred and distorted that it was hard to tell human from beast. Fear tightened her throat, not because she expected enemies to leap out at them, but because she thought she might be foreseeing a distant evil. She put away the images, trying to fill her mind with Hugh's face, with Eric's comical grimaces—and suddenly the wind veered and strengthened, and a sickening odor of burnt flesh choked her. Almost simultaneously they heard the dull thudding of a horse coming fast, and Audris saw Hugh reach for his sword. A low cry identified their own forerider, and Hugh dropped his hand to his destrier's neck.

"A burnt-out farm," the man said, "but all is quiet there now." He hesitated and started to speak again, but another gust of wind carrying an even stronger stench made him cough. When he caught his breath, he went on, "The Scots are mad. They did not drive off the stock. They fired the barn and burned the beasts—the yeoman and his sons, too."

"When?" Hugh asked.

"The ashes are cold. Yesterday or last night."

"Is it far around?"

"I am sorry, my lord, I did not look." The man seemed surprised. "I made sure there was no danger. We can pass." Then he saw the slight turn of Hugh's head toward Audris, and he realized his master wished to protect his wife. "We can cross the water here," he said. "It is not deep, and we will be well away from the farm. It is back from the river."

Hugh's attempt to spare Audris was worse than useless, unfortunately. Although they were less plagued by the foul odor of death after they forded the river, Hugh's horse suddenly jibbed and snorted, rising a little on his rear legs as he came alongside a thick patch of brush and bracken. Hugh's sword was halfway out when Audris's quick eyes made out the cause. She uttered a cry that was strangled by retching. There were four of them—a woman and three little ones—and the many black patches of dried blood showed they had not died swiftly or easily.

"Ride on," Hugh said harshly.

They obeyed, but they could not escape the horrors, which mounted as the farms became more numerous and as the sky lightened. The worst of all was in the tiny village where the source of the river met the Roman road. They should have gone around, but by then Hugh only wished to get by as fast as possible, and there was no way to know how far afield the victims had been pursued. Most seemed to have been caught right in the place, however. The corpses lay scattered all around the perimeter, as if the Scots had deliberately surrounded the place so that there would be no way for the inhabitants to escape.

By then Audris had no more tears, although she could not stop the dry sobs that racked her. All she could do was alternately clutch her baby and finger her knife, whispering softly between sobs, "I will cut his throat myself. It will be quick. He will never know. I will cut his throat myself." That was after they found a babe that had been spitted on a stick and half roasted.

Outside the alewife's house, the only building that had not been burnt, there was a little girl, not more than four. She had been so abused that her body had split apart almost to the navel. They galloped past as fast as they could, regardless of the uncertain light and the danger of a fall, so fast that they almost missed the forerider coming back down the far side of the road, half hidden by the trees. He signaled wildly at them, but it was already too late, for as they slowed they could hear the shouts of men who had heard the clatter of their horses' hooves.

"How many?" Hugh roared.

Audris heard the rage, the lust to kill in his voice, and she was nearly racked apart because she desired revenge for what she had seen, and yet she feared for her husband and for her babe and for herself if that rage drove Hugh to attack too many. And deep within her, too, she knew the men who were coming down the road had not committed the atrocities they had seen.

"Twenty... fifty... I could not tell," the man-at-arms replied, his first, short answer betraying his own desire to attack, governed by the better judgment of belated caution.

The shouts were growing nearer. Hugh turned his head to look longingly up the road, but then gestured ahead to the west, growling, "Ride! Ride! We must bring the women safely to Jernaeve first. But we will come back."

Chapter 25

IN ONE WAY THE HORRORS AUDRIS HAD SEEN WERE A HELP. SHE was so drained of emotion by the time they reached Jernaeve, just before the sun rose, that she only clung to Hugh for a little while when he told her he would not enter with her. She tried to beg him to be careful, to remember that he was precious to her—oddly, she never thought "needful," which was the first thing she would have said a year past—but she never did say any words.

They had forgotten Eric when they embraced, and he was squeezed between them and woke and began to scream. By then the three great bars that closed the gate had been pulled back. Hugh kissed her one more time, hard and fast, pushed her toward the opening gate, then mounted again and rode away. Audris hurried through the gate, leading her mare, with Lady Maud staggering beside her and Fritha driving in the packhorses.

Audris went only as far as the shed backed against the wall used to shelter the gate guards in foul weather. The captain of the troop doing sentry duty on the wall jumped to his feet and bowed as she came in. "Demoiselle?" he asked nervously.

"Demoiselle no longer," Audris replied, laughing, and then, almost shouting over the shrieks of her son, added, "I am Lady Audris now—and my son, as you may hear, wants to break his fast."

As she spoke, she unfastened the wrappings that had shielded Eric, sat down on the bench the captain had vacated, and bared her breast. The captain bowed to her, then, smiling, bowed to the screaming infant also, and left the shed. Lady Maud watched his retreating back, then turned and leaned wearily against the wall, staring at Audris.

"The maids whispered to each other that you are a witch," she said. "Are you?"

"No," Audris answered firmly. "Although you will hear all the folk hereabout say the same, I am *not* a witch. I know no spells and can cast no enchantments. All I know are the prayers that Father Anselm taught me to say when I make my potions for healing, and those are prayers to Christ, to Saint Jude, and to the Holy Mother. My weaving... That is too hard to explain."

"But all the men bow to you—"

"Why should they not?" Audris asked impatiently. "Jernaeve is mine, and my uncle is an honest man who has taught the people to respect me."

Then she bent her head over Eric in a clear sign that she did not wish to enlarge on the subject. What she had said was true. Every person beholden to Jernaeve knew that Sir Oliver would punish severely anyone who displeased his niece, but the alacrity with which they obeyed her and hung on her slightest word was more than simple respect. Audris had set her mind against acceptance, however, and she certainly would not discuss such matters with Maud, who seemed half mad sometimes.

There was a silence broken only by Eric's snuffles and grunts as he suckled. He was more than usually passionate about it, having slept longer than his regular time because of being cradled near his mother's heart and because, securely supported as he was, the movement of the horse was soothing to him. In about ten minutes, Audris pried him loose and transferred him to her other breast. He protested the transfer loudly. When she had him settled, she became aware, as one does, that someone was staring at her. She thought it was Maud and at first tried to ignore it, but the sensation grew more intense, and she looked up to find her uncle standing in the doorway.

"Uncle!" Audris gasped.

"Why are you sitting like a beggar at the gate?" Oliver asked crossly. "Do you think I have changed so much that you should fear to come into your own hall to suckle the heir to Jernaeve?"

"Oh, uncle, no," Audris cried, stretching her free hand toward him. Tears started to her eyes, but at the same time she smiled. "You heard Eric. I only stopped to feed him here because I did not wish to be deafened." Then she began to sob. "I am sorry to have angered you, uncle, so sorry. I beg you to forgive me—not because I fear you but because I *love* you."

"But you trust me so little that you fled your own place rather than tell me you had chosen a man at last."

"It is not true!" Audris exclaimed between sobs. "It is not! I explained in my letter—"

"But you did not explain to my face. How could you think I would deny you the right to marry the father of the child you carried? It was bad enough to let him take you without marriage or betrothal, but once it was done, it was done. And where *is* your husband? Do you suspect I would do him harm to keep my place as guardian?"

Oliver's words were bitter and his voice was harsh, but the bitterness and harshness were bred from pain, not rage, and Audris bowed her head, shaking with pain herself as she realized how much she had hurt him. Her mind spun, trying to find a new reason, a reason that would make what she had done more acceptable, and it steadied on an image—the image of a unicorn threatening Jernaeve.

"There was more, uncle." Audris lifted her tear-streaked face to him. "I wove four pictures that I never showed to you—all four of the unicorn—*la licorne,* Hugh Licorne. The first two were innocent, showing the meeting of the unicorn and the maiden and the ripening of their love. But the third showed the beast trampling this lower part and threatening the keep itself with his horn. When Hugh saw it, he vowed he would never enter Jernaeve again so long as he lived."

Oliver's expression changed, and an odd prickling passed over Audris's skin as she realized her uncle had accepted the inevitability of her relationship with Hugh the moment she mentioned the tapestries. She had an impulse to protest, but she saw the pain was gone from his face, so she held her tongue. Nothing she said would change Oliver's mind about her tapestries, and his belief had soothed him, which had been her purpose. In proof, although he did not reply, he stepped forward to take the hand she held out to him. Then he bent forward to kiss her brow, sighed, and bent still lower to look more closely at Eric, who was nearly full and turning his head this way and that as he toyed with the nipple he was still reluctant to relinquish completely.

"So, here we have the new lord of Jernaeve, do we?" Oliver said quickly, as if he wished to forget or bury what Audris had told him. "I see he takes after his father."

"In size and strength and looks, he does," Audris agreed, "but I hope Jernaeve will not be Eric's heritage. I hope to have more sons. Eric will have Ruthsson and—" Audris hesitated. "And perhaps something more." Then she peered around her uncle and, having found Maud, drew her to Oliver's attention. "This is Lady Maud of Heugh. She—"

"Hugh? Is she, too, related to your husband? Did not your letter say there was only a great-uncle living?"

"Oh, the names are so confusing!" Audris exclaimed. "Heugh is a place, not a person."

Oliver frowned, then, as he remembered, his voice rose unbelievingly, "Sir Lionel's wife?"

"Yes," Audris said, relieved that the subject of Maud's relationship to Hugh had been dropped. "It seems that Sir Lionel spoke the name Kenorn during the trial by combat. It is not so common a name, and it happens that Hugh's father was named Kenorn—"

"Hugh's father?" Oliver repeated. "I did not know Hugh knew who his father was."

"Yes, yes. It turns out that Hugh is not a bastard at all. There is proof that Margaret of Ruthsson was duly wed to Sir Kenorn—but Hugh could discover nothing more than the name. So when the quiet time in summer came, he felt he should ask Sir Lionel whether he knew Sir Kenorn. But when we came to Heugh—"

"We?" Oliver echoed pointedly. "Why did he permit you to travel with a newborn babe?"

Audris laughed, the laughter catching on a sob. "Because he is as indulgent to me as you, uncle. I said I wanted to go, so he took me. But it was not pure caprice on my part. I thought if I was near, Hugh would not dare begin a brangle with Sir Lionel. But it did not matter, for Sir Lionel was dead. Everything in the keep was very strange, but before Hugh could sift out what was what, the Scots—" Audris's eyes widened. "Oh, heaven," she cried. "I have been telling you all these tales and not told—"

"Never mind. We know the Scots are on the march." Oliver's face fell into angry lines. "I was out the day before yesterday, and we lessoned some raiding parties very well. I piled their dead in heaps all along the borders of your land, and they have stayed well to the east of Sandhoe since then. But they were only small parties, raiding. Alain has patrols out in the hills south of the great wall. Did you not see them?"

"Only raiding…" Audris shuddered and swallowed hard, but she did not tell him what she had seen. She knew his indifference to what happened on land that was not beholden to Jernaeve. Then she answered his question. "We came in from the north where the breach is near the bridge. Hugh wanted to be as far from Dere Street as possible."

"That was wise," Oliver approved. "There is an army going southeast along that road, perhaps to attack Durham or even intending to threaten York. Corbridge is taken, but no large force has come west from there. Young Oliver is by Hexham, and the Scots have not yet troubled the abbey. But they will not forget Jernaeve, curse them. They will come."

Suddenly Oliver stopped and blinked and Audris realized he was wondering why he had been telling her, of all people, such things. She was not certain herself, first associating this rare exposure of his concern with her own feeling, which had been growing steadily, that she was capable of doing anything necessary for herself. The notion had crystallized in her mind when she had wanted to go to Morpeth; it had been confirmed when—ignorant and all unknown as she was among the people of Heugh—she had hidden her fear, descended into the seething inner bailey, and chosen just the right woman in whom to place authority (backed by her own status as a noblewoman). Thereby, all the women had been organized so that the stock was penned, the children controlled, and a good meal produced for the men guarding the walls.

However, as she nodded and agreed sadly, "Yes, they will come," and her uncle stared at her for a moment, his mouth setting harder with disappointment, Audris sighed. Oliver had not recognized her change from girl to woman; he had only been hoping she would foresee safety. Well, she was silly to expect more, Audris thought. Had she not thanked God more than once that Oliver was not the most perceptive of men? She could not have it both ways. It was enough that he loved her. Let him see her as pleased him best, for in the end it mattered little. She was ripe to make her own life now.

While they were talking, Eric had stopped sucking. Feeling him release her breast, Audris pulled her gown up and rose to her feet as she lifted him to her shoulder, patting his back to bring the wind up. Oliver stepped back a pace and drew a long breath.

"Go up to the keep," he said. "Your tower is as you left it. Your aunt will welcome Lady Maud. I must send out messengers to bring in the yeomen."

Memories of the horrors they had passed rose in Audris's mind, and her eyes closed over tears as her arms tightened around Eric. "I pray God you have not waited too long," she whispered.

Oliver had started to turn away, but his soles gritted on the floor as he swung back toward her. "So? I will bid all make haste. And what of Alain and young Oliver? Shall I call them to Jernaeve to—"

"No!" Audris exclaimed in instinctive fear and revulsion— and then she was ashamed, for she had no present cause to dislike and distrust her cousins, so she kept her eyes closed. But she did not wish harm to come to them; Oliver and Eadyth would grieve. "Send them to their keeps to watch the southern croplands," she said. And when she did open her eyes, Oliver was nodding and looking at her with a kind of uneasy wonder.

"You are right," he said. "The army will settle around Jernaeve, but Alain's and Oliver's men cannot make the difference between holding the lower wall or losing it. On the other hand, they may make the difference between having some crops or no crops to harvest this autumn. From their own keeps they may be able to drive off the small parties foraging south for supplies."

Audris looked up at him blankly; she had known nothing of the reasons. She only feared her cousins—although it had been many years since either of them tried to do her a despite. But she could not tell her uncle; her aunt would not listen when they *had* hurt her and Bruno had been punished for protecting her. Had she understood her uncle better then... but she had not; it was much later that she had learned to love him. At that time she had feared Oliver almost as much as she feared his sons. And then Father Anselm had come, and she was mostly safe after that. It was all long ago, but still Audris felt relief that Alain and Oliver would not be in Jernaeve. She smiled to herself as her uncle left and walked toward the barracks. Hopefully he would be very disappointed in her, and the Scots would not come soon or, if God was merciful, at all. She had had no foreseeing—no vision, no urge to weave.

Unfortunately, however, Oliver was not disappointed. In fact, Audris's instinctive remarks fit the timing of events far better than she wished. Had Oliver's summons to his yeomen been a day later, many of them would have been lost. Moreover, his summons *would* have been just a day later, for the day after Audris arrived, a number of men who held small keeps along the North Tyne sought shelter in Jernaeve for themselves, their families, and their small troops of men-at-arms. Some had been driven out, and some had yielded on terms. All reported that Sir William de Summerville was bringing a large army south along the river from Liddesdale. Oliver had shrugged angrily. Summerville was bad news; probably he carried a grudge over his last attempt on Jernaeve.

There had been discussions that day and the next—while still more refugees of all types came to Jernaeve's gates seeking safety—among the knights who had gathered. Most of them wanted to attack Summerville's army near the breach in the great wall. They argued that it would not take many men to hold that breach, with the river on one side and Jernaeve's lower wall on the other. No matter how many men Summerville had, only a few at a time could come through.

"Yes," Oliver pointed out dryly, "but they can keep coming through long after you are exhausted."

"Unless Summerville has orders to bring his army south and he does not want to suffer losses or delay," one of the more hopeful knights suggested.

"If he fears losses or delay, he will not come through that breach at all, but leave the Tyne, turn east along the wall, and then go south on Dere Street," Oliver answered. "He must know that road has been cleared of resistance."

"And if that is his intention, had we not better stay quiet behind these walls?" another, less sanguine man asked. "If we attack, might that not draw down a vengeance on our host he might otherwise have been spared?"

Since Oliver was almost certain that Jernaeve would be attacked no matter what the dispossessed knights did, his lips twisted wryly at the "consideration for his welfare," which, he suspected, was a good part simple cowardice. That man would bear watching; despair could spread like a pestilence. But even from such as he, Oliver did not need to fear treachery. Most of the men had probably kept their lands the first time David had brought an army through Northumbria by swearing fealty to Matilda, but their current fury showed clearly that they had not been offered any choice this time. Whether the decision was David's or Summerville's own, now the intent was plainly to conquer Northumbria and make the conquest permanent by replacing the current holders with David's men. They would all fight, because fighting was the only hope they had of recovering their lands.

While they argued, Oliver considered their numbers, adding in the yeomen who had decided to take refuge in the keep. There were more than enough men to defend the lower walls—if Summerville was not prepared to take huge losses. If, on the other hand, Summerville threw his whole army against them, attacking on all sides simultaneously, it would not take many assaults to win a bridgehead on a mile and a half of wall. And once a safe passage was held, the rest would flood in. Fifty men would make no difference; probably even a hundred would make no difference. Moreover, there were far too many men to defend old Iron Fist itself. If they were driven out of the lower bailey and up into the keep, they would the sooner be starved out.

"Three men and their troops," Oliver said quietly, after slamming the hilt of his sword against a convenient metal buckler for silence—the argument between those who wished to attack and those who felt a passive course was best had been growing heated. "That is what I think can be safely spared from the defense of Jernaeve for guarding the breach and attempting to drive Summerville's troops along the wall to Dere Street. Will you cast lots among those who desire to try to drive Summerville east to Dere Street?"

It was a bitter irony of fate that they did not have time to cast lots. As they were arguing about the method to use—agreement even on that seeming impossible—one of the men Oliver had sent west of the river to hide atop the great wall and watch rushed in to report that the vanguard of Summerville's army was less than a league from the breach. Oliver hit the buckler again and, when relative silence had fallen and all eyes were on him, pointed to three men who had been among the most vociferous of those who wished to hold the breach.

"You three," he ordered, "take your men and go. Remember, we will not open the north gate to take you in again, no matter how hard-pressed you are. If we can, we will open the south gate, the one here near the river, where the bank is narrowest and fewest can attempt to rush the gate and keep it open—but I do not promise it. If we cannot take you back into Jernaeve, ford the river and ride south to Devil's Water. My son Oliver will shelter you there."

Shouts broke out—approval, protest, questions—and Oliver let out a roar that brought silence again. "I am master in Jernaeve. You came to me for refuge. While there was no threat, I was willing to listen. Now I command, and you obey without question or argument. If you cannot, go!"

In a sense it was a dangerous gambit. Each of the men was accustomed to being master himself, to giving orders, not taking them; in fact, more battles had been lost because leaders could not control their vassals than for any other reason. However, Oliver had two strong supports for his claim to mastership: the common sense of most of the men, who recognized the danger of anarchy and Oliver's right, and the knowledge that old Iron Fist, the last refuge in the keep itself, was closed as tight against them as against the enemy. The upper walls were held by Oliver's own men-at-arms under the command of his steward of many years, Eadmer, and all knew he would not permit *anyone* to enter unless Sir Oliver led them in.

An angry cry or two dwindled into silence as those who uttered them realized they had little support. Oliver noted who had made the protests, but he did not comment. His next remarks concerned which men should hold what posts along the wall. Without making obvious what he was doing, he set the protesters in among those he knew best and trusted most, and those he had marked as least willing to fight, he ordered to the northernmost wall, the great wall itself.

His reasons were simple: the great wall was higher and thicker than the east and west walls, and there was no way down from it, except by rough, ladderlike stairs at each corner where it met the lower walls. For those reasons, it was the least likely to be attacked; thus, it was best to have the weakest there; moreover, the north wall was farthest from the keep, so the other defenders would have more warning if the Scots did make a successful assault on it.

All hurried to their posts, but for a time it seemed Oliver's conviction that Jernaeve would be a main target was wrong.

Some troops did engage the men holding the breach, but most of the army hurried east along the north side of the great wall as if they were headed for the route south along Dere Street and would leave Jernaeve unmolested behind them. Insensibly, as the day passed, most of the men began to relax. True, the assaults against those holding the breach, which had been intermittent at first, were becoming more violent, but many blamed Oliver's stubbornness and the bitterness of those fighting there for that. Most no longer associated the desire to pass the breach with an intention of attacking Jernaeve. After all, early in the day between assaults, the Scots had called to be allowed to pass, saying they would do no harm to those who had fought them and would permit them to reenter Jernaeve in peace.

All knew, of course, that passing meant freedom to raid the lands south of Jernaeve—and it was that, the men thought, which Oliver wished to prevent. So, as the shadows grew longer and the breach was forced—those who had held it being driven back down the bank of the river—many who watched felt a bitter sense of satisfaction. Had not their lands already been lost to them while Oliver's were still untouched?

Some did not even order their bowmen to fire on the Scots when the bank between the river and the wall narrowed enough to bring them within arrowshot, to hold them back so that the weary defenders could be got in safely. But for all his hard words, Oliver did not desert them. He came out of the south gate himself, leading fresh men who were filled with rage and eager to strike some blows at those who had driven them from their homes. The charge drove the attackers back almost to the breach, so that the eighteen men—all that remained of the seventy-two who had gone out in the morning—could be taken in. Then, while the attackers were regrouping, believing that a new and equally stubborn force was pitted against them, Oliver led his men back inside Jernaeve.

By then the light was failing. Those by the north end of the wall, where the river was more than half a mile away, noted that men—none could say how many—began to come through the breach, but they stayed well away from Jernaeve's wall. None passed down along the narrowing strip of land between the river and Jernaeve while it was light enough to see, and if they passed at night, they did so very silently. It would not be very strange for the Scots to pass by night, because that would save them from being targets for missiles from Jernaeve when they had to be close to the walls in the yards-wide area near the ford and while they were crossing the river. The men on Jernaeve's walls had the whole next day to argue about whether the Scots had passed or not. They were glad of the subject, because it had begun to rain before dawn and they were wet and miserable as well as bored. There was no shelter on the walls, and all were growing resentful at being kept there under arms, feeling, as they did, that all danger had passed.

Even Oliver had begun to wonder. He himself would have judged from the behavior of Summerville's troops that his army was hurrying south to join King David. Yet Summerville was clever; Oliver did not trust him—and Audris had said there was little time. Oliver paced the walls and saw no more than the others saw. Summerville *might* be under orders strict enough to make him pass Jernaeve without a challenge—but Audris…

Shaking his head angrily, Oliver told himself he was a fool to give so much weight to her words when they were most likely spoken in fear and ignorance, but somehow he could not change the orders he had given—nor could he, filled as he was by doubt, enforce them. He distrusted himself all the more because he felt unwell. He had twice been wounded lightly in the charge he had led—a slash on the left thigh and a cut from an arrow that had not really penetrated on the shoulder. The wounds were nothing, but he had had an urgent desire to ask Audris to tend them—which was ridiculous, for he had suffered far worse and healed well without her help.

The long day passed, and still the rain fell. An hour before the evening meal, Oliver had resolved he would send messengers to tell all except a few guards to come down and take what shelter they could find. Many, he knew, had already done so. But he stood mute, watching the servants load wagons with bread and cheese and ale and start along the walls to deliver the food. He could have sent the message with them, he thought dully, and the men—those who were faithful—could have eaten as dry as those who were faithless. They would sleep dry, though, he resolved. Those who had done their duty would be relieved by the men who had abandoned their posts without permission. He would ride along the wall himself as soon as the meal was over. Those who had come down could sleep in the wet.

Had the rain stopped, Oliver might have yielded to his sense of foreboding, no matter how foolish it seemed, and changed his mind again. But as dusk fell, the skies opened in a new deluge. Thus, Oliver did as he had decided—but he could not sleep himself, and his heart was heavy as lead inside his chest. Sometime before midnight, he gave up trying, roused a groom to saddle his horse, and rode north to see if the weaker men had abandoned the wall altogether. The rain had finally stopped—the downpour at dusk seemingly having emptied the skies—but the air was full of a mist so deceptive that Oliver found his horse wandering off the well-known road. He would never have known it, except that the squelch of his stallion's hooves as they pulled out of the muddy road stopped when he got into a field.

Oliver cursed softly. The mist seemed to muffle sound, too. He should have been challenged as he rode, but he had not been. Were all the guards asleep? He called out and received a reassuring response, but the relief he felt did not last long. Soon his mouth was dry, and his heart pounded. Never in his life had Oliver been so frightened—and there was nothing to fear, nothing.

The shouts of warning cut through the miasma of terror like cries of salvation instead of threats of disaster. He responded at once, kicking his destrier into a dangerous canter and bellowing, "Up! Up! The Scots are at the walls!" And although he was well aware of how perilous the situation was, he was no longer sick at heart. The threat he had felt was real, no product of a superstitious and disordered mind. He had *known* Summerville desired Jernaeve and known he was a crafty opponent.

All along as he passed he heard men calling out, saw torches flame into life, saw some running eagerly to the stairs to mount to the wooden rampart—and noted a few holding back. A bitter, grim smile twisted his mouth. This time the cowards would find no safety on the ground. There was a blackness ahead, somehow more solid than the dark broken by the haloed yellow spots of the torches. Oliver slowed his mount's pace, knowing he had come to the great wall in the north. He had intended to turn right and ride completely around the wall, but when he drew breath to shout his warning again, he heard a voice cry "Quarter!" That drew a roar of rage from Oliver, and he flung himself from his horse and ran for the steps, pushing others out of his way but bellowing for them to follow.

At the angle where the great wall met the lower wall, Oliver saw a man descending. With another wordless roar of near-insane fury, he pressed forward, reaching the stair just as the other, who was looking back over his shoulder, was about to set foot on the last step. "Coward!" Oliver bellowed, and seized him and pitched him over stair and platform. Oliver heard him screaming as he fell—and still screaming as he finally drew his sword and climbed upward.

"Fight!" Oliver screamed. "Fight! For I will, and there is no entry into Jernaeve keep without me."

Chapter 26

HUGH BENEFITED IN MUCH THE SAME WAY AS AUDRIS FROM the horrors he had seen. He was not nearly as sickened or drained, of course, but he was sufficiently angered to save him any regrets at parting from his wife. She was as safe as it was possible to be in the midst of a war. Jernaeve itself was impregnable, and Hugh was certain that it was stocked with supplies for many months. Long before that, the Scots would be driven from Northumbria—and even if it took longer than he expected, Hugh knew that whoever else starved in Jernaeve, Audris would be fed while there was one crust of bread or one rind of cheese left.

They never did catch up with the troop whose path they had crossed on Dere Street, and neither Hugh nor the men with him regretted that, for as they rode south they came upon a number of smaller raiding parties on whom they vented their rage. All knew they were accomplishing more by salvaging something on the isolated farms they saved from utter destruction than they could have by attacking a troop far too large to be fought by six men. Nor, after the first few encounters, did they look for trouble, skirting widely any towns or large villages where they might expect a concentration of enemies. They had taken only one packhorse with them, lightly loaded with food and blankets, and they stopped only to fight when it was necessary or to rest the horses. South of Raby keep they found no more signs of the Scots, and they went east to the

Roman road and followed it to Allerton and then east again, across the moors and through a pass Hugh knew in the hills, to Helmsley.

They came to Helmsley, soaked and exhausted, just before the final downpour that ended the rain. Sir Walter's keep was closed tight but not under attack, and Hugh and his men were readily admitted, only to learn that Sir Walter was not there. Never had Hugh had such a welcome from his master's relations. He was warmed and fed and cosseted and begged fondly to remain for as long as he liked. At first he assumed it was because he was now known to have a heritage of his own, but later he realized Helmsley was very thin of men. They had gone with their master—and that meant an army was being gathered for a major battle. Yet when he asked where Sir Walter had gone, he was given only evasive answers, and when he insisted he *must* follow his master, he was virtually ordered to stay, on the grounds that Sir Walter would expect him to defend Helmsley.

Long practice in holding his tongue among these people kept Hugh silent. He probably could not have spoken anyway, he was so choked with rage at the selfishness of those who *should* love Sir Walter even better than he. Yet to add a tiny measure of surety to their own safety—which was at present not even under threat, and might never be threatened if the Scots were defeated—they would deprive Sir Walter of a strong and devoted protector and leave him with two half-taught boys to defend his back. Hugh would have left that night, but he could not ask it of his men and horses when York, which was the only place he could think of where he might find news of Sir Walter, was almost ten leagues away.

His initial silence raised hopes that were dashed when he said he was leaving, causing bitter recriminations, including angry promises to tell Sir Walter of his rudeness and insubordination. Hugh listened and then burst out laughing, remembering the anguish such words had caused him in the past and realizing how little they meant to him now. The threats and insults were, in fact, now a blessing, causing his heart to fill with warmth and a deep happiness that he had found his place in life at last. The acceptance and love he had found in his uncle and Audris had fulfilled him, and that fulfillment could never be lost, no matter what happened afterward from the sad chances of mortality.

At York, Hugh bade his men take what rest they could and feed and water the horses. He expected to travel on as soon as he saw Thurstan and discovered Sir Walter's whereabouts or, if that was impossible, King Stephen's. However, only a few minutes after he had found a secretary who knew him and sent him to ask for a few minutes of Thurstan's time, Sir Walter himself came hurrying across the guest's hall where Hugh was waiting, to embrace him hard enough to wring a protest from him.

"You are well come!" Sir Walter growled with tears in his eyes. "God be thanked! God be thanked you are here."

"What is wrong?" Hugh asked, breathless with sudden fear for his foster father—and a little from the air's being squeezed out of his lungs.

"Nothing!" Sir Walter exclaimed. Then he laughed and added, "That cannot be the truth, as you know. There is a great deal wrong, but my heart is much the lighter for seeing you, Hugh. Thurstan and I feared you had been caught by the Scots."

Hugh sighed with relief. "Then Thurstan is well?"

Sir Walter sighed also, but sadly. "I would not say he is well—but come with me. He will be much the better for seeing you with his own eyes and hearing what has befallen you. He speaks great praise of your wife, enough so that I find a great curiosity in myself to meet her. Is she safe?"

"In Jernaeve," Hugh replied, matching Sir Walter's stride as they left the hall and walked toward the archbishop's house. "It was not under attack when I left her there, and even if they come, the Scots will not soon open old Iron Fist."

"Nor will they have much longer to try to open it," Sir Walter said grimly.

"Is the king coming with an army?" Hugh asked eagerly.

"No, Stephen is enmeshed in a host of uprisings in the south," Sir Walter said, but Hugh noted that he did not look angry or disappointed, and his voice was quite cheerful as he continued. "There was a rumor that Robert of Gloucester was sailing for Bristol, and at once William Lovel closed Castle Cary, Paganel at Ludlow keep, William de Mohun in Dunster, Robert de Nichole in Wareham, Eustace Fitz-John in Melton, and William Fitz-Alan in Shrewsbury all cried defiance."

"But then—"

Sir Walter put a heavy hand on Hugh's shoulder and stopped him in the porch of the archbishop's house. "We shall do very well without the king," he said in the low grumble that was as soft as his voice could get. "Stephen is too easily swayed to mercy—and at the wrong times. I have heard that great ill has been done in Northumbria, and this is no time to stop with the work half done and make peace by giving away castles—or whole shires. I swore to Stephen, and I will not be forsworn. But also, it is our duty to defend ourselves and hold back the Scots." Sir Walter nodded sharply. "And that is better than to be forever fighting in the south in quarrels that mean little to us."

"If we are strong enough," Hugh said, "I can ask for nothing better."

Sir Walter pushed open the door and gestured to Hugh to go through. "We must be strong enough. Thurstan will preach this as a holy war, and men will answer." And then he raised his voice still more and called, "Here he is, my lord archbishop, hale and hearty. I have not asked him a single question, the sooner to bring him to you."

Several men standing before the archbishop's chair parted, and Hugh hurried through to kneel and kiss Thurstan's ring and then his hand. "It is *good* to see you, my son," the archbishop said softly. "I feared for you, feared you would be overrun—your lands are so far north, and there was, in the end, so little warning." Then he swept his gaze around the other men and smiled. "You must pardon me. This is my fosterling, and even in the midst of great affairs, no matter that I should know better, my heart still cleaves to him."

"No pardon is needed for that." Hugh looked up and recognized William, earl of Albemarle as the speaker. The earl smiled. "So sweet a flaw, which reminds us that you *are* human, my lord, can only make us the more obedient and admiring. After all, a blessed saint is by nature above us. You come there by your own struggle."

"And I will not stay long so elevated," Thurstan remarked with a chuckle, gesturing Hugh to rise, "if you tempt me with flattery."

Hugh began to sidle out of the forefront, but Gilbert de Lacy put out a hand to stop him. "You are from Northumbria?"

"Yes, my lord. Ruthsson, my uncle's estate, is west and north of Morpeth."

"It was taken?" a third man, William Peperel of Nottingham, asked in a sympathetic voice.

"Not when I left, and I have hopes not at all," Hugh replied. "We are very isolated, and there are no roads from the north passing by Ruthsson."

"You felt it was too dangerous to stay?" De Lacy's voice was too neutral.

Sir Walter growled, "Do not be a fool, Gilbert, or Hugh will bite off your head."

De Lacy made a gesture of negation. "No offense, Walter. I know your man. I was not questioning his courage but the reasons for his leaving his land."

"If you are talking about the havoc the Scots are wreaking, I did not know of it when I left Ruthsson—and only one day before they flooded over Belsay, there was no news of their coming at Morpeth."

"How could that be?" de Lacy asked.

Hugh shrugged. "De Merley himself was not in the keep the night my wife and I spent there, but if he knew, I am sure he would have left word with his steward. I think perhaps de Merley had no friends in David's court who would send warning because he had been so recently put into Morpeth by King Stephen."

Sir Walter laughed, but with a wry twist to his lips. "Very likely. Stephen put de Merley in because the previous castellan had too *many* friends among the Scots and yielded his trust a little too readily when called on to do so by David. The same might be true of Alnwick and the other royal strongholds."

"They were taken by surprise, you are saying." De Lacy nodded. "But even so—"

"It is idle to speculate on why," Peperel put in. "What I want to know is whether what we have heard of wanton destruction is true."

"Yes—and wanton is the word," Hugh said. "There is a senseless rage in what is being done. We have fought back and forth over these lands with the Scots for many years, and I have never seen the like—or, rather, never seen so much of it; there are always a few troops or a few men that go too far, but this… It is natural enough that they kill the yeomen who try to defend their farms, but to pursue the women and small children into the woods and torture them? Worse yet, I saw *cattle* burned in the barns and slain and left lying. There is *no* sense in that. The beasts should have been driven off to be sold or to feed the army."

"Where did you see this?" Albemarle wanted to know.

"From Heugh keep west to Dere Street and, mayhap, half a mile or even a mile west of Dere Street and south to the great wall," Hugh replied. "My wife, my son, and I were at Heugh keep when we heard the Scots were on the march. Since it was closer than Ruthsson, and the strongest place I know, I took my wife and son to Jernaeve. But south of Jernaeve I avoided the roads. Still we came on three farms where we dealt with small parties raiding or… I do not know what to call such wasteful destruction. South of Raby there were no signs of the Scots."

"Belike they have stopped to chew up whatever they could not swallow whole," de Lacy remarked angrily.

"You mean they will besiege and try to take those keeps and manors that have not yielded or been overrun before they come farther south?" Sir Walter mused, half to himself. "But they are likely to starve first if what Hugh said—and others reported, too—is widespread." He shook his head and said louder, "No, I do not think they will stop long. It might be that they will assault Newcastle and Durham when the different parts of the army come together, but I think they have so scoured the north that they will be driven south—and I fear the richer the land, the worse the rape of it will be."

"It is true that a madness afflicts them," Thurstan said. "They have slain priests on the very altars of their churches, and as if that blasphemy was not enough, they have cut the heads of Christ from the crucifixes and mounted the heads of the slain priests in their place. I cannot believe this is King David's doing." His voice shook. "I cannot believe it."

William of Albemarle's eyes narrowed. "It is entirely possible that David is as horrified as you, my lord," he remarked. "But whether it is by his will or because he has not the power to restrain these men, I think we are all in agreement that the Scots must be driven out."

"Will King Stephen send help?" de Lacy asked. "I know he cannot come himself, but—"

"No," Sir Walter interrupted. "On the other hand, he will ask no levy of us to help in putting down the rebels in the south, so…"

"So we come out ahead," Peperel stated flatly. "We defend our own lands. We pay no scutage. And we are not beholden. Yes, that is all very well, but *can* we drive out the Scots without help?"

"God will be our help and our support," Thurstan cried, struggling to his feet, his eyes alight. "I will make for you a Standard of such Grace that all men who love and fear God will flock together to fight under it, and those who oppose it will be stricken and blasted."

"No," Hugh whispered, catching at Thurstan's elbow to support him. But when the old man turned his head to smile thanks at him and he saw the light and glory in his foster father's face, he swallowed his protest and instead prayed, "Oh, God, give him strength," for one does not deny a man the right to glorification, no matter the cost.

The cost was high. Thurstan gathered the banners of Saint Peter of York, Saint John of Beverley, and Saint Wilfred of Ripon, and he fasted and scourged himself clean while he prayed over them and blessed them together with a silver pyx, which he had ordered made and consecrated, clean and new, to hold the body of Christ. Then he had brought a ship's mast, which was also blessed, and had the pyx mounted atop it and the banners fixed to it and the whole set into a cart so it could be moved with the army as a rallying point. And for each blessing he scourged himself and fasted.

Nor did Thurstan forget in the passion of prayer more practical matters. He sent out his bishops and his deacons and even his canons to every town and village and to every church and chapel, and those who had the right, preached, and told the priests to preach each Sunday after they had gone on, of the evil the Scots were doing and of the destruction they had wrought. They bade them preach, too, of how useless it was to think that any hold might stand against the horde alone, and that the only hope that remained was to join with those the archbishop had blessed and consecrated as angels of protection and vengeance and stand together to drive off the minions of the devil.

So a host gathered north of York, and Sir Walter lent Hugh to the archbishop to winnow out those who knew something of arms and had some weapon with which to fight. He set those to teach small groups whatever they could. There were others set to the same task, but still Hugh walked and questioned and explained from the bare dawn of each day until it was too dark to see at all.

Sometimes his spirit was exalted by the faith of those who had gathered and who knelt with passionate devotion to be blessed when Thurstan insisted on being carried through the camp. But at other times he was shaken with rage, knowing that these who hastened to answer the call in their simple belief could be little more than lambs for the slaughter, bodies to crowd and shout and die, distracting the enemy so that the mailed knights would have time and space to strike. And the pitiful knowledge drove him to try harder to teach them to defend themselves, to weave themselves shields of withies, if they could get no better, and to sharpen and fire-harden sticks to hold off a swordsman, which would give them a chance to swing their shorter, curved scythes.

He grew gaunt and worn, often forgetting to eat during the day and too tired to eat at night. Morel would bring food and follow him about with it or stand over him and shake him awake, or he might have starved; Morel was growing desperate, for he had not forgotten Audris's command that he bring her news of it if Hugh were hurt or sick. He would have gone to Jernaeve, but he knew there was no way he could reach the Lady or bring her out to her man.

News had come with stragglers that the lower walls had been overrun and Scots from mountain areas were making ready to climb the cliff and assault the keep itself. Even so, Morel was not worried about those in Jernaeve. As long as a strong leader held it, all threats except starvation were vain. The men in old Iron Fist would brush off those who tried to assault it as a man brushed off flies. Besides, the Lady was there, and if the men could not save it, she would; it was her place, after all.

Morel was far more worried about himself. The Lady was kind, but he was afraid she would curse him if he did not fulfill her trust. He looked at Hugh, who had only managed to swallow half a bowl of stew and was now sleeping, but very uneasily, tossing and muttering and gesturing. Morel could not make out whether he was still trying to teach those fools to fight and save themselves or whether he was dreaming of going to the relief of Jernaeve. Morel shook his head.

He was sorry for the louts who had answered the archbishop's call—but their fate was in God's hands—and he was worried about his farm, which might well be in ruins, and about his sons and grandson and even about Mary, but he did not let it spoil his pleasure in food or sleep. He snorted with a mixture of exasperation and affection—only fine gentlemen had the liberty to indulge themselves in a ruinous sympathy over what could not be helped. Then anger drew another snort—and his master's misplaced agony of mind would ruin him, too! He glanced once again at Hugh's haggard face, then gritted his teeth. He had to do *something*. The Lady had dared much to have this one man. Kind or not, she would not soon forgive the one charged with his well-doing if ill befell him.

Oliver was dead! Audris stood weeping above the torn body, her bloody hands still stretched toward it as if to stanch wounds that were too wide, too deep for closing. She realized he had been dead for some time, but she had refused to believe it, ignoring the priest who was giving the last rites, still working frantically to close the gaping holes, telling herself he could not be dead. He had come into the keep on his feet—she had seen that with her own eyes. He had walked as much as ten steps before pitching forward and falling. If he could walk, she insisted, he could be saved. Now she could lie to herself no longer. Eadyth, sobbing hoarsely, had finally pulled her away from the body by force and screamed, "Can you bring back the dead, witch?"

"Not dead! Not dead!" Audris had cried, but having been forced away from her determined concentration on the one wound she was sewing, she saw the blood was only lying in pools, not pulsing or welling out—and she saw her uncle's face, and she knew. "Uncle," she sobbed, "uncle. You saved me, why could I not save you?"

"He cannot save any of us now," Eadyth wailed. "The Scots will kill us all."

"Scots?" Audris echoed, her sobs checking, grief washed away in a flood of terror. "Where? In the keep?"

"I do not know," Eadyth wept, shivering, "but who will keep them out if Oliver is gone?"

Audris fled from the chamber, down the stairs, and out into the great hall. The word "Scots" had wakened in her visions of what she had seen on the journey between Heugh and Jernaeve, and all she could think of was getting to Eric to provide her baby with a merciful death. She was halfway across the great hall before she realized that there was no screaming, no fighting. In fact, all activity had stopped, as it always did in Jernaeve, when she appeared. It was that cessation of sound and movement that caught her attention and checked her panic.

Later she understood that it was her appearance—her gown, her hands, even her face streaked and splotched with blood, for she had unconsciously wiped away her tears with her stained hands—that had momentarily paralyzed everyone, even the strangers in the hall. Just then, the sudden silence was simply right and familiar; it calmed her fear, and she stopped running just opposite the huge hearth and faced the crowd.

She felt the tense expectancy and knew for what they waited. "Sir Oliver is dead," she said, into a silence so deep that her soft, grief-choked voice carried easily through the hall. "My—"

"Then I am senior here," a coarse voice interrupted, "and I say we send down a herald and make terms—"

He had come forward as he spoke, and Audris was so surprised at being interrupted that her response was slow. But when she heard what he said, terror seized her again. What she had seen convinced her that one could not make terms with the Scots; surely the women and children could not fight and would have yielded. The vision of impaled babes and mutilated women rose instantly in her mind.

"Take him!" she shrieked. "He is one of them, crept in with our own."

And before he could protest or draw his sword to defend himself, the menservants had leapt on the man and dragged him down. He roared with rage, shouting for help, but Audris was on him, her eating knife at his throat, hissing that one more shout would be his last. He stared up at her blood-streaked face in disbelief and horror.

"I am not a Scot," he whimpered.

"He is not," another man said, coming near. "How dare you, you slut of a woman—"

"I am threatened," Audris shrieked. "Call in my men-at-arms."

But some menservants had run for the steward as soon as Audris cried out that the man who wanted to yield was a Scot, and Eadmer was already entering the hall with a crowd of men, swords drawn and crossbows cocked, behind him. The crossbowmen ranged out along the walls from the door where they had entered; the swordsmen pressed forward. The servants not engaged with the man Audris was accusing fled to the protection of the walls between the crossbowmen.

Suddenly the center of the hall was empty, except for the group around Audris, Eadmer and his swordsmen, and five knights who had taken shelter in Jernaeve, one of whom had his hand on his sword hilt and one leg drawn back to kick Audris. He removed his hand very carefully, holding both arms away from his body, and stepped down on the leg he had drawn back, edging slowly away from Audris while she rose to her feet to face the steward.

"I meant no threat, my lady," the knight said softly.

Eadmer was staring at Audris, his face as pale as parchment. "Sir Oliver—" he faltered.

"Dead," she answered, her eyes filling with tears, "but there is no time now to mourn," she told him, choking back a sob. "This filth on the floor is a Scot."

"No, I am not," he protested, more strongly now that the knife was not at his throat.

"Then he is a spy for them or an agent," Audris insisted. "He was about to order Jernaeve be yielded."

Eadmer blinked. He seemed stunned. "Order? But Sir Oliver—" he began, then shook his head. "Yielded?" he repeated.

"No," three of the men protested.

"It is only reasonable—" the man who had nearly kicked Audris began.

She glared at him, and his voice faltered into silence, an expression of horrified revelation coming into his face. Audris laughed briefly and bitterly. "Yes," she said, "I am Audris of Jernaeve. You once *demanded* me in marriage and threatened that you would appeal to the king about my uncle's unwillingness to give up my wardship, but you did not take the trouble to look at me well enough to know me again."

"I heard you were gone from Jernaeve." He shrugged. "You cannot blame me for not knowing you, covered with blood as you are."

"My uncle's blood," Audris said bitterly. "My beloved uncle, who held Jernaeve for me all the years of my life and *died* to preserve it for me. And you would give it away, give it away while his blood is hardly dry in his wounds, give it away before we are even threatened!"

"Not threatened?" He sneered. "Only an ignorant woman could say that. We have been driven off the wall at the first assault. We have had huge losses—huge. We have lost over three-quarters of our men, dead, wounded, or prisoner in the lower bailey. There is an enormous army pitted against us. Is that not threat enough? If we yield at once, we can get good terms."

"What threat is an army, no matter how great, down below?" Audris returned his sneer, her voice high and contemptuous. "How will they come up? Up the road? Three at a time they will make prime targets for my bowmen. How many do you think can stand below the walls? Is there room there to raise up scaling ladders? Is there room to swing a ram? What say you, archers? Are *you* afraid of men who must walk *our* road three at a time and then stand beneath our walls?"

The men around the perimeter of the hall, who had begun to look worried over the knight's analysis, now shouted their confidence.

"Or do you think they will crawl up the cliff?" Audris went on, managing to appear as if she were looking down on her adversary although she was a head shorter. "Creep on ropes up the knuckles of old Iron Fist? These sniveling cowards"—her eyes moved from the standing man to the one still held by the servants—"seem to be afraid even to fight men with both hands clinging to their ropes and weary from climbing. Say, swordsmen, are you like them, or will you dare to go out the postern and cut down such dangerous enemies?"

The swordsmen roared with laughter. It was true that very few men could hold that cliff against a whole army, because no matter how large the army, only a small number could climb at a time.

"I *know* Jernaeve cannot be broken," Audris cried, "unless it be by treachery from within!"

Suddenly a touch of color came into Eadmer's face. "Do you—do you have a seeing, Lady Audris?" he whispered.

Audris saw nothing except the impalement of her son and

her own torture and rape by the lowest filth of the troops attacking them if the Scots were allowed into Jernaeve. In the past she had either ignored or done her best to explain away her "seeings." Now the idea was a notion she seized eagerly.

"Yes," she cried. "Yes! I have seen that we will be safe in Jernaeve. I do not see how long we must wait, for there is no time in pictures, but I see the lower bailey empty of our enemies, and the coming of our allies."

A cheer went up that almost deafened her. She had not known that so loud a sound of joy could be wrung from so few throats—and for so foolish a reason. When she had reminded them of what they must all know was the truth—that Jernaeve was virtually impregnable—their response had been no more than a show of courage. But when she lied, playing on their silly belief in her "seeings," they were convinced. Let it be, she thought; the important thing is that they defend the keep with good spirit. And while the idea passed through her mind, her eyes saw the bowman lowering their weapons and the servants relaxing their grip on the man they had pulled down, and she realized that the fools had leapt from a debilitating fear to an overconfidence that was even more dangerous.

"No!" Audris exclaimed. "Do not lower your bows. Keep good hold on that traitor, and seize that other one also. There is a shadow in my picture, a shadow showing the opening of Jernaeve from within. I do not know whether it be these or others who creep silently up the cliff or up the road to find a way in to open the gates to their friends. Jernaeve cannot be taken by battle, but it can be given away by treachery."

"Then what must we do, my lady?" Eadmer asked. "Must we slay all those we do not know and who cannot bring known witnesses to go bail for them? Some came to us for succor from afar."

Audris shuddered. "No! God forbid! Let us not make ourselves as evil and bloody as those who attack us. Only be sure that those who guard the walls are our trusted men and that they keep good watch for spies in the night. And set a double guard of trusty men by each gate and postern so they cannot be easily overwhelmed." She hesitated, trying to remember anything else Hugh might have mentioned to her when he talked of the experiences of his life, but no other precautions came to mind, and she could only add, "And do not rest only on my poor woman's knowledge, but do all else that seems to you best, Eadmer, to make us secure from within."

"And these men?" he asked.

"They desired to make terms with the Scots," she said, her lips thinning. "Well and good, I will not stand in their way. Take them and put them out—and let them make what terms they will."

The two cried out in protest, but their words were lost in the laughter of the men-at-arms, who thought that a very good joke. Even as the laughter died, however, cries of warning drifted down from the walls. The unbelievable was taking place. Summerville, who must have heard that Sir Oliver was mortally wounded or already dead, was seizing the chance that those within would be leaderless and panic-stricken and was trying an assault on Jernaeve keep.

Chapter 27

THREE WEEKS AFTER HUGH HAD LEFT AUDRIS IN JERNAEVE, Sir Walter returned to York with a tail of knights and men-at-arms gleaned from the East Riding of Yorkshire and from Lincolnshire. William Peperel and Gilbert de Lacy had arrived with similar tails, one in the early afternoon and the other in the evening, the day before, and the earl of Albemarle sent a man ahead to report that he would be a day late because of trouble with his supply train but that thirty knights and their meinies had answered his call to arms. On the same day, plagued by details of quartering and distribution, Sir Walter reminded himself that Hugh could take care of all such matters and sent a messenger to recall Hugh to his service.

Hugh did not know whether he felt like weeping with relief at being ordered to give up a hopeless task or with frustration because the men he was training were far from ready. Had Sir Walter been in his quarters, he might have protested his change of assignment, but Sir Walter was called away to a meeting with the other leaders of the army before Hugh could be found.

Then, in the rush and confusion of final preparations to move the army, they managed to miss actually seeing each other for the next two days, but Hugh did see Thurstan. He had heard that Thurstan had been "convinced" not to come north with the army, but to delegate his role to the bishop of Durham. That frightened Hugh so much, because he could only believe that the archbishop must be on his deathbed, that he dropped what he was doing and rushed to the archiepiscopal palace to seek out an aide who knew him well enough to tell him the truth.

Instead of simply giving him news of Thurstan's health, however, the aide almost fell on Hugh's neck and kissed him. He did not go quite so far, though, merely crying, "Hugh! What a fool I am not to have thought to summon you. How glad I am you came! I will just tell the archbishop you are here. He is at leisure."

"How ill is he?" Hugh asked unsteadily. "Is he much worse?"

"No, he is not worse," the deacon replied. "God be thanked, I think he is a little stronger, but he is not resting easily because he still thinks it wrong to leave this work he began half done. If you can only convince him that it is not for the sake of *his* comfort but for the good of the cause that he must remain in York, he would regain his strength faster."

Hugh's face lit with relief, flushing slightly with joy and with embarrassment. "I will do my best," he said, "but Thurstan—"

The deacon waved his hand in a gesture of acknowledgment and hurried through an anteroom and then through tall doors into Thurstan's bedchamber. In a few minutes he came out again and gestured for Hugh to follow, and a minute after that Hugh was kneeling by the archbishop's bed kissing his frail hand and then laying his cheek against it.

"What is it, my son?" Thurstan asked. "Why do you come from your duty now? Is something wrong?"

Hugh kissed the hand again, lifted his head to look at his foster father, and saw with relief that the deacon had spoken the truth. The pasty gray pallor was gone from Thurstan's skin, and though his eyes were still sunken and ringed with bruised-looking skin, they were no longer dim and glazed. He laughed with tears on his cheeks and said, "No, nothing is wrong with me."

As he said the words, however, fear squeezed Hugh's heart, for he remembered that Sir William de Summerville had broken Jernaeve's outer defenses and was assaulting the keep.

But there was nothing Thurstan could do about that, and it would be useless to mention it. Hugh reminded himself, as he had over and over during the past few weeks, that Sir Oliver would keep Audris safe and that Jernaeve could not be taken by assault while Oliver held it. Once again all he could do was try to close the fear out of his mind.

"Then what brings you, my son?" Thurstan insisted.

"To say farewell, for you know the army starts north tomorrow, to ask for your blessing, and"—Hugh paused, then grinned impertinently—"to say how glad I am that you have decided to stay in York, although I must admit when I first heard it I was almost frightened out of my wits. I was sure you *must* be on your deathbed. I could not imagine that anything except the final extremity could bring you to so sensible a decision."

"Dreadful boy," the archbishop said, chuckling and shaking his finger at Hugh. "You are not supposed to dispense with me so easily. You are supposed to 'regret' that I do not feel strong enough to accompany the army." He shifted restlessly in the bed, and the amusement died out of his face. "My bishops constrained me to this decision. It is their opinion that my tenure as archbishop is so necessary and important, I must not risk it even to lead this holy war to avenge the blasphemies and despites done the Church. And it is true that with a new king whose faith is not very strong, worse might befall the Church through an ill-considered appointment to the archbishopric than through the depredations of war. Still—"

He stopped and looked at Hugh, who was shaking his head energetically. "I was not thinking of the Church's welfare," Hugh admitted frankly.

Thurstan's lips twisted. "Oh, do *you* think like Albemarle and Peperel—and even Walter, who should know me better—that I would try to command the army? I know I am no soldier, and neither am I inclined to wish for or believe in miracles that make an Alexander of a priest who knows nothing of war."

He made an impatient gesture, and Hugh seized his hand and kissed it again, laughing. "Dear Father, of course I did not expect that you would be overtaken by a desire to don armor and wave a sword—and neither, I am sure, could Sir Walter have conceived so silly a notion."

"I did not mean that, and you are only saying it to make me laugh," Thurstan acknowledged wryly, "but I think I *would* have been a help—not by saying fight in this place rather than that or on this day rather than that—but in lifting up the hearts of the men, exhorting them to courage and reminding them of the evil the invaders have done. Yet Sir Walter and the others—like you—were glad when I told them I would not go." Thurstan stopped abruptly and bowed his head. "My pride." He sighed. "My cursed pride."

When Thurstan began to talk of pride, scourgings followed. Hugh restrained a shudder. "Father!" he protested. "Forgive me, but you are misreading a lack of faith for a lack of desire for your support."

"Whose lack of faith?"

"Albemarle's, Peperel's, Sir Walter's—and mine, too." Hugh shrugged. "You believe that God will give you strength for whatever duty you must perform and sustain you until that duty is fulfilled, but none of us have equal faith. We look into your face and see…" Tears rose in Hugh's eyes, and his voice wavered. "We see the hand of God on you, my dearest Father. Perhaps I mostly fear losing you, for my heart cleaves to you with the same need I felt when I was a child. Foolish it may be, but I have always felt no *real* harm could befall me as long as you were there. But the others fear for their mission. Forgive me, Father, but did you ever think what would happen to our army if you should die on the way?"

"But I *could* not," Thurstan said, astonished at the idea. "God would not permit it, unless for some unknowable reason of His own we must fail in this defense of our land. But in that case, we will fail whether I die or not."

"So your faith assures you," Hugh replied, smiling, "but Sir Walter's faith—though strong—is not so firm as yours, and Albemarle's and the others, mine included, are even frailer. Father, they would be *miserable* if you came, not because they think you useless but because they would be watching every breath in and out of your mouth, fearing every bump on the road lest it jostle you, every stream that must be forded lest it wet you, every mile they must go lest it weaken you. Men, you have told me many times, have free will. Is it not possible that in their concern to make your journey shorter or safer or easier, they might choose ill with regard to the field of battle and thus find defeat instead of victory?"

Thurstan raised his free hand, then let it fall. "I see. And I can see why they all looked so thankful when I told them I could not accompany the army." He shook his head and chuckled. "Old, vain fool that I am, I was hurt because they did not want me."

Hugh chuckled too. There was amusement and acceptance of his own foible in Thurstan's voice rather than revulsion. Probably he would pray long and hard to be forgiven his vanity, but it was pride the archbishop feared, pride and ambition, knowing them to be sins deep-seated in his nature, whereas vanity was not. Uplifted by knowing he had managed to ease Thurstan's mind and soothe him, Hugh once more kissed the hand he had been holding and then let it go.

"I must go back to the camp," he said. "We are making a final distribution of supplies for the march."

Then Hugh bowed his head and asked for a blessing, and as his personal terror welled up in him again, he begged Thurstan to pray for Audris and Eric also. Since Hugh managed to control his voice and his head was already bent so that his face was hidden, Thurstan fortunately did not associate the request with any special need.

To Hugh's relief, the archbishop gave both blessing and assurances of his prayers in a voice that showed he was smiling. Then he tugged gently on Hugh's hair and, when Hugh raised his head, gestured for him to get up from his knees, drew him close, kissed him fondly, bade him take good care of himself, and gave him leave to go.

The deacon, who had been waiting quietly in a corner of the room and had heard everything that passed, told Hugh, laughing, as he took him to the outer door, that he had wrought a miracle. And Hugh himself had felt a release of tension in his foster father that gave him hope that he *had* done some good.

That was one burden lifted from his mind and heart, and five days later, when the army had marched north to Allerton, where their foreriders were waiting with news that the Scottish force was only a few miles ahead, another burden was taken away also.

The news was passed quickly to the mounted troops, who hurried through the town and north of it about a mile, where the leaders took possession of a small hill, cleared by grazing, and directed the troops forward another quarter mile to secure the plain below. The clear ground was such that the area the left wing would defend was almost double the size of that on the right of the hill. Beyond the open area wooded land to either side closed off the possibility of open battle. It had been decided earlier that Sir Walter would hold the left, Albemarle the center, de Lacy the right, and Peperel the reserve. Hugh followed Sir Walter as he rode over the area he was to defend.

"It is wider than I like," Sir Walter said, "but I think de Lacy can spare us some men, and I think Albemarle will take the brunt of the attack. The Standard will be set on the hill, of course, which he will be defending. It is likely that the Scots will expend their greatest effort to secure the Standard as a prize of war."

"Even so," Hugh said, frowning, "the line is too long. If a force is sent through the woods to burst out at us while we are engaged with an attack—even if it be no more than a light feint—from the front, I am afraid so thin a line must fail."

"Teaching your grandfather to suck eggs again, eh?" Sir Walter teased. "You have learned apace, Hugh, but a wily old dog like me still has a lesson or two to give. No one will come at us unaware through the wood, because we are going to fill it with all those near useless yeomen and plowboys you have been mumbling about and instructing in your sleep for the past week."

Hugh, openmouthed with relief and surprise, looked at his master; Sir Walter's bellowing laugh rang out, and he leaned from his horse to wallop Hugh on the shoulder.

"There is not much the old man does not know," he growled with satisfaction.

"I am very sorry I disturbed your sleep," Hugh said, and almost immediately shook his head. "No, I am not sorry at all," he admitted. "I am glad, if it led you to think of such a use for those folk. They will be of real value in warning us of an attempted surprise and in delaying and holding off any force sent into the woods. With trees and brush to interfere with any real fighting, they can hold their own very well."

Sir Walter shook his head and sighed. "Hugh, I hope you do not plan to influence my military planning in the future by moaning all night. I swear to you that your night horrors did not persuade me to put the common folk in the wood. It was because the wood is there and because of what we have learned about the Scottish army. Gilbert de Lacy is doing the same on the right flank—and he was not kept awake by listening to you groan and grumble."

Hugh grinned at him impudently. "Mayhap, my lord, but dare I suggest that you put the idea into his head?"

"The damn fools would be of no use to us out on the field," Sir Walter roared. "And if I got too many of them slaughtered, we wouldn't have enough men to bring in the crops. And as for you, you shameless puppy, you had better put some steel into that soft heart of yours and use your head for more than carrying your helmet."

"Yes, my lord," Hugh replied in a very meek voice, belied by the curve of his lips and the sparkle of laughter in his eyes. "If your lordship would deign to instruct me about the Scottish army—"

But Sir Walter was grinning, too. "Oh, you will be instructed. You are invited to our council of war this evening."

"I?" Hugh exclaimed. "Why?"

"You are on the way to being a great man in Northumbria," Sir Walter pointed out, chuckling. "Ruthsson and Trewick are decent estates, and marriage to the holder of Jernaeve—"

"I have nothing to do with Jernaeve," Hugh said quickly, seeing the tapestry unicorn about to destroy the place. "Audris prefers that her uncle hold it—and so do I."

"I believe you," Sir Walter said with a wry twist to his lips, "but I would not bother trying to convince the others, who will nod and call you hypocrite in their hearts. But that is not important now. What is important is that because of the length of the left wing, you have been chosen to share the command with me and hold the far left."

Hugh looked out between Rufus's ears, frowning ferociously. He had barely prevented himself from crying out, "No, I wish to be with you." Sir Walter would understand too well that Hugh was offering, not seeking, protection, and to shake a man's faith in his ability on the eve of a battle was stupid. Sir Walter had been one of the great warriors of his day, but he was no longer young, and now he needed to be able to pull back and rest between bouts of violence. Two years ago both Hugh and John de Bussey had been at Sir Walter's side, ready to form a shield for him behind which he could take breath; now there were two boys—one sixteen, the other thirteen—who needed to be sheltered themselves.

"There is no need to glower like that, Hugh," Sir Walter continued when Hugh did not reply. "You do not give yourself enough credit. You are well able for this command."

Hugh was in no doubt of that; in fact, he knew he was more able than many—Peperel, for example, and several who had led assaults when he was with the king at Exeter. In other circumstances he would have accepted gladly, eager to make his name as a war commander. But Sir Walter's remark seemed to open a way for him to fight at his lord's side, and he said, "I have my doubts, and it seems to me that to doubt in such a position is dangerous. Surely someone else can be found—"

"No one *I* would trust to hold my left wing," Sir Walter said firmly. "Let it stand that I have no doubt of you—and that must be sufficient."

The frown blackened on Hugh's face, but he dared not say any more, and later, during the council, he learned that Sir Walter had not merely been trying to advance his favorite's interests, which was what Hugh had suspected. Sir Walter really wanted a person in whom he had perfect trust at the end of the left wing. But the first one to speak, after Albemarle reported that the Scottish force was far superior to theirs in numbers, was de Lacy, who plainly deemed it of little account, saying sneeringly, "It is no more than a ragged mob, without horses, without armor, and virtually without arms."

"Not quite without arms," Sir Walter remarked. "They use the shortbow and are brave spearmen."

"But the shortbow is little use against a man in mail," de Lacy said, sounding surprised by Sir Walter's remark. "Nor is a spear an effective weapon against a mounted knight."

"Unfortunately," Sir Walter commented dryly, "both have disastrous effects on *horses*."

"You mean they would shoot at or spear the horses apurpose?" A man Hugh did not know pushed forward, sounding unbelieving. "Nonsense. It is unknightly—and besides, horses are valuable."

"It is unknightly to impale children and dismember pregnant women, too," Hugh put in. "And I have discovered that the men of the far north have little use for horses—except for eating them."

"If we charge against that mass of footmen," Sir Walter pointed out, "we must become separated, whereupon each mounted man will probably have his horse killed or be dragged down and overwhelmed. We would do better to form a shield wall through which our crossbowmen can shoot and thin out their numbers."

Now Hugh understood why Sir Walter needed someone he could trust to fight to the death to keep the left wing intact. He was proposing a defensive battle in which it was of great importance that a cohesive, virtually unbroken line of defenders be maintained. If the line should fail, particularly the extended left wing, the English army could be surrounded and, most likely, exterminated by the Scottish force, which, in numbers, was vastly superior.

"Not attack?" Albemarle exclaimed. "But what if they ignore us and pass us by?"

"The Pictish lords will not do that, my lord," Hugh offered. "I went with Archbishop Thurstan when he made King David agree to keep the truce, and I heard them boast it was only because David forced them to retreat that they did not swallow King Stephen's army whole in the past. They say that one of them, unarmed, is a match for three or four Southrons in mail. In particular, they boast thus before King David's own men—those who came with him from the English court or who came from Normandy or France. They would not dare pass by an English army. They must prove themselves, to hold or increase their power with the king."

"I know little enough of the northern Scots," Peperel put in, "but I doubt King David would be willing to pass us by in any case. He is not fool enough to leave an intact and undefeated army between him and his own land."

A general murmur of agreement passed through the group, and Hugh thought that William Peperel might not be much of a soldier, but was a sensible man. From then on, all opinion moved in the direction of Sir Walter's suggestion, and it was not much longer before a plan for the knights to fight on foot was approved. Hugh, listening carefully to the details, remembered times in the past when he had attended similar councils with Sir Walter. Then he had scarcely attended to what was going forward, knowing he needed only to follow Sir Walter's lead. He had been scolded for inattention, too.

"What if I lost my mind?" Sir Walter had roared at him more than once. "What if I were killed and had not told my chief vassal the plans?" Hugh had answered meekly, promised amendment, laughed inwardly at the idea of his master's forgetting or acting in any way foolish. Sometimes he had almost regretted being squire to so worthy a lord, dreaming of becoming a great hero by replacing an incompetent master; nonetheless, neither the attendance nor the scoldings had been wasted. Not only did Hugh pay strict attention, now that the responsibility was his, but all the half-heard lectures and admonitions and after-battle explanations joined in his head. As if it were a game of chess, Hugh found he could visualize the two armies and see the result of this move or that.

The divisions of their forces were made, each man essentially leading those he had brought with him, with the addition of the best-trained and best-armed yeomen who had answered Thurstan's preaching. De Lacy passed a dozen independent knights and their small meinies to Sir Walter, and Sir Walter divided his force so that Hugh commanded nearly all the men-at-arms drawn from Sir Walter's own keeps. Hugh had opened his mouth to protest and been glared silent. He realized later it was the only arrangement Sir Walter could make since most of his knighted vassals still regarded Hugh as "Sir Walter's old squire" and would resent being told to take his orders. On the other hand, some of the men-at-arms had fought under him at Exeter when he had commanded his own troop, and all of them knew him and respected him. In addition, Sir Lucius, one of Sir Walter's youngest vassals, a solid, stolid young man, loyal and reliable, was designated as Hugh's second-in-command. Last, Albemarle suggested that Peperel's reserve be all mounted men.

Hugh nodded so vigorously at the suggestion that Albemarle noted his enthusiastic approval. Recalling Hugh's earlier remarks about what he learned when he was in Scotland with Thurstan, Albemarle reminded the others of Hugh's experience and asked if he had a special reason for wanting the reserve to be mounted.

"I am sure it is not needful for me to say this," Hugh answered, fearing to rouse resentment if he stated the obvious but not absolutely certain that what was obvious to him was equally obvious to others, "but I will say it anyway and ask your pardon if I sound as if I think you ignorant—that is not true. We need a mounted reserve, and, my lords, although we fight afoot, I hope all the knights will have their destriers close at hand as well."

There were smiles—Hugh was young compared with most of the men at the council—and nods. What knight in armor would be far from his horse if he could avoid it? De Lacy said, "Yes, to pursue them when they break."

"No," Hugh exclaimed—and drew frowns, but ignored them. "I think even if the footmen give way, there may be a second attack by a mounted cadre. There is envy and jealousy between the Pictish chiefs and the new men brought in by King David. I am not sure, but I think those David has given land and power may wish to show their worth if the footmen fail."

The frowns were gone now or, if they remained, were not directed at Hugh, and a babble of voices broke out as new suggestions were put forward, objected to, altered, reargued. Hugh began to regret that he had raised the issue; knowing how knights hated to fight afoot, he was afraid the original plan of battle would be radically changed, but Albemarle and Sir Walter prevailed with no more disruption than shifting some men between the front line and the reserve. Still Hugh mentioned his regret to Sir Walter as they returned to the small house they had commandeered in Allerton, and Sir Walter laughed.

"You mean that was said in innocence?" he exclaimed, shaking his head. "Too bad. I thought you were being clever and could hardly keep myself from cheering aloud."

"Clever?" Hugh echoed. "How?"

"Hugh!" Sir Walter reproved. "Think! When a line must be held, there are three dangers. First, the line can be over-whelmed. If the Scots are too many, the living will simply climb over the dead—or be pushed over—until we are buried under them. Second, cowardice can break the line; mostly if one or two flee, it does not matter, but sometimes panic will spread from one to the other, and all will flee. Third, when the oncoming enemy hesitates or retreats, the defenders must break their formation to pursue; if the enemy then rallies, there is no longer a defensive line, and the few can be swallowed by the many."

"I know that much," Hugh protested, "but I still do not see—"

Sir Walter leaned over as they rode and cuffed Hugh roughly on the head. "Then listen. About the first case, we can do nothing. If we are buried in enemies, then God, for reasons of His own, has seen fit to scourge us. I do not fear the line will break out of cowardice. The men who will stand with us are either already burning with hate and desire for revenge or have estates to the south and are desperate to drive back the Scots to preserve their lands. It is more likely that too many hotheads will rush out of the line to attack than that many will run away. In talking over your 'innocent' warning, we were able to mark out those who were too eager."

"But you put them in the reserve—" Hugh began, and then ducked and began to laugh as Sir Walter swung at him again. "I see. I see. The reserve was planned as a defense against any mounted group—I should have thought of that myself."

Sir Walter nodded and chuckled. "Mayhap I should stop telling you not to try to teach your elders. You may have sighted on a false image, but if you strike so near the heart of the real target, how can I complain?"

But Hugh's mind, relieved of immediate concerns, had immediately brought up the basic terror he had buried under worry about Thurstan and the ill-equipped yeomen. "If we prevail," he said, "is it decided what next to do? I mean, will the army follow David north to relieve the sieges on the royal castles? Or—"

"You are worried about Jernaeve," Sir Walter said kindly. "I know you need not be, but"—he smiled wryly—"my words cannot ease your heart, and I am sure I would feel the same if our positions were reversed." He frowned and then added slowly, "No plans are made. Truly, from what I have gleaned about the size of the army descending upon us, I do not think there are many sieges under way. David's army must contain all, or nearly all, the force he brought from Scotland. The question of what to do next was raised, but most thought we would need a day or two to lick our wounds and then we could decide."

Hugh said nothing, but his expression was bleak as they both dismounted and one of Sir Walter's squires led the horses away. By habit, he held back for Sir Walter to enter the house before him, but he did not follow. Hugh knew there was a good chance that the army would simply disintegrate; some would pursue the Scots north; some would feel they had done their duty and, having aborted any danger of the invasion continuing south, would quietly go home.

Only the troops bound to each major battle leader would wait for orders. Hugh did not *have* to wait; he was no longer bound by oath to Sir Walter, but to go without his master's leave was still impossible to him—and all Hugh had was six men—if they survived.

Instead of going through the door, however, Sir Walter turned to face him. "When the battle is done—one way or another," he said, "do not wait for orders from me, but take my troop north to Jernaeve. You will not have enough men to drive off an army, but if you can find some fleeing Scots and herd them before you into the besiegers' camp, they may cry of a great defeat and frighten the besiegers away."

And before Hugh could thank him, Sir Walter turned on his heel and strode into the dim room, shouting for meat and drink and to be freed from his armor. Hugh hesitated, fighting a chill. There had been something odd in his master's face and voice. He thought for the first time with doubt of the huge army coming against them and of the first "case" Sir Walter had mentioned—that they might be buried by the sheer number of their enemies. A dreadful suspicion rose in his mind: had Sir Walter sent him to hold the far left not because he wished to be sure it would be well defended but because it was farthest from the Standard and nearest to the wood? Escape through the wood would be easy if their army were destroyed and holding his ground became pointless.

Love and irritation warred briefly in Hugh, only to be replaced by frustration. If what he feared was true, there was nothing he could do about it. To protest would only earn him another clout on the head and an angry growl about being a fool. Sir Walter always managed to make his favors to Hugh seem a benefit to himself. Sighing, Hugh turned around and looked north. The low hill was not visible over the roofs of the houses, but Hugh could just make out a gleam of silver— the pyx—and below it the movement of the saints' banners stirring in the breeze. He remembered the horrors he had seen along the Scots' route down Dere Street. No, he told himself, we will *not* be the victims of God's scourge. My father in God said we would be angels of vengeance. We will prevail.

Chapter 28

COMFORTED BY HIS FAITH THAT GOD WOULD SUPPORT THE army that the archbishop had gathered and blessed, Hugh had followed Sir Walter into the house, eaten with good appetite, and slept, as any soldier should whenever opportunity arises, until about two hours after midnight. He woke as he had set his mind to do, dressed quietly, saddled his horse, and rode out to the camp. The men were rolled in cloaks or blankets within feet of where they intended to fight. Fortunately on this August night the weather had been mild and dry. To Hugh's relief, he was properly challenged several times; the sentries seemed to be awake. He did not speak more than to identify himself, but he learned later there was good reason for their watchfulness. The Scots had arrived and were very close.

Nonetheless, when he found his tent, Morel reported that all was quiet; there had been campfires not more than half a mile away starting at dusk, first a few and then so many they seemed to light up the whole plain, but aside from a few clashes in the woods, there had been no fighting. Hugh was not worried about the Scots coming in force through the wood; a few men might get past to spy, but from where they were to the river, it was thick with yeomen. He did not put overmuch weight on Morel's report about the numerous campfires either, reminding Morel how the besiegers of Heugh had tried to magnify their numbers by setting many fires and having servants run back and forth fueling them. But in the morning, as soon as there was enough light to see, he had to admit that had been a false judgment.

At first glance, Hugh thought there was a dip in the plain that was still in shadow; then he realized the ground was black with men. Instinctively, he turned his head to look at the Standard. The pyx had caught the first rays of the sun and burned red instead of shining silver, and the saints' banners hung limp in the dead calm that often marked that hour of a summer morning. Then, softly, softly, almost like a murmur of love, a sound rolled toward him from the Scots. His head snapped around, but there was no movement yet. They must be cheering, he thought with an odd sinking at heart, and looked back at the pyx.

It was still red as blood, but the banners were now snapping merrily in a rising breeze, and Hugh saw a brilliantly garbed form climbing into the cart, raising a crosier, blessing the flock. Thinly but clearly, above the sound from the Scots army, Ralph of Durham's voice floated out over the troops he had blessed. Hugh could not make out the words, but he was well aware of what they must be. The bishop must be praising the past exploits of the Norman lords, listing the lands they had conquered, telling them that the Scots were cowards and fools, designed by God to be defeated because of the outrages they had committed.

To confirm his thought, either the breeze shifted slightly or the bishop turned his head and words became audible: "...by divine permission... tell you that those... violated the temples of the Lord, polluted His altars, slain His priests, and spared neither children nor women with child shall on this soil... punishment... crimes. Rouse yourselves... bear down on an accursed enemy with courage... in the presence of God."

There was another period in which only the voice, rising and falling, could be made out. Possibly the men, some kneeling, some standing, all watching the bishop and the Standard above him with devoted attention, heard more; Hugh's eyes were on the dark blanket that was the enemy army, which seemed to be heaving and twitching. They were forming to attack. A cry of warning rose to Hugh's lips, but he stifled it. It was too soon. The bishop, atop the hill on the cart, could see better than he could, Hugh reminded himself.

Words formed in the sound again: "Numbers without discipline… hindrance… often victorious when they were but a few against many… renown of your fathers, your practice of arms, your military discipline… make you invincible against the enemy's hosts."

Hugh bit his lip; the whole black mass was stirring now, its forward edge raveling out as the swiftest and most eager surged ahead of the others. He turned his head to look at the bishop, suddenly wondering if Ralph of Durham was one of those who believed that since God foresaw all it did not matter how long he talked because they would be victorious if they were meant to be. But just then, Durham raised his crosier and pointed with it: "…perceive them rushing on… advancing in disorder… now avenge the atrocities committed in the houses of God against the priests of the Lord… should any fall in the battle, I, in the name of the archbishop, absolve them from all spot of sin, in the name of the Father, whose creatures the foe hath foully and horribly slain, and of the Son, whose altars they have defiled, and of the Holy Ghost, from whose grace they have desperately fallen."

The whole last passage, giving the defenders absolution, was clear. Durham must have been facing them, Hugh thought, and stole a glance toward the bishop from watching the blanket of enemies heave and roll toward him. He saw that Durham had not climbed down but still stood on the cart with the Standard, pointing his crosier at the Scots. His voice came faintly now, without words, and Hugh realized that Durham—either with natural courage or with the strength of faith—was repeating the absolution over and over in each direction so that every man in their force would hear and be shriven. One last time Hugh raised his eyes to the pyx and whispered his own brief prayer to Mary, begging the Mother of God to preserve and protect Audris and Eric if by the will of her Son he should not survive.

From the look of the masses flowing inexorably toward them, it almost seemed as if all of them must be trampled down and overwhelmed. Yet the sound of his own men crying, "Amen, amen," to Durham's exhortation briefly drowned the shouts of the oncoming horde, and none of them flinched. A moment later, Hugh could make out the Scots' answering challenge of "Alban! Alban!" He looked right and left along the line and drew his sword as he bellowed, "Archers! Ready and hold!" He could hear troop leaders down the line repeating his order and Sir Lucius some way behind him doing the same. But the force charging them was behaving oddly; the black wave was developing a definite point, curving away from his wing toward the hill on which Durham still stood. Sir Walter had been right; they wanted the Standard.

Hugh sucked in a deep breath and shouted for the leftmost end of his line to come forward so they could shoot into the flank of oncoming men. A few minutes later what had seemed a solid, moving mass disengaged into individuals. Hugh took another breath and opened his mouth to order the archers to begin firing, but as the charging figures became clear, he was so surprised that the words hung unsaid for an instant.

The Picts, the wild northmen, headed the charge, and the madmen had either discarded what little armor they had been wearing when Hugh saw them at Heugh or this was an even more barbaric group. Bareheaded, bare-chested—except that some of them wore what seemed to be a broad scarf of many-hued cloth—even barefooted, most without shields and armed with no more than a long spear, more fitted for hunting a defenseless doe than for attacking an armed soldier, they came running as if they were invulnerable.

"Shoot!" Hugh roared, finding his voice although his mind was still fixed in a dizzy alternation of admiration for the insane courage and disbelief at the simple insanity of the attacking men.

A cloud of arrows arced forward, not only from his men but all along the massed line as far as the base of the hill, beyond which Hugh could not see. Some figures stumbled and fell; others stumbled, righted themselves, and continued the charge. Hugh shouted again, a wordless paean to bravery, but his next cry was a warning to the swordsmen stationed among the archers. Although the main thrust of the attack was toward the hill, the sheer mass of oncoming men was forcing a substantial number outward toward the wings. Hugh risked one more glance at the center, knowing it would be the last he would have before he and his men were either buried in enemies or too busy fighting them to look elsewhere.

The ground was littered with still bodies and struggling ones, but the movement forward seemed to be no slower. Hugh thought he could hear individual bellows now and again rising above the shouts of the attackers and defenders and the screams of the wounded, and he had a single glimpse of a long, bright sword held high, waving the enemy onward. Beyond, as Hugh's eyes swept away from the front lines and outward, he saw two separate groups of men on horseback. Hugh dismissed them as not being any immediate threat. There was no way they could charge through the mass of footmen dividing them from the English.

In the brief time he had looked elsewhere, his own flank had become a near-image of what he had seen in the center. The archers were taking a terrible toll, shooting, dropping the discharged crossbows, turning and reaching for a reloaded bow from a man—or more often a boy in training—crouched behind him. It was only when an archer two men down from him sprouted an arrow in his back that Hugh realized the Scots were shooting at them, too. But the bowman did not fall; he uttered a curse, reached back, and brushed the arrow away with one hand while he grabbed for his newly loaded crossbow with the other. At the distance the shortbow had not the power to pierce the hardened leather jerkins the archers wore; however, somewhere up Hugh's line of men there was a shriek of pain. At closer range the shortbow could be effective—or if an arrow struck a man in the face or on an unprotected arm or leg.

Still, compared with the crossbow, the shortbow was ineffective, and the closer the enemy drew, the more deadly the crossbow became as its accuracy increased. Now the attackers had to leap over dead or wounded comrades every second or third step, but they came on, seemingly fearless, shaking or stabbing with their long spears, screaming their war cries.

Hugh's heart lifted as he saw the Scots' front rank decimated again and again and realized that he and his men would not be overwhelmed and killed, but under the relief was a tinge of horror at the numbers of fallen.

The sense of dreadful waste increased as a few—so very few—of the incredibly brave men charging so hopelessly passed through the hail of shafts. One stabbed at Hugh with his spear. Hugh's first blow cut the head from the weapon; his second cut the head from the man. He nearly wept as his enemy died, for he knew he had killed a hero—or a madman—and it was a pitiful thing for either one or the other to die so uselessly.

Another and then another came and died—ill armed and unarmored, they had no chance at all. Nor was Hugh alone in what he felt. The cheers and jeers that had rung out from the men-at-arms as the first Scots fell began to change into angry shouts of warning. They could not stop killing, for to do so meant that they themselves would be killed, but many were revolted at the defenselessness of their enemies.

Time stretched as it does when one's task becomes more and more unpleasant. Hugh's long shield and tight, thick rings of mail were invulnerable to the Scots' spears, whereas the short, round shields some of them carried were useless in opposing his long blade. Hugh felt as if he had been lopping off limbs and heads for hours. As the main body of the enemy army reached them, many more escaped the archers, and Hugh often had two and sometimes three to fight at a time. He never felt in any danger, even when the clever ones recognized that they could do him no harm by stabbing at his armored body and went for his face and feet. It was too easy, too pitifully easy, to foil those attempts. He only felt sick and sicker as more escaped his killing blows and lay nearby or writhed away, moaning or screaming or silent, to die slowly. Hugh had fought in large and small wars often, but never before had he felt like a killing machine, a butcher.

Later—Hugh had no idea how much later—the sound of the battle changed. He had no clue to what it meant, for the words, if they were words, were meaningless, and he did not dare turn his head from the three men advancing on him. "Look at your dead!" he bellowed. "Go back! Courage alone cannot pierce mail." And while he shouted he raised his bloody sword; his throat was sore with shouting those words or similar ones with no effect. But this time there was no need to strike. Those coming at him had paused, turning toward the hill of the Standard, where a strange, wordless wail that sent chills up Hugh's back had burst out. His head turned also—the sound was weirdly compelling.

In the brief time Hugh dared look, the scene at the base of the hill seemed unchanged, except for larger heaps of dead, but even as he pulled his eyes away, an afterimage struck his mind. The long, flashing sword no longer waved. An unreasonable pang of sorrow made Hugh lower his own weapon; he knew a great leader had been struck down. Lament, he thought, that was the cry—and then jerked his sword up and focused his eyes, thinking, they will need to cry one for me if I do not mind my own affairs. But the men who had been ready to attack a moment earlier only shrieked some gibberish—curses, perhaps—and ran away. All along the left wing that same cry was rising, and most of the Scots were retreating. But the English line was buckling in response, bulging outward as the men-at-arms moved to pursue those who fled.

"Stand!" Hugh roared. "Stand! Archers, forward. Stand and shoot! Drive them on. Swordsmen stand."

Up and down the line the command was repeated, and the bulging stopped. Only a few swordsmen, caught up in the lust of killing, followed. They were soon lost among those they pursued, except for one or two who turned back. The men had been warned of the danger, but it was no surprise to Hugh that they needed a reminder that a withdrawal might be no more than a feint to destroy the line that the huge army arrayed against them had been helpless to break by force. Another time he might have been surprised that so few had rushed in pursuit, but he was sure that some of the men-at-arms were as sick of killing as he was and that the others did not wish to waste energy in following naked savages who were not worth looting.

The thoughts did not interfere with the sweeping glances Hugh cast around the area of his responsibility. Their own force was thinned, and moans and cries of pain came from behind the English lines as well as in front of them. Scots arrows had struck home, and lances and swords were more effective against the short leather tunics and round shields of the men-at-arms than they had been against Hugh's long-sleeved, midcalf-length hauberk. Still, the losses were not dangerous. They could withstand another wave, although that did not seem a danger in the immediate area. But there was a bulge in the wood to the left that troubled Hugh. The Scots might be reorganizing behind it.

He shouted his concern to Sir Lucius, who had moved into the front rank farther to the left as losses brought his men forward, but the young knight responded with a yell of excitement and pointed urgently to the right. Hugh looked toward the hill and saw the mounted reserve coming full tilt down and around it, waving their swords and shouting for the men on foot to make way. As his eyes took that in, Hugh's head was already turning to seek the cause, which was coming across the plain—more than twenty, perhaps fifty, mounted men flanked and followed by several hundred footmen.

Lucius began to roar, "Horses! Horses!" and the yeomen who were acting as grooms ran forward. Even as he seized Rufus's rein Hugh had a terrible freezing moment of doubt that Lucius had forgotten the need to hold their line. That doubt was briefly overlaid when he tried to jump for his stirrup and failed and had to haul himself into the saddle. He was shocked by the refusal of his muscles to obey; he had not realized until then how tired he was.

But concern for breaking the defensive line swiftly over-came Hugh's sense of weariness. Atop Rufus, he could see that Sir Lucius had not succumbed to battle fever. A second troop of horsemen had emerged from the bulge of wooded land and was charging across the ground directly toward them. Hugh shouted for the captains not to let so many mount that their troops were thinned too much, and then gestured for Lucius and perhaps ten more, who were already ahorse, to move out ahead of the shield wall. By then, the enemy were close enough for him to see they had lances, and he snarled a curse. If they waited close to their line to receive the charge, they would be spitted like pigs.

"Charge!" Hugh bellowed, waving his sword. "Spread out and charge."

He did so himself, turning Rufus toward what seemed to be the center of the group. He could hear someone calling orders among the oncoming men and had just enough time to think that the riders were being warned to open their formation to attack Hugh's widely spaced men lest they be taken from the flanks and the rear. He was among them before he saw the result of the order, striking aside one lance and slatting another off his shield. Both were ill aimed, not through any fault in the riders' abilities but because if both angled their lances sharply enough at Hugh, they were likely to spit each other or their companions' horses.

Hugh was past those riders, striking fiercely at a third, who had not been able to lower his lance, being too close behind the man ahead. A shriek told Hugh that his sword had struck true, but he had no idea where it had hit. He could only pray he had disabled that man, needing to look the other way to catch a lance on his shield, but the angle was all wrong, and Hugh flung himself forward in the saddle, shrinking in expectation of being pierced sideways through the ribs. Instead a blow across the back pushed him painfully into his pommel, and two loud screams rang out on either side. Hugh did not try to look; he laughed grimly, almost certain the lance aimed at him had caught the rider he had already struck with his sword—the second cry being one of horror as the lance struck friend rather than foe.

There was nothing to laugh about a moment later as a lance from the right caught the inside of his shield, which he had extended to slat off a blow from the left. For one instant Hugh had the choice of having his arm torn off or letting go of his shield, which meant that his left side would be defenseless and likely hacked to bits in minutes.

In that instant a violent jolt on Rufus's hindquarters propelled both man and horse ahead. Rufus shrieked with rage and tilted forward to kick out powerfully with his rear legs, and the lance point came free of Hugh's shield. Simultaneously, Hugh was aware of a burning pain across his left shoulder just as a horse and man behind him screamed with pain. Had he not been gasping with pain himself, Hugh would have thanked Rufus aloud. That kick had probably broken the rider's leg if it had not succeeded in staving in the ribs of his mount.

Then for a minute Hugh found himself outside the knot of fighting men. As he turned Rufus back into the fray, he saw that most of the attackers had broken or cast away their lances. He saw, too, that more horsemen were pushing past the lines to assist him and his men, although the fighting seemed to have intensified all over. Then Rufus was up, striking with his forefeet, snapping and screaming at an oncoming stallion, which shied away, giving Hugh a clear stroke at the rider.

Pain lanced across his back as he swung his sword, and the blow went slightly awry; more pain tore him as he raised his shield to ward off the counterblow, but he was already backing Rufus, turning him away before he would need to strike again. He had recognized the shield, and he had no intention of letting his hand be the one that injured—or, heaven forfend, killed—Henry of Huntington, prince of Scotland. And despite his pain, he could not help laughing again as the prince shrieked imprecations at him, calling him coward and worse. Poor Henry must know that any man from the northern shires who recognized him would draw off; he must have the devil's own time getting anyone to fight against him.

A feeling of sympathy for the frustrated prince swept over Hugh as he saw a mounted troop coming from the English lines near the hill, shouting and waving their weapons. Rather reluctantly, he looked around and called out for Lucius and his other men, knowing he should try to block Henry's escape. To kill or wound the prince might be a disaster, a cause of permanent enmity with King David, but to take Henry prisoner would be a great coup.

Nonetheless, he was relieved rather than disappointed when there was no reply to his call before Henry was surrounded by his own men, urging him away. The prince shook his sword and shouted at them, but the men closed in around him, and he acknowledged defeat, set his spurs to his horse, and galloped away after his retreating army. Prince Henry and his men were the last to leave the field, except for those wounded who were creeping or staggering toward whatever shelter they could find.

By then it was certain there would be no rally by the Scots, and Hugh returned to his tent, astonished to discover that it was still quite early. The battle had begun before Prime, and from the position of the sun, it could not be later than Tierce. Two hours or three... could it be possible that so little time had passed? If his physical weariness were a measure, it would be the next day's Tierce that was sounding. Yet he could feel a desperate energy building inside him. One more duty, just one more, and he would be free to go to Audris. Sir Walter had said to take his men and go, but Hugh could not, not until he knew his master's fate.

A voice had been nagging at him while he marveled at how short a time had passed, and now he looked down and saw Morel, who was begging him to dismount. "You be all over blood, my lord," Morel was saying. "The leech be here. Let us tend to you."

"Later," Hugh replied. "The hurts are nothing. Go bid the captain of Sir Walter's troop see that the men eat and rest. He is not to let them scatter seeking loot."

He almost smiled when he saw the expression of disgust on Morel's face. Doubtless some of the men had already been out and had discovered there was nothing, not even good weapons, to be stolen from the dead. Usually Hugh was glad the men-at-arms could glean some profit after a battle; this once he was better pleased by the poverty of the dead. There would be less angry muttering when he ordered the men to march. He had already explained to the captain what must be done, warning him to reserve supplies for the march north, but he had not expected they would be able to leave that day—he had not been sure any of them would be alive to go at all.

A stirring of breeze wafted the distinctive odor of blood to him; Hugh's smile twisted. He had forgotten the August heat.

Likely the only men who would mutter would be those left behind. By the end of the day a slaughterhouse would be a lily compared with this field.

"But my lord—" Morel began desperately.

"I must see how Sir Walter fared this day," Hugh went on, ignoring the interruption. "When I return, the leech can see to me, and then we go to relieve Jernaeve."

"Jernaeve!"

Morel's eyes lit. He had been sick with worry ever since he had first caught sight of Hugh's bloodstained armor. The Lady had said to set his master in a safe place if he were sick or hurt—that would be no trouble with Sir Walter close by— and then to fetch her to him, but the latter was not possible. To bring Sir Hugh to her would be next best. He had already found a leech and bribed him with one of the coins Lady Audris had supplied to leave his other patients. If his master could be patched well enough to get to Jernaeve, he would have fulfilled his trust. If... But Sir Hugh looked more likely to die of bloodletting than to be healed, since he would not let himself be leeched.

"My lord," Morel pleaded, "let me go to Sir Walter for you. I can carry a message, or—"

Hugh was about to say he wished to see his lord with his own eyes, when he recognized Sir Walter's younger squire working his way through the troops, his head turning right and left, clearly seeking someone. "Ho! Philip!" he called, "how is it with Sir Walter? Is he hurt?"

"Hugh?" Philip's voice climbed and cracked. "Is that you? You are all bloody."

Hugh laughed aloud, for he knew from the surprise and concern in Philip's voice that Sir Walter must be safe. Had he been wounded, Philip would not have been so surprised at Hugh's condition.

"That is a not uncommon result of a battle," Hugh responded, and then, seeing Philip's slight shudder and realizing the boy's face was very pale and that he was, as much as possible, avoiding looking at the battlefield, Hugh added consolingly, "but I am not much hurt, and I think most of the blood is other men's. You will become accustomed, Philip—I once felt the same as you. But let me hear you say it. *Is* Sir Walter unhurt?"

"Yes, he is well, and in high good humor. He says he is disgusted by his lack of faith, for he admits now that he believed they would be too many for us. But he sent me to ask after you, Hugh. What shall I tell him?"

"That I will start for Jernaeve near Sext—"

"Start for Jernaeve?" Philip echoed. "Hugh! You belong abed."

"No!" Hugh exclaimed forcefully, fearing that Sir Walter would descend on him and—for his own good—withdraw his permission for the use of his troop. "I tell you the blood is mostly of others, and I will murder you if you give Sir Walter a false tale that I am bleeding to death. You can hear my voice. Do I sound weak?"

"No," Philip admitted, but he sounded troubled, and after a moment he said, "And *he* will murder me if I say all is well with you and you die on the road."

That made Hugh laugh again. "I will not die on the road. You tell the truth—that I have a slash on my back and another on my shoulder, neither deep nor dangerous."

It took a little longer to convince Philip, and Hugh was not at all sure he would stay convinced; moreover, he was certain that if Sir Walter asked *any* questions, Philip would burst into tears and babble about Hugh's being drenched in blood. Therefore, as he dismounted from Rufus, he sent Morel to tell the captain to make ready to leave, and he bade the leech pull off his armor and tend to his hurts right there.

"But I have no cautery—"

"The hurts are from clean steel and not deep enough to need a cautery," Hugh said, shuddering inside at the idea of having a hot iron dragged over the long slice on his back. "Sew them up and slap a poultice on them. If they do not heal, my wife will see to them—"

He stopped abruptly, aware that a tremble had come into his voice. The leech shrugged, wondering not for the first time how it came about that the same men who rushed into battle laughing and did not seem to regard the wounds they received were utterly terrified of the curing of those wounds, flatly resisting the leech's recommendations until the last extremity, when usually it was too late, and often striking those who attempted to treat them. Nonetheless, he made no comment, merely gestured to his two assistants to unarm Hugh and remove his arming tunic while he himself made preparations to sew up the wounds—and to avoid being kicked, bitten, or otherwise injured while he did so.

Actually, he had misunderstood the unevenness in Hugh's voice, which was owing to fear for Audris rather than unusual fear of the leech's ministrations. Hugh did hate to be treated worse than he hated the original hurt—largely because being treated was more painful; in the heat of fighting one often did not notice being wounded—but just now, without distractions to control it any longer, his anxiety about Audris was reaching the panic state. In a way that fear was helpful, so occupying Hugh's mind that he was somewhat less aware of the pain being inflicted on him. In addition, Morel had chosen well; the leech was skilled and quick, pouring wine on the wound to wash it, and knotting and cutting his silk between stitches so that the flesh would heal smooth.

When he was done with both wounds, Hugh thanked him brusquely and beckoned to Morel, who had returned with word that the troops would be ready whenever he was. The captain had been more eager to leave the battlefield than to eat or rest. The bodies were beginning to stink already, and the groans of the wounded were no sweet music; it would be better, he had said, to eat and sleep on clean ground after a few hours' march. That welcome news had also distracted Hugh from the leech's ministrations so that his work seemed even more efficient. Thus, he bade Morel give the man a silver shilling.

"I am not done, my lord," the leech protested.

Hugh looked at him in surprise and then down at his bare body, wondering where he had been wounded without even noticing—and gasped. Now he knew why everyone had been so horrified and cried that he was covered with blood. In fact, he must have been. His chest, arms, and thighs had scores of small cuts, none large or deep, but all showing they had bled. Because he had been sweating heavily with heat and exertion, the mixture of blood and sweat must have soaked his tunic and oozed through his armor.

"But how——" he muttered, and then shook his head disgustedly. He had been too sure he was invulnerable to the long spears of the barbarians; it was true only in the sense that they could not kill him. Apparently the tips had been sharp enough to force their way through the links of his mail and his tunic far enough to prick him. He looked at Morel and uttered a short laugh. Apparently the leather and scale of the men-at-arms had been a better protection.

"I must wash you and salve you," the leech said severely. Seeing that he was being paid about five times his usual fee, he felt obliged to give as good service as he could. "It is true that no single cut could do you harm, but all together——"

Hugh frowned, quivering with impatience to be gone but restrained by common sense. "Very well," he growled. "Do what you must, but be quick." His breath hissed in as the leech began to pour wine over him, but he turned his head toward his servant. "Morel, tell the captain to get the troops and the supply wagons started northeast toward Gilling. We can pick up Dere Street near there without fording the Swale. I will follow and overtake him long before he comes to Gilling anyway. Are any of my own men hurt?"

"Only one too bad to ride," Morel replied.

"Let him stay with Sir Walter's wounded men. See that he has some money and tell him he will be welcome in Ruthsson—if it still stands—whenever he is strong enough to come."

Morel shook his head. "He will not come," he said.

"You are sure?" Hugh asked sharply.

"The wound be sucking with each breath," Morel replied.

"Then save the coin," Hugh said practically, "but be sure to see him and tell him his place in my service will be kept for him—it may cheer his heart. And when you return, you may set the men to packing." Hugh smiled suddenly. "They have been sitting while you run hither and yon on my orders. I am aware, Morel, and you will not lose by it."

Morel was not about to tell Hugh the whole secret of his devotion, but he grinned and said, "I profit already in a good master, a stomach that never be empty, and more of interest in my life than what manure be best."

Hugh looked after him as he went out, a little puzzled by Morel's care of him, which was more like that of a servant bound from early youth than a man hired in his own middle years. By natural association, Morel's hiring brought Audris to mind again, and Hugh urged the leech to hurry, shifting impatiently when he said he must anoint each cut and then wind on bandages so the salve would not be rubbed away. At that, Hugh growled, saying he had no more time to waste on little nicenesses, ordered the man to smear on his salve, and told one of the assistants to find a clean shirt in the leather bags on the floor. "The salve will be on the shirt. The shirt will be on my body. What comes off one place will be rubbed on another."

The leech protested, but Hugh silenced him. He knew he was being foolish, that a few minutes more or even an hour more would not matter. He and his men could overtake the foot soldiers and the wagons easily, and it was their pace that would determine how long it would take to reach Jernaeve. Still, he could sit still no longer. He had to be up and doing— even though when he did stand up his knees felt uncertain and the muscles of his thighs quivered as if he were supporting too much weight.

He felt better, though, after Morel came back and insisted he drink some wine and eat something while the men took down and packed the tent. The food stayed down, although the stench from the battlefield was growing, and once mounted on Rufus, who had been fed and watered under his eye, he was steady enough in the saddle. But he was aware that he had lost more blood than was good for him, and when they overtook the marching troop he was willing to keep to their slow pace. They were moving; that soothed him. Nor did he protest when the captain came and asked if the men could rest and eat. They had reached the track that ran near the river, and he comforted himself with the idea that they would move more quickly even though the road was rough. He ate again, sitting with his good shoulder propped against a tree, and realized he had dozed, only becoming aware that time had passed when a low-voiced discussion between Morel and the captain roused him. Then he went on with the troop, although Morel pleaded with him to go back to sleep.

By nightfall when they made camp, they had come to Dere Street and traveled along it, making good time on the hard surface. Hugh knew the men on foot could go no farther and said no more than that a watch must be set around the camp, and particularly on the supplies, to guard against any group of Scots stragglers; they had come upon a few single men, most badly wounded, and Hugh had regretfully ordered that they be killed. He had no way to transport them, no men to spare to guard them; to leave them behind meant, likely, only a slower and more agonizing death—or, if by chance any recovered, the certainty that they would steal from or murder innocent people in order to stay alive themselves.

Personally, Hugh was sorry to stop. He did not feel well— he was already hot and thirsty with fever—but he suspected he would feel far worse the next morning. And he was right. He had eaten what he could, but that was little, and, although he dropped asleep as soon as he had quenched his thirst, he did not sleep well. He woke in misery each time he moved, and whatever position he took hurt him.

By morning his head was pounding, and although he did not look, he was sure his wounds were inflamed. Nonetheless, he choked down a little bread and drank—that very willingly— three or four cups of watered wine. When Morel brought his armor, now cleaned and gleaming with oil, though Morel had no way to mend the broken rings on back and shoulder, Hugh groaned aloud with anticipation of the pain it would cost him to don it. It was too dangerous, however, to ride without it. By now the defeated Scots might have gathered into groups large enough to present a serious challenge.

Once mounted and moving about an hour after sunup, Hugh felt better, but as the heat increased so did his misery, for he felt as if he were burning, and the sweat that poured out of him stung his wounds. He almost prayed for rain, until he remembered that rain would make mud. Even Dere Street had patches where the stones had been uprooted or washed away, and those patches could become bogs.

They stopped to rest men and horses about an hour before noon. Hugh remembered that clearly, remembered drinking and drinking and feeling that he could never quench his thirst, but after that his memories became hazy. Perhaps they stopped once, perhaps twice more; he was not sure of anything until suddenly he was conscious of a tearing agony and realized that Morel was pulling off his armor. Then he found himself shivering so hard his teeth rattled, and knifings of pain pierced his back and shoulder as the tremors tore at the stitches in the wounds.

It was dark, and he was propped up against his saddle in his tent with Morel trying to force some hot wine between his teeth. As soon as he could unclench them, he drank what was offered and let Morel ease him down. He must have slept on and off afterward; he remembered throwing off the blankets, then crying out with pain as he groped for them later when he began to shake with cold again.

In the morning Hugh found himself almost clearheaded. There was a singing in his ears, and his back and shoulder were very painful, but he was rational enough to ask Morel how far they had come the previous day and to rejoice when he heard they were, in Morel's judgment, not much more than seven leagues from Jernaeve. He was also rational enough to be surprised that Morel said nothing when he could not eat at all. Later, he remembered they must have passed an abbey along the way, and he wondered why Morel had not tried to drag him in for treatment. He puzzled at that from time to time as he rode—it was better than thinking about the pain each step Rufus took cost him—and he began to laugh and also to understand how muddled his mind was when he finally realized that Jernaeve was Morel's home, too. Of course the man was eager to get there and learn whether anything was left of his farm and his family.

As the day passed, Hugh often wished he had not solved that little puzzle so easily. He remained conscious and aware, alternately burning and freezing, his body racked with pain and his mind with fear for Audris and Eric. The dull misery of the previous day began to seem like a restful haven, and he had to struggle constantly against two opposing and equally irrational desires—to insist that the men be driven faster so they could arrive sooner, and to stop altogether so he need not know the worst, if the worst had befallen. But at last, just when Hugh was beginning to worry about how much longer he could control the impulses to shout out crazy orders, they came to the bridge south of Corbridge and turned west toward Hexham without going near the town. Although they had not seen any organized group of the enemy, Corbridge might still be in the hands of the Scots.

"Go ahead," Hugh said to Morel, "and see if the abbey is taken. If not, ask the monks what they know of Jernaeve."

Hugh was afraid to go himself, afraid that between his fear of learning that Audris was lost to him and the pain that gnawed at him, he might yield to a brother that offered him the oblivion of drugged sleep. But the news that Morel brought back was no help at all. The only Scots in the abbey were wounded men who had staggered in begging for shelter and sanctuary. They were no threat and knew nothing.

The abbey itself had not suffered more than the minor damage of carelessness and filth, although it had lost all its stores and most of its cattle and sheep. The monks could tell Morel no more, for they had fled in terror, carrying what they could, when raiding parties came south from the siege of Jernaeve. Then on 20 August a lay brother who had hidden in the village told them that he had seen a large army of Scots marching south in great haste. Only then had the brothers dared to return to their church and buildings.

To save himself from going mad as they turned north to cover the last few miles to Jernaeve, Hugh mulled over the news Morel had brought. Had the army that went south been the same that had attacked Jernaeve, or was the keep still besieged? No, the siege must be lifted, one way or another,

Hugh thought, or foragers would still be coming to the abbey. So the army that went south must have come from Jernaeve, but if so, had they abandoned the siege in response to an urgent summons from King David—or had they somehow found a way into the inner keep and left some men to hold it while the others went, as they thought, to complete the conquest of Durham and Yorkshire. Hugh shook with fear and fever. He could not believe Jernaeve could be taken, could not believe it, and yet would the Scots dare leave such a prize, such a strong point blocking one of the main roads between their realm and the territory they hoped to conquer?

The last ideas went round and round in his head until the words made no sense and Hugh was back to clinging to his saddle, his chin on his chest, his eyes fixed unseeingly on Rufus's mane. Then Morel cried out, and Hugh looked up, knowing that the sounds he had been hearing were not in his head but were the river. The sun was low in the west, and Jernaeve's cliff was a threatening black mystery, only the tops of the walls and the bulge of the south tower gilded by the light. Instinctively, Hugh's eyes went to Audris's window, but it was blank and black, the heavy shutter closed. An icy chill washed over him. With the siege lifted, the window should be open. And no challenge rang down; Hugh strained his eyes, but he could not see any movement on the wall. Frantic, he gestured for the troop to move on, shouted for them to run. They reached the ford—and a hail of quarrels arced out from the walls at them. Hugh sat watching, frozen in despair. The impossible had happened. Jernaeve had fallen.

Chapter 29

IN THE LAST LIGHT OF THE SUMMER EVENING, HUGH RODE alone up the long winding road from the lower bailey toward the keep. The saner part of his mind expected a hail of crossbow bolts to finish him, but another part was full of grim rejoicing. The shock of learning that Jernaeve was in enemy hands some two hours earlier seemed to have steadied his mind and numbed his physical pain. Despite the shower of arrows, he and Sir Walter's men had crossed the ford and entered the lower bailey, where Hugh stared around at the ruins.

He should have been horrified, for it was obvious that most of the wreckage had not been caused in the attack and was mere wanton destruction, but what struck Hugh most forcibly was a sense of familiarity. All during the discussion he had had with the captain about what was best to do, that familiarity nagged at him—for each time he had visited, Jernaeve's lower bailey was in the most flourishing condition—until he remembered with an almost physical shock that he had seen the bailey in ruins in Audris's tapestry.

From that moment a terrible kind of joy seized him. There was, of course, no indication in the tapestry of who had destroyed the bailey; the unicorn was standing among the ruins, and he and Audris had assumed it was the unicorn that had caused them—but that assumption might well have been wrong. All that was unmistakable was the unicorn's rage and threatening attitude toward Jernaeve. But if Jernaeve were filled with enemies, that attitude was perfectly reasonable. The more he thought about it, the firmer grew Hugh's conviction that he must get into the keep. Audris must be a prisoner there, and if she was not—Hugh shuddered and then stiffened to control himself. She must be there; in the last tapestry she was in the garden with the dead unicorn. Hugh sighed, remembering the peace in that last picture. Once in, he was sure he would somehow find a way to open Jernaeve to Sir Walter's men before he died.

Burning though he was with fever, Hugh was not so much out of his head as to mention the tapestry or the wild conclusions he had drawn from his memory of it to the captain. What he had proposed was that he go alone and try to parley with whoever was holding Jernaeve. Possibly they had not yet heard of the defeat King David had suffered at Allerton. With that news, he might be able to arrange some terms on which they would yield the keep.

The captain was doubtful, but aside from warning Hugh that the Scots were barbaric enough to shoot him even while he called for a truce, he thought it worth a chance—since he also was convinced that the Scots were stupid wild men who could be easily cheated. Of course, the captain had no idea how sick Hugh was, and Morel, who did know, had not uttered a single word since the flight of crossbow bolts had come at them. He was paralyzed with disbelief, so shaken was his world at the idea that the Lady could not protect Jernaeve.

Thus, Hugh started up the road, fully armed but without his sword or any other weapon. When no bolts had flown at him at the halfway mark, he called out that he desired a truce to come higher and speak to whoever held Jernaeve keep. He stopped there and waited, and after what seemed like a long time but had to be only a few minutes because it grew no darker, a voice called back that he might come. Something stirred in Hugh's mind, something to do with the fact that the voice spoke in fluent, cultured French, but he could not think about that. He started up on the road again, thinking only of reasons that would get him inside Jernaeve.

"Who are you?" the voice from the wall called down when he reached the last turning in the road.

"Hugh of Ruthsson," he called back.

There was a brief silence, and Hugh wondered if it had been a mistake to tell the truth. Would he be shot out of hand? Hugh started to lift his shield, but the voice came again, high and shocked.

"Take off your helmet—and say again who you are."

Take off his helmet? The better to kill him? Still, what choice did he have? Painfully, he lifted his hand and pushed off the helmet, not even trying to keep it from falling to the ground. With teeth gritted over the agony of pulling the stitches of the suppurating wound in his shoulder, he undid the fastening of his hood and pushed that back.

"Hugh of Ruthsson."

He tried to shout so that he could be heard, but his voice was just a croak. The numbness to pain that hope and high excitement had granted him had ended, and it seemed that the agony had returned a hundredfold in revenge for the hours it had been held at bay. He was aware that it was growing dark too suddenly and felt himself swaying in the saddle. And then he thought he heard a woman scream his name—no, it was the screech of the portcullis rising. He made a last desperate effort and kicked feebly at Rufus to start him forward, clinging to his seat in the saddle with the last remnant of consciousness. And there were hands holding him, helping him down, and—and Audris's voice. He blinked, and for one instant saw her face. It disappeared in the growing blackness, but he could still feel, and there were lips on his.

❧

For a long time after that, days and nights were little more than black and white bars in which Hugh had horrible nightmares of tearing down Jernaeve or of being tortured in its dungeons. Later, the black and white bars stretched out into days and nights again. The horrors receded, leaving only a dim discomfort. Hugh became aware of pain, of being lifted or washed or of having food or drink or some horrible, bitter potion pushed past his lips, but mostly he floated in contentment, for each time he managed to open his eyes for a moment Audris was there, smiling down at him. And, at last, when he forced his lids open, they stayed open.

"Audris?" he whispered. "Are we prisoners?"

"No, beloved," she said. "It was all a mistake, dearling, all a mistake. Jernaeve was never taken. We thought you were the Scots returning. Never mind that now, heart of my heart. Eric and I are safe, and you are safe. Rest."

He was going to say that he had been doing nothing but rest for a long time, but somehow his eyes were closing again. He did sleep, but when he woke, this time to a room softly candlelit, he was ravenously hungry, and his first words were, "What is there to eat?" And Audris, who was sitting by the bed, laughed like a bird singing.

Almost as soon as the words were out, Fritha came running from the small hearth, carrying a bowl. Hugh intended to ask a great many questions, but he found it strangely exhausting to be lifted and propped against pillows and to swallow what was put into his mouth, although it was delicious. He knew there were important things to say, but somehow his mind would only fix on silly things like how strong Fritha was, to have been able to lift him, and his intense desire to see Eric.

Still, he barely managed to stay awake long enough to admire his son, who gurgled happily at him in spite of being suddenly wakened, and he fell asleep before he had quite finished saying, "You were right, Audris, he does have a sweet temper."

The next day, he did manage to ask questions, and all the news was good—so good that he felt uneasy. But he was too tired, even after hearing only good news, to probe for what he felt might lie under it. After all, he knew he could do nothing, even if everything Audris had told him was a pack of lies designed to calm him. It was better to try to believe what she said, to eat hugely—he seemed to be constantly hungry whenever he was awake—and to spend whatever time he was not eating or sleeping that day idly playing with Eric, who wriggled and waved his hands and feet in delight at being free in the big bed beside his father, and watching Audris work at her loom, which Fritha turned so that he could watch the picture grow—a happy scene of a hunting party setting out.

The uneasiness stayed with him, however, and he must have slept restlessly and had bad dreams—although he did not remember them—for soon after he had broken his fast in the morning, Audris brought his uncle to see him.

"You were so very ill," Audris said, her eyes filling with tears. "I thought…" Her voice failed, and she shook herself and laughed at past fear. "I thought you might die, so I sent for Uncle Ralph."

"I told her there was no danger," Ralph said, smiling, although his own eyes looked suspiciously wet. "I knew that anyone who survived a battle with Lionel Heugh was not going to succumb to pricks from Scottish lances. But I must say I am very glad that Audris no longer needs the support of my strong spirit."

"Strong spirit," Audris interrupted, wrinkling her nose. "He wept more than I." But she put her arm around his waist and leaned her head on his shoulder lovingly. "Still, it was true I needed him."

Ralph pretended to look down his nose at her in disdain, but he was hugging her tight, and then he laughed suddenly, kissed the top of her head, and let her go. "Well, whatever the reasons, I am glad you are all but well again. If I do not go back to Ruthsson immediately, nine-tenths of the lush crops you worked so hard to get into the ground will disappear into private hoards."

"Then Ruthsson is safe?" Hugh asked, stretching a hand to his uncle and drawing him close to kiss.

"There are advantages to being buried in uttermost Thule," Ralph said, first clinging to Hugh for a moment and then straightening and producing an indifferent shrug. "No one came near us." And seeing Hugh still frowning, he added, "I swear it, on my own soul—and if you think I would not mind adding a sin to my already substantial burden, I will swear it on the soul of King Henry, on whom you know I would lay no sin."

Hugh smiled at that and admitted, "I believe you."

"Trewick has had some damage, although it was not burnt out like Belsay. One of the raiding parties breached its defenses, but there were enough men to drive them off before they put torches to the place. And Heugh is safe, too." Ralph shook his head in wonder. "I never thought I would set foot willingly inside those walls, but Audris wrote that Lionel was dead and our Louis was holding the place and asked me to discover, if I could, whether it had been taken. That Louis is a good man. He took in the yeomen who managed to escape the Scots and gave them weapons. He told me the Scots that attacked while you were there never came back and no other group large enough to be dangerous challenged them. Only a few raiding parties tried to threaten him, but Heugh was more than strong enough to hold them off, so he did not yield it."

"I am glad of it," Hugh said. "It is a fine keep, and no matter to whom it belongs, I would not like to see it despoiled."

Hugh started to ask another question, but Ralph shook his head. "That is enough, Hugh. You needed to be assured that all is well—and truly, all *is* well. For the rest, you know I care very little. So long as he does us no despite, King David is as welcome to me as King Stephen—perhaps a little more welcome. The Scots are gone from Northumbria and the people are picking up the pieces of their lives. There is nothing you can do now except rest, so that you will be ready to act when you must."

He kissed Hugh again and left, and while Hugh was still protesting that he was not at all tired, he fell asleep. He woke only an hour later and sat bolt upright, this time remembering his dream. "Your uncle," he said to Audris, who was at the loom and came running, anxiously asking what ailed him. "I must speak to Sir Oliver. I must thank him for his hospitality and assure him it was not my intention to come here as if—" But the words died in his throat as Audris stopped and he saw the expression on her face.

She lowered her eyes. "He is dead, Hugh." Then she ran to him and threw herself into the arms he opened to receive her. "He is dead," she sobbed. "I could not save him. I tried. I swear I tried with all my strength and all my skill."

"I am so sorry, my love," Hugh whispered, holding her tight. And then "hearing" what she said, he added fiercely, "Of course you tried with all your strength and skill! Who says you did not?"

"No one," Audris sobbed. "In fact, my aunt says he was dead when they brought him in and laid him down, but I felt his body move with breath, I am sure of it, and I keep wondering if deep in my heart I envied him Jernaeve and did not do all I could or ought."

Hugh shook his head. "Hush, love. You wanted to believe him alive, and so you did. I have seen the newly dead seem to sigh with breathing. I do not know what it is, perhaps the soul passing. But for all your skill with potions and salves, dearling, I think your aunt has seen more death than you. Is it not true that in ordinary times you only came to those for whom there was hope?"

"Oh, yes," she sighed. "That is true, but..." She started to cry again, more softly, hopelessly. "But I hardly ever told him I loved him—only once or twice—and he was so good to me. And I was often disobedient and vexed him, and... and..."

Hugh kissed her silent, rocking her comfortingly. "So we all feel when those we love die. So will I say to you, no doubt, when Thurstan is taken."

"Thurstan?" Audris echoed, her sobs stopping abruptly. "Hugh, no! Oh, what will I do? You are not strong enough to travel."

"No, no," Hugh soothed. "I am sorry I frightened you. I hope he will have some years among us yet, but he is very frail and will not spare himself."

"When you are well," Audris said, brightening, "we will go to York so that he can see Eric. And we will take Uncle Ralph—"

Hugh laughed aloud. "Now there you have a truly brilliant notion. Perhaps Thurstan can save Ralph—and it might be that Ralph can insinuate a little balance and reason into Thurstan." He was quiet for a few moments, and Audris moved tentatively. Hugh tightened his grip. "Lie with me," he murmured, and then, in response to her wordless protest, he laughed gently. "I did not mean that—although I soon will, I think—but my body has been nothing but a trial to me for so long. It is good to feel pleasure in it again."

By the end of that week, Hugh had made good his promise, although Audris insisted on mounting him so that he would need to exert himself less. When they were done, he protested in a playfully die-away voice that he was sure it would have been less exhausting if he had plunged and been done instead of being played with until he was half crazy before being allowed to spill his seed. But the next night it was he who gasped that he was too weak to climb atop; Audris made no protest, but later she meanly pointed out that his request cast some doubt on the complaints he had voiced the previous night. Whereupon, to her genuine concern—and equally genuine pleasure—he reversed the process and agreed, when he had caught his breath, that he was *not* too weak.

Hugh had made giant strides in recovery that week. His wounds had closed and lost their scabs, showing clean pink flesh where oozing sores had for so long resisted every poultice Audris could devise, and feeling no more than a little tender. He had sat up, been helped a few steps to a chair, walked by himself, and at last—with Morel walking backward in front of him and Fritha with her hands out to catch him—he had tottered down the stairs to eat dinner in the hall.

Hugh had to laugh, for his entry was—except for his slightly drunken weaving—like a triumphal procession. Eadyth had insisted he sit in Oliver's chair, making the first jest he had ever heard from her when she commented that if he did not have the arms of the chair to support him, he would surely tip over, fall on the floor, and spoil everyone's dinner because they would all have to leave off eating to fuss over him. And to make their joy utterly complete, just as Hugh had taken the seat offered, a messenger came from Bruno with the news that he had been knighted by the king and granted a pension. He had other news, also, the letter said, but he would save that to tell himself, for the king had promised him leave to visit his sister in a fortnight.

The only sour note was from Maud of Heugh, who came to the table, saw Hugh sitting at its head, and fainted dead away.

She revived before Audris could even go to her but began to weep hysterically, and Eadyth took her to her chamber. "I cannot imagine what is wrong with Maud," she said when she came back. "She is the most sensible creature ordinarily."

"It is something about Hugh," Audris said, looking troubled.

"Oh, he is not as ugly at *that*," Ralph remarked blandly. "His face gave *me* quite a start, too, the first time I saw it, but it did not knock me unconscious…"

Hugh began to laugh; Audris gasped in pretended outrage, insisting that Hugh was not ugly at all and that Eric, clearly the most beautiful baby in the world, looked just like him. Whereupon Hugh began to commiserate with his son, and Ralph took back his remark, agreeing that Eric was the most beautiful baby in the world. The servants, in response to a sharp gesture from Eadyth, began to bring the meal, and between the food and the nonsense, Maud's peculiar behavior was temporarily forgotten.

Unfortunately, it could not be permanently put out of mind, nor was Ralph in Jernaeve much longer to divert attention from Maud's fixation. There had been a week of bad weather after Hugh first came down to the hall, but on the first bright day Ralph left for Ruthsson to oversee the sharing of the harvest. Maud had not been much in evidence while Hugh kept to the hall, where he listened to Eadmer, supported his decisions, and infrequently offered a suggestion about the restoration of the damage done by the Scots.

However, as Hugh regained his strength and spent more and more time in the bailey and storage areas of the keep, he seemed constantly to encounter Maud. She did not faint again, but would stare and run away, often weeping. A few times, Hugh tried to stop her and speak to her, to assure her that he did not blame her for whatever had happened to his father in Heugh keep—but he never got that far.

At last, exasperated, for Hugh had been sensitized to people who did not like him and he was beginning to have bad dreams about the woman, he mentioned the matter to Audris one day before he went down to break his fast.

She was suckling Eric and looked up from her peaceful

contemplation of her son's greed with a worried frown. "I know," she said. "Maud follows you about."

"Follows me?" Hugh repeated, astonished. "From the way she acts, I would think she would do everything to avoid me. Curse the woman. If she follows me, why will she not stop and speak to me? All I wish to do is tell her I have no ill will to her and ask her the name of the girl who is heir to Heugh and the name of her guardian. Something must be done about Heugh or it will fall into the king's hands, and I do not want a royal castle so close to Trewick."

But Audris shook her head and would not discuss Heugh. All she said was, "You exert a fatal fascination for Maud." Then she sighed. "I suppose we will have to send her back to Heugh, but I hate to do it. She is treated with such contempt there, even by the lowest servants, and here she is a comfort to my aunt."

"Then do not send her away," Hugh said harshly. "We will not be here much longer ourselves."

Audris looked at him levelly but said nothing, and Hugh turned hurriedly away, knowing that Jernaeve could not be left masterless any more than Heugh, but Hugh had no idea what to do about it. He did not really wish to leave Jernaeve. The more deeply he became involved in restoring the damage done by the Scots, the more he loved old Iron Fist and desired to care for it and rule it himself. But try as he would to put that tapestry out of his mind, as long as he was the unicorn, he dared not call himself master of Jernaeve.

When he was gone, Audris went back to staring at Eric, but she was not seeing her son. She knew well enough what was troubling Hugh, but she could not think of a way to undo the damage she had done when she showed him the tapestry. Why had she ever done it, she wondered, and then closed her eyes over tears. She had done it to protect her uncle—but her device had worked too well. Now that Oliver was dead, she knew her husband was no danger to her keep, but nothing she said seemed to convince him. Yet Jernaeve was too important a stronghold to place in hands that might become untrustworthy; there were not many Olivers in the world, who, for honor, would yield up what they had loved and cared for. Somehow, she *must* find a way to convince Hugh that the image of the unicorn no longer applied to him.

The trouble was that Hugh still really thought of himself as Licorne. He called himself Hugh of Ruthsson, but that was his mother's name, what he would be called if he were a bastard. Hugh needed his father's name. And as the idea came to her, she gasped. What a fool she had been not to put the two things together! Maud knew who Kenorn was and what had happened to him. Eager to rush off and bring Maud and Hugh to a confrontation, Audris looked down at her son impatiently, but he was still sucking, and to take the breast from him would only cause chaos. The enforced stillness gave her second thoughts. She was so sure that Kenorn was some relation of Lionel's—but what if she was wrong? What if the secret causing Maud's misery was shameful to Hugh? She had better wring it from Maud herself and then decide what to do.

At last Eric sighed, gave a last pull on Audris's breast, and let the nipple slip from his mouth. She lifted him to her shoulder, quite willing to wait while rumbles shook Eric's body as the air he had swallowed with his milk came up. Audris continued to pat him patiently, until she felt his head droop heavily, and then she bade Fritha watch him and went down to break her own fast.

To her chagrin, she discovered that Maud had asked to go to Hexham and Eadyth had arranged to send her there. And Hugh was gone by the time she entered the hall, too, which worried her a little, but he came in to dinner in a better mood, not having come across Maud even once. He looked tired, though. Audris knew he was impatient with what seemed to him a slow recovery of his strength, so after dinner she deliberately enticed him out into the garden. Intending only to make him willing to stay and rest, she chose a spot with tender memories—the sheltered grassy plot where they had suddenly and unexpectedly made love when he returned from taking Thurstan to Roxburgh.

She had hardly begun, "Do you remember—" when Hugh

began to demonstrate that he remembered all too well. He started to caress her in jest, and she responded as playfully, expecting that they would draw apart naturally at any moment, but somehow the caresses soon became more immediately important than the eventual fate of Jernaeve, and they found themselves half undressed, as passionately entangled as if they did not have a private chamber and a comfortable bed in which to disport themselves. Then it was too late, and besides, the chance that some member of the household might come there lent spice to their passion, so they finished their lovemaking where they were, half laughing, half ashamed, and too lazy and satisfied when their love had been consummated to do more than straighten their clothes and collapse again onto the grass.

In minutes Hugh, who had been tired to begin with, was deeply asleep with his head pillowed in Audris's lap while she rested her back against the bench—the same bench, she remembered, which they had been sitting on when her uncle came upon them, frightening them so much. She had stopped crying every time she thought of Oliver, but memory made her eyes sweep the garden, and she stiffened and hissed, "Stop!" And then softly, but with such authority that she was obeyed, "Come here."

Slowly Maud came around the rosebushes that sheltered the grassy plot and into the open. "Forgive me," she said. "I did not mean to spy on you, but—" Her face twisted. "I once thought to have that—to love my husband and take joy in him. Kenorn—"

"This is Hugh, not Kenorn," Audris said, glancing down at her husband, but their voices did not seem to disturb him. His body was flaccid in total relaxation, his face turned slightly inward toward her body, his breathing deep and even.

"No," Maud said. Her eyes were also on Hugh, and tears were leaking down her cheeks. "I meant Kenorn—your husband's father. I was supposed to be betrothed to Kenorn, not Lionel. Kenorn was nothing like the other Heughs. He was always laughing and kind—so kind to me when I first went there, not quite thirteen and frightened to death." Then her lips hardened, and she dashed the tears angrily from her face. "At first I only thought he was being kind when he refused to marry me. I believed it was because he thought me too young—but he had another woman."

Audris had scarcely heard Maud's angry remarks. She was thinking about the earlier statements, putting together the fact that Maud was meant for Kenorn with what she had said about Heugh belonging to Hugh. In general it was the elder brother for whom a wife was found first. "Sit down here on the grass," she directed, gesturing to the place she wanted Maud to sit, then paused while Maud sank down facing her but near enough to touch. "Do you mean Sir Kenorn, Hugh's father, was Sir Lionel's elder brother?" she asked.

"Yes, the elder—and I had a rich dowry, far richer than what that other woman could have brought."

So Heugh keep did indeed belong to Hugh. But this time Maud's bitter tone came through to Audris, and she put that consideration aside, hoping she could soothe Maud and perhaps persuade her to act more rationally toward Hugh.

"That was so long ago," she said. "You must try to forget it. I am sorry Hugh looks so much like his father and brings back sad memories, but I hope you will try to put those memories away and come to love Hugh. You see, he will be very glad to learn you are his aunt, because—"

"No!" Maud gasped, shrinking in on herself. "No! He *must* hate me!"

Audris remembered that Maud had used those very same words when they were in Heugh and she had tried to comfort her. "Lady Maud," she pleaded, "you are making my poor Hugh very unhappy by your unhappiness. You must try to believe that whatever the past holds, Hugh will not—"

"No," she repeated, her eyes wide and fixed. "You do not understand. We sinned against him—against him and against Kenorn, Lionel, and me. We hated each other, but we were bound together by sin, and by sin heaped on sin."

"It was so long ago—" Audris began, but Maud did not even seem to hear her.

She looked down at Hugh, and there was such torment

in her face that Audris's eyes filled with tears. "Long ago? Perhaps, but the evil is still new. That evening—it was after the evening meal, but the light had not yet gone—I saw Kenorn ride in, with only two men, but he did not stop to speak to me. He went directly to—that place no longer exists in Heugh; the keep was not yet built then, and Heugh was not so great. Later, I was summoned, and Lionel was already there in the old man's private place—and as I came in, I heard the old man screaming that he would have the marriage annulled, that Kenorn was pledged to me. And Kenorn just laughed at him—he always laughed at his father's tantrums—and reminded him that he had *not* gone through with the betrothal and it was too late. Not only was he married, but his wife was heavy with child."

Maud hesitated and drew a shaken breath. "It was like a knife in my heart when I heard him," she continued. "He had given me gifts and called me a pretty child—and all the time he had a wife. For a minute I hoped again when the old man screamed, 'A bastard! A bastard!' but Kenorn laughed again and said that proof of the marriage was in a safe place, and his father should be glad of it because he had mended the feud with Ruthsson for good. Then the old man struck him! He grabbed up the iron poker from the hearth and struck Kenorn right across the face from here to here."

Maud made a line from the forehead across the cheek and down to the jawbone. Audris gasped, remembering the flaming bruise that had marred Hugh's face after the battle with Sir Lionel. It had traced a line just where Maud's finger had run. She shivered, thinking that the Lord had taken His vengeance, as it said in the Bible, in His own good time.

"Hugh will not blame *you*," she soothed. "You were no more than a child yourself."

Tears ran again from the tired, reddened eyes. "But we never told," Maud whispered. "Lionel helped his father carry Kenorn out in the dead of the night and bury him. I could have confessed to a priest, brought him to the grave and had the ground blessed, but I did not. I hated Kenorn then, for scorning me, for wedding another." Sobs broke her voice, but she struggled on, and Audris no longer tried to stop her, knowing she must confess it all before she could be comforted. "They buried him in unhallowed ground, unshriven," she sobbed, choking but keeping her voice low—and her eyes were still on Hugh. "They killed his *soul*, kind, laughing Kenorn."

"No," Audris said firmly. "Christ and his Mother are infinitely merciful. So I was taught by Father Anselm, and so I believe. They would intercede for a good man with the stern Father. Kenorn would not be damned for trying to make peace between two warring families."

Maud dried her eyes and looked up at Audris. "Is that true?" she asked. "I was so afraid, but I never dared so much as hint, not even to a priest…"

"Yes, it is true," Audris stated. "Father Anselm was a very, very holy man, and if he said so, it was true."

"But still," Maud sighed, "still it was a dreadful sin. We never tried, even after the old man died—and that was only three years later—we never tried to find out if the child had lived. We knew if it was a boy, it was the rightful heir to Heugh. We hoped it was dead; we *prayed* it was dead. Yes, although I hated Lionel and he hated me—" She hesitated again, and her eyes grew distant. "Perhaps that was my fault too. He was a hard man, but if I had not showed him I thought him loathsome, perhaps… No, it was the evil in us that bred hate and more hate. I—I prayed that the woman *and* the child would die… in the beginning, before I realized how great a sin it was to pray that a child would die."

"But you see Hugh came to no harm," Audris coaxed. "So you *did* no harm. And you were only a child yourself."

Maud did not seem to hear her. Her eyes were fixed ahead, blind, and she rocked a little back and forth. "I was punished for my evil," she whispered. "*How* I was punished! *My* children died—all of them. Some were born dead, some lived a few days, some lived a year or two to wring my heart the harder before they were swept away. But I could not repent, for *if* a child had lived, I wished Heugh to belong to *my* child. But none lived. My children died. All of them."

"Oh, my God." Audris sighed, weeping too. "Oh, no, no. Oh, do not put that burden on Hugh's life. It cannot be his fault—"

"Hugh's fault!" Maud seemed to wake from her trance of grief. "No! The fault was mine!" She stared at Audris, at the tears running down her face, reached out and touched her wet cheek with a timid finger. "You weep for me? Yet it was your husband I prayed would die."

"But he did *not* die," Audris cried, sniffling.

"No, I did not," Hugh said, sitting up suddenly.

Audris gasped, and Maud twisted around desperately, trying to rise. Hugh caught her and held her as gently as he could.

"Aunt Maud," he said softly. "Do not run away. Only let me say one thing to you, and then, if you wish, you need never look on me again. I wish to offer you an explanation for my father's behavior. If he looked like me, as all say he did, then he was an ugly man. I know it, and he must have known it. Even though Margaret Ruthsson came to love him, I do not think that it entered his mind that, young as you were and with no reason to favor him above other men, you would come to care for him. I have done much as he did with young girls of Sir Walter's family. Try to forgive him. I hope you can, because I would value an aunt who could love me."

Maud was crying helplessly, but she was not trying to escape Hugh's hold, and he drew her closer, leaning across Audris, who wriggled out from between them, rising and stepping backward over the bench. She came around to the other side and knelt so she could also embrace the weeping woman.

"You can confess now," she murmured, "and free your soul of this burden. You have done penance enough."

Her eyes met Hugh's, and he nodded slightly so she saw he understood what she meant. "In a while, when I am stronger," he said softly, "we will go to York to see my father in God. Thurstan, who is archbishop of York, raised me. God moves in His own ways to mend the ill that men do to each other, and my life has been better than most men's. Thurstan will shrive you, and we will find my father's grave and consecrate the ground, and Thurstan will pray for his soul. Come, aunt, you have wept enough for the mistake of a child. Come, be comforted."

Eventually Maud's dreadful sobs quieted, and Hugh and Audris helped her rise and half carried her back into the keep and into her chamber. She clung pathetically to Hugh, and he remained with her while Audris found Eadyth and explained and then mixed a soothing potion. It was nearly time for the evening meal before Maud was willing to release Hugh's hand and turned to Eadyth, who waved Hugh and Audris away.

"My poor dearling," Audris said when they were out of the chamber, pulling Hugh's head down and kissing him. "I never meant to put you through such torture."

He shook his head. "It was not so bad," he said thoughtfully as he walked to Oliver's great chair by the hearth and sank down into it. He waited while Audris got a stool and settled beside him, leaning on his knees. "I am sorry for Aunt Maud," he went on, "but I think she will be better now that she has told us and we have accepted it. Or even if she is not"—he smiled wryly at Audris—"she will no longer haunt my dreams, because I understand."

"Heugh is yours," Audris said. "Did you hear that much?"

"Yes, and I am glad of it," Hugh admitted, smiling again. "At first I did not want it, but that, I think, was because of the shock Maud gave me. It is a fine place."

"I think so too," Audris agreed. "And it is conveniently close to Jernaeve." She saw Hugh's face tighten and put a gentle hand on his, which had clenched into a fist. "Soul of my soul, listen to me," she pleaded. "You are no danger to Jernaeve. You have been no danger to Jernaeve since you discovered who you were. We have had sign after sign of it. Remember when the unicorn shield was broken in the combat with Sir Lionel? I knew then, but I should have realized earlier, when you came back to me after we had coupled. A unicorn can only come to a virgin maid, but you came back to me. Hugh, the unicorn is dead—or, rather, there never *was* a unicorn."

"I do not know," he said uncertainly.

"I know." She laughed up at him softly. "Oh, Hugh, did you not recognize that scene in the garden? You stretched out with your head in my lap and Maud telling us that your name is *not* Licorne but *Heugh*."

He frowned. "Of course my name is Hugh. What are you talking about, Audris?"

She laughed louder. "Oh, dear, how can I say it so you will understand? You are Hugh Heugh, or Hugh de Heugh. Your poor, poor mother was trying to tell Thurstan your name, yes, but not your *Christian* name—what good would that be? She must have known she was dying—and she struggled so, but Thurstan could not understand."

"Good merciful God," Hugh breathed. "She must have been trying to say 'tell Kenorn' or perhaps to give my grandfather's name, Lionel—and my father's, Kenorn, and it came out li-corne. But it was God that stopped her tongue. Do you realize that, Audris? If Thurstan had understood her and had sent me to Heugh, I would not have lived a week. If the old man had not killed me, Lionel would have arranged it."

Audris shivered. "There are not many Olivers and Eadyths in this world, I fear." But she blinked back her tears and smiled. "And, perhaps, dearling, the unicorn was meant to pique my curiosity to bring us together?"

This time Hugh laughed. "I am sure of it, dear heart, for without God's direct intervention—or, more likely Blessed Mary's, for the Mother always did like a merry jest—it is not possible that a woman like you would look at a man like me."

Audris cocked her head to one side. "I am not sure," she said as if seriously considering Hugh's statement. "Just now with your face still white as a bone and that color hair, I admit you are shocking, but"—she levered herself up by leaning on his knees and kissed his prominent nose—"there are some fine, upstanding features about you—" Balancing on one hand, she slid the other between his legs.

"Hush, you lewd slut," Hugh whispered, putting both arms around her and crushing her to his chest, then dumping her firmly back on her stool. "We are supposed to be considering what to do about Heugh. There may be a contest for possession with the girl heir's guardian. I am not much worried, with Thurstan, the abbess, Maud, and the servants to speak for me, but I think I heard Maud say there was proof of the marriage in a 'safe place.' I wonder where. It was not with my mother's possessions."

"I think I know," Audris said. "Margaret must have sent it to her sister—what was her name?"

"Ursula," Hugh replied, surprised at recalling the name and then realizing that everything about that letter had branded itself deeply into his memory. "At least, she had taken the name Sister Ursula—no, Ralph called her Ursula too. But the convent was not named."

"Ralph will know that," Audris assured him, "and marriage lines will have been kept."

Hugh nodded. "I think you are right. You are a clever minx. I will write to Ralph tomorrow. Hmm, remind me to send someone for Morel. I gave him leave last week to help his sons restore their house. He said they only had to rethatch, that the place had not been burnt to the ground."

"And the family was safe inside Jernaeve," Audris remarked with satisfaction. "They even saved their cow and most of the hens—and with what Morel has earned, they will be able to buy feed and grain and seed, and not have to eat the animals and be left with nothing. They were among the most fortunate."

But Hugh's mind was on his own affairs, and he paid little attention to the fate of Morel's family. "I will go to the convent when I have an answer from Ralph—if it is not too far. And then to York, before the weather gets too bad." He frowned. "We will be traveling much of the autumn, it seems, but—"

"But first," Audris said quietly and rather sadly, because she was afraid that she had failed and Hugh was talking around the problem that really troubled him, "we must decide what to do about Jernaeve."

To her surprise, Hugh settled himself more firmly in the great chair of state. "We will live here," he said. "I will find a good man to hold Ruthsson for me and another to hold Heugh. Jernaeve is different. Jernaeve cannot be left in other hands. It would be too hard to pry out a treacherous castellan."

"Hugh?" Audris's question was tremulous with hope.

He smiled down at her. "In that last tapestry—the one that shows the unicorn dead—there is a man's shadow stretching out a hand to you. I hated that picture, until I saw the shadow. I did not know why that shadow comforted me—but now I know. I am the shadow. A man. Audris, only a man, holding out my hand to lead you away from a beautiful dream. Do you regret the tapestry of dreams?"

"No!" Audris cried, her whole face alight with joy. "No. I was a silly girl when I dreamed of the unicorn. I am a woman now."